# CAROL
# BRUNEAU

# Berth

**A NOVEL**

*Cormorant Books*

Canada Council   Conseil des Arts
for the Arts   du Canada

ONTARIO ARTS COUNCIL
CONSEIL DES ARTS DE L'ONTARIO

The publisher gratefully acknowledges the support of the Canada Council for the Arts
and the Ontario Arts Council for its publishing program. We acknowledge the financial
support of the Government of Canada through the Book Publishing
Industry Development Program (BPIDP) for our publishing activities.

Printed and bound in Canada

This is a work of fiction; any resemblance of characters to persons living or dead is coincidental.

LIBRARY AND ARCHIVES CANADA CATALOGUING IN PUBLICATION

Bruneau, Carol, 1956–
Berth / Carol Bruneau.

ISBN 1-896951-85-6

I. Title.

PS8553.R854B47 2005   C813'.54   C2004-906520-3

Cover design: Marijke Friesen
Cover image: Early Morning 1 © Margot Metcalfe
Author photo: Bruce Erskine
Text design: Tannice Goddard
Printer: Friesens

CORMORANT BOOKS INC.
215 SPADINA AVENUE, STUDIO 230, TORONTO, ON CANADA M5T 2C7
www.cormorantbooks.com

*To the lightship of friends*

*O abyss, O eternal Godhead, O sea profound,*
*what more could you give me than yourself?*

— SAINT CATHERINE OF SIENA (1347-1380)

# CONTENTS

## WINDS

You can have a heart as big as the sky, and hate flying. I have always hated it. The turbulence. The take off: that upwards thrust like an orgasm backwards. Like being blown awake, penetrating the clouds. That blind faith, a sweaty belief almost that you've sprouted wings. Feathers. And then the landing.

Go figure, then, that I'd married military. Air force, to be exact.

I hated flying so much, I'd just driven four thousand miles to avoid it. My boy and me, the station wagon loaded down like the Clampetts' truck. "Pedal to the metal," Sonny — Alex, his real name — sang out the whole way across Canada, from Vancouver Island to Nova Scotia. "What d'you think Dad's doing right now?"

Charlie flew, our little family uprooted like a dandelion. A new base, a new edge of the country. Four thousand miles.

Our lives still in boxes, barely time to shower. Blown in like weeds, Sonny and me. And guess what? Just in time for Family Day.

The tarmac felt like moving metal, my foot still bent from the accelerator.

Sit down, shut up, and hold on: to quote the famous bumper sticker. Advice I wanted to follow right now, gazing up at spacious blue. At least the sky here looked the same; that was one small comfort. *Up, up, and away. Up where the air is clear. Up, up into the atmosphere. Let's go fly a kite.*

Holy good shit. As if you could trust the sky, something that sucked and vacuumed things up, all that blue. Water, spirits. Up into heaven, if you believed in that sort of thing, which I didn't. And here I was with Sonny waiting in a line-up to fly, of all things. One of a flock of moms and kids getting a taste. A chance to go up in a helicopter, a taste of what made our husbands high: the work they did to feed us.

The chopper looked endangered, a prehistoric dragonfly buzzing on the concrete.

There was a lady flipping hot dogs, handing them out on serviettes. "New posting?" Her brows lifted.

I'd have chatted with her, if not for the roar of rotor blades. *Operation Get Acquainted*, said the badge on her apron. "Kind of late, isn't it?" I nudged Charlie. He was clapping a helmet on Sonny's — Alex's — head. It slid down Sonny's forehead like a basket that was too big.

The sun beat down, the runway like a beach with sand the colour of old chinos.

"I'm Joyce," the lady said, swatting flies. "Joyce LeBlanc. I'm three doors up on Avenger." The relish was green and sticky. "'Nother dog, sweetie?"

Charlie helped Sonny into a vest, one made of Kevlar that fit like a dress. His shorts drooped below it, his calves like white baseball bats. All nerves and bounce, he pushed to the head of the line.

"Keep your shirt on," Charlie hollered. Then, to me: "Coming?"

The hot dog lady beamed. "Just hope for the best." She, I noticed, was staying grounded. It wasn't clear who she meant it for, me or the gal behind cradling a toddler. "Always hope for the best."

Charlie laughed. Sweat wormed under my T-shirt. "Coming?" he yelled again.

Maybe it was PMS, maybe I'm a little bit crazy. But I'd have done anything to grab those tongs, serve wieners, and swat away flies. Anything to keep my feet on the runway.

Fears are just thoughts, I told myself. Just thoughts.

Charlie was giving me the eye, that look that says pee or get off the pot.

Just then the sky filled with shadows, birds cutting the glare.

"Willa!" Charlie's voice was worse than a traffic jam, worse than a fleabag motel with no pool. "You coming, or not?" His face bloomed from the hatch — his face, and the navigator's. The helo had swallowed Sonny.

Fear tasted like hot dog as I climbed the metal steps, let myself be eaten. And only because of Sonny.

Inside was a dingy sauna, but instead of bodies and sweat it stank of fuel. Instead of benches there was a seat like a canvas sling. Sonny grinned, a freckle-faced jack-o'-lantern. I grinned back, a death grimace.

The roar throbbed overhead, gnashing engines bearing down. We were in a cellar; any second we'd be bombed. A blast like the end of the world.

Charlie grabbed my wrist, pulled me down, strapped me in. The seat sagged like a camp cot. Sonny patted my knee. Families did this kind of thing all the time, his grin said. Look at Disney World. People pay money to get scared shitless. This is free.

My teeth ground together. All that weight, million-dollar engines pressing down. Metal fatigue, I thought. Charlie smirked with pride: no life like it. The air as heavy as an ocean flooding down. Clouds. Our skulls, tender as eggs fallen out of a nest.

As we rose, my stomach lagged. My face was frozen. Lock-jaw. My back clammy with sweat.

Through the cockpit windows, between the pilot's and co-pilot's heads, a swath of concrete flashed. The hot dog lady, then the tops of trees: tiny dots growing tinier and tinier.

You're in a car, I told myself. On a bus. Clenching Sonny's hand.

Such a good kid, he didn't pull it away. Charlie stared straight ahead, being kind.

My innards flew forward. The taste, again, of hot dog. We hovered, pressing up and up and up. Like Martians in our head-sets, their weight holding in our brains. Then we thrust forward, like a kitten picked up and lugged by the scruff of its neck.

Out of body, out of mind. Drifting higher, higher. A kitten with its eyes not opened yet; no looking down.

Was this the art of detachment?

Sonny let go, rubbing the dents in his palm. The back of my shirt and green canvas were like the same cloth. Shaken loose, soot sifted down. Breathing, I tasted grease.

Then the mother cat yanked us short, jerked us sideways. Someone peeled back the cargo door. A blast of cold. The wrinkled blue sheen of water, the Atlantic a carpet rolling up into smooth, hazy azure. I glimpsed the green sprawl of an island, its shoreline a necklace. Pearls.

My stomach was helium, a black balloon. The rest of me an island like the one below, my heart a lagoon wrapped around Sonny.

Charlie's jaw twitched. His lip curled in satisfaction. The feeling of leaving earth. Leaving it upside down maybe, boring through crust.

Pressing my knees apart, I strained against my harness, tried hanging my head. Shut my eyes as if, opened, all of me would leak through them. Something bumped the roof of my brain. Maybe this is what dying is like, the amoeba inside you that dreams pushing to get out.

Chugging in cold, I waited for it to be over.

When I looked again we were flying over glass and concrete towers. Capillary streets, cars like bright, beaded chemicals. We scooted along at a leisurely clip (faster, make it go faster!), our shadow below an escort.

"Having fun?" Charlie bellowed.

The peaks of a bridge loomed: steel mountain tops.

Charlie fitted a monkey tail to Sonny, a gunmetal-grey cable and boom. Manoeuvered him towards the gaping, rectangular light.

"No!" The engines chopped up my scream.

Sonny knelt there, that hazy blue melting by, an aura. A flash of green girders. He was sticking his head out, yelling something. *Geronimoooooo!* His body snapped tight against the edge of the hatch, his shorts and vest flapping back. He was screaming. Laughing.

Charlie hauled him back, slapping his knee. Sonny shouting.

My heart jackhammered. Tasting nitrates, petroleum, I anchored my eyes to wires running up the wall: arteries. Then studied circles on the floor, something to do with sonar: nerves. I searched for other circles, gauges, dials — the ones out of Charlie's range.

Clumsy as a pup, Sonny patted my arm, his mouth opening, closing like a fish's. "Don't be a wuss, Mom. It's not that scary. Not the Tilt-a-Whirl or Scrambler."

Jerking forward, I kissed his cheek. Not the wisest thing to do, but some things you can't help.

The warm-cool blush of his skin.

My worst fear suddenly vaporized. We'd made it. A gift, a reprieve like a magic bauble: a sun-catcher, one of those glass things people hang in windows. We banked and started descending. Slowly, like a crippled geriatric going downstairs.

Touchdown. Relief was a hot-cold flash, with something else chafing inside. A hard little gem. Now I knew. This was it:

where Charlie went when he disappeared, evaporated from our lives.

As my soles felt cement, somebody yelled: "Say SEX!" It was the hot dog woman still in her apron, aiming her Instamatic. Snap. The three of us caught there, in helmets and headsets. Like the Robinson family from *Lost in Space*, or Cold War-style aliens.

"Welcome aboard," she squealed.

Two days later I was back on the tarmac — on terra firma, but no more grounded. The Dodge had died en route to the grocery store: the transmission? It was Sonny's — Alex's — first day at school, his new school, and any second he'd be out for lunch.

Where the heck was Charlie?

The sun baked down, hot for October. I'd left my shades in the car and had to shield my eyes, stepping from the hangar. The only shade was from the building, not a bush or tree in sight other than a blur of woods in the distance. A plastic banner flapped behind me, yellow in a riff of wind. *Foreign Object Damage. Stay Alive. Be F.O.D. Smart.*

The men formed a dragnet, a chain across the runway. Clones in their blue coveralls. Shadows pooled at their feet. I couldn't make out a face, let alone anything so quirky as a moustache — if there'd been one. No weak links in this chain, not one straggler. Even their laughter sounded the same, snatches of it against the engines droning overhead.

Heat rippled as I stood there waving, hoping somebody would notice.

Every now and then one of them would rib another. Like guys on a ball field, or in a pub. Time out from the enemy, I thought: kids and wives. The Boys. The F.O.D. squad. Great.

A boxy woman in uniform eyed me as she slid past.

"Excuse me —?"

She kept going.

"Attention!" a voice barked and the chain tightened.

"Advance!" The chain inched forward, taut as wire, then knotted as someone stooped to pick something up. Nothing you could see with the naked eye.

Charlie's voice boomed inside my head. *One tiny stone, Willa. One ti-ny stone flies up, hits a compressor — you can kiss that engine goodbye. Not to mention the entire crew! Entire*, he would stress. Charlie was the type who got ticked if you left crumbs on the counter.

I tried harder to make him out, waving frantically now. All I could think of was the Dodge sitting on the shoulder, the beefy guy in a truck who'd been good enough to stop. Shit.

Someone touched my arm. The uniformed woman. There were wings on her shirt.

"Personnel only. D'you have a pass?"

"My husband —" I threw up my hands.

"Wait inside. I'll see what I can do."

I followed her into the cool of the hangar. Five grey-green helicopters were parked inside, a couple missing tail sections. Another had lost its rotors; a hole gaped in its roof. Dragonflies, dead ones. Dismantled, they were even more awkward, quaint. At home Charlie called them relics; in a good mood he compared them to a sixties Corvette.

The servicewoman disappeared and I flagged down a brush cut who smelled of fuel.

"I'm looking for Charlie Jackson, my husband, and I'm —"

Cupping his mouth, he stepped outside, hollering loud enough to cut through anything. "Jackson? Buddy, your wife wants to talk to ya."

Amazing, how it carried.

One of the links in the chain split off, shambling towards me. As Charlie's features grew I forced a smile. He walked right past without saying hi, wiping something from his hands. Disappearing into an office, ducking out again, he gave me a pained look.

"The transmission, maybe?" I mouthed and heard him ask for the phonebook.

He took forever — calling a garage, I hoped. When he came out, the look on his face wasn't good. "There'll be someone down at one. Can you handle it?" Then he strode outside again — that is, if you can imagine someone that stocky, five-nine with a rolling gait, striding.

It was well past noon when I cleared the gates and made it down the hill to our house on Avenger Place. Sonny was on the front steps, kicking the concrete. He'd taken off his shirt; his stomach rolled over the top of his sweatpants. His backpack lay on the walk, a black banana poking from it.

"What took you so long? I've been waitin' for hours."

"How was school?"

"School stinks. My stomach hurts."

I pushed past to let us in.

"I'm missing *Batman*. What's for lunch?" Switching on the TV, he flopped into Charlie's recliner. "Hey — wha'd you do with the car?"

The volume rattled the window, rocked the furniture on the tiles.

"Turn it down, would you?"

I boiled hot dogs and flung them on a plate. Sonny was sprawled upside down, watching the news. An uprising in the Caribbean, people teeming through the streets like ants.

"Cool." He chewed with his mouth open.

"Manners!"

"Why? No one's watching." He handed me his plate.

The next item involved missing people — runaways — the lack of "closure" for families. I was already grabbing my purse; it was a good twenty minutes back to the car.

"Don't forget to lock up. Can you do that, d'you think?"

Outside, the sun had relented and it felt slightly more like fall. Our street, a long crescent, followed a rusty fence up a slope overlooking the water. It was as if God forgot to put trees on this side of the harbour or the wind had blown them to the opposite shore. Our neighbourhood, if you could call it that, clung to a hill, the whole thing hemmed in by barbed wire and WARNING signs.

The houses were the same, greyish pink, green, and turquoise shades, as if fog had seeped into the siding. We'd just moved in, so I should've been more forgiving. Except for the sameness, they almost looked like regular houses, but with no landscaping, no attempts at gardens or decks, things that had to be rooted and nailed down. There was grass though, short and yellow, with bursts of lushness near steps and foundations. And weeds, plenty of weeds, still thriving. If it was grim, the view redeemed it. Our first night, a windy one, you could feel the spray. On a day like this the harbour sparkled like crushed glass and looked almost warm.

I followed Avenger back to the gates, where the highway cut the base in two. Hard to figure why those gates existed; they were always open and rarely manned. Maybe to give the impression that we lived like civilians, which Charlie and I had yet to do. Moving was hard enough, Charlie said. Imagine living off base: it would be like having a cold that wasn't bad enough to keep you home. If you were going to be sick, best to let it keep you in bed. In nearly ten years of married life, we'd known nothing else.

Reaching the highway I walked briskly, following the smell from the oil refinery. With any luck I'd arrive before the tow truck. A woman with a row of baby seats in her van slowed and waved. Sandi, her name was; she'd been traipsing up the street with a gaggle of toddlers the morning our moving van pulled in. She lived around the corner on Sea Fury (or maybe it was Spitfire). On Family Day, after our chopper ride, she'd invited me for coffee.

I waved back — a ride would've been great, but she was in a rush. Watching her drive off made me walk faster and I passed a row of spruce trees, the only greenery for miles. The petroleum smell got stronger, and the blue and red signs for the Superstore loomed closer, almost wavy in the heat from the pavement. Just ahead on the roadside sat the Dodge — baby-poop brown, Sonny called it — its *Beautiful B.C.* plates looking exotic. A guy in a ball cap was hitching it to a truck.

"You the owner? Jump in."

It wasn't the transmission, but a belt. The car was sitting in the driveway by the time Charlie got home, and supper was waiting. Chicken picked up on the fly, and frozen fries. It was sticky and warm in the house. "What's the temperature?" Charlie asked, as if I should know.

Sonny wolfed his food down, then took his dodge ball outside. Charlie ate without talking, afterwards changing into sweatpants and his favourite T-shirt, the one that said *Gravity is for sissies* across the front. When he flopped in front of the TV, I took his glass in to him, half a beer he'd left on the table.

"Oh — thanks. Sweetie." He barely glanced from the screen. There were voices outside and sliding past Charlie's chair I peeked through the sheers, which, just out of a box, needed ironing. Sonny stood in the driveway hugging the ball while a swarm of boys swooped around him on bikes. He was a chunky kid, big for his age, not exactly shy but not great at making friends either. The ball was a magnet; how else had the kids found our place, with its picture window and walk and patch of lawn like everyone else's? Maybe Sonny'd met them at school.

I sat on the couch, deciding to leave the dishes — there weren't many — and during a commercial asked Charlie about work.

"Busy. Fine. The usual," he answered, cutting things short when the program resumed. A nature show about the Australian outback, it kept flashing back to some guy wrestling a crocodile.

"Sonny should see this," I said, stretching my arm along the back of the couch. I caught a glimpse of him outside. One of the kids, a scrawny blond boy, had grabbed the ball and was bouncing it off Sonny's butt. I went to rap at the window.

Through a mouthful of beer Charlie murmured, "Leave him be. Last thing the kid needs is his mom treating him like a dweeb."

"Did you find anything today?" I asked. Charlie looked up, baffled. "That exercise — it looked like a blast." It was meant as a joke: I knew why he'd joined the military, and it wasn't to clean runways.

"How many times have I told you," he said, setting his glass on the rug. "It might seem like crap to you, but it's serious business, Willa. People's lives depend on it." He glanced around. In the TV's glare his face was almost the same sallow green as the walls. His eyes had a pleading look. "There's more to things than fun, you know. You might try the same approach to, I dunno, vacuuming."

We'd just moved in and already there was dust, true enough. I tried keeping things tidy for him and Sonny, I really did.

People like my father said: Get a man to put a roof over your head. No one said you had to keep a sterile zone underneath it: a home like a runway, dirt and hazard free. If we'd stayed anywhere long enough, I'd have got a job, a real one, and paid someone to clean.

"I know, I know," Charlie waved at the TV. "No one likes grunt work."

"But we all have to do things we don't like," Sonny brayed from the entry, bouncing his ball up the stairs.

And who would give a damn fifty years from now if our house was clean? I wanted to say, but, as Sonny flopped to the floor between us, I rose instead to straighten the kitchen.

"You got homework?" I heard Charlie asking him, and the usual reply: "Nope."

"Sure? You check this guy's backpack?" he hollered to me. Hanging up the dishtowel, I didn't answer, just slipped out the back way to take a walk.

Already it was dusk. From the street you could see inside other living rooms identical to ours — the same greenish walls and square, overhead light fixtures. TVs in one corner, the same jumpy glow. I could picture the husbands inside, like Charlie, slumped in La-Z-Boys; the backs of their cropped heads, and moccasins on tiled floors. A couple of places had boxy couches like ours, and others, pictures and plates too high up the walls, the odd formation of Blue Mountain geese.

Rounding the curve and crossing onto Sea Fury, I picked out Sandi's house, notable for the ride-on toys piled outside. Marching past, I imagined the echoey sound of TVs up and down the street, bouncing off walls and ceilings. It should've been a comforting thought, the repetition of rooms and voices, TV voices, and silence as people tuned in to their shows. But tonight, in this sticky, unseasonable warmth, it wasn't.

At least from the sidewalk you couldn't see the dirt inside, if there was any; or smell what they'd had for supper — onions, I imagined, hamburger, Ragu sauce. Outside a couple of places you could hear babies crying and little kids having fits, which cheered me up considerably, spurring me into a power walk. At least I was past that, Sonny being older. The most anyone would hear passing our house, in the daytime anyhow, would be the radio. I slowed down again. Too often airwave voices wooed me from the sink, the suds going chilly; or from laundry balled up on the bed, or rings on the furniture.

Gazing in at those living rooms, I felt a bit like a sightseer. Like someone who had followed signs, even got the trip mapped out by the CAA, yet missed a turn, ending up in a place that should've been familiar but wasn't.

Ahead of me, something shambled from under a parked car. A cat, I thought, but it was a raccoon. I tiptoed closer and made kissy noises. Across the lawn, a face bloomed in the window — a little girl in pyjamas. For a second I saw myself there. This small white face, the last time my mother had come home from the hospital, when I was three or four. The little girl stared, but I didn't wave. Instead, I turned and headed home, steered by the fence and the black stretch of water.

# CURRENTS

Sandi phoned again to invite me over, this time for coffee and a stitch-and-bitch, or that's what it sounded like, above the squall of children. At ten o'clock in the morning? I yanked some burger out of the freezer, contemplating the hours ahead, and thought of my dad — whom I hadn't thought of in ages — how he'd taught my brother to fling fish sticks in the oven when our mom wasn't there to cook any more.

"What can I bring?" I asked Sandi, pinning the phone with my shoulder. *Don't let her say Phentex.*

"Just yourself," she said, and I pictured an infant in her arms, clawing her mouth. The image opened something else inside me, also remote, but fresher. The miscarriage I'd had before our second-last posting. I'd only been a few months along. The fetus was miniscule, but it was a girl. A girl, Charlie had marvelled, which sharpened the disappointment.

I took my time getting ready and arrived around eleven. Sandi greeted me wearing Reeboks and pompommed socks and a sweatshirt with cuddly looking animals on the front. Dread nipped at me as we moved to the kitchen.

She introduced me to her friends, four or five gals sitting around the table perusing catalogues. Babies gummed toys at their ankles. Their names flew out of my head the instant Sandi spoke them; these women did seem awfully alike, with their curling-ironed hair and sooty-looking eyes. A couple of them I'd seen by the school pushing strollers, wearing tights that showed heavy thighs and knobby knees. The strollers were the kind with umbrella handles that looked as if they'd fold with the baby inside, like sandwiches made of squishy bread. (*A Fluff sandwich*, Sonny might've argued, in the same breath asking why he couldn't have one.) It's bitchy of me to say, because we were probably the same age, Sandi's friends and I — thirtyish — but having an older child plus losing a baby made me, well, different, didn't it? If not smarter, then wiser.

"Where'd you get your Snugli at?" someone asked, ignoring me.

"Same place I got the Jolly Jumper. When Donnie's away I go nuts, you know."

"People ask what I do and I tell 'em: I shop."

"You're new, aren't you?" someone interrupted; she might've been a Debbie. "What's your name again? Willa?"

"That's different." The woman who said so smiled at me.

"Oh — *oh*, girls! Did you hear the latest Sharon, Lois & Bram?"

"Well. Don't quote me. But I heard the Elephant — you know, the Elephant? — is a frigging tyrant."

"Marsha!"

"It's okay — isn't it, Taylor?" The woman shrugged, stroking her child's hair. "It's not like she talks yet."

"Joshie does. Don't you, bud? Say 'da-da' for Auntie Sandi — you can do it. Come on, for Mommy ..."

Plunking a mug in front of me, Sandi shifted the catalogues to make room for some cookies. A toddler clung to each of her legs.

"Have you had her to the doctor? I mean, at eighteen months she should be talk —"

"Donnie called last night. Says not to worry; she's saving it for when he comes home."

"Dads, right?" They all snickered, and I couldn't help thinking of my father and Sharla, the woman he'd married. "Don't call me dad," he'd said at their wedding. Joking and slapping Charlie on the back. "Taking care of my girl, eh? Now she won't need to worry about the old man any more." It'd been almost two years since I'd seen Don't-Call-Me. He and Sharla golfed a lot. I was glad for him, though. He deserved to be happy, after raising Jason and me on his own all those years.

"Donnie's back when?" someone piped up.

The coffee was bitter but I drank it anyway, flipping politely through a catalogue of lingerie with Irish lace.

"*When?*"

"Oh. Same as Jarrett. Six months."

"Sex months, was it?"

Cartoon laughter rattled from the living room, and there
was a mushy sound — a child in a playpen? I put down the
catalogue and steadily sipped coffee, ignoring the Care Bears
on the cup. The smell of Similac was making me queasy. That
whole family thing: it was like the elastic in underwear that got
stretched so much everything dangled. My brother Jason was
somewhere up north. People have lives, right? I had Sonny and
Charlie to worry about.

"Yeah, right. With Petie in our bed every night," this woman
was saying.

"Oh, he'll outgrow it."

"In time, you think?"

"Hope so, eh. I *could* send him to my mother's. Hey, Sandi
— where do you order this stuff from, again?"

"Nursery supplies?"

"Accessories. You try those Velcro diapers yet? Look, they're
a dream."

"Nothing like 'em."

"I *hate* that effing Elephant, myself."

"Sandi — you on a diet or what, girl?"

"Diet cookies — right, Sandi?"

"Don't laugh. I lost two and a half pounds last week."

"Get out."

"*I'm* aiming for twenty, by the time Donnie gets —"

A splutter erupted from an infant in a moulded seat, and I
thought back to when Sonny was that age.

"Oh frig. Marsha, could I bum some wipes?"

All those infant needs and taking care of them. Being someone else's lifeline and food source: their oxygen, really.

"Stay put — I've got some." Sandi scurried from the room.

When Sonny was a baby, life had been all about needs. When he'd napped, Charlie and I would rush to bed, not even bothering to draw the shades. We'd do everything in fast forward; never mind that I'd felt like a walking breast.

I stared at the clock by the fridge and stood up. "Sheesh — lunchtime already."

"Oh my God, is it?"

"Your little guy's in school, right? How's he like it?"

It sucks, I felt like saying, but smiled. "Oh, we're adjusting." Sonny better than I, perhaps. His being at school left me more time to think, and seeing him off in the morning made me feel as if I'd neglected something, like when you grocery shop and return home only to realize that the item you've forgotten had been the reason for going in the first place.

"Donnie keeps talking about home-schooling —"

"Oh GOD! Don't mean to interrupt, but did you *hear* about the poisons in apple juice?"

I pointed to the clock and mouthed: "Tell Sandi thanks *so* much but I had to run."

There was a knock. Sandi intercepted me at the door. It was Joyce, the woman who'd done the Family Day hot dogs; she had brownies with her, and an envelope.

Sandy tugged at my sleeve. "Oh, but we're just getting started!"

BERTH

"It's been lovely, really," I said, "but Sonny — Alex — will wonder where I am."

Joyce opened the envelope and pushed something at me. It was a snapshot showing Charlie, Sonny, and me squinting at the camera. My face ashen, Sonny's jubilant. His look was vaguely like my father's, the sort of resemblance only I would notice. I turned it over. F.D., October 1986, she'd penned in.

Outside, the day opened again, the cracked grey street before me with its pastel houses and the ruffled harbour for a back-drop. In the distance, up beyond the school and the runways, was a pencil line of woods. Overhead, you could hear the beat of rotor blades, a helicopter circling in, preparing to land. It was close enough that I spotted the starboard door opened wide and two men up there, like tiny G.I. Joes in helmets and headsets, their legs dangling over. One of them waved.

I wondered if it could've been Sandi's husband returning from a mission, mistaking us for each other. My jeans for leggings, my straight brown hair for her highlighted perm. Guinea pig chip hair, Sonny called it, when we'd run into her at the grocery store. Charlie was off getting himself a doughnut. Sandi had smiled distractedly, peeling her baby's fingers from a bag of Oreos. Her smile had brightened a bit when Charlie ambled up, tossing something into the cart. "I'd like you to meet my hus —" I'd begun, as her little boy made a grab for some Coco Puffs. Before I could finish the introduction, she was off chasing him.

"Who was that?" Charlie had wanted to know, his mouth full of fritter.

21

"A mom from around the corner. Air force."

Who knows why he asked. A new place, fresh faces? There'd been a hundred Sandis on each base we'd known. Seeing her chase the toddler made me feel odd, deflated. As if I had a pair each of perfectly useful hands and feet — but for what?

After the coffee party, the rest of the day I amused myself sorting through boxes in the basement, jumbles of stuff packed in a hurry, non-essentials. The sort of stuff you could lose in a fire and not miss. There was a framed photo of my father and his new wife Sharla.

The last people in the house hadn't been too tidy; the storage space was so cobwebby I put on a bandana to do my work. It reminded me of a neighbour on our last posting, a woman who cleaned each Tuesday, a pillowcase over her mop like the head of a condemned man.

By the time Sonny got home I had half the stuff sorted — a teapot located, winter clothes put away. There were still books and tapes and kitchen gadgets. But then I stumbled across some photo albums, shots of Sonny taken over the years. Sonny as a baby, gumming a teether in his high chair, crawling across various floors, and, later, winging a ball at his dad, starting school — in all the various places we'd lived. I looked happy in the ones of me, in a tired, delirious way. Happy, distracted. Except for the last place — on Vancouver Island — the backgrounds had a sameness, one blurring into another. I was trying to remember which living room was which when Charlie arrived home from work.

"Hey!" I said, running upstairs. The burger wasn't quite thawed, sitting in the sink. He was getting a Pepsi from the fridge.

"Where's Alex?" he wanted to know, unzipping the top of his coveralls.

I had to stop and ask myself the same thing. Charlie stood there drinking, looking kind of disgusted. "What's wrong, hon? That thing wrapped around your head too tight, or what?" I pulled off the bandana. Even being funny, Charlie could be like a burr, so prickly around the edges it was sometimes hard to credit what was inside.

Sonny was in his room, of course. A poster of Hulk Hogan glowered down as he kneeled on the carpet playing with Lego. He'd gotten so big he almost looked funny bent over the spaceship in his hands. My boy, who teachers said couldn't sit long enough to learn multiplication. Who still had trouble writing his last name legibly: Jackson. Jackass, some kids in his last school called him, when I was right there picking him up. It was a hard thing to watch, your kid being teased, like a bear suffering wasps. Especially when you knew what was inside him, what he was capable of.

Charlie had built him a special table for his Lego — the airstrip and hangar and spaceships and jets he'd brought all the way from B.C., mostly intact. Charlie hadn't seen the little Tupperware container of people, though. Dozens of tiny yellow bubbleheads, torsos with the arms and legs nipped off. "Boys," he'd said, when I showed him. "That's what they do."

To his credit, he'd gone out one evening and bought Sonny a bike with a light, saying a ride after supper might be good — better than dodge ball.

"But with a ball, we know where he is."

"For God's sake, Willa. He's nearly nine years old. You can't put him in a bubble. He has to make his own way." Fine for him to say, when I was the one who saw Sonny getting teased, on whom Sonny vented. What kid wouldn't act out, wearing Sonny's shoes? "How're his marks?" Charlie changed the subject, and I said it was too early to tell.

"Hungry?" I asked Sonny now, and he looked up from his Lego. Those coffee bean eyes.

"What're we having?"

"What would you like?"

"Pizza pockets and Sara Lee?"

Sonny's love of junk made cooking ridiculous. I could've been a microwave — or the reverse of Jeannie slipping from her magic bottle in that sixties TV show. Turning on appliances, then slipping down the drain instead. This *was* twenty years later.

"You're out of luck, Sonny boy."

"I don't know who you're talking to," he said, and mumbled into his fist, "Earth Base to Flight Zeeero-Zeeero Nine: is there a humanoid on board?" Then he made a siren noise and pressed a button. The light on the spaceship's nose flashed red. "Emergency landing! Personnel clear the runway, unless you want your heads blown off!"

"Willa? What the hell is *this*?" Charlie yelled from the kitchen.

He was standing by the sink with burger blood dripping from his wrist.

"I was planning to make —"

"Some of us like to eat at suppertime?"

Idiotically, I felt the prick of tears.

"Charlie?" I grabbed the package, ran it under the tap. "Do you think it'll be good for him, this place?" He looked at me, baffled, and without a word got out a leftover pork chop and disappeared to the basement.

"Dad's had a rough day," I told Sonny when the two of us sat down to eat.

Charlie had never been the talkative type. But his silences were like weather fronts, breezes that blew into gales or petered out. You just had to excuse them, because his moods were a storm that mostly never hit. Still, that coolness dampened everything it passed over. This wasn't the first time Sonny and I — *Alex*, Alex, I repeated in my head: *call the child by his name for God's sake* — sat alone at the table almost hating to chew in case the sound drove his dad deeper into the basement.

Maybe he was down there looking for something to unpack, or fix. That's what Charlie did when he wasn't away or at work or watching TV. It was good that he had a purpose, things to do. It made me jealous.

And it wasn't that we feared him, exactly. He loved Sonny. I guess he loved me, if love was a wind that blew hot and cold. A propeller that beat the air, invisible enough that it was easy to doubt it existed.

But as we munched our burgers, as the clock ticked and a

tap dripped, it was like the floor was tin. The last thing in the world you wanted was to disturb Charlie. God knows he did his bit for us every day. The least we could do was let him tinker in peace.

 3

## TIDES

Charlie took me dancing at New Year's — a party at the mess. A slew of people were invited, everyone connected to the squadron. There were pilots, navigators and AESOPS — airborne electronics sensor operators — and technicians like Charlie; even snowplough drivers, and their wives. Wet snow fell like cow flaps that evening. We were late and he was fidgety, worried about missing the free drinks because the babysitter, Joyce's daughter from three doors up, took forever coming over. Not that Sonny was a baby. He was in a snit, figuring he could mind himself even though he knew he wasn't old enough.

"I can get my own freaking 7-Up," he said as the three of us paced in front of the living room window. I'd bought barbecue and sour cream and onion chips and there were Twizzlers in the cupboard. Sonny said he was going to watch videos all night, frig what Carleen the babysitter asked him to do. She could pass out and pee herself in the basement, he said, going on and on; what were we doing anyway, spending good money, when everyone knew she'd just lock herself in the bathroom and smoke dope. "Yes she does," he insisted. "You can hear her in there choking — oh, wait, now I remember: it's her boyfriend sucking on her neck like a vampire —"

"Sonny. You have some imagination. Carleen must be a whiz if she can jam all that into an hour." I was thinking of parent-teacher night, the one other time we'd hired her. The sole occasion Charlie and I had gone out alone since the move.

"Jumpins," Charlie blurted, fed up. "Give it a rest, son." He adjusted his collar, not used to being dressed up. He probably would've been happier going to work.

"Rest in pieces!" Sonny shot back, taking over his dad's chair and gluing himself to the screen. Swear to God, at times he was like a forty-year-old trapped inside a kid's body.

"Makes you wonder about reincarnation," I mumbled to Charlie, when Carleen had arrived, finally, reeking of gel, and we were heading to the car. "If I get to come back, it's gonna be as a bee." I poked his arm. Once, he would've laughed. He'd have made a buzz in my ear and said, "Frig that, I'm coming back as a — never mind." Now he grimaced — a migraine smirk — as if he were working on an engine, cleaning and greasing parts. His look didn't change as we entered the hall.

There were already quite a few people there, party-doll couples like the kind on top of wedding cakes; and all of us miniatures in this big, hollow room. It could've been an old hangar, with its girdered ceiling. But it felt good just to be out.

I spotted Sandi with a short, stringy guy who must've been her husband — I hoped he was, the way she kept tailing him. A lot of the women were dressed like her, in slippery-looking dresses so skimpy they must've been freezing. They looked smaller somehow, slighter, without their kids. The men were decked out in sports jackets and pants knuckled from hangers, and there was the distinct smell of Brut in the air. Charlie had just shaved, and his skin had that pinkness that made it easy to forget we'd been married this long. He smelled faintly of my Nivea.

The dancing hadn't started, partiers drifting around like bits of tinsel in the echoey room. Someone had set up rows of stackable tables. On one wall was a giant poster of a Sea King, its nose painted like a red and blue target. Someone had taped streamers to it, a limp burst of colour over the big propeller. Bands of crepe paper dangled from some lower rafters, and strung above the bar — another stacking table covered in blue — was the year in gold numbers: 1987. A new year: this one would be better. It made me think of Sonny's first day of school, of holding my breath in hope while fighting a loose, sinking feeling. The way it felt being out. Like regaining the use of your legs after having them in casts, and hoping you could still dance. Or run.

Right now I was worried about my slip showing; my dress climbed the backs of my legs, plus I'd put on a pound or two, which dragged at my pantyhose. It was the only pair I owned — there wasn't much call for pantyhose, frying burgers or scouring the sink. Minutes before Carleen had shown up, a run had started in one heel, which I'd caught with a dab of Cutex.

Charlie was the best-looking guy in the place, pink-faced and bull-necked in his blue sports jacket, his sandy, not quite silvery crewcut glistening. Each table had a hurricane candle in the middle, and crepe paper streamers taped to the sides. The ends swished the floor, the lights bobbling every time someone set down a drink. Charlie beelined to the bar where two of his buddies were serving beers from coolers, and shots from the table set up behind. Somebody'd cut 87s out of Christmas wrap and stuck them to the tablecloth, and one of the bartenders had the numbers painted on his forehead in blue glitter.

Joyce drifted over with a glass of something red, cooing about the job they'd done decorating. She asked me if Carleen would be very late, her eyes all the while fixed on Charlie downing a beer and laughing at something Mr. 87 was saying. I looked around for her husband and saw him carrying in a stack of chairs.

"Someone's put in a lot of work," I said to make conversation, as she nudged me towards a punch bowl and an assortment of glasses that would've rivalled a spring fling sale. I took one patterned with clubs and diamonds and she ladled in an inch or two of punch, stabbing a cherry with a plastic sword and poking it in.

"Hubby looks happy," she said; and suddenly, who knows why, I imagined Sonny watching TV while Joyce's daughter sat on the edge of the tub and inhaled. I pictured him on the couch, his hand paused in a bag of Lays, guzzling his fifth glass of pop. It made me forget my skirt riding up and Joyce raising her glass.

"A'right!" she exclaimed, clapping her hands, then lighting a cigarette. The hall had filled like a tank, making it less drafty; already the air was blue with smoke. "I was scared there for a bit," she said.

I followed her twinkly gaze. The band had arrived with their instruments and were starting to set up. One fellow had a guitar the colour of the car Charlie dreamed of — a red Mustang. Another, dressed in a turtleneck, scowled as he assembled the drums.

After a while, a fellow in a suit arrived lugging a bass and an amplifier, and a few minutes later, a lanky, gaunt-looking man appeared carrying a brown case. He looked wet and kind of rushed, as if he'd been waiting outside somewhere. His cheeks were ruddy, almost like Sonny's after a bike ride in the wind, and he kept blowing on his hands and rubbing them together. It almost looked as though he'd gotten the address wrong, or shown up by mistake; he was wearing jeans and hiking boots with red laces, and when he took off his jacket he had a sweater underneath. Grey, with red and white around the neck and cuffs, like the kind I'd sent my brother one Christmas. Maybe he was the manager or, in a pinch, the singer. He wasn't a roadie: a chunky fellow with a mullet had arrived and was moving about, plugging things in. The two of them disappeared, maybe outside for a smoke.

After a little while they came back, the guy in jeans joking with the others as they tuned up. When he finally opened the case, he took out a saxophone. It was sleek and brassy, with buttons neat as engine parts. He blew a couple of notes, aiming at the bassist's ear, then threw his head back, laughing.

"Ladies and germs — the amaaaazing Hughie Gavin!" the bass player razzed, giving the sax a shove.

Saxophone wasn't my favourite instrument. We were paying Carleen *how* much an hour? At least it wasn't trumpet, and with any luck we'd be home in bed when the crowd requested reveille.

Sandi drifted by with her husband, hanging off him like a coat. "Jesus," he muttered, and she backed off a little, reaching to fix her strap. He lit two cigarettes, poking one into her mouth. Charlie was on the other side of the room, deep in conversation with another guy, the two of them swigging beer.

I found two seats at an empty table and listened to the band warming up. Jangly notes bounced from the ceiling, the way you'd imagine music might sound in a prison. Then the sax player started in. He angled himself sideways as he blew. After a few bleats, he stopped and pulled off his sweater. He had on a blue button-down shirt underneath that looked new: it was stiff and still held the folds from the package. I couldn't help noticing how it stood out from the waist of his jeans; as he swung sideways, his body almost looked concave, like a satellite dish, or bellows with lots of room for air. And as he played, his cheeks flexed, almost like the sides of an animal breathing. He didn't get that googly look of a trumpeter, like Louis Armstrong, as if he'd explode. He looked wiry, tight, as if all the work was in his mouth.

Finally the band struck up a tune I vaguely recognized. Possibly from childhood: trips to the grocery store before my mother got sick. "Fly Me to the Moon"? Jazz, anyway. No wonder I didn't quite get it. Honking like the sound of geese fleeing winter. Charlie had a few tapes like this, but I never played them. I liked music with words you could latch onto. Charlie wasn't big on words, but when I glanced over he was still going at it with that buddy of his. A good old good old, a heart to heart.

I was hoping he'd come and dance. Once in a while, at functions like this he would — with coaxing. Though he didn't have great rhythm. He'd pump his hands like pistons, making me think of that golden oldies tune "The Loco-Motion," then move them to my waist as if I were a cocktail, his hands a shaker — or a cellulite-reducing gadget. But he tried, and tonight I was game.

More than once the sax player blared his horn my way. I don't think I imagined it. Quite possibly I blushed. Each time was a little like being pinched, like having a stranger touch your waist, no chance at all to suck it in. I kept looking around for Charlie, who was talking to a short, dark-haired woman now, the captain in charge of training pilots. She looked older, serious, and probably had been pretty once.

To anyone who noticed — the Sandis and Joyces — I must've looked stung with boredom, humming with it, my eyes on the rafters, mentally swinging from them, waiting to leave.

But that wasn't quite true.

The band played on and Sax Man took a little break, snapping his fingers and nodding along. Perhaps his eyes wandered over to Charlie talking to his friends again, sitting on the floor with the wall for a backrest, his tie undone. Maybe. Because he looked right at me and smiled. Not a friendly smile; and certainly not an "I feel for you" smile. More one of curiosity, or maybe contempt. Suddenly I was witheringly aware of my metallic dress and the net of spray holding back my hair. It was easy to lump me in with everyone else, the crewcuts and their spouses. Maybe, quite simply, he was on the lookout for someone to sleep with. A nature girl, as Charlie called them: girls who slept under the stars. But everyone was married; why else would we be there? Never mind the slipping straps and rundown bitch sticks, as Charlie called high heels. We wives aimed to please, which wasn't easy in out-of-date shoes dug out of boxes once a year.

The band tooted out something Herb Alpertish, the guitarist swinging right into it. I tried to focus on the drummer and the bass player — everyone but the saxophonist, who had his eyes closed and was blowing at the ceiling, one long, screechy raspberry. My eyes kept flicking to his shirt.

Waving to Charlie, I tried concentrating on my drink, stabbing the ice cube with the little sword. I was on my second drink — ginger ale — when he came and put his hot hands on my shoulders, pulling out a chair with his foot. He smelled of beer and his face was flushed. As he sat down, I reached for him, my hand brushing his side. His ribs, through a pad of flesh and his jacket. Or the memory of his ribs. I thought of them almost as if they were my own, neither taking them for granted nor feeling any particular attachment. It was so different from when Sonny was a baby, sleeping, when I'd counted them in the sun streaming through the window.

He rocked back in his chair, then, after a minute or two was off again in search of more punch and another beer.

Breathing in, I glanced up at the band. The sax player was leading a slow number, the bell of his instrument buffing the air. The dance floor was empty, laughter and chit-chat so loud the notes got lost. But he didn't look as if he minded; he could've been telling himself a story.

Charlie returned with our drinks, and we watched a couple, quite drunk, doing the monkey, then the bump. "Hold me back," he joked and his eyes glazed as he picked the label off his Keith's. I patted his leg. After a little while he said, "That's enough. Let's get out of here."

For the five minutes it took to drive home, I felt a rosy kind of hope inside; I wouldn't quite call it expectation. But I thought of sunlight playing over his chest while the baby snoozed in the other room.

In bed, I put my hand on his stomach, left it there. Waiting. He kissed me gently on the forehead then rolled to face the wall. Almost instantly, his breathing became a snore, and a tightness spread through me, moving from my thighs right up into my lungs.

4

# TRUE NORTH

A snowstorm turned the base into a Fluff sandwich, as Sonny remarked, gawking outside. He still had to get dressed. It was one of those mornings there wasn't much in the house besides ketchup. I made porridge and left some jam and the last of the milk on the table, then slipped out to the store while Charlie was showering. A purpose, I thought. A mission.

A drift and a two-foot bank left by the plough blocked me in. I managed to dig the car out, a plank of snow sliding off the roof as I backed onto the street. Didn't they ever have storm days in this place? Making it to the highway was tricky, but it was pretty clear sailing to the Superstore, with hardly any traffic. The sky looked like fibreglass insulation gone mouldy. At least the supermarket was bright, with all those huge, blown-up photos of fruit. For a moment I felt right at home, almost cosy, the way I had moving with Charlie into our first married quarters, back at the ripe old age of twenty.

Empty of people except for a stock boy and some check-out girls, the store was like the inside of an orange, or the sun turned down low. The endless aisles and raftered ductwork made me feel tiny. I was checking through a carton of eggs when I heard humming. That Beatles song, "Across the Universe," competing with ABBA on the PA. I'd just put the eggs in the cart when someone came around the corner. He looked vaguely familiar, despite his navy toque pulled low. His jaw had a bristle of beard; his cheeks were ruddy as if he'd been outside forever. He had on a brown canvas coat that, even from a distance, smelled like a tent — not unpleasant. He stared at me, blue eyes fixing on my plaid scarf. He looked puzzled, as if he'd seen me before.

He had. The PA had switched to an instrumental of "Hotel California" before it hit me. The guy from the New Year's dance — the sax player. I caught a whiff of something else — wet wool, and fuel. Gasoline? I reached for some margarine. He was poking through a family pack of eggs. When I glanced back our eyes met and he smiled. I felt myself go as pink as the child safety belt on the cart. What's her problem? I imagined him thinking as I scooted to the next aisle.

Throwing some coffee into the cart and some Quik for Sonny, I remembered the milk and scuffled back to the dairy aisle. He was still there, selecting butter. Pounds of it. Must have a pile of kids, I thought, picturing them. A wife, too. A female version of him in hiking boots. No make-up. The type who ate organic grains and used lichen shampoo, not tested on animals, or humans either. I pictured them in a kitchen with jars of beans and plants in the windows, the smell of nut butter and sprouts steeped into the woodwork. I envisaged the wife nursing a baby, and tried to imagine her name. Penelope? Elizabeth? Sandra — no, that was too close to Sandi, with her sweatshirts and feathered bangs.

"Where've I seen you?" His voice was a pinch. He was holding two pounds of butter as if they were hot bricks. Maybe he didn't have kids; someone with kids would've been three aisles over by now, whipping pizza pops into his cart and pushing for the checkout.

One kid, maybe — like us, with Sonny.

I gave him my base girl smile.

"Pardon?"

"It's just — I'm sorry — I've seen you before. Just can't place it." He'd put the butter in his cart, was holding an economy slab of cheese. "I don't get to shore too often," he said, almost apologetically. "God. When I do I'm like a kid in a video store."

I glanced at his cart, feeling myself redden again. There wasn't much in there a kid — a normal kid like Sonny — would eat. Canned beans and stew and packages of fancy dried bean and rice mixes, and canned tuna and tomatoes, a lot of cans, and regular white noodles and even a box of Hamburger Helper. There was a family pack of Mars bars, and, oh, yes, canned milk. The biggest size box of tea bags they sold. Peanut butter, a vat; smooth. An extra large box of laundry soap.

"Forget something?" he asked.

I must've looked baffled. "Oh … I, um —"

"I *remember* — you were at that dance we did. That's it, that's where I've seen you." He sounded almost relieved. There were fine lines around his eyes and his face was windburnt; the redness couldn't be from the cold alone. Right, I thought. A wife, about to appear any second. Emily. Maybe something less flowery: Ann.

"Am I right?" he was saying, and my mind flew to Sonny and his dad in coveralls, inspecting things.

"Sure. That must be it." The ruddier his face seemed, the hotter mine felt. "Great music," I lied. "Gosh, what time is it? I left the house in a … I just hope my son made it to school."

Even as I glided away, my pulse quickened and dull regret attached itself to me.

Leaving the store — it took no time at all getting through the checkout — I loaded up the trunk and slowly pulled out. Remembering we were out of toothpaste, I stopped at a drugstore. Back on the road, a red truck fishtailed ahead of me. Maybe I'd stop for coffee; I'd left the house without making any, since Charlie had been out of cream. As the Tim's came in sight, I thought that he and Sonny would like some doughnuts, so I turned in. The truck had turned in, too. It was parked next to a Mustang with smoked windows — the only vehicles in the lot.

A guy with badly permed hair had beaten me to the counter, and was ordering three double-doubles. I asked for a Boston cream, a chocolate dipped, and a medium black. The clock said 8:58. Oh go for it, I thought, and took a seat. It had started snowing again, a fine white spray ticking the windows. Poodle Hair made his way to a spot, lighting a cigarette. As he sat down near the disposal bin, I noticed his friends. One was the man from the dairy aisle — the sax player, again! — and the other seemed vaguely familiar. It was the husky guy with the mullet, who'd been helping the band with its equipment that night. The three of them were folded around a tiny table.

The sax player must've sensed me looking. Glancing up, he blinked, appearing surprised. He mouthed something like "Hey!" — it was hard to tell exactly through the cloud of smoke. When I shrugged, he left his friends and came over. He waved his hand in front of him as if apologizing for the smell, explaining, "My buddies. A colleague, you know, and my good friend Wayne. Drives me around when I need it."

The one with the poodle cut rose, stubbing out his cigarette, and left; the other, the big guy, brought their coffees over.

"I'm his chauffeur," this one said. "Good thing, Hughie, otherwise you'd starve on that fuckin' island."

"Aw, get out." The sax player winked at me.

It was odd; for a second I felt like someone on TV meeting two talking heads onscreen — or how I imagined that would be. It was sort of like being underwater. Not quite real, despite the background noise of dishes clanking and coffee hitting a burner.

Hugh pointed to the seat beside mine. "You look like you could use company."

*That bad?* I almost said, hearing Charlie's voice inside me. I would've said it, had Hugh been someone like Sandi fishing for an invitation; I'd barely managed to brush my teeth that morning.

I looked at my watch. The friend, the shaggy one — Wayne — shuffled closer to let someone with a tray go by. There was a stringy silence.

"You live on an island," I finally remarked, for something to say. It sounded instantly dopey, like saying, *Soooo — you have one arm and you're applying to the circus.*

Wayne sniggered, fidgeting. He seemed anxious — for another cigarette maybe, or to hit the road. "Hughie's a light-house keeper. When he's not blowing his brains out on that fuckin' horn."

"A lightkeeper," I said idiotically, picturing the Tim and Ginger books Sonny'd read before moving on to *Goosebumps.* My mind filled with cartoon images of rocks and waves and craggy old men. "That's ... different."

Hugh eyed me, amused or disappointed, it was impossible to tell.

"I'm surprised, you know, they still have people doing that ... kind of thing."

He was staring now, with the hint of a smile, his eyes a startling blue. He rubbed his jaw and I noticed his fingers. They were long and tanned with nails that were clean but not too clean.

"I don't know your name," he said. Wayne was slapping at his coat pockets, rooting for matches.

"Willa," I said. "Willa Jackson."

He nodded and stuck out his hand. "Hugh Gavin. And my

best bud," he said. "Wayne Tobias." His eyes warmed as they locked on mine; there were grey flecks around the pupils. "I'm over on Thrumcap," he explained, the way I'd tell Sonny there was pop in the fridge. "Wayne's got the boat." He sipped coffee. "He's my taxi."

"An island." I was still taking it in. Thinking how I'd go nuts on an island, and how for Sonny it'd be even worse — like life without TV. "I don't know how you stand it."

"Lots of time to practise." He tootled his fingers over invisible keys. "Lots of time to fart around, figure things out." He rolled his eyes good-naturedly, that blue shifting like the snow at the window.

Wayne shook his head. "Drink up, you friggin' bastard, if you're expecting me to get you back there any time soon."

Ignoring him, Hugh seemed in no hurry. "It's grand out there," he said. "You should see it sometime. Especially in a storm." He stood up slowly, finishing his coffee. "You could come check out the light."

There was a pause.

"I could call you sometime," he said, crumpling his cup.

"What?" My voice seemed to come from the cup in front of me.

His friend flipped a matchbook onto the table and Hugh dug for a pen.

"Buddy's bored." Wayne smirked, stomping his feet.

Like a machine — a floor polisher or a dishwasher or something out back — Charlie's voice grumbled inside me. I wrote down our number. Just like that. My hand trembled, and I hoped no one noticed. It was like entering a raffle for a prize I didn't even know I wanted. Wayne's eyes bored through me as I slid the matchbook over to Hugh.

"I'll give you a tour," he said.

"A tour would be great ... sometime. My son would love it."

He didn't look at all put off by that, wearing the grin he'd worn on New Year's Eve when the crowd applauded a solo.

Sweet God, what had I done?

Watching them trudge outside, I remembered the groceries sitting in the trunk, and wondered if keeping a light was anything like housework. Whether there was someone always running a finger over things, sizing up your efforts. At least he hadn't asked about me, what *I* did. Good thing, I thought, stuffing the napkin into my cup. There wasn't a whole lot to tell.

The news came in February; the Sea Kings would be going out on an exercise for three months. I shouldn't have been surprised; it's why they say there's no life like it in those recruitment ads that make enlisting sound like a leap to glory. Twelve weeks. Word came the day the washer died and the car's muffler went. "But why you?" I asked Charlie, throwing up my hands. The answer was plain. He and the other technicians were to the choppers what I was to Sonny. Well, not so much Sonny now as Sonny just out of the womb. Milk-machine, handmaiden, and guardian rolled into one. A human remote controlling a black and white TV.

Charlie waited till after supper that Friday night to say

they'd be shipping out the following week. He waited till I'd swallowed dessert, springing it on me between rising from the table and scraping his plate.

"But we've only been here five months," I protested, even as the Jell-O pudding curdled in my throat. "Isn't there anything you can tell them?"

He looked at me as if I had carrots for brains. "I don't know why you're so upset. It's not you who has to go up in those things. Think about the guys, Willa! Life is rough," he mocked, "get used to it."

Sonny skulked to the living room and turned on the TV.

Charlie put his hand on my hip to move me away from the garbage. Then he went and shut himself in the bedroom. I could hear the clock radio while I cleaned up. My mind wheeled through all kinds of excuses for him. He was lying there reading a magazine when I went to bed hours later.

"I'm sorry, hon," he said, without looking over. He turned the page and kept reading. "Three months isn't that bad. It could be worse. We'll be with a destroyer in the Mediterranean. Thank your lucky stars it isn't some godforsaken place like Haiti."

Three months can feel like three years; if anyone knows that, it's a no-life-like-it wife.

After the muffler, the car needed a valve job. I was coming in one lunchtime from the garage and collecting Sonny when the phone rang.

"Charlie?" I jumped in. There was always that second between picking up and wondering: is this it? The news that he'd been lost or hurt, and was lying somewhere like a jigsaw puzzle.

There was a pause which set my heart racing, and for a second everything stopped, even Sonny opening some Twizzlers at the counter.

"Is this Willa?" a man asked, clearing his throat. "Honk, honk," he said, and hummed something into the phone. My mouth went dry. I was about to hang up when he said, "It's Hugh." He paused and a little chill leapt between my shoulder blades. "Remember?" he said. "You drink your coffee black."

I tried babbling something about Charlie, but the words died in my throat. It was as if I'd spent my whole life casting out excuses in a long, billowing line; and suddenly the line had spun itself out. There was nothing to do but start reeling, madly.

Sonny wasn't impressed when he heard we were going on an adventure. He was ticked off because there was a WWF match on TV that he wanted to watch.

"Let me guess," he said, sucking a Cherry Blaster. "We're going to Beirut? Germany? I know: Slobodanlovakia!"

"Guess again," I said. "An island."

"Australia!"

"Um, closer."

He stuffed more candies into his mouth, scowling.

I bribed him with Kentucky Fried Chicken to get him in the car. He ate his snack pack while we followed Hugh's directions to the Passage. It was a ten-minute drive, which wasn't bad. You could see the tip of the island from the base, standing at the top of the hill; it was the one I'd spotted from the chopper the day of our ride. But you couldn't see the light; it was on the opposite side on a spit pointing like a finger into the harbour. Wayne's boat was docked near a government wharf.

"We're going to visit a friend," I'd told Sonny. "He's a musician."

Sonny's face had a sour look as I pulled up to the rickety marina. It was a few yards from a big wharf with fishing boats tied up alongside it. The red truck was parked nearby, beside a trailer that looked like a French fry wagon, with the sign: Charters. Eco-Tours. Deepsea Fishing. It had a faded picture of a figure like Captain Highliner painted on the side. Wayne emerged, cursing to himself as he locked up and sauntered ahead of us down to the open boat. He just grunted when Sonny asked if there were sharks, and mumbled about Hugh owing him.

It was early April, a drizzly day grey as flannel; Charlie had been gone six weeks. The island loomed close enough to shore that you could see the trees. As we got into the boat, the drizzle thickened to a slow white rain and Sonny and I hunched together for warmth. Wayne didn't seem to notice it, starting the outboard. He had his red and black hunting jacket undone, and his shirt was unbuttoned so you could see dull looking hair and pasty skin. Snowflakes dissolved in his mullet as he lit a cigarette. He smoked the whole time; maybe that was how he kept warm, lighting one cigarette off another. We kept our backs to him, motoring along. It was as if the boat was a

Chevette and Sonny and I were a couple of hitchhikers he couldn't wait to unload. The water was choppy and I thought of "The Minnow," that theme song stuck in my head from *Gilligan's Island* reruns. What had gotten into me, to put us in such a spot, at the mercy of this greaseball who didn't even carry lifejackets?

*Shit!* I could imagine Charlie yelling, if he'd known, though he'd have said *sugar* in front of Sonny. *You trying to drown my son?*

This wasn't the half of it. If Charlie could've seen us — chugging across the water in a Boston whaler to meet somebody who could've been a madman for all I knew. Except that Hugh had those eyes. I'd seen pictures in the paper of crazies, murderers, and people with no conscience: that fuck-you look in their eyes. Hugh's, if I remembered, were wide open, clear and calm as a lake.

5

# THE COMPASS

There was a man waiting on the wharf, which listed badly into the water. I hoped it was him as we motored closer. An echo of Charlie's voice droned with the engine: *If you're so bored, go do something. There must be some class you could sign up for. Decorating?*

Hugh seemed thinner than I recalled, and taller in that canvas coat. He reached down to help me as I clambered up the rotting ladder. Sonny balked at first, rocking the boat as Wayne stayed put in the stern. "Don't look down," I said when he started climbing. Hugh reached for Sonny's hand and hauled him up. Sonny eyed him as if he were some kind of misfit but mercifully kept his mouth shut. Hugh jumped down to hand his buddy some bills, and told him to come back in a few hours.

"I'm not waiting over the house all day," Wayne groused.

"Me and Reenie are going out to the club for a few. If you want a ride back it'll have to be soon." It was meant for us, though he said it to Hugh.

"Whatever." Hugh shrugged, standing with us on the dock. "We'll have our tour, then Wayne'll pick you up. Right, bud?"

You couldn't hear Wayne's reply above the throttle. As the boat skimmed off, it was as if Charlie were in the clouds, looking down. Here we were in the middle of the harbour with nobody around but this guy I'd known for all of five minutes at the Tim's.

"Call me Hugh," he said to Sonny, shaking his hand. Sonny gave him the same look he'd given the teacher on his first day at school. Here we go, I thought.

"Hugh's a saxophonist," I told him, as if it made any difference. "Hugh, this is Sonny. *Alex*."

Sonny kicked stones into the water.

"Well," said Hugh. "First stop's the light, I guess."

"How far is it?" Sonny glowered.

Looking amused, Hugh pointed towards an opening in the woods, what appeared to be the head of a path. "I don't get a lot of visitors," he said. "Well, except Wayne and fellas from the band. Mostly I go over to jam. Too big a pain hauling gear over here. We don't practise enough." He glanced at Sonny. "Your mom can tell you that."

Sonny took out a packet of sugar he'd got with his chicken, and shook some onto his tongue. As I elbowed him he piped up, "We have to walk? That sucks."

"No cars out here," Hugh shouted. He was slightly ahead now, starting up the trail. His voice caught in the wind. "It's not that far."

"It looks far," Sonny grumbled and I gave his arm a little wrench.

It ended up being farther than I expected. Hugh walked fast; we almost had to sprint to keep up. He could've been a runner; he had that tautness about him, that compactness, and he didn't seem in any real hurry plodding ahead. The woods thickened — mostly crowded spruce, their boughs breaching the path — and I was getting winded when finally the water came in sight, a pearly gleam through the trees.

The trail ended at a beach where waves beat the greyish sand. Sonny poked behind, filling his pockets with dull-looking shells. The sand gave way to a stretch of blackish mud and rocks like teeth with seaweed and litter caught between them. Sonny went to pick up a feather and I gasped. It was attached to bones — the carcass of a gull pressed flat as a duck in a Chinese restaurant, one eye gazing up.

At the start of a boardwalk, silver timbers banked against boulders, Hugh paused and we leapt from rock to rock catching up. Ahead was a barn-like house and just beyond it, the bright white tower with its red top. The wind pushed us towards it, and reaching the tower we huddled there for a moment, pressing ourselves to its cold concrete. Behind us, a clothesline ran from the house to a telephone pole, its pulley squawking like a bird. You had to shout to hear yourself.

Hugh unlocked the door and we stepped inside. It was cool and still as a cellar, the cement floor painted grey, the walls white. There was a dusty-looking broom propped below a window, and a bulky piece of machinery on a trolley — a generator in case of power failure. "A lifesaver, that thing," he said.

It was like being inside a toilet paper tube, Sonny murmured as we climbed three steep metal ladders to the top. Our footsteps rang below as we squeezed through the hatch, emerging into the lantern. The air up there was warmer, almost stuffy. There was barely room for the three of us to squeeze around the lens or file past the radio. Propped on a shelf, it was a dusty contraption the size of a shoebox, its microphone dangling. Beside it sat a roll of paper towel and a green spray can of window cleaner.

This part felt like being inside an eyeball, I couldn't help marvelling, squinting at the brightness. Light poured in all around, absorbing the smooth revolving flash that was so green it could've been under water. The lens dwarfed us, like the eye of a gigantic insect, the fly in an ancient sci-fi film, its reflectors like scales. It turned silently in a trough of silver liquid that made me think of the ring of fire in that Johnny Cash song — except the liquid couldn't have been hot. Sonny went to test it with his finger.

"Don't touch," Hugh said. "It's mercury. The stuff inside a thermometer?"

Sonny bent and peered down at his reflection blurred and stretched like in a midway mirror.

"Couldn't I have a bit? A tiny blob?" he said, and though I told him to put a lid on it, I understood. There's something about shiny things; perhaps we're all crows at heart.

Ignoring his pout, standing very still I watched the clouds, bolts of grey against the peach-coloured horizon. For a moment it felt as if we were part of the sky, moving.

"I just want to see how it rolls," Sonny persisted. Hugh brushed my elbow. Too soon he was leading us down again.

"Tea'd be good, to warm up," he said, more an observation than an invitation. Below, as he locked up, I studied the red and white No Trespassing sign, and he remarked, "Visitors are supposed to be licenced. Good thing we didn't go out on the platform. I'd be in deep shit if you'd fallen off." He smiled broadly, teasing?

"I thought lightkeepers had to be on watch all the time," I yelled above the wind.

"She's on autopilot, mostly," he yelled back, steering us towards the house. "I'm here making sure nothing fucks up." Wincing, I glanced at Sonny still staring up at the lantern — orbiting Jupiter. Good thing, though. Like Charlie, like any parent, I tried to watch my tongue around him.

We followed Hugh to the back porch, where he braced the door against the wind. We found ourselves inside a creaky kitchen. It had a wood stove and antique-looking wiring running up the walls. He put on the light and crossed to the stove, lifting a burner and warming his hands.

"They only got power here ten years ago. Can you imagine?"

I couldn't, actually, and wondered how anyone survived here, with or without electricity. Not many men would, women either — none of the ones I knew, anyhow. I remembered Charlie the time the power went out during *Hockey Night in Canada*.

There was a hotplate in a corner and a sink with the space underneath curtained off. A cracked mirror hung above it, and along one wall stretched some shelves and cupboards painted surf green. The fridge was curved — like a fifties Chev, I could almost hear Charlie saying — and there was a red table with the leaves folded down, and a pair of dinged-up kitchen chairs. The walls had a yellow tinge, as though they could've used washing, and the baseboards around the linoleum needed paint.

There was running water — hallelujah! — and Hugh put on a kettle that shrieked when it boiled. I waited for Sonny to make some crack about what a hole the place was, and how everything was new in Patricia Bay where his last school had been. But he'd found a flashlight and busied himself flicking it on and off, aiming it at my face.

"I'm the devil," he croaked, holding the beam under his chin.

Hugh knelt to stoke the stove. He'd taken his coat off and I admired the spread of his shoulders through his grey sweater. His hair, messed by the wind, looked longer and darker, curling behind his ears. As he went to the cupboard for cups, I couldn't help noticing how his jeans rode on his hips, faded in spots that emphasized not just his leanness, but a loose kind of vigour, strength.

"I don't see why I couldn't have a *teeny* bit of mercury. A sample," Sonny started in again. "I don't see how it would hurt anything."

"Give it up," I muttered, as Hugh passed us each a mug of scalding tea. "Ever hear of the Mad Hatter — you know, from *Alice in Wonderland*? Wasn't that mercury poisoning?" Something uglier, something I'd seen once in *Life* magazine, swam up from my adolescence. Photographs of people with fish eyes and twisted bodies. There'd been one of a girl my age being bathed by her mother; the picture still haunted me.

"Ever hear of a place in Japan, Minamata, or something like that?" I started. "Some kind of poisoning, in the sea, in the fish. That was mercury."

It couldn't be healthy, having the stuff out in the open like that, and being around it.

Smiling, Hugh shrugged. "A speck of tea, bud?" he offered. Sonny looked confused; he never got tea at home. Taking a slurp, he blinked and swore. "Shit," it sounded like.

"Wha'did you say?"

Hugh gulped his tea, watching us.

"Not in front of an audience, please," I tried to joke as Sonny took another sip.

"You ever hear of loony lighthouse keepers? Someone did a study — the mercury, and that." Hugh made a face. "I dunno. Some guys, it's the isolation gets to 'em. In real remote places. Not like this. And it's not like we eat the stuff, right."

"Got any munchies, like, I mean, a snack?" Sonny piped up,

and I could've smucked him. Hugh went to the cupboard and set a pack of Fig Newtons on the table.

"Tttttt," Sonny said in disgust, and, truly, I could have clocked him.

Hugh laughed. "Lucky you, having a comedian for a son. More tea, bud?" he asked. "Willa?"

When he took my cup our hands touched and I felt myself blush, aware of Sonny soaking everything up.

"So," said Hugh, taking a cookie and pushing the package away. "Do I call you 'Alex' or 'Sonny'?" He was trying to be serious. "Can't help it — that name makes me think of Cher. Sonny and Cher? You know that old song, 'The Beat Goes On'?" He gave me a look, not quite a wink.

"Right," I said.

"Your ma's better looking," he said matter-of-factly.

"My dad calls me Alex."

"Right," said Hugh. "I can see why."

"My dad's on tour," Sonny said. "Exercises."

Something about his tone made me picture Charlie skipping rope on the landing deck of a ship. Doing calisthenics, bicep curls. Sweating. Nothing was halfway with Charlie. I looked at my running shoes.

"How long's he gone for?" Hugh asked.

But Sonny clammed up, helping himself to the Fig Newtons. Before I knew it, he'd eaten a row.

"I owe you," I said, and Hugh smiled. A funny expression that probably meant nothing, but seemed to take everything in. His eyes lit on me, dark grey in the dimness.

"Nah," he laughed, "I'm glad for the company. Now, about the tour." *Tore*, it sounded like, and I must've looked puzzled. "You like forts, Alex?" he said, putting our cups in the sink. It'd been months since his dad had spoken to him that way, not since Family Day on the base.

It felt twice as drizzly and cold going back outside; I'd have just as soon stayed put. But Hugh lent me a slicker and Sonny a huge pair of rubber boots. This time we headed up behind the beach, along a swampy path through the trees. It was a bit warmer in the woods and for a few minutes the sun peeked through. Sonny's boots made a slogging sound as he traipsed behind. "How much longer?" he complained — once.

We passed a couple of shacks — cottages, Hugh explained — that looked flattened by weather, silvered shingles and porches sagging into the wiry bushes. Finally the path came to a clearing and a hill with the concrete ruins of fortifications built into it.

"All right!" said Sonny, clambering along a crumbling ledge.

"Be careful," I yelled automatically.

"There used to be horses," Hugh said, "before my time. Ponies. Might've been wild, I'm not sure. They might've belonged to a midway or something — pastured here."

"Hi-ho Silver!" I watched Sonny leap from a wall, boots sailing off in mid-air.

"He's got some energy," Hugh remarked. "How old's he, now?"

"Nine and a bit."

"Ah. You've been married a while, then." It sounded sympathetic. He was watching me, his eyes like the flash of harbour through the treetops. "It must be tough on Alex, your husband being away."

I was thinking more about the car just then than about Sonny, or Charlie.

"You must miss him, eh."

It was a question, any *eedjit* could've seen.

"Well," the pulse thumped in my ear, "you get used to it."

Sonny was watching us, perched like Spider-Man on top of what might've been a powder magazine.

"Frig," I let loose. "Get down off there, Sonny, before you break something and Mr. Gavin has to call for help! Kids," I sighed.

Hugh's look made me blush again as he cupped his mouth, hollering, "Hey, Al!" Suddenly there was the thrum of an aircraft overhead, getting closer. A chopper. "Coast Guard," he said, his eyes on Sonny. "That'd be timely, eh?" Then he yelled, "Quit scaring your mom. She's got enough on her plate, I think."

Sonny had retrieved his boots, and came running as fast as he could. "What on a plate?"

"Mention food, well, chips and pop," I said, "and Sonny's the best eater on the planet."

Hugh grinned as if he'd read Sonny's mind.

"Sorry, bud. No Burger Kings over here. Best I can offer is liver and onions."

"Gross," said Sonny. "Crap." But Hugh had turned and was heading back towards the woods.

"It's not what I'd choose: single-parenthood," Hugh said over his shoulder.

Choice was never the issue, I thought, ducking a branch.

"Mom says you play the sax," Sonny cut in, a little out of breath. "When I'm ten I'm gonna play 'lectric guitar."

"Oh yeah?" Hugh actually sounded interested.

It seemed quicker getting back to the beach. The tide had come up quite a bit, and we started across the pebbled strip between the wet sand and dune. A far-off roar grew louder, and we stopped to watch a container ship churn past. It was the size of an apartment building, a tug kicking alongside like a tiny grey boot. Once they'd passed the light, Hugh led us back along the path that climbed the island's spine to the wharf. There was the whine of an engine, the flat shape of a boat with a single person approaching. Hugh squinted at the clouds; the sun had all but disappeared again.

"Mr. Punctuality, or what? God help anyone who messes with Wayne's plans. Ah, but he's a good head. I'd be screwed living out here without a buddy like that."

Which made me want to ask why he bothered, except that the island did have a certain, I don't know, charm. And it was closer to civilization than a lot of places.

Sonny was already on the wharf as the boat shuddered alongside. I didn't want to hold Wayne up, and wasted no time climbing in. Hugh squatted above, ready to give a hand. I had the silliest feeling — like I'd had with Charlie early on — that nothing bad could happen with him around, that neither Sonny nor I could fall in. Sonny even glanced up and muttered, "Thanks."

Wayne seemed in a better mood. "Take 'er easy, Hughie," he yelled. "Don't go too crazy, all holed up." As we motored off, it was obvious he'd been drinking. You could smell it.

Hugh stood for a long time waving. I watched him get smaller and smaller as the wharf disappeared and the island shrank, riding the whitecaps like a porcupine.

This time Wayne was quite chatty. "Dunno what buddy sees in it," he said, and I guessed he meant Hugh. "He could get other work, guy's been around, you know. Not much call for sax players, though." He didn't wait for an answer, just kept talking, shouting at our backs.

"That life would drive me nuts, I mean it. Crazier than a bagfullahammers. 'Specially after what happened to one guy. Holy jeez. Used to be two of 'em out there, fella and his wife? She found him hanging one day. Suicide."

My teeth were chattering and Sonny's lips had gone blue. "Pull up your hood," I nudged him. "That might help."

Wayne kept at it. "Hughie didn't tell you?" No chance to lie and say yes.

It was as if he'd been saving this up. "You never heard of Double Alex — Alex Alexander?" He sounded incredulous. I looked at Sonny, nudging him again. "Story goes, when a guy's hanging, it's up to whoever finds 'im to let some blood. Relieves the pressure, eh. That's if buddy's still kicking. You let the blood, buddy lives; you don't, he croaks — of course."

Sonny had a frozen, surly look. Who knows what was going through his head.

"Frig, if old Alex's wife wouldn't let his blood! Maybe she didn't know to. Or maybe he was already dead. Anyways, upshot is, you find someone hangin' and don't do nothing to save 'im, his ghost'll stick around till it makes you do the same."

*Skkkkttttt*, he went, as if choking himself. He pulled a beer from his duffle bag.

*Sssskktt*, I mimicked to Sonny, rolling my eyes.

"So Hughie's got someone to talk to at night," he joked, guzzling, wiping his mouth on his sleeve. "Not much of a life, though, unless you count that goddamn horn-blowing."

"Seems like a nice person," I said blandly, as if describing a bank teller. The way I would've to Charlie. Despite the acid wind, my face warmed.

"See any sharks, kid?" Wayne hollered, ignoring me. "Seen a hammerhead, coming over. Keep an eye out, now."

"So Hugh's pretty much on his own, then," I said, fishing.

Wayne flicked his hair from under his collar, snickering. "I'm always telling him he needs a woman, keep 'im on the straight and narrow."

Maybe I looked worried.

"From goin' bananas, I mean. All that time alone's hard on a guy." He gave me a long, itchy stare. Thank God the dock was looming, and the trailer with the Charters sign. Wayne polished off his beer and dropped the bottle overboard. Then, steady as a nurse, he eased us up to the wharf and helped us out. He followed us to the car, breathing down my neck as I unlocked it.

"An '82, is she?" He slapped the hood then brushed his hand against his jeans. He stood there as I got in and dug through my wallet. I handed him my last ten.

"Thanks, miss." He licked his lips, and I wondered how it was he and Hugh were friends.

"Anytime you need a ride over. Tobias — it's in the book."

"Not likely," I said, brushing some salt off the seat. "Today was just a little tour."

"A tore, eh?" You could see he was amused. "Oh yeah, that'd be Hughie. Bona fide tore guide."

It was raining by the time we got home, and we changed into pyjamas and ordered pizza. There was a message on the answering machine from Charlie. His tour had been extended by four weeks, and he hoped there was nothing we needed. "Tell Alex I love him," he rasped before the line clicked dead; it seemed so brusque and obvious. He loved Sonny, of course; we both did. But who doesn't love their own flesh and blood?

We fell asleep in front of the TV, and sometime after midnight I herded Sonny to bed. I dreamt about him riding around on the back of a dolphin, like something you'd see at Marineland.

Except it was the harbour, and his father was hovering above in the fog, chopper blades whipping the air like meringue. A light sliced through and a horn blew. Not a foghorn but a bugle playing reveille. Then the dolphin sounded, taking Sonny with him. But as Sonny bobbed to the surface, the chopper's hatch opened and the horse collar descended, winching down, and he caught it and up he went, swinging skywards to safety.

 6

## LATITUDE

I didn't hear from Hugh again for two or three weeks. I'd wake every day with a dry churning inside, like an engine in need of grease. I got PMS, the TV went, and a couple of days later, a coil in the dryer. It was almost May, but you still needed gloves. It stayed so damp nothing would dry outdoors, and I had wet laundry hanging everywhere in the house.

Sonny was at school when the phone rang. I was expecting a repairman, was thrown a bit when the voice said, "Willa?"

He'd come ashore to get stocked up and he wanted to know if we could meet at Tim's. I couldn't, of course; I was waiting for someone. On the spur of the moment, at the tail end of a breath, I invited him for lunch. Why lunch, who knows? The second it popped out I regretted it. Picturing the three of us, Hugh, Sonny, and me, wolfing Kraft Dinner, Sonny making rude noises with the ketchup.

He hesitated, then said okay. I could hear a voice in the background: "Welcome, shoppers. In Holy Smokes we have genuine Cuban cigars on special. And in Meats ..."

"I'd come and get you, but," I offered lamely.

He sounded surprised. "Oh, it's no problem. I've got the truck." He paused. "What time, then? Soon?"

I got the panties and T-shirts out of the living room — just in time, too, as the truck came creeping up the street. Sandi had just gone by with her double stroller and a gaggle of little ones dragging behind. I'd ducked behind the sheers as she passed; she'd glanced up a few times as if meaning to stop in.

There was a T-shirt of Charlie's — Sonny had taken to wearing it — draped over the TV. I threw it in the closet.

Hugh got out and came slowly up the walk. There was something in his hand — a rose, of all things. Yellow. I bit my nail, just waiting for Sandi to reappear.

When the buzzer went, I jumped — imagine — then counted to five before getting the door. I tried acting surprised, my eyes snapping from his face to the rose.

"You shouldn't've," I said, marching to the kitchen for water. He waited in the living room, standing there in his brown coat and boots until I came back, setting the vase on the coffee table and switching on a lamp. He took off his coat and sat down on the couch, which was still damp from Sonny's pyjamas. His dark hair had a reddish tinge in the light, like a black cat in the sun.

"Get your errands done?" I asked, at a loss. How lean he looked, settled back against the plaid upholstery. His face was longer than I'd remembered, more weathered, the hollows of his cheeks lined. He seemed older, too, and despite his outdoorsy look, his skin seemed fairer — that complexion that turns pink before it tans. In the lamplight, overkill on this partially sunny morning, he had freckles.

It was as if I hadn't really seen him that day on the island, or the fog had blurred his features. It was like this man in my living room was someone I'd known in another place, on some previous posting, and was meeting for the first time in ages. It's strange what moving does: puts the world in a shaker and spills it out, randomly you think, until —

"How's Alex?" he said, looking at me.

"What? Oh ... he'll be here at lunch. You can see for yourself."

"Shit. I'm early, aren't I. Look, if I'm holding you up from —"

"No! I mean, no ..."

He followed me into the kitchen, watched me make coffee.

"I've been wanting to see you," he said quietly. Oh, God, was I hearing right? "Ever since you came over, you two. I didn't want to butt in or ... How's Charlie doing?" he asked, smooth as water over sand. "That's your husband's name? I figured he'd be back by now."

A fuzzy warmth buzzed in my ears, and I realized in a blur that I'd been hoping for this ever since my dream, the one with Sonny and the dolphin. The last man I'd talked to was the mechanic at the Ultramar, a guy with hands so dirty you barely wanted him touching your car.

Hugh slung his coat over a chair and sat, his elbows on the table, hands clasped in front of him. His eyes were that steady blue.

"If this isn't a good time," he began, though it looked as if he meant to stay for a while. It was a bit early to start lunch. I poured us each a coffee and sat down. He kept eyeing me as if reading a poster with odd graphics. I rose to get the milk.

"I shouldn't say it," he said slowly, "but I've been thinking about you. A lot."

I splashed milk into our coffees, too flustered to ask what he took. My neck felt hot, and somewhere in my head a voice like Sandi's said, *You had a visitor, I hear. Joyce LeBlanc saw someone driving in.* I thought of the truck parked at the curb. Cluelessly, I rose and opened the window. It might've been half sunny, but the draft felt frigid.

"Take me someplace warm," I joked.

He held up his hands, like a minister officiating at a christening — or a funeral.

"Would if I could." His gaze shifted, focusing on my mouth. Forgetting when I'd last brushed, I put my hand over it. But found myself watching his fingers, and imagined them flitting over his sax.

*A bird in the hand is worth two in the bush,* looped through my mind. A ridiculous mantra. Except that he had beautiful hands, big but not clumsy.

Perhaps he didn't even play, perhaps I'd dreamed all of that, too.

"Good thing Alex has you," he said. "A stay-home ma." For

a second he looked almost embarrassed. "So Wayne didn't lose you guys overboard." He coughed.

"He said he'd take me over any time." I waited, holding my mug.

"That's what I figured he'd say." He looked pleased; he was smiling, a bit uncertainly, though, as if I were a logo that needed decoding.

"God!" I said, jumping up. Wishing I'd got groceries. Sonny was like a central vac; Lord knows how I'd feed him when he got to be a teenager.

"I'm really sorry," I said, taking out hot dogs and the remnants of a bag of buns.

"I should've brought a picnic," he said. Not a criticism.

Sonny wouldn't be home for another half hour, but I put the wieners on to boil and mixed some berry-flavoured punch. I could feel Hugh watching me and taking in the varnished cupboards, the chipped woodwork and the crocheted dishrag hanging from its plastic hook.

"Do you worry about him, Willa?"

"Sonny?" I put down my wooden spoon. "He's doing okay, I think. Three schools in five years isn't ideal, but —"

"Charlie, I mean. D'you worry about him?"

I thought of the car, the dryer with the clothes spinning around and around, wet. And I thought of Charlie's silences and hammering in the basement. I looked at Hugh, my face like cement, and shrugged. Glugging punch into tumblers, I plunked them on the table, laughing.

"Ah! 1987! *Il est un an très bon.* Vintage Sonny. If he makes it to ten with all his teeth, I'll —"

"Willa," he took a sip, "well, it hits the spot." He slid his hand across the sticky wood grain and rubbed his fingers over mine.

"Willa? If I had someone like you, I wouldn't leave for all the money — all the mines and shells and choppers — on the planet."

"Thanks a lot," I said, feeling sick.

"Wait," he said nervously. "Let's try that again."

But there was a bang and Sonny blew inside, pitching his knapsack down the basement stairs.

"Why'd they make you bring that home at lunch?" I started in. "Not like you won't be back after —" Then I saw Sonny's friend, a scrawny little guy half his size. Derek.

"Me and Derek'll both have two," he said, eyeing the hot dogs. "You can bring 'em in to us. Oh, and drinks, too."

On went the TV in the living room.

"Sonny?" I yelled. "You and Derek can eat in here, with *Hugh* and me. We've got company, in case you didn't notice."

I heard Derek say, "Is that your dad? *My* dad's on a sub. When *he* gets back he's gonna take me to sea with him."

Hugh raised a brow. I stabbed and slid the wieners into some flaccid buns and handed them out on paper towels. We hunched around the table to eat, Sonny glowering at me.

"Oh, all right," I finally said. "You and Derek can watch TV. Try not to leave crumbs. And don't forget your pack when you go back to school."

Hugh got himself a drink of water. "I could run them up."

"Sonny needs the exercise," I said quickly. "He's hardly been on his bike since ..."

"What?"

"Since, um, Charlie left. The tires probably need air."

Hugh nodded as the boys reappeared and began rooting through the cupboards.

"Nothing to eat," Sonny moaned. "You never buy anything decent."

"You should live with me," Hugh teased. "Tuna — breakfast, lunch, and supper."

"Disgusting," said Sonny.

"It's not that bad," Hugh said, grinning at me. His eyes had dark flecks around the pupils.

"Is it hot in here, or is it just me?" I switched on the fan above the stove. It roared like a jet.

"There's that kid in grade five tradin' hockey cards. Let's go," said Derek, nudging Sonny. They kept eyeing Hugh as if Hugh had been airdropped. "Are you in the squadron?" Derek asked.

"Sorry?"

Minutes later the kids were out the door. "I hope you're wearing your jacket!" I shouted, too late. You could hear them tromping down the back steps, their voices travelling up to the window.

"A force to be reckoned with," Hugh said, shaking his head.

The house seemed so instantly quiet it was as if a plug had been pulled on the sound, all of it drained but the fridge's hum and a tap dripping. Hugh was studying me as if he knew me, had known me since I was a teen and could peel back my years with Charlie.

"Hope I'm not keeping you from anything," he said, and his eyes held me, making my knees rubbery. He came to the sink where I'd started washing dishes, and took over. We stood elbow to elbow as I dried.

"How long has it been?" he asked.

"Excuse me?"

"Since Charlie left."

Whatever had been soft and melting inside me stiffened. It was painful, those syllables rolling off his tongue, Charlie's name. I didn't answer, just kept drying the pot. Our hands bumped as he wiped the drainer; then he took the pot and set it down. He put his hand on my shoulder, the way my brother Jason might've if we'd kept in touch. But then he did something definitely unbrotherly. He drew me closer and kissed my forehead, and as I looked up he moved his mouth to mine and we kissed. For how long I'm not sure. There was just the fridge's hum behind me and a thudding in my ears.

When we stepped apart, he laid his palm on my other shoulder and drew me back, his arm like a crook. And he hugged me close, in such a way that the smell of him, the buzz of him, swelled and surrounded me.

"I can't believe this," he murmured.

"You can't."

"Willa?"

I waited.

"Let's get out of here — take a drive or something." Now he was the one who seemed like a teenager. How old *was* he?

My heart sagged. The dryer guy was supposed to be coming. But it was driving down Avenger Place in that candy-apple red truck that worried me. Passing Joyce or Sandi — worse, their husbands. I imagined their stares, though maybe that was a bit paranoid. Still I felt the familiar jab of frustration, a feeling always winding up or ticking down. What was the point of anything if you were caged in? That was Charlie's motto. The thing that kept all the engines going; the thought that some-one's freedom was threatened. Like thunder rumbling through an empty sky, crossing everybody's radar screen.

I thought dizzily of the dryer repairman.

"We could put some air in those tires," Hugh coaxed.

"Why not," I said finally. "A drive would be good."

He waited in the living room while I brushed my hair and put on a bit of make-up. My eyes had a jumpy, giddy look in the mirror, the look of a teeny bopper sneaking out to drink lemon gin and neck with someone in the woods.

He carried the bike up from the basement.

God. GOD, I thought, as we stepped out into the sun which was trying hard to warm things up. Following him to the truck, I imagined Sandi approaching with her brood — hers and half the neighbours', mothers off bowling or bingo-ing. *I didn't know you had a brother here,* you could just hear her saying, a slyness in her voice. *No point hiding things. We're all in this together. It's our duty to keep each other apprised ...* Sandi was my scapegoat as he lifted the bike into the back, and I climbed into the passenger side.

The woman across the street was outside with her little ones, huddled against the wind. She glanced over and waved as we pulled from the curb, yelling something to her baby. "Yucky!" it sounded like. "Don't eat dirt!"

Hugh waved back, then pulled a U-turn and headed to Sea Fury. I focused on a tanker gliding past in the harbour, its midship obscured by a yellow house with one of those collapsible clotheslines out front. It looked like a dead umbrella or some instrument of torture from the Khrushchev era. Dandelions bloomed on lawns, and there were buds on the puny lilac a few doors down. Mostly what sprouted were toys, bright bits of plastic strewn over the yards. As we drove up the street, the wind blew swirls of dust and you wondered how it could be so dry after months of sleet and dampness. You had to marvel at it — the gritty breeze off the harbour — even as spring burped along, making faint progress.

But none of this mattered as Hugh and I pulled onto the highway and drove away from the base, away from the oil refinery and the alleyway of grocery stores and fast food places leading to the city. Behind us, the oil tanks looked like English mints stuck into the hillside. We stopped at the Ultramar and he filled up the bicycle's tires, then we kept going.

We passed the autoport, a ship as tall as a high-rise docked alongside compounds packed with new cars, every model and make you could dream of caged behind electric fences. Eventually paved lots gave way to yards and houses, places with swing sets and baby barns and satellite dishes. We passed the wharf and trailer where Wayne had his business, slowing when we came to a beach with a weathered sign and a boardwalk over low patches of dune.

"Too cold for a walk, you think?" Hugh said, and I shrugged.

The harbour branched here, wedged apart by two islands, Thrumcap and another, smaller one closer to shore — the pair of them spooned together like lovers, or a mother and child. A narrow channel with quite a rip separated the baby island from the mainland, but it was near enough that I could make out the trees. It looked uninhabited, a hillside pasture showing yellow through the ruins of an orchard. The hardwoods were in tight bud, groves like grey fur against black spruce.

"Mine's the next one over," Hugh said, pointing, and I nodded.

"Any place else, wouldn't they build a bridge?" It seemed crazy, to be so close yet cut off.

"Six of one, half dozen of another. Gives Wayne something to do; otherwise he'd spend all his time drinkin'."

We walked the beach towards the point. Seagulls stood in the steely shallows. I couldn't tell if the tide was coming in or going out. The birds looked planted like those birthday flamingoes on people's lawns (*Lordy, Lordy, Gordy's forty!*) except they were grey — grey against grey.

The wind twisted my hair into my mouth and I picked it out. Hugh moved closer, a windbreak. Tilting away from the breeze, I rested my head against his shoulder for a second, long

73

enough to take in his coat's canvas smell, almost like dubbin, and the smell of his hair and skin — that man smell, not of sweat or dirt but fitness, unsullied by aftershave.

The feel of his hand at my waist startled me as we turned towards the boardwalk. "It's a lot warmer in the truck," he said, but we kept walking, rounding the point and pausing to gaze at the horizon. There was a third island etched there, grey and flat, with what looked to be a lighthouse and a barn on it, and not a single tree.

"Devils," he said. "Now you wouldn't want to be stuck there alone."

"God." I rolled my eyes. "You locals and your demons. A ghost on every corner."

"A friggin' ghost," he joked. "I wouldn't know." Then he took my arm.

I squinted at the spit of land jutting out towards that island, a point almost level with the sea. When I turned, he drew me closer and I blinked as he kissed me. I blinked like a baby. I opened my mouth and felt his tongue.

"Does spring ever come to this place?" I said, stunned, as we moved apart. I did a three-sixty to see if anyone had been watching. There wasn't a soul in sight. But the wind had eyes, or seemed to. Ears also.

He looped his arm around my shoulder and we walked, my hip bumping his thigh. My neck pulled. I wasn't used to looking up.

We hurried back to the truck, but then Hugh spotted an ice cream place across the road. "I scream, you scream," he said, and though our teeth were chattering, we went over. He got mocha fudge. I got black cherry cheesecake. We ran back to the truck and sat licking our cones with the heater running.

"Who needs spring?" he said. "At least this way the stuff doesn't melt." He bit the end off his ice cream and sucked the dregs, like Sonny would have.

"Is that the time?" I gasped, noticing the clock. School would be out any minute.

"Wayne'll have my balls, thinking I stole his truck." He crumpled up his serviette, hunching forward, and twigged us into reverse. "Isn't it shitty, how treats run out," he said, and his voice was full of something, not quite disappointment. "So how come we don't eat the good stuff all the time?"

7

# LONGITUDE

Charlie sent postcards. One for Sonny, with the Leaning Tower of Pisa on it, and another for me, showing an olive grove. "Love ya," said Sonny's. Mine talked about cheese and was signed "Charlie" in a rushed sort of scrawl. Sonny stuck his to the fridge with a magnet. I slid the other one into a cookbook.

The next time Hugh called, he seemed in a hurry. I could hear music in the background. Loud. It sounded live and not too professional, and there was laughter and shouting. A party. It was a Friday night, after all. Sonny'd gone for a sleepover at Derek's.

I was alone watching *Jeopardy*. Does it get any lonelier?

"Run away with me. Just tonight," Hugh said out of the blue, matter-of-fact as if asking me to a movie, something as safe as *Star Wars*, or *Rocky*.

"What?"

"We can be there in half an hour."

"*We?*"

"Wayne's driving."

I pictured Sonny in the Johnston's rec room wolfing chips, glued to Derek's television. Charlie bolted into my thoughts. An image of him on leave, someplace hot and sunny. In a taverna, drinking and laughing with his comrades. His captain.

"I'll be waiting," I said.

It was still quite light when they pulled up. *Please God, don't let the neighbours see.* In the distance, through a gap between the refinery and a drill rig, the buildings of the city flashed gold in the setting sun.

It was like boarding a bus with no doors.

We didn't talk much. I sat in the middle, holding my breath as Wayne rode the bumper of the Chevette ahead. It had a sticker that said: *Danger, Toxic Love*, with nuclear waste symbols on it. Hugh turned the radio on, singing along under his breath. Wayne hardly opened his mouth; he seemed like a guy who didn't much care for women, not to talk to anyway. A couple of times he elbowed me and didn't notice or apologize. I could hardly complain, though.

"We're taking Wayner from a party and everything," Hugh joked. "You're the boss, bud."

Thoughts of Charlie crept back into my head, and I pushed them away.

When we came to the chip-wagon/office, instead of pulling in Wayne kept going, up a short hill and around a bend, finally turning in at a yellow bungalow. The yard was packed with cars and motorcycles; I could hear things in progress. Wayne pushed inside ahead of us, and a thin woman in tight jeans came up and slid her arms around his waist. "What's goin' on?" she yelled above the noise, turning, not exactly friendly. Her eyes froze on me.

"Lemme grab a beer, then I'll take youse over," Wayne said, brushing past her.

Somewhere in the house, maybe the basement, someone was playing guitar, loud, wailing metal, and I could smell pot. Charlie would've had an absolute bird. *You're the mother of my child, for God sake!* I imagined his voice. Then pictured him once more, sitting someplace hot and arid, near a tarmac somewhere in the world, with his shirt off, listening to his buddies' jokes. I wondered what else happened on those leaves of his, where he and the others went. Suddenly I didn't care.

We never got past the hallway. The case with Hugh's sax sat beside a table, an antiqued piece with a doily on it and a fake-looking oil lamp. A swag hung on the wall above, made of artificial blossoms and twigs. There were a lot of tole-painted ornaments and dried flowers.

The thin woman acted like she didn't see me. "Beer's in the fridge," she said, but Hugh didn't seem to hear. He'd taken out the sax and seemed to be working something out, not playing but wiggling his fingers over the keys.

"Willa?" he said after a bit. "Drink?"

I started to say yes, smiling at the hostess who kept fidgeting with an earring, one of a slew of gold-coloured studs in her ear. She had a hardened look, her brows plucked so severely she appeared startled, caught off guard.

"We'll pass, Reenie," Hugh said before I could answer. "We're just hanging out, waiting for bud." He grinned at me, waving his saxophone along with that awful music — was it AC/DC or Black Sabbath they were trying to copy? A couple of women appeared, younger and fresher-looking than Wayne's wife or girlfriend or whatever. One of them eyed Hugh like a cat fixing to rub against him.

"Got a present for me?" she said, her smile fading when she saw me.

"Tell Wayne we'll meet him down the boat," he shouted past her to Reenie, putting the sax back in its case.

"What was that all about?" I nudged him.

"Oh, you know." He just grinned. "Some girls. Always on the lookout for a party favour. Loot bag."

Minutes later we were slouching downhill in the twilight, Hugh lugging the sax. I thought of Sonny with a sudden pang, and wondered if he was having fun. We got halfway to the dock when I remembered my backpack in Wayne's truck.

"He'll bring it." Hugh's hand was on my shoulder. "The man wouldn't walk an inch to save his life."

I hated to think what shape Wayne would be in, meeting us at the boat.

"Don't worry." Hugh seemed to read my thoughts. "He could steer that thing in his sleep, and he's only been drinking since seven."

"What?" I tried to joke. "Out here the rules of the road don't apply?" It was a last-ditch effort at being adult. An image of Sonny sprawled on a hide-a-bed in his Batman pyjamas spun off into thin air.

"Tsk, tsk." Hugh elbowed me. "You think I'd get in with a drunk? Willa, there are about a thousand other places I'd rather capsize."

I mustn't have looked convinced. Once an adult, always an adult. Once a mother, always a —

"What time do you have to be back?" he asked. "In the morning — for Sonny?"

I was about to say eleven when the truck purred alongside us. Wayne peered out.

"You owe me big time, Gavin. Get in, guys." He actually moved over, making room. "Nah, I'm just shittin' ya. Look, if it weren't for Reenie, I'd stay the night with youse. That is, if a guy could get anything stronger than tea to drink." He smirked at Hugh and something tugged inside me: fear. Shame. The only guy I'd kissed in years — besides Sonny — was Charlie.

"Already she's makin' noise about cleaning up," Wayne ragged. "Well. Let's get a move on before it's tot'lly dark."

They talked for most of the ride across, about music, mostly. Guitar riffs and bands I'd never heard of. Then Hugh started discussing jazz. Wayne listened intently as he steered us in. The man's mood swings were hard to figure. And I'd thought Charlie was moody; those spells when he'd hide out downstairs or in the bedroom, so quiet I'd almost forget he was there. Wayne's silences hung like clouds. From what little I'd seen, I imagined he'd have the kind of temper that'd swing a person like a monkey by the tail.

Hugh got out first, helping me from the boat while Wayne sat smoking a cigarette and talking about makes of guitars and Reenie's tole-painting lessons and how it was a good thing they didn't have kids. Who knows how much Hugh had told him about Sonny and me. It was hard enough figuring out why they were friends, let alone what else they talked about on all those trips back and forth in the boat and in the truck, running errands like an old married couple. Men. On a certain level they mystified. Figuring them out was like analyzing the chemistry of a plank. There was wood, and there was *wood*. And then there was Hugh.

Waving Wayne off, he took my knapsack, hooking his arm through mine as we left the wharf and headed into the trees. A sliver of moon lit the path. Magnified by the stillness around us, the distant thunder of the container port rumbled overhead. Despite Hugh's presence, the noise made me edgy, alert, and I was glad when we arrived at the beach with the lighthouse perched out there on the spit, the dark shape of the house beside it. As we crossed the sand, the tower flashed its solid beam, almost like that of a cruiser, lighting our faces every so often.

"It's on a thirty-second rotation," he said, gripping my hand. Hoisting the sax in his other one.

For an instant the light was a strobe, and I was in high school, the sand underfoot a gym dance floor. I was holding hands with a boy I had a crush on, one I would've dropped acid for, stolen for, done anything for.

Dotted with moonlight, the water raked in and out, a slow

waltz. It breathed with us, licking our shoes. Hugh started to whistle, a tune vaguely familiar. The Carpenters: "We've Only Just Begun." I picked up a stone and pelted it, just to hear the splash, something besides the hissing waves and his whistling. Then he laughed.

"Don't they piss you right off," he said, "songs like that."

This unleashed a rush of names, every bad song we could think of.

"The Bee Gees," I said. "'I Started A Joke.'"

"Neil Diamond," Hugh topped me. "'Cracklin' Rose.'"

"The Village People," I blurted out, giddy, my ears numbed by the wind and the pulling sound of the surf. "'YMCA.'"

"You win," he said, whistling bits of each through gales of laughter.

Squeezing my hand, he blew on my fingers to warm them. Where the sand gave way to stones, he let go and stopped to open the case. Gently, as if it were an infant, he lifted out the sax. Planting his feet, he started to play. A low, soft, smug sound. It took me a moment to catch the tune: "Moondance." A gust of wind lifted the notes and spilled them back. I closed my eyes and for a second it was a woman singing. A woman with ropy hair, I imagined, flecked with seaweed and mother-of-pearl.

When I looked up, the moon had slit the clouds. Hugh kept on playing. If it hadn't been so chilly, I'd have taken off my sneakers and danced barefoot, a slow, hippie spiral over the sand.

This can't be real, I thought; any of it. The moon, the harbour, the moaning notes mixing then with a thrum from the marsh behind us — a sound like aliens landing.

"Nee-deeps," Hugh stopped to tell me, "also known as frogs." The noise rushed in, stemming all other sounds. "Listen," he said, wiping off the mouthpiece, then snapping the sax back into its case.

"It's a chorus," I whispered.

"Great backups, what?" He took my hand again and we laughed, stumbling along like drunks. The tide had come in over the rocks, and only the light kept us from missing a step and falling in. But we made it without getting a soaker.

In the kitchen blue light fell from the window, brightened every now and then by the tower's flash. Hugh moved about quietly making a fire. We stood in silence, holding hands and watching the distant glow of cranes moving containers. Leaning against him, I shut my eyes. I imagined the harbour rising to the sills and spilling inside, filling the room like a fish bowl. I pictured chairs and pots floating out to sea.

"Is something wrong?" he asked, and then I imagined Charlie airborne, harnessed inside the belly of a chopper, listening raptly to each sputter and spin.

"Not really," I said, swallowing.

"Tea?"

Standing on tiptoe, I shook my head, reaching my arms around him. I could feel the vertebrae under his shirt. Gently I untucked it, sliding my hand over his skin, pausing at each ridge of muscle. I thought of Sonny going on about wrestlers, their abs and their pecs, and somehow a giggle escaped.

"You're sure you're okay?" He caught my hand and pressed it to his lips, then led me past the table towards another threshold. Indigo light spilled in across the bare floor and a corner of the old-fashioned iron bedstead.

I made myself breathe.

There was a stubby red candle on the sill, which he lit; and as we undressed I caught our reflections in the glowing pane. Naked, he seemed even more ... unlikely. Taller, longer-limbed and taut-bellied. His hands seemed bigger. I had to look away at first — away from his chiselled arms and the soft dark hair at his navel.

But his eyes never moved from me, as if he was greedy, almost, studying each pore.

I wanted to curl away and cover myself, until he put his ear to my breast as if sounding each heartbeat. He touched my stretch marks — what no woman wants — and asked about the spot on my arm where, when I was twelve, a girl had dug her pencil in. As I lay there, he traced every bit of me with his tongue.

A pearl gleamed at the tip of him, and I tasted it. And we lay on our backs, mute, catching our breaths, our skins just touching, until he drew me to him again and slid inside, stroking quickly until we both came.

He shuddered and lay still, gently winding a strand of my hair about his finger.

As a dampness settled around us, we listened to the harbour's noises, sounds made as if in its sleep — of bell buoys tolling, and groaners. Before dropping off, he whispered about lanes and channels charted and marked like runways with navigation aids. He'd only got the job on a whim, he told me. It was the sounds that drew and kept him: their music.

By the sound of that music I tried to sleep, lulled by the creaks of the house and the waves shushing outside the window.

8

# THE SEXTANT

Charlie worked his way into my thoughts, much as I tried to lock him out. It was as if he'd climbed through Hugh's window and sat watching, and the draft creeping in was his breath. But it wasn't guilt I felt so much as a sense of having jumped, blind, and bobbed to the surface.

I lay under the covers — a tangle of afghans and quilts smelling of wood smoke — and listened to Hugh's breathing. His breathing and the night seemed measured by a sort of conversation; the ringing of a buoy answered by a moan. The mattress felt like a bog, our bodies like footprints. Eventually I fell into a half-waking, half-sleeping stew of dream and memories stirred by the wind's creaking.

I was barely twenty years old again, meeting Charlie for the first time at a Red Cross shelter in Calgary. There'd been a mini-disaster, a gas leak; a tanker truck had spilled its load.

A neighbourhood was evacuated, the people put up in a gym. I was volunteering. My job was setting up cots.

The military came to help, though besides making sandwiches there wasn't that much to do, and still a stocky guy with a moustache rushed over to assist me. We'd stopped for coffee, when, his mouth wrapped around a Timbit, he asked, "Wha'd you think of Sly Stallone — the Eyetalian Stallion? What, you haven't seen *Rocky* yet? I've seen it twice … wouldn't mind going again." And he'd asked me out.

Hugh shifted in his sleep, the mattress sighing like the waves curling just outside. His features looked softer, smoother in the revolving light.

I'd been put off by Charlie's hair at first, or lack thereof, and his age. He'd seemed at least thirty, though he was only twenty-three. But then I'd had a phobia about people in uniforms, maybe from watching nurses tend to my mom.

While he and I were dating, the Red Cross gave me a job in a blood donor clinic. This was before AIDS. The blood was the easy part, even when bags burst and I felt like Bela Lugosi holding them. But there was something clean about it, healthy, as it went through a centrifuge, being spun into plasma, platelets. It could save people, after all. Accident victims, chemo patients. Except for my mother; nothing had saved her.

The house around me creaked like a ship. Hugh's mouth twitched in a faint smile.

The blood never bothered me, but the uniforms did. Polyester pantsuits, aqua for inside, navy for outdoors, like the ones worn by Sally Ann folks ringing bells at Christmas. "I'm allergic to polyester," I'd told the supervisor. "Excuse me?" she'd said, unamused.

I'd stuck it out three whole months when Charlie proposed. His wasn't the kind of proposal you read about in *Glamour*. He was being posted, and wondered if I'd like to see the country. "Sure," I said, with no idea what that meant. By the time I figured it out, Sonny was on the way.

A bun in the oven. Blood. I gazed at Hugh's sleeping face, the strangeness of his features, their fresh familiarity. The doctors had ruled out more children after my miscarriage. A good thing now. Not that I'd planned any. Thinking up meals had become the extent of my planning, how to serve chicken six ways to Sunday. Which pretty much described base life, I'd learned soon enough after getting married. It didn't matter where you lived, the fare hardly varied. What differed was the sauce, depending on what spices you added.

Watching Hugh, the soft rise and fall of his chest, my mind flitted then circled back to Charlie. At first, his absence had sharpened my longing. I'd slept with his clothes. A T-shirt scented with deodorant, a ball cap smelling faintly of mowed grass and barbecue. Those first couple of years, when he'd go away on exercises for five or six months at a time, his home-comings were honeymoons, the kind we'd missed when that first posting got bumped up by two weeks.

You can get used to anything, other women would tell me. As if they'd sampled Spam and felt qualified to say, *Well, it's not half bad, once you get a taste for it.* Someone compared sex to potato chips; eat one and boom, you're addicted. It made me think of dogs getting a taste for blood, which reminded me of my old job. Life would've been so much easier being hooked on carrot sticks.

But dogs and blood were the least of my worries the first time Charlie left on a tour. I was pregnant and much as I'd have loved an animal for company, he was right; pets were a millstone when you moved.

Charlie got called out again, a week before Sonny's birth. The only familiar face was the doctor's. She stitched me up — I was awake, it was a Caesarean done with an epidural — chatting as if over coffee about how hard it must be for guys coming home to an instant family. Instant, like soup mix or pudding.

After that, Charlie's homecomings seemed different. Less kissing, more pounding in the basement. The last few years, they'd been more like the way you'd feel when you've just had something fixed on a car, say, the radiator, and a tire blew. Just when you'd hoped for a smoother ride.

Hugh turned in his sleep, his gentle snore in sync with the groaner rocking out there in the dark. The wind was a soft shush.

I pictured Charlie eyeing himself in the mirror. Once, he'd come home and shaved his head bald as a baby's. I was almost scared to watch him undress in case he'd shaved his chest, too. By then he'd put on weight, got thicker, softer; his blond stubble began coming in a bristling grey. He'd lost the moustache; until then, I'd never seen him without it. When he shaved, his upper lip was like land cleared for a runway.

Studying Hugh's face, the hollows of his cheeks washed

every few seconds by that watery light, I felt a ghostly regret. What I'd have done, the last few years, for a kiss — a real kiss — the warmth of an embrace. How it had felt watching Charlie watch the news, the latest world crisis, and hear him bark at Sonny to put his bike away. How I'd wondered; who *is* this guy? He looked and talked like Charlie, left the seat up and the tissue holder empty, like always — but where was he? The guy who'd set up the cots had been hijacked. So what, if women like Sandi still turned to look when he walked by? That thickness of his had built up slowly, like the rings of a tree. Maybe it had started when he became an air technician. Less time on tour, he'd promised. But the choppers were useless without people like him.

Lying there, on the cusp between waking and sleeping, I quit trying to pinpoint who and where Charlie was. He was Sonny's dad, was all. I imagined a Sea King taking off, then hovering over an ocean. Engaging in some sort of war game, something that made sense to him but meant squat to the rest of us.

My heart lifted with the whistling of Hugh's breath. Charlie was in his heaven, and I ...? Well, being alone had advantages: Cheerios for supper when you didn't feel like cooking. But more than that, so much more than that, I was floating now, floating as if on a giant Cheerio, a life ring, kicking my feet and swimming.

Tracing Hugh's ear with my finger, a feathery touch so as not to wake him, safe, I allowed myself a few more memories. Images drifted up like Polaroids. Charlie throwing a Frisbee to

Sonny; Charlie cutting the lawn. His washboard ribs as he showered. His arms; Charlie had nice arms. But it was as if they belonged to someone else, and he wasn't at home in his skin. Maybe I hadn't been at home in mine, either. I wondered, vaguely, if he missed me, what he might be thinking now, high above the Mediterranean, somewhere under the sun. He wasn't at home any place but in the tail section of a chopper. And where had that left me?

I lay close to Hugh, my cheek to his chest, breathing in his smell. Pressing against his moist softness.

I thought of the times in bed when nothing had worked, and Charlie'd rolled over, sighing, "I don't know what's wrong." Something in his voice had blamed me. One morning Sonny had been in the living room watching cartoons so loud the walls shook. "Leave him be," Charlie had said when I threw on my nightie to speak to him. "It's the noise," he said, "the fear of interruption."

"What else is new?" I wanted to say, but put a sock in it instead, as Charlie would've said. *Put a sock in it, Alex. Listen to your mother.*

Now Charlie was a string of vapour, a jet stream. A patch of fog lifting off the horizon.

The dampness in the air deepened, and I moved against Hugh's warmth. I drifted off and, sometime before dawn, woke feeling faintly sweaty and sick. Easing myself out of bed, I crept slowly upstairs to the bathroom. The floorboards felt cold and slivery. From the little window I watched the waves slap like ink against the breakwater.

Nothing prepared me for what happened next: a blast that rumbled through the floor, shaking the panes. The foghorn split my ears, caught my lungs in mid-breath. It froze the air, its mournfulness bellowing over the ocean, chased by a squealing echo that pierced my brain.

Rattled, I crept down the dank, slanted staircase, my ears ringing as I crawled in again. Hugh's hair was like a bird's nest against the pillow. Without opening his eyes he slid his arm around me and we sank together. I'd just gotten comfy when the blast went again.

"Foghorn," he murmured, pressing my ear to his chest. "Runs on remote." The steadiness of his heartbeat grounded me, our skins somehow blotting out the noise. But the possibility of drifting off again was wrecked, and we lay whispering. As if the house was bugged, as if Sonny were nearby, might hear and walk in.

"Tell me about yourself," I breathed, steeling myself for the next blow. Between blasts, the only sound was the waves.

"Nothing to tell," he said, his voice gravelly as he twisted my hair around his finger. "We moved a lot. My old man sold insurance. Hardly stayed anywhere long enough to start and finish a year at the same school, my brothers and me. Three of 'em — my poor mom. You?"

"One father, one brother. I hardly see them. My mother, um, died when I was five. So you'd know, then — about moving." I ran my fingertip over the jut of his nose, a motherly sort of gesture, I realized, embarrassed.

"Alex, you mean? Yeah, I can relate, I guess." He pressed his palm to my ear, stroking my hair away.

"You weren't born here?" I murmured, just in time. We waited out the noise. "So where'd you grow up, mostly? There must've been some place —"

"Out west, sort of," he said. "Okay. How about you?"

Greyish light had leaked into the room, and there were birds outside the window. Gulls, making an awful racket. My mouth felt woolly, my eyes as if full of sand. Our clothes lay on the floor, my jeans and Hugh's, a comb sneaking from a pocket, and his wallet.

I shrugged, naked, feeling the silliness of our questions.

His breath was warm, almost salty, as we kissed and he moved on top of me, gently sliding inside. We made love quickly, cosily. No words. His movements a silent praise.

"Hallelujah," he said afterwards, studying me under the blankets. My body like a stretch of sand at low tide, Hugh combing it. Every bump and curve, as if overnight a new crop of things had washed up.

"What time is it?" I inched myself up, hugging an afghan. It was like something a grandma would knit, itchy and smelly.

"Only early," he said, kissing my knee.

His watch was on the floor. It wasn't quite seven.

"Alex's out like a light, I'll bet," he said, reading my mind. "Ten more minutes. It's Saturday." He laughed. "Let me at least make you something to eat. Tea and seaweed?"

I imagined Sonny smiling in his sleep, dreaming about some gag on TV. Then, like a video fast-forwarding, an image of Charlie shot by, an image of him shaving. The pair of us in the bathroom, me hogging the mirror to put on make-up. Not just lipstick. Blush, mascara, the whole deal. Sonny liked watching me do my face, said it reminded him of people doing shop windows, those painted decorations. He didn't like the results, though; he said I looked different, not like his mom at all. Charlie liked me in make-up, though he never said so.

"Stay put," Hugh said, yanking on his clothes. I snuggled back under the covers while he went to cook breakfast. I could hear him moving around, getting things. Cooking was something Charlie hated doing, unlike those guys who enjoy the novelty of it. He'd never been one for cooking. Or looking. With Charlie the bedside light stayed off. He went for certain spots the way you went to the fridge for milk, though maybe it hadn't always been like that.

Lying there, the smell of bacon drifting in, I tried to remember when things had changed. Probably when Sonny was an infant and hardly slept out of my arms.

I'd gained weight being pregnant. Maybe I'd been too easy with the way Charlie started treating me — politely, as if nothing had stretched or loosened. Back then he was polite. But it was hard, feeling invisible night after night.

Maybe he'd been seeing someone else. The scent of coffee wafted in, and I thought of Charlie's captain at the base, who had to be in her forties. But that was a non-starter; aside from tours of duty and search-and-rescues, most nights he'd come home for supper. He'd watch TV with Sonny, unless Sonny nagged him into playing Lego. If he was really tired, he'd close his eyes and pretend to be asleep — a trick from when Sonny was in diapers. Back then, Sonny would crawl onto his lap and peel back his eyelids. Wake up, Daddy.

Wake the fuck up, I'd thought — how many times? Who knows what Charlie had been feeling. Resentment? Anger, maybe, burbling away like a faulty compresser.

I shut my eyes and listened to Hugh out there in the kitchen, singing under his breath. An old Elvis tune: "Love Me Tender"? And I imagined Charlie flying over Avenger Place, seeing me in the yard hanging laundry, and parachuting down. Like a doll attached to a red-spotted toadstool, floating from a cartoon sky. Landing by the fence wearing nothing but his Jockeys and that grim smile.

Hugh appeared with a cup of coffee. Behind him I heard the snap of fat and, beyond that, imagined the roar of wind overhead. I pictured the sky again: empty.

"You okay?" he said, and then: "There're things that can make a person crazy, Willa. You know what they are, best to just avoid 'em." He watched me dress. Fastening my bra, I thought of laundry fluttering on a line. Pink panties, socks, and military greens: a shade matching spruce. Camouflage.

9

# BUOYS

Fishcakes, bacon, and warmed-up beans awaited, their smells driving out the kitchen's dankness. I was starving. The coffee was instant and the food had a disappointing musty taste but I devoured it like candy, perching on a wobbly chair with my knees up.

"How old you say you were?" he asked, and I stopped chewing. Seeing he was teasing, I squinted at the grease-spattered clock above the hotplate. Call Sonny, I thought. Talk to Derek's mother, invite Derek for a month of sleepovers.

"What is it?" Hugh said, and I felt a tingle, like wet sand on my skin, and a sudden heaviness. I imagined Sonny phoning, the sound jangling in the empty house. *Where the frig is she?* I could hear him, and see Derek's mother frowning as she flipped pancakes.

Hugh leaned over his plate. Butter congealed with ketchup.

His face was full of curiosity, sympathy even. None of Charlie's *What's your problem?* impatience.

"I'll give Wayne a shout. Buddy's probably itching to get out of the house. Don't worry." Hugh massaged my wrist. "I hate for you to go." His hand crept to my bicep, lingering there, gently squeezing.

I was thinking of the night before, the wail of the sax above those singing frogs. The foghorn had stopped, for hours now, it seemed.

"Play me one more tune," I said, leaning closer, my hands tucked under my chin. As if I had all day to listen.

Then I pictured Sonny dragging his sleeping bag up to the door and finding it locked (naturally he wouldn't have the key I'd finally given him after he pestered me) and pounding till he did himself damage. Without a sound I rose and went in and made the bed. It smelled of us. I shook out the afghans, hideous by daylight, crocheted from red and brown Phentex God knows how long ago by somebody without enough to do. Folding each one, I laid them over the bedstead.

The sax sat in its case by the door. Hugh sauntered in, tucking in his Levi's shirt, and bent over me, kissing my nape. Turning, I started to undo his buttons. Then imagined dented wood, Sonny's swollen fist.

"Can you call Wayne soon?" My voice was a minnow darting through shallows.

He nodded good-naturedly, then I heard him in the kitchen, dialling. When I went out, he was pulling on his jacket. He had to check the light.

I started the dishes, rinsing off ketchup. The water smelled brackish, and only got lukewarm. The detergent was green and sticky, clinging to the plates in globs. You wondered how he managed to bathe, how he got along out here, period. I couldn't wait to shower.

When he returned, he walked me quickly to the dock, where Wayne was waiting. Kissing me, he "muckled right on," as his buddy said, muttering as I got in. It was nearly eleven-thirty; with any luck, Sonny had slept in. I made myself picture him sitting on a hide-a-bed eating Cheerios. Isn't that what you're supposed to do? Visualize what you want, think hard, letting your brain lap over whatever it is: a bowl of strawberries or new shoes. Knowing what you want is half the battle — I'd read it in a magazine.

Wayne's eyes seemed to drill through me, and I concentrated on the scenery, the cranes at the container pier poised like giant crab legs; the red and white bulk of a Coast Guard cutter heading to sea. His silence shamed me, as if he could picture Sonny. The only time he spoke was to offer a cigarette.

As we approached the marina, with a leaden feeling I remembered the car sitting in the driveway at home, a decoy. I'd have to ask Wayne for a lift. But as we docked, he mumbled something about "the wife" having stuff to do, and invited me for the ride.

I felt exhausted as we pulled up to the bungalow. I got out of the truck, waiting for Reenie to come outside. Wayne sat there smoking, the engine running. After a while she appeared, her wet blond hair in a ponytail, the trace of a smile on her thin face. "Where's Hughie?" she wanted to know, elbowing Wayne as she slid in beside him.

"Shut up, Reenie," he said. Nobody spoke as we sped past a collection of houses and what looked like a convenience store.

"I have to get back for my son," I explained, and Reenie shrugged. Our thighs almost touched, hers like sticks in her black stone-washed jeans. My jeans would go into the wash the minute I got home. She kept staring at my knees, as if she could read the past few hours in each grainy thread.

"How old's he?" she asked dully.

"Nine — ten come January."

"Uh-huh," was all she said, watching the car ahead.

For the rest of the drive nobody talked, except Wayne grunting the odd question. "We need milk? Bread? How 'bout them egg rolls, you know, that kind ..." It was as if I were invisible, but it didn't matter. Maybe it was a good thing. I was feeling like I'd been run over — that tiredness that starts in your hips, works its way up. Yet, it was a good tiredness, a lightheadedness, like being hungover without the queasiness.

"Take 'er cool," Wayne said, letting me off. I wanted to pay him for going out of his way. But when I held out a curled-up bill he clamped his mouth shut and waved.

"It's no problem," Reenie said in a bored voice, "we were coming this way anyhow." She didn't say goodbye as I slammed the door; and by the time I reached the steps they'd peeled off.

It was like being fourteen again, honestly, turning the key, tiptoeing inside. Half expecting a voice like my father's to bark,

*Where've you been?* I clapped my hand over my face and breathed in, as if I'd been drinking. "Sonny?" I called out, which was silly — of course he hadn't taken his key. The house felt empty and watchful and unnaturally quiet, that sort of stillness that precedes a cloudburst.

I ran a bath and checked the phone machine. Two messages: someone wanting squares baked for Spring Fling; someone else trying to sign me up for bowling. I dialled Derek's, hoping a kid would answer. But his mother picked up, listening as I explained who I was.

"Oh," she finally said, "they're not here right now. They've gone fishing."

"Fishing?" She'd as easily have told me they'd stolen a car. "Excuse me?"

"You know, you get a line, I'll get a pole — that kind of thing? What kids do? I'd be surprised if they caught a Sobeys bag, myself." She laughed — suspiciously, it seemed. Remembering the tub, I asked her to send Sonny home whenever.

Falling asleep in the bath, I didn't hear the car outside, or the door, just footsteps in the hallway and whimpering, a shell-shocked sort of crying, a woman's frantic comforting. "MOM?" Sonny roared through the crack of the door, and in a heartbeat I was out of the tub and into my robe, dripping everywhere.

He was standing there with a fish hook in his temple, half an inch from his eye. The woman — Derek's mom, I guessed — was nearly hysterical. "It's okay honey, it's okay," she kept saying. "Mrs. Jackson, it's, it's ..." Her words skipped past me, not quite registering, as if addressed to someone else.

"Let's get in the car," I heard myself saying calmly, after throwing on dirty clothes. "It's all right, Sonny," I repeated, hearing a door slam behind us, Derek's mother making helpless, apologetic noises.

"Thanks for having him," I yelled mechanically, rolling down the car window. Waving. Sonny sat in the passenger seat, his face tear-streaked and sullen but calm — too calm, maybe.

At least there was no blood.

At Emergency the nurse cracked jokes. "Nice jewellery. Popular this time of year." Sonny glared back, a tear leaking out. By and by an intern arrived to remove the hook and swab the pinprick wound.

*Half an inch closer* pulsed through me, my heart still pounding as we got back into the car. Thank God it had started. As we pulled out of the hospital lot, I remembered Derek's mother, the poor woman.

"What happened, anyways?"

Sonny shrugged, sucking a Popsicle, the fish hook wrapped in a Kleenex on his lap, a souvenir like the baby teeth I'd find whenever we moved, squirrelled away among other keepsakes, single earrings and safety pins.

"Derek started casting and, and ..." Sonny's voice trailed off as he caught a drip. "It's okay, Mom — he didn't mean to."

*Half an inch.* My heart beat even faster.

"It was just an accident, for crud sake."

Lord, if he didn't look just like Charlie then, forget his teary cheeks and the fact that his voice had miles to deepen. Where was his father at that moment — ducking rotor blades or hovering over equipment or standing around a ship's deck telling jokes? I pictured him smiling through his Ray-Bans up at the sun. It jabbed at me, that we had no idea, really, what he was doing or where he might be. The only sign of him was in Sonny's look, the cowlick at his part like a patch of grass that had been slept on. It was just like Charlie's, if Charlie'd let his hair grow.

With a pleasant little jolt I remembered Hugh, the way you remember someone on a wharf, tiny but still waving.

That night I dreamt about painting the hallway yellow, a deep canary yellow, and keeping on until the whole upstairs was like being inside a forsythia bush. The glow spread over the tiles and furniture. In the middle of my project Charlie walked in, dropping his duffel bag. He eyed me standing on a chair also painted yellow, and shook his head. "Go towards the light, Willa," he said, and left. But that's what he said, honest to Jesus. Go towards the light.

I woke with his voice in my ears and a chill as if the window had been left open. Sonny was sleeping like a mummy, the effects of his overnighter. The house was a tomb. I turned on the TV but the cable was on the blink. Nothing but white noise and music playing. On a whim I found the duster and whirled around the living room with it. Hugh's smile kept flashing through my head; an image of him making toast. I must've started singing, because Sonny shuffled in, puffy-eyed, in his pyjamas.

"What're you dancing for?" he asked, switching off the TV. Staring as if I had two heads. It made me think of Charlie doing the Loco-Motion. Maybe his dance moves weren't so illogical, since he loved engines, understood them. It still knocked me out that he could look at something and know how it worked.

But that made it harder to figure out how he could be so thick, too. He'd never understood, for instance, why I liked sugar on oranges and shows like *Jeopardy*. Had never comprehended why I put clothes in the dryer on nice days, or why I wouldn't let Sonny have those Fluff sandwiches he wanted for lunch. It was beyond him why I avoided things like kaffeeklatsches, and wearing pastels. "Couldn't you wear something besides jeans?" he'd asked once, meaning, what have you got against looking *feminine*? That word that reminded me of tampons and douching and "feminine" deodorant spray.

People said things happened for a reason, even when my mother had gotten sick. Though it was hard to see inside clouds, sometimes good things lay in the shadows. Having a boy exempted me from girl stuff. No daughter to disappoint, no one to discuss periods with. It was after the miscarriage I'd started dressing like Sonny: jeans, sweatshirts, sneakers. "There are so many things to feel bad about," I'd told Charlie once. "Why would you care if I don't wear pink or aqua?"

We'd treated the miscarriage as if I'd had a flu. A week or two later, a chopper from his squadron had crashed on a routine mission and the crew was killed. We watched it on the news, Charlie and I. Not even a war, and there were pictures of flack vests hanging from branches, rags of metal everywhere. The

November woods still smoking.

Shaking Cheerios into a bowl for Sonny, I thought of the funerals. I'd pressed Charlie's uniform beforehand, polishing the buttons with Brasso. He couldn't or wouldn't do it. There were more important things, he'd said. Standing outside the small brick chapel, I'd watched a shred of newspaper lift and tumble along the curb. Before the burial, one of the crew — an AESOP grounded by appendicitis before the mission — tapped each of the flag-draped caskets and barked: "Have a good one, bud." A couple of the wives were French, and I'd wondered if they understood.

The wind had messed our hair and blown grit into our eyes, and I'd seen how adrift they were, all these widows: parachutes without air. I could never say I envied them, not even the one with perfect legs and a beautiful black suit. But in their grief you saw relaxation. Easier suppers and only the complaints of kids to contend with, easily silenced complaints.

When we picked Sonny up from school afterwards, he'd asked, "How was the funeral?" as if it'd been a barbecue. Such a grown-up question. People died all the time; so why not make the most of things? There was no such thing as eternity. And I'd gone in and lain on our queen-size bed, staring at the wall, thinking not just of the crewmen but of my mom. Not long after, Charlie was transferred; and so it went.

Cereal wasn't good enough; Sonny wanted Kraft Dinner. I was stirring in the orange powder when an aircraft rumbled overhead, loud as a snowplough. From the kitchen window I watched the chopper coming in, trotting sideways like a dog. Rotor blades hacked the air and the house shook as it passed.

Sonny sat at the table picking the scab near his eye, in a snit because I didn't want him watching TV.

"When's Dad coming home?" he whined as I whacked some macaroni onto a plate. We'd been through this a couple of times, me repeating the message Charlie had left weeks ago, that he loved him.

"D'you love Dad, or what?" he asked, when I didn't answer. "How come he never calls?"

"That's not true," I said, licking the spoon. "What time'd you guys get to bed Friday night? You're overtired."

"Tttttt," was all he said, digging in.

## 10

## FOG SIGNALS

The phone rang several days later. It was Charlie. Though I'd been up a while, his voice slugged me awake, dead familiar yet disembodied. Touching down from another world. A ghost, had I believed in ghosts then, as I came to later, or at least in how the dead resurface.

"Charlie ...?" It was as if I'd been slapped. There was a pause, an intake of breath.

"What's going on?" he wanted to know, as if calling from the hangar to see how Sonny'd done on a test.

"Where are you?" I half listened, a lump in my throat, as he described the weather, the colour of the Mediterranean. His voice seemed to pulse, fading in and out. For most people, the Mediterranean meant wine and olive oil; for me just then, it conjured a hopelessly WASPish man in shirtsleeves stumbling over words in Italian. To whom hardly mattered now. I pictured him in a grounded chopper, legs hanging out the side like a kid on a stalled midway ride — the Zipper, for instance. Waiting for someone, anyone, to flip a lever.

"Willa? You say something? Connection's lousy, can't really hear you. Why don't I hang up and call back?"

"Oh ..." I glanced at Sonny, dawdling over his milk. "Listen, I'm just getting breakfast."

He sighed — disappointed? Pissed off?

"I'll try later. Tonight?" he said grumpily.

"Okay."

"Okay," he echoed.

"Charlie ...?" I held my breath.

"Yeah?"

"Love you," I said crazily. As if holding out one last chance, the softest way to say goodbye.

Sonny heard and perked up. "I wanna talk! Dad, *Dad*!" he clamoured. "Tell Dad about my eye thing!"

"Catch you then at ... what? ... twenty-one hundred, your time?" Charlie was saying.

In my mind, I'd already hung up. "Sure. Okay. We'll be here," I said, putting down the phone.


We weren't, though, as it turned out. Just after six that evening Hugh called, asking how Sonny'd like to sleep out on the island.

"Under the stars? Kind of chilly, isn't it?" Plus it was a school night, a Thursday.

His laugh tickled like a feather. "He can have the room

upstairs. To himself. There are a couple of beds up there. Or you could stay with him. If you'd feel better."

"Hmm," I said, hiding my disappointment. Ticked at myself for feeling that way.

"Charlie phoned," I said, low enough that Sonny wouldn't hear above the TV. I'm not sure what I wanted — advice? Someone to take note, perhaps, to see ... what?

But all he said was: "Yeah? So when can I get you?"


Hugh had the truck again; no sign of Wayne or his woman — a relief. Sonny didn't say much sliding in between us, though you had to figure things weren't too bad if he kept his mouth shut.

Wayne ferried us across; it was touch and go, the four of us in the whaler, and a couple of times we found ourselves in the wakes of boats from the other wharf. This time he and Hugh kibitzed over the merits of Zeppelin versus Motley Crue, Billy Cobham, and Steely Dan. Sonny listened with a funny look, not quite bored the way kids get around adults, but almost envious. "Can you play 'Everybody Have Fun Tonight'?" he asked. "You think I could play that?"

Hugh shook his head, pretending to cuff him. "What, on sax?"

"Teach me?" Sonny persisted.

Wayne hacked into his fist, stifling a laugh. Hugh looked surprised.

"Sure. I guess. Sometime." He looked at me. "Yeah, Alex. I could show you, why not?"

I tried to gauge what was going on behind Sonny's freckled face. Maybe it was better not to; he was probably thinking about his father.

Instead of heading back, Wayne tied up and came ashore. It wasn't the same, four of us tramping through the woods. I felt jumpy, worried Wayne would stay and say something, I don't know, inappropriate in front of Sonny. He seemed harmless enough, though, and he'd done me those favours. His coming along would've made sense if Hugh had beer. But Hugh wasn't much of a drinker, except for gallons of tea and water. That was clear from the night of Wayne's party.

We sat in the kitchen, Hugh rustling up an extra couple of chairs from somewhere. We kept our jackets on. It stayed light a long time, and I realized with a shock that it was almost summer. Hugh made tea and we sat drinking it in the twilight. The sea swished in and out of our talk, its murmur just outside the window filling the lulls. Hugh and Wayne rambled some more about music, and Sonny kept asking if they liked so-and-so. Mostly I listened, pushing back the sleeves of my jean jacket and gesturing at Sonny to pipe down. What is it about kids that they have to yell? The room wasn't that big, though it took up the back of the house; and his mouth was just inches from our ears. It wasn't like they were ignoring him. Every so often Hugh would give me a look as if to say, it's okay.

Wayne went out to the porch a couple of times for a smoke. When it started getting dark, he slapped his thigh, announcing, "Well, guys, time to boogie." You couldn't tell if he was serious or not; something about Wayne made you think of John Travolta trapped in the last decade, the disco era. His hair, for starters. Though you couldn't imagine him dancing, not with his wife; and especially not slow dancing, not with that gut of his, and her like a praying mantis. God, it's hard to figure what brings people together.

Hugh followed Wayne outside; he stayed out there a while before coming back in. His eyes shone as he smiled at me.

"What about your band?" I asked, curious. "You never mention them. Don't you practise?"

"Now and then," he said vaguely, watching Sonny rocking his chair. Sonny was bored out of his tree now but trying not to bug me. He kept playing an imaginary guitar and humming some jumpy tune under his breath.

"You must be bushed," Hugh said, but he didn't answer.

"Ready to hit the hay?" Hugh tried again.

Sonny looked up. "Show me that song. You know, the one I wanna learn to play."

"Tomorrow," Hugh said, with that faith the childless have that kids listen. Sonny opened his mouth, but before he could speak I jumped up.

"Let's check out the upstairs — there must be a bed you can use. C'mon, get your backpack and we'll see what's what."

"Help yourselves," said Hugh, smiling broadly.

There was one big bedroom up there facing the beach,

with a couple of saggy iron beds. Across the narrow hall was a room full of stuff — a storeroom crammed with junk: broken furniture, a steamer trunk with Hugh's initials, H.G., painted on it, and some odds and ends that might have been lifesaving equipment, all quite decrepit. There was a rusty spear with a hook at one end — a gaff; a life preserver and a couple of those orange pylons used in road construction; a sagging metal rack hung with rain gear, and quite a few pairs of ancient rubber boots. There was a doll, of all things, a naked, armless baby doll lying in a corner, its eyes half open in a nod. Beside it was a carton with Keep Cold printed on the side.

"Willa?" Hugh's voice echoed from the dusty landing. "Need any help?"

"You take the one by the window. And I'll sleep here," I said loudly, dropping my pack on the bed nearer the door. Sonny went over and flopped down, the mattress bulging around him.

"Piece of crap," he complained matter-of-factly. "I'll never get to sleep."

"Sure you will."

"No I won't."

"Yes, you will."

"I want *my* bed."

"Sonny —"

"Why'd we have to come here? Doesn't even have a freakin' TV. What kinda worthless piece of crap place …?" It was almost like he was enjoying this.

"Watch your mouth, for Pete's —" There was a creak.

Hugh appeared in the doorway. "Problems, Alex?"

Sonny made fish lips, and shook his head.

"Good," said Hugh. "Make yourself comfy. And that tune you were asking about? Show you in the morning, promise. Right now I need to borrow your ma. Willa? Coming downstairs?"

Bending over Sonny, I tried to fluff his pillow. It felt doughy. Crawling to the window, I pulled the faded curtain. There was something on the sill, a little square of brown leather tooled with flowers, with holes in it. One of those hair clasps, the kind held together with a sharpened stick, that made you think of geishas, or cavewomen.

Sonny yanked off his T-shirt, in a snit or not it was hard to say. I glimpsed his belly. Baby fat, prepubescent pudge. But he almost had breasts, it struck me with a kind of wonder; why hadn't I noticed?

"I'm changing, can't you see?" He covered himself with his shirt.

I tried shutting the door behind me; it wouldn't close completely, as if it was too big for the frame. Giving up, I slipped downstairs. Hugh glanced up from something he was reading, a little green book the size of a person's hand.

"Everything okay?" He laid the book down.

"Kids — you know. He can be a bugger sometimes."

*Navigation*, I read from the spine. *The People's Books.*

"Hope it wasn't something I said." He covered my hand with his, then brought it to his lips. "You're a good mother, I can see that."

It made me blush. "Oh, everyone's a good mother."

"Right. Saint Teresa," he said. "Did you know she was nuts?"

"What?"

"Teresa. Of Avila. She saw things. Visions." He waved his hand extravagantly.

"Okay?" The last I'd heard of saints and visions was at that funeral, a hymn that went, "Be thou my ..."

"Then again," he laughed, "she wasn't a mother. Not even like the one in India who tends the poor."

He had me stumped; where was this was going, and what had it to do with Sonny?

His smile shifted. "My mother packed her suitcase once, at dinnertime. The bunch of us around the table — my dad, me, and my brothers. She ended up eating alone later, in her hat and gloves. Had to take 'em off to do the dishes."

"Then what?" I said, a catch in my voice. If he noticed, he didn't let on.

"Nothing. She just, ah, looked like the Queen, you know? Good old Brenda, refusing to sit with us."

His joke was interrupted by hollers. "Mom? MOM?"

Sonny thumped downstairs. He hobbled in, rubbing his eyes. "I can't get to sleep," he grumbled. "How'm I supposed to get to sleep?"

Hugh pushed his hair back, smiling with those eyes that seemed to see right through me.

I sighed as if forcing myself to breathe. "What's wrong?"

Sonny looked from me to Hugh, waiting. The elastic was gone in his pyjama pants and he kept hauling them up. "It's so ... quiet."

"You want to see quiet?" Hugh sounded amused. Charlie would've hit the roof by now. *Gimme a break, Alex*, I could just imagine him muttering.

Hugh rose and went upstairs; we could hear him creaking around up there. Sonny scowled at the floor, avoiding my eyes. After a while, Hugh came back with a battered Scrabble game, the box a faded violet.

"Great." Sonny looked about to cry.

Hugh unfolded the board and set up three little wooden stands, shaking the lid full of letters. He turned them over one by one. It was like watching rice cook.

"I'll keep score," he said, folding his arms. "Take a letter, Alex. Closest to A goes first."

I sucked my teeth to keep from laughing. The look on Sonny's face! As if he could've overturned the board, possibly the table. Instead he gave in. "*C*," he said glumly.

"All right," said Hugh, picking letters as if he knew what they'd be, arranging them on his stand. "Go for it."

Sonny overturned a letter in the box, peeking.

Hugh raised an eyebrow. "Cheaters get to sleep in the tool shed."

*C-R-A-P*, Sonny spelled without hesitation.

"Double word score." Hugh winked at me, jotting it down. Sonny grabbed more letters.

"Willa?" Hugh's eyes locked on mine. They seemed dark in the dingy light, and full of patience.

Oceans of patience, I thought, fussing with my letters. Six consonants and a blank. I hadn't played since I was Sonny's age, when my dad thought it'd help my spelling.

"Pass," I said.

Hugh leaned closer to peer at my stand. I felt his breath near my ear. "You've got a blank — use it." His fingers brushed mine as he reached in to shift my letters.

*T-R-U-S-T*, I spelled. "Say it's a *U*."

"Or a *Y*," he shrugged, "whatever. Ten points."

Sonny twisted in his chair, concentrating, his tongue sticking out.

*F-O-R-G-E-T*, he plunked down, planting the letters like seeds.

"Wait a sec." Hugh grinned at me. "It's my turn."

"Triple letter!" Sonny crowed.

"Oh all right." Hugh walked his fingers up my arm. I was having a hard time concentrating, and it didn't get better. "Hang onto a *U* in case you get the *Q*," he whispered loudly into my ear. I leaned closer.

"Any more advice?" I whispered back. To my amazement Sonny paid no attention, gazing at his letters.

The game progressed, a patchwork of words creeping over the board. Hugh came up with ones I'd never heard of, words like "qua" and "ti," totting up our scores with a chewed-off pencil. He had one arm looped over the back of my chair, his hand gently brushing me after each turn. I kept glancing at that greasy clock. Sonny's eyes looked increasingly heavy. "We can always finish tomorrow," I suggested, but he pretended not to hear, arranging and rearranging his letters.

Finally we got to the last letter, mine: the Zed.

"You're sure you can't fit that in?" Hugh rubbed my shoulder. His thumb brushed my strap.

Sonny pored over the board. "Oz," he murmured, practically in his sleep. As he leaned forward, the crack of his bum showed; he'd pretty much given up on those pants. "Right there, Mom. Zed."

"No proper nouns." Hugh smiled, nudging him. "Okay, Tessie, toss 'er back."

Gratefully I gave up the letter. Hugh yawned, tallying the results. He gave a big stretch, hugging me. "Sonny: one hundred and ninety-seven. Willa ... Willa? One hundred and twenty-two."

"And?"

"Beat you both: two hundred and sixty-nine. No contest."

Sonny flicked his letter-stand in disgust, then, saying nothing — incredibly — trudged upstairs. I remembered that he hadn't brushed his teeth and started to call out. Hugh stopped me with a kiss, a long, slow one that might have lasted forever. His mouth tasted like tea. Above us, as if from somewhere out of time, I heard rustling. Mice. No, Sonny going to bed. Hugh's lips moved to my throat. Somewhere in the night there was a churning sound: engines. And from upstairs, one last, feeble holler:

"*Mom?*"

"I'll be right back," I whispered, untangling myself. By the time I got there, Sonny was asleep. He'd almost pulled the curtain off. When I went to fix it, the little hair clasp was gone.

The lights of a passing ship splashed the landing. Pulling the door to, I tiptoed back downstairs.

Hugh was lighting that stub of a candle in the bedroom window. I blushed again.

"Tell me about yourself," I said softly. "How you got here, what you did before — ?"

"Same way you did, Tess. By boat. Nothing that matters, okay?"

Before I could blow out the flame, he had his arms around me and we were sinking into each other, our voices shushed by surf.

I woke early, but not before Sonny. Slipping out of bed, I felt a draft. The back door was ajar, a dampness sighing through the kitchen.

Oh, shit.

Hugh hadn't stirred. He lay on his side, his arm flung out as if still encircling me. The light from the window tinted everything green as I threw on my clothes. Imagining the plop of stones behind the breakwater. Picturing him slipping, a close call, then running, barefoot, wet, into the woods.

I listened to Hugh's breathing, a soft, untroubled backup to the whisk of surf, an echo. A clamminess spread through me as I thought of Sonny waking in his strange bed and seeing the smooth one across from it, then tiptoeing downstairs and peeking in.

*Alex.* I had to let go of that baby name I'd saddled him with. Except, then he'd seem less mine, somehow. As if you can own a child. There it was: the urge to hoard something close to your heart, wrap your arms around it, as if hoarding made it more sacred, secure.

I imagined Sonny climbing the hill to the fort, crawling under wet boughs, reindeer moss in his hair.

There wasn't time to wake Hugh. But as I climbed the path, the air dripping around me, I wondered about my boy and me: where our being together and being separate ended; whether there's a bottom to the loss you can feel. Sonny was only nine, but as the cool moisture seeped through my clothes, it struck me that as long as I could remember I'd been grieving something, and not just my mother. It was the simple fact that people grew up, grew apart, grew old. Aspects of Sonny already outgrown like sleepers, like snakes casting off old skins, and what was I supposed to do?

Maybe at that moment I wasn't thinking straight, wanting only to find him; embrace him if he'd let me, and say that no matter what, as long as I breathed, I'd be his mom. I imagined him firing a rock, kicking the ground. His grown-up voice saying: *That's supposed to make it better?* Speculation, of course; but it only hurts the heart guessing what someone else will do.

The beat of a chopper pulled me out of myself. The sound came closer, then faded, the aircraft out of view. I wasn't religious, had no time for stuff like that, but it reminded me of locusts, invisible threats infesting the air beyond the tree buds.

What was I doing here? The feeling shuddered through me

as Sonny appeared, a reddish bloom in the misty tunnel of green ahead. "Alex!" I shouted, barely able to keep from screaming. "Wait up!"

"H-how could you ... do that? Don't you *like* Dad?" he blurted out before I could catch my breath. He had his Nike jacket on over his pyjamas. His face was pale in the needled light. "Why are you doing this to *me*?" He made a choking sound. "Are you and Dad ... getting divorced?" His words were like an axe. He was almost my height; pushing hair out of my eyes, I went to touch him, let my hands drop.

"Sonny. Listen."

"Sonny, listen," he mimicked, bending to squash a June bug. He sniffed, looking away, then sniffed again and spat, "So," it could've been Charlie talking, "when're we going home? There's a *Star Wars* thing on channel ten and I gotta —"

My thoughts flew to Hugh, awake now perhaps. Moving around the kitchen, shirtless, fixing coffee. And Sonny, the night before, bent over Scrabble. The candle flickering in the window, like a tiny face reflected in the pane. Hugh's words as I blew it out: "Wouldn't it be nice, sometimes, if the world would just back off?"

I imagined Sonny and me tramping up the steps at 12 Avenger, Charlie's voice on the machine. *Hi. It's me. Calling, like we said. Guess you slipped out — for a video or something?* His edgy laugh dissolving to dial tone.

"We don't need to go home. It's a little holiday, from school," I told Sonny. He broke away, climbing a grassy ledge, a rampart. A couple of dandelions bloomed at my feet. When he was tiny, he'd have picked them. *Catch!* he'd have said.

"Come back, now, and get dry," I yelled, turning towards the path.

There was no rewinding: the damage had been done. How could I explain: Grown-ups have needs, too?

"When's the boat coming?" he hollered, following grudgingly, kicking at the bushes.

"Whenever," I shouted back, walking faster. My voice echoed from the ruins like a stone down a well. As I reached the path, pushing back raspberry canes just in bud, a chorus inside me mocked: *Make your bed, you lie in it, sweetie.* Those voices from earlier postings: *Get used to it — you married it.* But the whisking of my jeans through the grass sang out something else: Hugh's name. It wove in and out of my thoughts like a dragonfly. There'd never been anyone quite like him, not in my universe. My heart floated at the notion. Chances were there'd never be again.

"What's for breakfast?" Sonny called, slowly catching up.

"We'll see," I said, seizing his hand.

11

## CHARTS

Hugh had a fire going in the woodstove, porridge bubbling on the hotplate. The ruckus we made coming in wrecked the quiet, but he grinned in an accommodating way, moving to kiss me as we peeled off our jackets. Patting Sonny's shoulder, he asked cryptically, "Wha'did you find?"

"Find?" I waited for Sonny to sneer, *Wasn't looking for anything.* But he sat down, poking at last night's Scrabble on the table, the way his dad would've poked at a faulty gauge. He gave the board a shove, then folded it roughly, dumping all the letters over the red tabletop, picking through them.

PORDGE SUCKS, he spelled with great care, the tiles clicking on the scarred paint.

Hugh made a face, rummaging through the pile. Stealing Sonny's O, he laid out THE BIG ONE.

In spite of himself Sonny smirked and began flipping over tiles in search of another combination.

BEIN HUNGRY SUCKS TOO, Hugh spelled painstakingly, then dished out a bowlful of cereal for each of us, spilling some.

Slowly I put down: SOMEONES BEEN EATING MY. As if Sonny were two again.

Between spoonfuls, picking some new letters, Hugh swept the last two words away and put SLEEPIN IN MY.

Sonny dumped brown sugar on his cereal and began miserably to eat it.

"Nothing like having company," Hugh said, taking our dishes. "See? You've saved me from goin' looney. So if I crack up, you'll *know* it's the mercury talkin'. Right, Alex?" He winked, then let out a sigh. "Look, I've got a buncha stuff to do, but there's no need for you guys to take off."

Sonny started in about Darth Vader and Han Solo.

"Haven't you seen that?" Hugh said.

"Six times." There was pride in Sonny's voice. Like father, like son.

"You must have it memorized."

"Like it's branded on his brain." I laughed, but thought of the steps at home, the rusty railing coming away from the concrete, how it wobbled under your grip. I thought of the phone and some leftover chili in the fridge, and the grass growing up to the walk, and about bingo and bowling and Friday night TV.

Hugh leaned back, lanky in his green T-shirt, his hands folded on the table. A vein stood out ever so slightly on one forearm. I caught his eye. His look was nothing but calm.

"You said you'd show me that song," Sonny crowed out of the blue, almost badgering.

"Okay," Hugh agreed, "but up in the lantern, how 'bout that? Somewhere the noise won't get to your mom. She looks tired, y'think, Alex?"

"No."

"Bet she wouldn't mind us out of her hair." His eyes were on me, not smiling but warm — warm as a bath.

"Go make your bed," I told Sonny.

"Bed?" Hugh pulled a face. "Willa, the guy's got an agenda — a tune in his head. Nothing like a song that won't go away, hey, bud?" He swaggered a little, swooping up the sax. I bit my lip to keep from smiling; he was dizzy with the same hangover as me.

I helped myself to the last scrape of porridge while they went off. As I watched the whitecaps from the window, the odd bleat travelled in — that, and birdsong from somewhere over the marsh, a mile off, it seemed. *Heee-haaaaar*, it went, as if such joy could be parsed into syllables.

Going in to make the bed — Hugh's bed — I figured, why not? and stretched out in my clothes. A sweet mustiness seemed to fall over me.

Who knows how long they were gone, Hugh and Sonny. Their voices in the kitchen shuffled me from a dream, the kind of dream that stays with you for hours, even days. In the dream were beach stones, round and white and nested like eggs in a field of long, dewy grass. They formed a track leading up to some woods, an overgrown, grassy track that I had to follow.

The spruces ahead were dense and lush, not sparse and stunted like real ones. The sun beat down, and I longed for shade. But the stones lay in my path, and I didn't dare step on them, afraid they would break.

In the kitchen, Hugh had the sax out. He was showing Sonny how to wipe the mouthpiece with a small yellow rag, and mentioning the reed. The word sent a tingle through me, conjuring the whisper of grass, the warmth and coolness of stones.

"Listen to this," Sonny bellowed straightaway. Clutching the sax, he squawked out a few sad notes.

Hugh slapped his thigh, counting invisible time. "Charlie Parker, look out." He grinned at me, nodding along.

Disgusted, Sonny ducked free and thrust the sax at Hugh. Without wiping off anything, he honked out that song Sonny had been on about, "Everybody Have Fun Tonight," bending and twisting as if we were a hall full of people, fans out of our seats. He blew and blew with his eyes squeezed shut, till you wondered what was going on behind the lids. But it gave me a chance to look at him, really look, the way I'd studied Sonny as a toddler taking his first steps. Suddenly I longed for dusk and candlelight, to see Hugh naked. Asleep. To count the freckles on his windburnt skin, the lines around his eyes; brush my fingertips against the shadow of his beard.

Hugh opened his eyes and stopped playing, the sax flagging against him like a dead duck, and I felt myself being drawn in. It was the kind of feeling Alice must've had being sucked through the rabbit hole. The opposite, maybe, of being born;

and possibly this was exactly it, what I'd been waiting for, had always wanted. To be taken in somewhere, some place dark and mysterious, and never have to leave. Oh my God.

"Willa? Tessie?" His voice encircled me. He had a surprised look, incredulous, as if a bird had hit the window. I felt naked, as if my clothes were drying, flattened to the boulders outside, and Sonny could see me: *Ew! Mo-ther! Gross! Get dressed!* I imagined a squall crossing his face, tears. Had Sonny known what I was thinking, he'd have rounded up our backpacks and dragged me away. Sonny was a smart kid; at home, he could be my extra eyes.

A chill lit my spine, like granite touching the top of it: a cold granite egg.

Sonny was asking Hugh about climbing the rocks behind the tower.

"Pffft," Hugh brushed him off. "You take a slide into the sea, who's gonna fish you out? What do you think, Willa? Would we fish this guy out?" His voice went serious. "*Don't* try it."

Laying down the sax, he told a story about some daredevil girl, the daughter of another lightkeeper, who'd treated the railing around the lantern as monkey bars and tobogganed on the breakwater after ice storms.

"Did she die?" Sonny was mesmerized.

Hugh opened a can of Chef Boyardee, shook the contents into a frying pan. "I don't think so. Last I heard she was in law school, something like that." The way he said it made me feel funny — old yet undeveloped, like something still growing under a lens or in a Petri dish.

"Ravioli?" His voice lapped, far away.

The clatter of cutlery roused me. Once more I was ravenous — it must've been the island's air. The red sauce coated my tongue; how good it tasted. Sonny licked his plate.

"Don't," I said, catching his arm. Rising to rinse my dish, I glimpsed the clock. "Good Lord, the time!"

Hugh licked his spoon. "Does it matter?"

I ran a deep bath upstairs in the blue-stained tub. The room was grey and chilly. Through the pipes you could hear Hugh and Sonny — scraps of conversation, Hugh's deep voice and Sonny's high-pitched one. Their talk lilted like the waves below, and lulled me. My skin looked yellowy white in the dingy water and the light from the bare window. It wasn't a room to linger in. Not far off a bell buoy tolled, that miserly, gloomy sound not quite an alarm but a warning. Lying there, I listened to all the harbour sounds out of sight and reach, like dogs in a neighbourhood conversing: an invisible chorus of barks and yips. How odd, to be tired but not sleepy, full yet empty. Hungover without having drunk anything. But it was okay, everything was okay as I shifted in the tepid water, closing my eyes. For a moment the bath was a hammock; any second the wind would come and tip me out, but just then it was fine to sink and swing.

As I climbed out, letting the water run away, the foghorn rattled the salt-streaked panes. It shook the boards underfoot, like a blast heralding the end of the world, as if the plaster might shake loose, the walls fold in. The noise scalded my eardrums, squeezed my lungs, but as it ebbed, ploughing the air, the thump of my heart replaced it.

There was scuttling, pounding on the door. "Moo-oooom! Hurry up, I gotta go. Hugh says if you don't come out soon we'll hafta bust the lock."

Hugh's voice was like chocolate: "That scare you or what? Can't believe you're still in there, Willa, after that."

Sonny cackled.

"Hang on, bud. She doesn't come out soon, we'll give 'er another little toot."

"Thought you said it ran on autopilot — the horn, I mean." Shivering, wrapped in a ragged pink towel, I was quite awake now and not amused. The terry felt like dried sandpaper. As I dressed, their breathing came through the panelled door.

"Manual override." Hugh sounded gleeful.

Sonny snickered through the crack. "I see England, I see France —"

"Okay, okay. You guys are evil, absolutely evil."

"You mean like Darth Vader?"

"Must be why you're hiding," Hugh sang out.

Sonny choked back laughter. Next came humming: "The Camptown Races." Who could figure how Sonny's mind worked? With a funny pang I wondered if, just then, he could've described his father's face or smell, or whether he missed his Lego or anything else about Avenger.

Yanking on my jeans, I listened to the two of them thunder down the stairs. By the time I got there, the kettle was screaming. "Jeeez-me," I imitated Joyce LeBlanc back on the base. "We'd better call Wayne." But nobody moved.

"Forecast calls for clearing," Hugh said. "We could do a bonfire tonight on the beach."

Sonny gave me a beseeching look.

"But, Wayne —"

"Too late to call now. Buddy'll be out on a tear, if I know him."

"We're not really ... prepared." I was picturing dresser drawers; mentally stuffing things into bags.

"We'll do snoots — hot dogs. It's not a big deal."

I was thinking of Sonny, two days and nights in the same clothes.

"Can I light the fire?" he was already pestering. "I'm good at lightin' fires. Mom knows, she's seen me. Can I? *Can I?*" His pleas banged around in my head, just as they would have at home. Which was where, and what? A house with a phone and an answering machine and maybe a flashing light and ... Charlie's voice. His silence.

"All right." I made it sound like a sacrifice, as if giving in for the first and only time. Sonny was already rooting around for matches.

"There's a spare box in that upstairs room," Hugh said, and Sonny pounded up the stairs. Hugh put his arms around me and I pressed my cheek to his chest. "That'll keep him busy for a bit." He massaged the little bump at the top of my spine with just the right pressure. As if each pore was a button on his sax; what tunes those fingers could coax.

"I believe I'm in love," he said, sniffing. When I looked

into his face, it reminded me of the moon: open and clear, unmarred by foot or fingerprints.

After supper we beachcombed for wood. The sun splashed the sea and sand with orange, the beach blooming with rockweed and litter. There was part of a chair I could picture in someone's kitchen, a fence picket, and the ribs of a lobster pot. There were grocery bags that might've been washing around since their invention, condoms like shed snakeskins, and tampon applicators, Gatorade bottles, and rusty beer caps.

When we had enough wood, we huddled in the lee of the dune, and Hugh helped Sonny roll pages of the *Herald* into tight little sticks and ease them into the teepee of twigs they built on the rocks.

"This is crappy," Sonny grumbled. "Why can't we do it on the sand?"

Hugh wasn't listening. I wanted to poke Sonny with a piece of driftwood to make him behave. But then I tried to put myself in his place, missing TV and wondering where his dad was and how long this little camping trip of ours would last. It should've made me feel guilty, like a stowaway, one of those immigrants you heard about crossing the ocean in containers: people packed into crates with holes punched in the sides. Except they were usually men, with buckets to pee in and hardly any food or water; and the air — well, you could imagine what a shortage of oxygen did to the brain.

Hugh had brought along a Thermos of tea. As the flames licked the paper, shooting past his face and Sonny's into the velvety dusk, I warmed my hands on my cup and sipped. I didn't mind the canned milk or the chipped china. I was Robinson Crusoe. We were the Swiss Family Robinson. Hugh was the Professor, I was Mary Anne. Except it wasn't clear where Sonny figured in the equation. He threw on too much wood and Hugh gave him a look — bemused, perhaps. I listened to the flap of wings over the pond behind us, breathing in that smell of swamp.

I imagined Charlie coming home — from where, God only knew. I pictured him going into the kitchen, finding a note: *Lasagne in the freezer, zap on high one minute or two. See you in heaven. In some other life. In your dreams.* The writing wasn't mine: I've never believed in eternity. Maybe it wasn't a note from me at all, but something someone else had scribbled to make him feel ... better? Then I imagined him not coming home, the note sitting there beside the toaster, unread. Charlie drinking in a mess somewhere with his buddies, drinking all night and playing darts and shuffleboard. His hair fading from grey to white, as the hours ticked by in military time, so that by dawn he was an old man. And I thought of that disease children can get that causes them to age and wither before your eyes, dying before puberty. The disease has a name, but the name hardly matters. It's as though their bodies are mad at the world and aiming to get back at it, in a soul-shrinking fast-forward.

I sipped my tea and felt the fire warm my cheeks. Hugh and Sonny squatted close by, the three of us watching the stars poke holes in the sky. The lights of the city leapt across the harbour. Somewhere inside myself I tapped out a message to Charlie, bolder than any note. One last cry to wherever he was, the voice inside me displaced and feeble as a voice inside a container. *Help.* Before I slip under waves of seasickness, of thick salt water. *Are you listening?* I wondered. The only reply was the snap crackle pop of flames eating wood and dried seaweed.

As the fuel dwindled, Sonny got antsy.

"Take a hike, why don't you, and see what you find," Hugh said, giving him a friendly nudge. Grudgingly Sonny wandered off — not far, just over the rocks towards the pond. He soon returned with a warped piece of board. His back to the fire, he laid it across two boulders and knelt before it, playing it like a piano, humming along. That bloody song again, "Everybody Have Fun Tonight."

Hugh's face lit up; there was something kid-like and tender in his expression. He started strumming an air guitar, losing himself. Forming chords, his eyes squeezed shut, and wincing as if the notes were needles. Then he broke out laughing, and Sonny laughed too, that gurgly laugh I'd been missing since our move; the kind of laugh kids reserve for each other. Snorting, giggling, he launched into another one, "The Way It Is" — Bruce Hornsby and the Range — till the board flipped sideways. Hugh howled, lying back against the shifty stones. Just as he was looking helpless, Sonny pointed across the blackness to the city and said, "Man, we have an audience. Look, Mom — they're all sitting there waving lighters. See? They're watching us!"

"Yes, yes," Hugh bellowed, laughing up at the stars. The flames crackled; somewhere out there in the dark the buoy rocked and tolled.

The wind fanned me alive, the air cold now, rubbery against my skin. "I could sleep out here," I said, not quite meaning it. Already the dampness had begun to creep up my arms and my butt was numb from the rocks.

"Your mom's a nature girl, I *knew* it!" Hugh yelled.

"Shhh!"

Sonny looked up from his lopsided keyboard, sniffing. Puzzled. "Mom hates camping." His voice was tired but stubborn. "The time me and Dad and her ..."

Firelight scrubbed Hugh's face. Looking at me, he waited. Then he said, loud enough that Sonny wouldn't miss it: "You *could* stay here."

12

# THE LOG

Charlie came home eight days later on a leave. He had forty-eight hours before his next tour, routine exercises just offshore. He looked different to me, tanned and thinner. His head was shaved, and there was a strange hunger in his look, a new remoteness. He kissed me — "Damn, it's good to be here!" — then asked what was for supper, what homecoming treat we had waiting.

He glowered at his chicken nuggets. "Sheesh. You usually make those ribs, that's all."

Sonny got out the ice cream cake — his idea — which we'd picked up on the run. Charlie's face lit up and he clapped Sonny's shoulder.

"You shouldn't've."

"Mom wanted to," Sonny said. Then, "Gotta be at Derek's

for seven. There's this project for math, and a wrestling special on TV. Can you drive me?"

"Walk," said Charlie.

Once the cake was back in the freezer, we found ourselves in the bedroom, just the two of us.

"Willa," he said, like a wind-up toy, the kind that beats a drum. "I missed you."

An image of his captain flashed through me, that fireplug dynamo with highlighted hair, and the way she spoke from the side of her mouth, like Jean Chrétien.

It was as if we were reading from a maintenance manual: a three-month checklist.

My jaw clenched when he kissed me. When he slid his hand inside my jeans I got up, leaving him lying there. He looked like the ceiling had just opened and a pipe burst.

In the kitchen bits of uneaten cake left beige pools on the plates. I cleaned up. The phone rang, and my heart seized. A wrong number: someone looking for pizza.

When I slipped into the bedroom again Charlie was asleep, sprawled on top of the covers. I picked up Sonny, and that night made my bed on the couch. The two days before Charlie left again, we were countries on opposite sides of the world.

"We need to talk. There's something I've —"

"Not now, Willa. For chrissake, put a sock ... I'm a little preoccupied? Beat is more like it; can't you see?" As if it were up to me to fix it.

"You're right," I said, tearing up. In spite of everything.

"It's this goddamn job." But the way he spoke, I knew he didn't mean it.

*You've always been married to your job*, I wanted to tell him then, but couldn't. Not with Sonny, my confidant, lying there watching cartoons. Sonny who could've laid bare everything, my cranky little soldier. Peacekeeper.

"See ya, Dad," was all he said.

The day I picked to leave was foggy; it was right after school ended. It's almost obscene, really, how easy it was. I left a note, but one that said little — blood-from-a-stone little — signed, simply, "Willa." No *love*, *sincerely*, *regrets*, or *yours truly*. It took three tries to get the wording right, a barebones explanation with no hint of apology. The remark that Sonny was my biggest concern, that in the long run he'd be better off, too. I'd met somebody, I said. Hedging on an address and phone number, finally including both in case of emergency. No point coming after me or thinking things would change, I wrote. This was love and it meant everything. You would know about that.

I left like a thief, whispering to Sonny as we moved through the rooms grabbing last minute items, as Charlie surely would've, in my position. A few times Sonny said, "Mom?" too loudly and I shushed him, as if speaking in normal voices would trip an alarm, deter us.

The only thing I waffled over was Joyce's snapshot from Family Day, the day my heart had nearly failed, watching Sonny dangling from the cargo door, two thousand feet up. The day I'd learned a little of what it meant having wings. I couldn't decide whether to bring the picture or leave it taped to the fridge; it was the only one taken since our move east, the three of us together, Charlie, Sonny, and me. I peeled the photo from the fridge and put it in a drawer.

I called a cab, leaving the Dodge in the driveway. It would only be a burden. The taxi came, as if to take us shopping or to the airport. I'd have liked our exit to be invisible, leaving nothing changed or amiss, as if we'd gone on an errand and would be back in a few hours. Charlie wasn't due home for two weeks, but I left the fridge well stocked, the kitchen and bathroom spotless. Not a crumb or speck of dust to be seen.

Crossing over in the boat that morning, I couldn't see five feet in front of us. As we zipped along, the water was like shale, the air completely still but for the engine's whine and the port's distant rumble. It was early — too early, I guess, for Wayne, who as usual didn't speak.

It was like being in a vacuum, the only certainty the feeling of speed. I worried about slamming into something, another boat or an animal in the water; couldn't help imagining a wall of steel or shiny flesh breaking through the fog suddenly. Still, there was something — and I hate the word — appropriate about going by open boat, as if all the world should see us, Sonny and me. The underworld, too, as if the creatures below should've had periscopes. But the only thing popping the surface was a cormorant, its skinny black neck and bill like the mouthpiece of Hugh's sax. It made me gasp, a spectre jutting from the water like the tip of a shipwreck.

Wayne looked hungover. It was hard to tell if his face was dirty, or he was growing a goatee. I closed my eyes and felt the dampness pinging my lids. An image of Hugh swam up: the reddish tinge of his beard, the roughness of his cheek. And I thought of Charlie: how, if he'd grown a beard, I mightn't recognize him, except for his eyes, that simmering impatience. What colour would his beard be? The question stung as we skipped along, a smooth stone over smoother water.

Sonny hung over the side, trailing his hand in. It must've been early; he was so quiet. You could feel Wayne giving him the once-over, taking in his holey sweatpants and sneakers with the rubber badge peeling off one ankle. Wayne seemed pissed off, as if the ten bucks I'd handed him weren't nearly enough, though it should've been. Within minutes the trees loomed, the pier with birds dotting it like clean socks. But he'd taken note of our knapsacks, heavier than usual, the garbage bags of clothing, not to mention Sonny's grocery bags of comics, and other paraphernalia including his bike — all the stuff a kid would need to amuse himself in an island paradise. Of course, the water was too polluted for swimming and already, with summer barely started, the bugs would be murder. *What bugs?* I thought gleefully. As we swung about to dock, the fog broke at the end of the channel and on the spit-blue horizon I could just make out the light and houses on Devils Island. It looked so flat I could imagine it sliding under the ocean, disappearing like Atlantis.

Hugh had told a story one night about a boy finding the print of a cloven hoof there, pressed into the island's gravelly sand. No way could it have been an animal's, he'd insisted. Devils was too far out and hard enough for people to land on, let alone deer. Curled close to him, I'd imagined the undertow pulling stones — that sucking clatter — and fog, endless fog. Now I thought how lucky he wasn't the lightkeeper there. I couldn't have done that to Sonny. Imagine, fearing the devil and nowhere to run but in a circle, an endless circuit of sneaker prints in the sand.

As he cut the motor, Wayne eyed Sonny's blue CCM lying in the bow. The "sissy" bell on the handlebars, my idea of a necessity for riding on the street, wasn't an issue now.

We stayed put while Wayne hoisted the bike onto the wharf and tossed up the rest of our stuff. An osprey watched from its nest atop a telephone pole, a nest the size of a Little Tykes wagon. "Look, Sonny." I pointed. "It has babies!" You could see the little heads poking up.

But Sonny wasn't impressed. He was watching the woods for Hugh, who emerged suddenly and walked slowly towards us. Wayne had already started the engine. "Hey, buddy!" he yelled and Hugh waved. I was clutching at bags, balancing the bike and hauling on my knapsack while Sonny sauntered ahead with his comics.

The water licked the sand as I dropped everything and waited. Hugh was smiling, taking his time. It looked like he was limping. He squeezed Sonny's shoulder and pointed to something rusting in the sand, the ribs of a hull. Soon he was beside me, grabbing our packs and shaking his head, laughing.

"You look like two fucking runaways," he teased. "Like the guy on *Bugs Bunny*." Amid the jumble he kissed me — a kiss that turned my knees to kelp. The feeling spread, as if I were swimming. My heart floated, it did, as if I'd sucked in water. If Sonny hadn't been there, I'd have taken everything off and lain on the sand. But as I watched Sonny kick at a rusty spike, the urge drifted away, leaving an ache as the fog parted overhead, showing a glimmer of blue. It was like the sea and sky cracking open, and there we were, everything spread before us.

"I didn't think you'd do it," Hugh said quietly, strapping on my pack. "Jesus, what've you got in here?" Already I was wondering what I'd forgotten, running down a mental list: shampoo, hairbrush, soap, et cetera. Earrings, bug dope, sunscreen, the special comics that wouldn't fit in Sonny's pack.

"I still can't believe it," Hugh marvelled, rubbing my arm and leaning close. "You're here, I mean. Please. God. Don't let me wake up and find I dreamt it. I've been going stir-crazy without you." We'd been apart for days, waiting for school to be over. His face danced before me, so close I could see each bristle on his jaw, and smell his smell of wood smoke and leaves and salt air. As we reached the path he whistled to Sonny.

"That your bike?" Sure enough, there it was back at the dock. "You might have a time riding it, Alex," Hugh shouted. "Least you won't get lost." I thought, guiltily, that was too bad. How much easier, were Sonny still small enough to nap.

CAROL BRUNEAU

He scowled at the dock.

"Go on. We'll wait," Hugh said, and for a second Sonny looked about to argue.

I waited for it: *Ah, Mooom, no one'll steal it. Who'd want a blue bike anyway?* In my other life, the one I'd stepped out of, I'd have gone back for it and wheeled it home.

"Alex?" I let myself be pulled along, the warmth of Hugh's hip against me. Hesitating, kicking sand, Sonny ran back. There was the ticking of spokes as he caught up.

"You'll figure out the trails," Hugh said, glancing over his shoulder, smiling into my eyes. "They all lead pretty much to the same place. That's the beauty of it."

The fog lifted as we cut uphill. The woods were dense and lush with moss and ferns and thickets of knotweed alive with birds. The only sounds were the bike's swish through foliage and the wafting roar of the city a million miles off, punctuated with birdsong. It was so sweet and startling, exotic as the call of birds at the world's first dawn it struck me as I slapped at mosquitoes. Enthralled, I barely noticed when the path forked and Hugh picked a different route. My heart lifted with each perfect note. If not for the bugs, we could've walked naked. We could've been Adam and Eve and Pinch Me, the three of us.

Then we came upon a swampy trench. It was full of rusted frames and gears and pulleys half hidden by trees — a rifle range, Hugh explained, for training soldiers in one war or another.

"Bloody military owns half of Thrumcap, like it's this big playground or something."

"Sweet!" Sonny burst out, despite the mosquitoes and the

burden of his bike. "I'm coming back here!" Like a vow to revisit a comic book store. He stopped for a closer look at some gears, then poked around inside a crumbling cement bunker.

It clouded over again, the sun like a white-hot marble trying to burn through.

"Place's got quite the history," Hugh said, explaining that, once upon a time, the island had sheltered cholera victims. Luckless Irish immigrants nursed by the Sisters of Charity, their corpses dumped at sea.

"Shit, you must've brought the friggin' kitchen sink," he said. "This stuff's getting heavy."

"ALEX!" I yelled. "Let's go!"

The path widened to a mossy track between some tamarack trees. Their tiny red cones were miniscule roses among the feathery needles. "Look," I said to Sonny, but he didn't care. When the trail straightened, turning gravelly, he swung onto his bike and pedalled ahead.

"Wait up!" I called as he disappeared.

Hugh poked me. "It's okay, Willa. Tessie. He can't get lost."

"I know, but ..."

The woods gave way to a thicket of rose bushes with masses of dark pink blooms. The scent was sharpened by the salt air, and I turned to Hugh, locking my arms around his waist. I closed my eyes, drinking it all in.

"What're you takin' so long for?" Sonny's voice drifted towards us. He'd gotten off his bike. My face felt warm as the sun suddenly bloomed through the clouds. Hugh breathed into my ear.

"It's all right — he's gonna have to get used to it."

When we caught up, Hugh ran his palm over Sonny's head, letting it hover as if gauging the height of his fresh buzz cut, enjoying its feel. I loved it when Sonny got his hair cut; the day before, I'd watched his face in the mirror as the barber combed and snipped. The best part came later, in the parking lot, touching that silky, springing hair — until he'd yelled, "Quit it, Mom. Someone'll see."

Hugh blinked; he seemed almost dizzy. "Here we go," he murmured as the lighthouse came into view. We took a sandy path that separated the wide green pond from the marsh, and as we headed towards the spit, the wind picked up and the clouds pulled apart, showing stitches of blue.

"Almost home," Hugh said, squeezing my hand.

Sonny had dropped his bike on the rocks and was pelting stones at the waves. I let the breeze fill my lungs. It was like being little again, even younger than Sonny: the feeling of lightness. Like being walked back along the block to early childhood, some open-ended place of safety. Where time — summer — was water spilling over loose, green stones, a place where everything was cool and green.

"Thank you," I whispered to Hugh, clutching his arm and not letting go.

13

## THE CHRONOMETER

The rest of that first day — our first day living with Hugh —
floated past. By the time Sonny and I emptied our bags and
found spots for our things, the sun was blazing. That afternoon, the three of us took a walk to another fort, retracing the
route behind the pond and following the path to the island's
highest point. Cutting through a grove of knotweed, we passed
a cemetery, the stones worn smooth and slanting into the
bushes. Nothing like Memory Gardens where my mother
was, with its black, polished monuments.

The path led to the centre of some crumbling ramparts.
Sonny ran ahead, aiming an imaginary machine gun, spraying a
pretend battalion with bullets. Hugh and I found a grassy spot
overlooking the harbour and stretched out. The sun beat down,
moulding my spine to the earth; I could feel the ground's
warmth through my T-shirt as Hugh leaned over and I shut my

143

eyes. His kiss felt cool as mint. The sun beamed through my lids, a dance of warm light. Hugh moved away, then pressed close.

"Open up," he said, and I blinked. As I started to speak he put something in my mouth — a tiny, melting burst of sweetness. A strawberry. He had more in his palm, each no bigger than the very tip of an asparagus spear. He placed another on my tongue, laying the rest in a row down my front like teensy red buttons. One by one he ate them, as if undoing me. Sitting up, he started picking another handful. I sat up too, shielding my eyes against the sun, which was blinding now, and looked around.

"Oh, God, where's Sonny — ?"

Hugh planted another berry in my mouth.

"That taste," he said softly. "You could almost say it's music, Willa. What we all should aim for." He had an odd smile I couldn't quite figure out.

"Whatever you say."

I lay down again. The wind twitched his hair. His face was close to mine, lean and tanned with a rosy sheen. His hand was on my stomach, the fine reddish hairs on the back of it sparse as maram grass.

"You're so patient, Willa."

"Patient?"

"Good things come to them what wait," he said, and his joking voice only made me want him more. But I lay still, closing my eyes again; the sun was a scarlet flame now. *Waiting.* He opened my lips with his tongue and slipped another berry in. His mouth tasted like jam with a salty tang and —

"Mooooo-oooooom!" Sonny's holler arced overhead. Like

a boomerang it bounced off the sun, spinning back.

"Ooops." Hugh's breath was like grass tickling my ear. Pulling me to my feet, he murmured, "Tonight?"

After supper Sonny wanted to play Scrabble — go figure. It stayed light forever. When it finally got dark, I said that the fresh air must've tired him. Slow as an eighty-year-old he poked upstairs, lingering on each step. Hugh and I sat in the kitchen till moonlight spilled across the table, waiting for him to quiet down. I liked to wait till he was sleeping. Taking my hand, Hugh held it as if reading my palm.

"Let's take a walk, Tess. Not far."

I went up and stood at the landing. It was stuffy, the day's heat trapped there. A slight draft stirred from Sonny's room. He seemed to be asleep.

"Just in case he isn't," Hugh said, tugging me outside.

The night was still warm, only a trace of dampness on the breeze. He gripped my hand and we walked quickly without talking. Glancing back at Sonny's window, I thought I glimpsed his pale face behind the panes. But it was nothing, and want quickened my pace. Above the beach we entered the woods, stepping briskly over roots stretched like limbs across the moon-lit ground. After a while we came to a clearing and the outline of a cottage bordered by flowering trees — an abandoned tea house, Hugh said. In the blackness, the boughs appeared laden with snow, luminescent. The air was heavy with their perfume, so still not a petal fell.

We undressed quickly and lay in the grass alive with insects; who knows what animals were lurking. Hugh moved on top of me, and as he entered I felt the muscles of his back tense, and I was lost in it, in the haste and need of what we'd put off all day. It was like we were rushing to get somewhere, and afterwards, hearts still racing, we fell from each other, surprised.

The house was silent when we tiptoed in.

"Talk to me," I whispered in bed. "Tell me everything — about you, your friends." My body thrummed, resisting sleep even as Hugh drifted off. I prodded him gently, wide awake, though it must've been late. The newness of being together made time zip by; the prospect of tomorrow mirroring today was almost too gauzy, too amazing, to load with expectation. Who wanted to waste any of it sleeping?

"Who?" he mumbled, spooning against me.

"Reenie and Wayne." I stroked his chest.

"Been together forever. A shame."

My hand idled. "Why'd you say that?" I thought of Reenie's skinny brows, the constellation of rhinestones in her ears.

"Wayne's not what you'd think," he murmured. "Not what most people would think. Underneath it all he's a puss, a lamb of a guy."

"O-kay," I said, unconvinced.

Outside the window something creaked — the clothesline, it sounded like.

"Reenie's a piece of work." His breath was a whisper against my neck.

"How'd *they* meet?"

"Huh?" He was struggling to stay awake.

I could've lain there all night talking, listening to fog rub the shore. He kicked off the quilts and we lay with just the sheet covering us.

"Give me a break," he laughed sleepily, kissing my breast. "How do most people meet growing up in a two-house town? At the ball field?" He snuggled close. "The cemetery. Fuck, the playground — I dunno. You'd have to ask them."

I imagined Reenie's face smoothed with make-up, the hard beige ridge of her chin.

"She keeps him in line, boy. Without Reenie he'd be fu —"

"Listen." I put my finger to his lips. There was that creaking again, like rope swinging from wood. It made me think of a tree. A Joshua Tree, like on that U2 album that'd just come out. Someone swinging from it. God knows where this came from; there wasn't so much as a two-foot spruce out on the spit. As suddenly as it started, the creaking stopped.

"And what about you — how'd you meet them?"

"Reenie an' Wayne?" he slurred, sighing into my hair. "Same way we met, at a dance. The guys — the other guys — said Wayne could make things happen."

I raised an eyebrow.

"When I was trying for this job. Lotta guys with way more experience. Wayne figured I could help him out, you know. With business."

"Um ... I'm missing something?"

"Think he pays for that house and truck and boat and all those tole paints and earrings with his ferry service?" He laughed, swallowing. His eyes closed, he rubbed his thumb and fingers together. "Oh, Tessie, all the eco-tourists in the world couldn't keep Wayne afloat. A little of this, a little of that. You don't wanna know," he murmured. "You could call him an entrepreneur. Unlike moi." He stroked my shoulder.

"Thank God," I said, turning onto my side.

"Thank who?" He tickled me. "Sheeesh, Willa, don't tell me you're tired?"

Then he kissed my ear, sliding his arms around my belly. "You're really here," he whispered, moving gently against me. "How lucky is that?"

We woke to fog, and the rest of that week it rained. A lousy start to summer, Sonny complained, though you had to hand it to him; he could've been a lot worse, what with no TV or kids around. He spent a lot of time in his room reading comics and drawing. Drawing what? I wanted to know, but he wouldn't say. A couple of times I caught him sliding papers under his bed, but there was nothing there when I went to make it.

"Leave him be," was Hugh's only comment.

The foghorn roused me one morning. Hugh was already up; a bulb needed replacing in the lantern. I heard him upstairs rooting through the storeroom and hoped he wouldn't wake Sonny. We were going to have coffee first, the two of us, but before we could, Sonny appeared. He flopped down with an *Archie* comic, glancing up with mild interest when Hugh showed him the big mercury bulb. Its filament made me think of a ship in a bottle.

Sonny watched as Hugh kissed me on his way outside.

The day started off drizzly, but after breakfast the sun peeked through. I did a wash — jeans, underwear, socks — in the ancient wringer washer, and hung them out, stiff as dried kelp. The wind tore at the saggy line. Still in his pyjamas, Sonny charged at it like a bull, snorting and pawing the ground. My hair stuck in my teeth from the wind. A fine mist hugged the whitecaps and spray spiked the air. From the lantern above I could hear snatches of "Blue Train," the notes gliding and muffled, smothered by Sonny's shouts and the smashing waves.

The sun climbed, already baking. A beach day, had the water been swimmable. You could imagine the heat in the tower, cooking the mercury, vapour rising. I wondered if you could see or smell it, pictured it moving like cirrus clouds.

A picnic day, I decided, watching the wind twist our clothes. I slapped together a lunch. Peanut butter sandwiches, Cokes for Sonny and Hugh and a beer for me, a lonely Keith's found in a cupboard. Oranges for dessert, and some dried-up jujubes Sonny had got his hands on somewhere. I imagined Hugh's surprise; he always looked amazed when such things turned up, as amazed as when we'd find new paths or plants or evidence of wildlife on our hikes. A beaver lived in the pond, we'd discovered one grey morning, with the same delight we'd felt watching red-winged blackbirds flutter above the reeds. I'd never seen a beaver before, except on a nickel.

"Years ago," Hugh had said, "the poor bugger would've been turned into a hat. One of those tall things like Abe Lincoln's?" Then he'd told a story about mad hatters, real ones, long ago in Connecticut. Their shaking hands dyed red from the mercury they'd used to make the felt.

Hugh took forever changing that bulb. Maybe he'd decided to polish the lens too, or clean the mercury bath. I thought of the trough, that liquid metal as bright as a mirror, and of Alice and her Mad Hatter. Along with keeping things spic and span, Hugh was supposed to strain the quicksilver now and then, to pick out dirt and dead flies, anything that impeded the lens's smooth turning. Though from what I'd seen, the job was mainly babysitting. The Coast Guard controlled most of the operations by computer. But Hugh worried about the sailors passing the light, port or starboard, and putting their faith in it. Hoping there was someone looking out for them — a human eye — which is what he tried to be. There was something about a man's presence, he said, even if the Coast Guard didn't think so. Even if all you could do was watch from shore and radio for help, or wave and hope some poor bugger out there took comfort believing he wasn't alone. Of course they weren't, he'd told himself. There were hundreds of people at sea, keeping each other amused with card games and pictures of naked women and enough to drink and toke.

"How do you know that?" I'd wondered early on, the night of Wayne's party, what Hugh had against drinking. He hadn't answered right away, so I guess it was out of vigilance, some knowledge of his that disasters dropped from the sky, got spat up by waves.

"You never know," he'd said. "The last thing you'd wanna be, if someone's in trouble, is passed out at the switch. You wouldn't want to be spilling your cookies, either, making the rounds."

"Rounds?"

"Beachcombing. Used to be what keepers did, especially on islands. Daily walkabout? Checking for washed-up bodies."

I threw the lunch into a bag and went and hollered up to Hugh. After a few minutes he came down, locking up behind him. Again I read the sign: *DANGER. KEEP OUT. This is an aid to navigation and persons found tampering with this equipment will be prosecuted.*

Sonny ran ahead as we strolled down the beach and up the tea house path. The three of us, a real family. The clearing looked bigger in daylight, and you could hear the usual squeals and rumbles from the port, that ever-present hum. The branches bowed like fishing poles, the frothy blossoms like lace against green and the sky's aching blue. The sun burned directly overhead.

The wind ruffled the long grass, showering confetti as we approached. The ruined garden opened like a door in a movie, as though we'd drawn back the woods' gloom, stepping into sunlight. Daisies sprang from the spot where we'd lain that first night, and I had the oddest feeling I was viewing things through the wrong end of a telescope.

Hugh's hand moved at my waist as we whisked through the grass. I noticed each blade, each tasseled head. Tramping uphill, Sonny stopped and stripped bark from a tree. Above that distant hum, flies buzzed, the sound pierced by cawing. Ravens? In the heat you could almost hear the sun crisping rotted shingles on the tea house roof. I *felt* these sounds as we passed a foundation of fieldstones half buried in the grass, the thorny sprays of a hedge gone wild.

"Here?" said Hugh, flinging down the striped blanket beneath a massive tree. Its leaves were the burnished copper of an Irish setter and its bark was scarred with initials. Scabbed with lichens, the limbs swung upwards like elephants' trunks. Hugh lay back, leaning on his elbow, and curled around me. Opening his pop, he closed his eyes and drank, then lay back once more, arms cradling his head.

"They're calling for rain again," I said, repeating the morning's forecast. "Should you stick around?"

He moved closer, laying his head in my lap. He squinted up at that hapless blue — not a hint of cloud. Upside down, his face reminded me of Sonny's.

"You worry too much. God's in her heaven, Willa."

I unwrapped the sandwiches, balancing mine on my knee. Sonny squatted in the shade, overturning rocks at the edge of the garden. He ambled over with a salamander between his palms; it was charcoal with brilliant orange spots.

"Hey," said Hugh, "let's find something to put it in." Dropping his sandwich, he got up and poked through the weeds beside the crumbling cottage. He managed to find a jar with half a rusted lid. Sonny deposited the creature inside, stuffing in leaves and dirt.

"Seek and ye shall find," Hugh tickled my side. "Everything you need, when you need it — hey, Alex?"

"Sonny," I called, "come eat your lunch."

"I ain't hungry." That dude talk again; my boy flexing whatever muscles he could. He'd lost some of his chubbiness, even after just a week and a half of being out here. Though his bike still sat in the shed where he'd left it — out of the weather, at least.

Hugh put his thumb to my lips. "Alex? C'mere."

Sonny set down the jar and the two of them took off up the hill beyond the snow-white trees. Wrapping their food, I caught up to them in a grove of chestnuts.

Something made Sonny jump. A snake, a green thread wriggling through the clumped grass.

"Don't be a wuss." Hugh laughed, bending to watch its progress. "It's just a grass snake, buddy."

Under his tan Sonny looked pale; sweat beaded his lip.

"Grab it," Hugh said, and I waited. I hate snakes, have always hated their squiggle and the thought of their sliminess. Those books from the school library lied when they said the scales were dry and that human hands passed on deadly diseases. Death by touching — it had to be a lie.

Sonny's chest moved under his T-shirt. As he chewed his lip, his face changed. His shoulders tightened as Hugh scooped up the snake and dropped it into his palm. He flinched and might've let it go. Instead he held still, cupping his hands, not wishing it harm. Did snakes have bones? You could see his mind working as the creature twitched and flicked; he closed his fists around it and held it out. Its tongue flickered, lightning forking from its tiny jaws.

Probably I screamed — a totally stupid reaction — and felt instant shame. You were supposed to teach kids the opposite of fear, that everything was somehow good and lovely and worthy of awe.

"Now your mother's a wussy!" Hugh walked his fingers up my back. Sonny stooped to let the snake go. It hairpinned sideways and vanished into the grass, apparently unscathed. I wiped my palms on my shorts, running back down the hill ahead of them.

When I reached the ruined hedge, there was a shriek and I turned to see Sonny barrelling towards me. His shoulders were scrunched up and his mouth was open in a howl, his face a sickly shade.

Hugh brayed with laughter. "Jesus!" he kept saying. "A little thing like that — totally harmless!"

As Sonny caught up to me, his mouth trembled and there were tears and a little trail of snot starting from his nose.

"If I w-wanted a snake down my shirt, M-Mom, I woulda asked." He was trying to be brave.

"Oh ... sweetie." I went to loop my arm around him. Hugh was smiling and tamping the grass with his feet. Something about his expression stopped me. "It's okay, Sonny, really. Be a brave soldier. You're not a baby."

Squinting, Hugh shook his head. "Figure if he likes sala-manders ..." He seemed confused, blank.

As I turned to hug him, Sonny wriggled away, wiping his face on his shirt. Hugh and I watched him run towards the tea house, then comb the ground by the blanket as if he'd lost a loonie.

When we got there, the jar was empty; the pet had escaped.

"Sneaky little bastard," Hugh said, opening Sonny's Coke and passing it.

That night in bed we waited till all was quiet before making love. Instead of being sleepy afterwards, we lay wide awake.

"You still haven't told me," I said, "what you used to do. How you and Wayne got to be friends."

"Me and Wayne?"

There was a pause. I nudged him.

"It was over a girl, actually." He was dismissive, tracing my side with his finger. "A bit of a case — the kind you feel sorry for? A street kid, kind of ... you know." I didn't.

"She worked for us — for Wayne, I mean. For a bit. No big deal. She might've had the hots ... well, I palmed her off on him."

This took a second to sink in. "You *palmed* her off?" I pictured Wayne in his ball cap, his burly fist around a beer.

Hugh's eyes were as liquid as the mercury in the tower. "Well, not just like *that*." He snapped his fingers. "Not till after ... look, I was lonely. You have no idea ..."

"That was then, right?" I snuggled closer, and his embrace absorbed me as if our skins had dissolved and his spirit moved inside mine.

"Don't worry," he sang against my throat, a deep, melodious thrum like a gospel singer's. "Be happy, Willa, my sweet, sweeeet wisp."

"What about Reenie?" I murmured after a while.

"What about her?" He paused, his fingers drumming a silent beat on my arm. "She and Wayner have an agreement. They've been together so long, you know. They're good friends." His breath warmed my shoulder.

"I bet."

"It happens, Tessie, I guess. Don't get me wrong. Wayne worships the ground Reenie walks on. She says jump, he says how high."

"Nice," I said drowsily. "You still haven't told me."

"What?"

"Why they're such buddies of yours."

His eyes widened. This time we both heard it: the creak of a rope. I wondered if I'd brought everything in, those jeans of Sonny's that'd flapped all day like dried salt fish.

"We knew each other before," he said, "that's all. Would you knock it off and go to sleep?" Breathing softly, he put his hand over my mouth. I slid my leg over his, pushing against his warmth.

"Tell me more about you," I said, feeling him harden. He pulled me closer.

"Nothing to tell, really."

"First person you kissed, first time you got loaded, stuff like that," I coaxed, joking.

He didn't laugh. "Don't remember. Don't want to. There. You?"

My body stretched taut against his, that little voice swinging in and out of my thoughts: *don't waste it.*

"Whistlestop, Alberta. A kid in grade two. He brought his G.I. Joe collection to school. The grad dance at Whistlestop High; lemon gin," I snorted. "Tom Collins was my date." The bed shook with my laughter. Hugh hardly grinned, which made me try harder. I loved how his teeth showed when he laughed, his teeth but not his gums. "I literally fell out of his car."

"Whose car?"

"My date's!"

"You're lucky, then." He yawned, and I felt him softening.

"So ... how 'bout you?"

"Lucky?" he said. "Shit, if you knew ... "

"This ... girl." I walked my fingers over his chest and under his chin. "How'd you cross paths with her?"

He didn't answer right away, closing his eyes and appearing to drop off. After a minute or two he inhaled slowly. "Out west. The three of us were out there at the time." His voice was tired. "Me and Wayne ... and this chick."

"Chick?" I mimicked. "She was his *tore* guide?"

"Well, you know." His breathing grew slower, deeper. "Hell on wheels, Willa; that's how it was at the time." *Don't even ask*, he seemed to say, stopping me with a kiss.

14

## MERIDIAN

One morning we overslept, all three of us. It was almost lunch by the time we got up. Setting out Corn Flakes, Sonny spotted them first: a pair of black and orange boats in the curl of the beach, a few hundred yards offshore. We ate our cereal watching divers bob and disappear. Hugh went up to the lantern for the binoculars.

"Knock yourselves out," he teased, plunking them down between us. "Jeez, I've never seen such nosy parkers as you and your mother, Alex!" He rubbed my arm. "It's just the navy doing routine stuff. Practice dives."

"What for?" Sonny asked like a normal kid, not a military brat.

"Defusing bombs, checking dumped artillery? Who knows, Alex. The military works in strange ways. Youse would know."

"Maybe they're diving for treasure," said Sonny, too

earnestly. "Or bodies."

"You guys figure it out. I've got work to do," Hugh said. "Oh, hey, the sunscreen's under the sink. You'll want it if you're heading out."

"Feel like a hike?" I asked Sonny, peeling him an orange, laying out the sections like dories.

He had the binoculars pressed to the window, his cereal gone mushy. "How can they be 'frogmen' if their gear's black?"

Here we go, I thought. Next he'll ask about his dad. We'd been out here more than three weeks, and not a peep from Charlie, not so much as a note or a phone call for Sonny. Not that I expected anything. But thinking about it threw a shadow like that of a passing container ship.

"My turn," I said, taking the glasses from him and focusing on the divers huddled on deck. They looked like carpenter ants, too small to make out faces.

They were still there when I hung the laundry out, and when Sonny and I went to the pond to feed the ducks. As we cut back past the marsh, we watched the boats weigh anchor and steam slowly around the island's northern tip.

The ancient phone was ringing when we reached the porch, Hugh nowhere in sight. Its clanging filled the kitchen as I ran to grab it.

"Hello?" Catching my breath, I started to explain that Hugh was working.

The person on the other end drew a deep breath and cut in. "Bitch."

My hand tightened around the clunky receiver. "Y-you

must have the wrong —"

"Goddamn bitch," his voice gouged the air, then the line went dead.

Sonny had poured himself some Coke and stopped in mid-sip. "Mom? Who was that?"

"Nobody," I said, though he must've seen me trembling. "Will that be canned soup for supper, or canned soup?"

For once, his groans were like Noxzema on a sunburn.

"You okay?" he kept up, in a way that wasn't like him at all.

"Fine." To prove it, I grinned. "Do me a favour. Run next door, would you, and see what Hugh's up to?"

He made a gargling sound. "Do I have to?"

"Sonny!"

Opening cans calmed me, and by the time they came in the Campbell's was bubbling.

"Whassup?" Hugh wanted to know.

"Hm? Oh — we missed you, that's all."

We were crossing the beach late one day, returning from one of our picnics, when it fell: a silence that thrummed like a bird inside an egg. Hugh squinted up at the sky, the clouds packed like traffic. Sonny was by the water, dropping rocks on jellyfish that had washed up.

"Where's a bucket?" he shouted. "I could make jellyfish stew."

As I yelled for him to hurry up, the stillness broke. Rain began to spit. At the first drops we stuck our tongues out, laughing, barely noticing the squall chugging up the harbour.

But as it closed in we started to run. In minutes the spit was wrapped in mist that blotted out the lighthouse. Waves churned the sand and thunder boiled from the opposite shore.

"Better move it." Hugh grabbed my hand and Sonny's, propelling us over the rocks. Fog wisped past our shins like a gas and way out on the water the buoy clanged. The pounding behind the breakwater rumbled through our feet.

"Nasty!" Sonny winced, skidding over seaweed stuck to tarry feathers. I started to laugh, but Hugh's expression stopped me.

This wasn't your average squall, it hit me as he shouted, "Move it!" The words were barely out when hail the size of mothballs flew down, pinging from the rocks.

"Jesus, Willa, I've seen you move when you have to," he hollered, with no hint of fun. He grabbed Sonny's arm roughly.

The hail thickened. "Ping-pong balls!" Sonny yelled, as it pelted and ricocheted. I threw the picnic blanket over him and tried to duck, stumbling along. As we neared the house — Hallelujah! — we could see that a kitchen window had been smashed. Foam seeped between the giant boulders beyond the tower, dotting the gravel like spit.

"Get in, quick!" Hugh shouted. "For chrissake, stay clear of the windows!"

I bristled; he was overdoing it, surely, to get a rise out of us. His voice had a sharpness I didn't like, a roughness as he pushed us into the kitchen, and left to check on the light. Through the rattling panes I watched him run to the tool shed and grab a jerry can, then dash to the tower, ducking baseballs now.

I tried the kitchen light. Nothing. Then I picked up the phone. It still worked, thank God. After a few minutes there was a grating roar, and light flashed from the lantern again.

"Scrabble?" I kidded, hunkering down with Sonny. There was a thud outside, a crash like something giving way. As I fought panic, Hugh appeared. His hair a wet tangle, his face looked almost bruised.

"Fuck," he said.

"A duck," Sonny chorused. Nobody moved. Then came a groan, a grinding that drove a needle of fear through me. Hugh's face was gaunt as the waves slammed.

Like an idiot I slunk to the window.

"Get the *fuck* away from there!" Hugh seized my wrist, pulling me away — but not before I glimpsed water encircling the shed. It slid under the clothesline, swirling around the pole.

We were being cut off, it seemed, an island off an island, a clutch of buildings surrounded by the ocean. I put my arms around Sonny. He was shaking. "It'll be okay," I kept murmuring, a mantra to push back the waves.

A slo-pitch from heaven hit the pane and burst in, showering glass. It rolled across the linoleum like a foul in outfield. Sonny's eyes widened and he leapt to grab it. It dripped through his fingers as he raced to the freezer. From upstairs came a steady pummelling. It was like being attacked by pitchers at batting practice. Maybe just then Sonny had the same thought, or maybe it was out of fear. We both let out a jumpy laugh.

"Hold tight," I think Hugh yelled, staring as if we'd lost our senses. "Hang on," he ordered, a bit more calmly, walking the floor as if it were a rolling deck. Opening the door to the cellar crawl space, he fished out a kerosene lamp and lit it. I could hear water lapping.

As the dirty light broke the gloom, something bizarre happened. The pelting ceased, and as the smashed window filled with a strange, peachy glow, the wind stopped. After a while, the sea subsided to a normal hiss, a rustling like leaves. *Hiss and swell, hiss and swell*, the sound stilled my swaying brain.

As fast as it had risen, the storm passed.

Hugh came and wrapped his arms around Sonny and me. *Group hug*, Sonny would've sneered and weaselled out of it, any other time. Now he rested against Hugh's shoulder, grabbing a handful of wet flannel; and for once, that smart-assed mouth of his left him high and dry.

Venturing out the next morning, I felt like Noah's wife leaving the ark after the flood. All that remained of the boardwalk were twisted planks, the spikes wrenched from them. The yard was a garden of rotting net, garbage that had washed up, and reams of kelp. There was even a crate of bananas, black and disgusting.

"Bet you a buck you won't guess what they are," I said, coaxing Sonny outside.

Some of the boulders shoring up the seaward edge of the spit had shifted.

"What if you're out here, and I'm over there in the woods or something, next time a storm comes?" he asked warily.

"Better to stick close," was my reply, though the thought rankled.

It got awkward having him underfoot all day, especially with no TV. He wasn't much of a reader, except for comic books. And you could only play so much Scrabble, though as summer wore on, we took to playing cards, charades, and Risk. Sometimes at night Hugh told stories, mostly to get Sonny to turn in early so we could claim the dark. I was always afraid he'd hear us, even from that upstairs room, with the waves for a lullaby and the honks of passing ships. Though I'd brought him here, I never meant for Sonny to be my witness.

We started sneaking out at night, Hugh and I, like teenagers parking. The grass was our back seat, the darkness our blanket. The wind blew the bugs away. The paleness of our skins made us ghosts moving against the woods' velvet backdrop. When the stars came out, they were eyes watching us, but without judgment. It was as if they were winking, a party to our craving. And though helicopters — Coast Guard and military — often chewed the air above, approaching and leaving the base, I never thought of Charlie up there looking down.

Except the night of the storm, once things subsided — then I did. Impossible to watch breakers and not feel my heart swim out. An image pushed and pulled inside me, of Charlie leaning out of a chopper, feeding down a lifeline — a basket or horse collar — to a sole survivor bobbing on the sea. Impossible not to think of him and his buddies, all hands, searching and rescuing.

Seeking but not finding?

I thought of that phone call: *Bitch*. It was only right that I'd given up on him. And that he'd given up on me. But on Sonny?

I could count on one hand the times that we went ashore that summer. Only when we needed groceries. Then, I felt like a castaway craving greens. Hugh would phone Wayne who'd ship us over, then chauffeur us to the Superstore. It felt strange going back there, to that shiny world of plastic and chrome. None of it looked real. It hurt my eyes. Even the air hurt — the hot whirr of cars in the parking lot, the store's air-conditioned chill moving up my arms. Sonny, though, stepped inside as if we'd never left. He clamoured for Coco Puffs, chocolate bars, frozen cakes and pizzas.

"No problem," Hugh said. "Fill your boots. No, really, Willa. Whatever he wants."

Once Sonny put a big box of Drumsticks in the cart, which escaped notice till they'd been rung through. They were a sticky white soup by the time we got home. Hugh handed him a spoon. "Have a blast," he said.

Money wasn't an issue. Hugh kept a wad of it inside his wallet, which made me uncomfortable.

"I feel bad, you footing everything."

"Tttt." He eyed me. "Listen, Tessie. What's it for, then? I got cash to burn, no place to spend it."

Returning to that abandoned world — the mainland — made me feel like a fruit bat leaving the jungle, temporarily blinded. Hugh, like Sonny, had no trouble. He moved as easily through frozen foods as he did an aisle of ferns. It was as though his feet didn't touch the ground; no signs of shock or adjustment, of resetting his inner rhythm to a faster, jerkier one. In the supermarket I was all thumbs, terrified of seeing someone from the base; stepping back on the island, all knees and elbows following Hugh up the path, weighed down with cans while slapping at insects. But by the time we got to the beach, my limbs would relax, my stride almost matching his until I'd stop and wait for Sonny hauling his share.

A small inconvenience, the awkwardness of re-entry in exchange for paradise.

Maybe Hugh's ease moving between two worlds could be put down to practice, and had little to do with a chameleon spirit. Not long after Charlie's bitch call, the phone seemed to ring regularly, though the sound never stopped jolting me, bringing back the venom in Charlie's voice. It was members of Hugh's band, hoping to get together. He seemed uninterested at first, his days so entwined with mine — like the morning glories twisting around the rocks above the high-tide mark. He didn't like to leave us out here alone. I didn't much relish it either, the threat of a storm always lurking off the tip of my imagination. He started spending more time playing, though, afternoons in the tower, the buzz of notes like a chorus of bees in perfect pitch. He played jazz tunes mostly, a few weeping, wailing blues, and sometimes Van Morrison, which made me want to dance out there under the blistering sun. Sometimes in the evenings before we escaped, he'd play in the kitchen, music waxing and waning to the rush of surf and the wind tapping the curtain rod against the open window.

One night he played a slow, mournful tune new to me. "'Motherless Children,' Blind Willie Johnson," he said. "Though Eric Clapton gets all the credit."

In spite of my happiness, a tear snaked down.

"Tell me," he said.

"What? About my mother?"

The sax dangled between us. At the table, Sonny was all eyes.

"Um — she had brown hair, blue eyes. Smelled like green Jell-O." Something caught in my throat. "Don't remember a whole lot. I was only …" An image flashed of my brother and me eating breakfast, our mother at the sink. A dribble of blood down her bare leg. This terrified look on Jason's face, our mother saying, *It's nothing*, and running upstairs.

Hugh stroked my arm. Sonny went back to his comic.

Then I saw myself, not much bigger than a doll, crying and sucking on my fingers. Wearing a pale pink dress, standing all alone on a corner of our suburban street, lost. *Bad, bad girl, wandering away. How's Mommy to know where to find you?*

"Spider-Man sucks, y'know that?" Sonny griped.

Next I thought of my mother lying in bed. I'd taken her sewing scissors and lopped off my bangs. The room was dim and shadowy, and she herself hardly had any hair left, save for baby tufts sticking out here and there, like my doll's when I gave her a trim. *Thank you my darling.* Her voice a dry, cough-ing whisper. Its sound, a papery whisk, and the memory of her sobbing moved through me, a dull ache settling under my heart. It dissipated as Hugh started playing again. Something fun, cocky, and my mother was gone. Even Sonny was bopping along. I lost myself, watching the slow swing of Hugh's body, the sway of his head, the way he opened his eyes as if surprised, then squeezed them shut to the instrument's lift and thrust. It made me jealous, the way they possessed each other, Hugh and his sax, as though with each bar he wrestled to make it behave. Perhaps it was all about taming, bending the thing to his pur-pose. He could've charmed cobras with that music, his playing was pure erotica — the opposite of guitarists', who seemed to play with themselves instead.

Closing my eyes, I felt him playing me.

Sonny was still awake when I picked up the blanket and went outside, holding Hugh's hand. We didn't make it as far as the field.

But when something roused me in the middle of the night, Hugh was gone. Checking the light, maybe, or polishing that new tune. Drowning everything out, the sea put me back to sleep. He was there when I woke in the morning.

The last week of August we went to a house party over in the Passage, not far from Wayne's. Some friends of Hugh's were hosting it: Kenny, the drummer in the band, and his wife, Paula. They had a barbecue and live entertainment — a glorified jam.

Kids were invited. Wayne and Reenie were there, and the other band members and their "partners."

Reenie was outside having a cigarette as we drove up, the four of us squished into the front of Wayne's truck. "Long time no see," she said coolly, raising an eyebrow at Sonny. He had his nose in the latest *Punisher*. He hadn't wanted to come, arguing that he could watch the light while we partied.

"Not likely," I'd argued back, trying to keep it down as Hugh and Wayne loaded stuff into the boat and waited for us to get in.

Even with the engine whining, Sonny'd kept it up, glum as a rattlesnake as we landed and climbed the ramp to the dock. "Dad never made me do crap like this."

"Behave," I'd muttered, and when Hugh glanced back, impatience had flicked over his face. Who could blame him? He'd gone ahead to the truck, lugging his sax and a bag of munchies.

It was a short drive to Kenny's, a small, grey-sided house with a whale weather vane, a shaky white deck out front, and a barrel by the driveway, spilling flowers. Kenny looked vaguely familiar and it made me blush, remembering New Year's Eve. Paula, his wife, was slim and perky in white jeans and a skimpy top. She had a new baby and a little boy of two or three. When introduced, Sonny scowled and waved.

Reenie led me to the kitchen where three or four women scurried around getting food. The room was newly renovated, with blond cupboards and an island and crisply black and white tiles. Some little kids were building a plastic castle — two girls and a boy who barely looked up at Sonny.

"You're too big for castles?" Paula asked my boy. One of the kids spilled juice and another dripped Popsicle on the floor. Sonny sat down at the pine table, clutching his comic book.

A blond woman came up to me. "You must be Julie ..." She had an infant in one of those backpack things and looked like she'd just finished a hike. "You're with Hugh?"

The chatter stopped. Reenie disappeared. Paula was rinsing vegetables; the only sound was the tap running. The blond woman looked a bit dazed, then smiled, sticking out her hand. "I'm Emily," she said, tipping forward, "and this is Johanna. We haven't met. I'm Bob's wife. The bass player?"

Paula drifted over, patting my arm. "Could I get you some wine?" Her hand felt wet.

"Veggie?" interrupted another woman — Shayla — passing a plate.

"Guess I'm confused," said blond Emily, eyeing me while dangling a carrot stick over her shoulder. The baby grabbed it and spit bits into Emily's braid. "I was sure your name was Julie," she said, rubbing her cheek.

Paula pushed a glass into my hand. "Does your son like Cheezies? Everybody!" she called out above the chords vibrating from another room. "This is Wil-la. Willa ...?"

"Jackson." I smiled at Emily. "This is my son Alex." I willed him to look at me but he just kept staring at his comic.

"My husband Bob plays bass," Emily said. "I guess we haven't met before. It's this baby stuff, right? Hormones, they screw your memory."

I sipped wine and unloaded our snacks: chips and Bits &

Bites. They looked poisonous beside all the vegetables and dip. I felt everyone staring at Sonny. At least summer had melted off most of his chubbiness.

"Party food," someone said, digging in. Emily nibbled a Shreddie. "Mmm," she said, being nice.

"Better take the guys some beer, eh?" Paula rooted through the fridge, thrust a Keith's at me. "Oh. Right. Hughie doesn't drink."

Emily covered her mouth. The baby chewed her braid.

*Julie*, I thought, the name stirring from nowhere.

I helped myself to more wine and escaped into the living room. It was small and dark with heavy carpeting and a beach stone fireplace, a row of small, high windows along one wall and a picture window facing the road. The sofa and a matching chair were shoved aside to accommodate the drum kit; its cymbals and toms were a sprawl of brass and chrome like something from the *Ed Sullivan Show*. Wayne squatted over a mess of cords and mic stands, adjusting things. His shirt came untucked, and you could see his crack. Getting up he staggered a little, almost stumbling into an amp and Hugh's sax.

The other guys and Reenie were out on the deck drinking. Hugh sipped from a tumbler — Coke? — winking as I peeked outside. He turned and kept talking as Paula appeared with her baby glued to a breast, her top pulled up, showing her midriff. She beckoned, "Can I ask you a favour?" A car turned in, some guy in a Mustang. Darrell, I heard someone say.

I was on my third glass of wine, slicing lemon when the music started. Sonny had finally put down *Punisher* and was playing a game with the other kids, shooting them with a wooden spoon. Oh God, I thought, as the little ones fell, giggling their heads off. As the sax started in, I let it go. Drifting to the doorway, I stood beside Reenie, listening. The newcomer, a bearded guy with poodle hair, was rolling a joint. He looked out of place with all these upscale granola types, his lizard eyes darting around. I'd seen him before, but it took a moment to realize where: at the Tim's that snowy day, months ago.

Caught up in the music, the women had stopped talking. Emily and Paula swayed babies on their hips. Their eyes were locked on Hugh, just like mine. We were like remote control cars with the same beautiful kid at the switch, mesmerized by his moves, moves that should've been for me alone. Now they belonged to this room, these wives, girlfriends and babies, and to a past, it jabbed me, probably full of other such rooms.

It hurt to peel my eyes away. The music bubbled and broke inside me, and someone yelled, "The volume! The kids! They really oughta tone it down!"

At the end of the set, Hugh dripped with sweat. The other guys too, but who noticed? All those women watched as he scooted over and kissed me, the kind of kiss that singles you out like that one hailstone falling from blue sky. Suddenly the room was ours. The women and their little kids, even the men — all but Darrell, the burly guy, who coughed.

"C'mon out to the car for a sec, Wayner," he said. "Hughie?"

It must've been the wine. By the time we ate — me perched on Hugh's knee out on the deck, Sonny running around throwing Cheezies — I was properly pissed. Otherwise I mightn't have been so easy about what happened. The neighbours had a dog with a litter of pups. Sometime between dessert and coffee the kids wandered over for a look, and Hugh and Sonny disappeared. They came back with a black and white puppy wrapped in a pink towel. "It's a boy," Sonny said, to reassure me. No babies to worry about. "Oreo," he named him, kneeling on Paula's floor as Hugh kept shooting me looks.

"My whole life I wanted a dog," Sonny said, rubbing his face in the pup's fur. He let it crawl over his lap as it tried to escape all the tiny, mauling hands. The pup hijacked the party. The band regrouped for a few more tunes, but things lacked drive after that.

"You're not mad, I hope," Hugh said as we were getting into the truck. Wayne's eyes were glassy. Reenie was on the deck, holding somebody's kid — Johanna, the backpack baby. She looked out of place and fed up, turning as we pulled out of the driveway. I tried not to lean into Wayne, but it wasn't easy packed in like that. The puppy squirmed from lap to lap, peeing on Hugh. Sonny hooted as Hugh threw up his hands. Wayne slapped the wheel, and it seemed to me as good a moment as any to blurt out, "Who's Julie?"

Wayne's eyes slid to the rear-view. The only sound was the pup licking Sonny's finger. "Ow!" he yelped when it nipped.

Hugh's arm rested along the top of the seat; he kneaded my shoulder, nudging Wayne.

"Hey, loverboy," Wayne scoffed, turning down to the dock. "Got your stuff all right, eh?"

Hugh tapped his sax case. His eyes were on the water. Like

Sonny, he was sober. "You want to know who Julie was?" he said, matter-of-factly. "I've already told you. An old girlfriend —"

"Right," Wayne chimed in, blasting the horn at a gull.

"— that's all," Hugh added, jumping out.

"Okay, Wayne," he said, once we were in the boat, "Let's see you drive 'er, buddy."

As we shot from shore, Sonny cradled the pup like an infant, kissing its muzzle. It occurred to me that we had nothing to feed it. *Tomorrow,* I thought hazily, burping wine and Cheezies, and gripping the side. Maybe Wayne thought I'd barf; he eyed me nervously, with new interest. Then it struck me, the meaning behind his look. One of a string, it seemed to say. One of a flock. He was wrong, of course. I knew better. Hugh just wasn't the type to love a pack.

15

## LEARNING THE ROPES

Sonny carried Oreo on his shoulder, that little white snout poking from the towel like a rat's. It was dark by the time we reached the spit, and I had to stop and pee in the dunes. Chilly and damp, the wind had that edge that signalled summer's end. The puppy blinked feverishly as we hiked along, picking our way around the ruined boardwalk.

We made a nest of old blankets and a life jacket, and laid it near the foot of Sonny's bed, beside a swath of newspapers. Sonny splashed milk into a saucer and shook flakes of tuna into an old margarine tub.

"It's up to you, bud, to train him. You have to take him outside to do his business," Hugh said.

"Like having a baby," I slurred.

"Wouldn't know about that." Hugh flicked my ponytail off

my neck. "Your ma and I are beat," he told Sonny. "We're off to bed. You and Mr. Christie okay?"

"His name's Oreo. Nerd," Sonny started, as Hugh headed downstairs stiffly, almost limping. He paused on the landing to get his balance, stooping in the greenish light flashing in.

I lay on Sonny's bed for a while, watching him play with the pup. It waddled and staggered, attacking folds in the news-paper. My throat felt dry and my head ached above one eye. Sonny flicked a bottle cap across the floor like a puck, barely noticing when I got up and slipped to the bathroom.

A cruise ship glided past as I splashed my face; you could feel the shudder through the floor before its reflection danced in the mirror. Glowing like a chandelier, it slid over the indigo water like a Hollywood phantom. Captivated, I watched it float into the night till it was just a firefly on the horizon.

Downstairs, Hugh was in bed with the light on. He pushed back the covers to let me in.

"Tell me about your girlfriend," I tried teasing, sliding into the crook of his arm. He kissed my hair, then took a big, long drink from the glass of water at the bedside.

"Which one, Tessie?"

It had to have been the wine; in my dreams that night I took a joyride through the circuit of streets on the base. The Dodge had pedals instead of an engine, like a car on *The Flintstones*. Gaining speed, my feet scraped the pavement; my sandals had fallen off. Blood oozed from my toes. Coasting past the house on Avenger, I nearly ran down someone walking. She was wearing a brown leather jacket and jeans, all you could see from behind. The street narrowed suddenly and I swerved to avoid her. She turned and I froze. She had a face like mine. I think it was my mother.

As soon as we were up and dressed, Sonny and I got the pup outside. Hugh stayed in bed, his sax abandoned on the kitchen table, no sign of the case. I sat on a rock drinking coffee while Sonny tried teaching Oreo to sit. A chilly haze blew in off the ocean — so much for the clothes I'd left on the line. Soon we were engulfed in fog. Someone with the Coast Guard had taken charge of the foghorn; every few minutes it blared.

Oreo trembled and pressed his belly to the ground, leaving a wet spot. He'd already had a few accidents. Hugh had almost slipped in one, going to the bathroom. We'd soon be out of newspaper. I was thinking that we'd have to call on Wayne to get dog food, when a noise burned in the distance. A purr at first, it mounted to a roar. As it got louder, the fog broke and a helo skimmed towards us. At the same time, a destroyer glided past the boulders at the end of the spit, its sonar orbiting slowly in the mist.

The chopper swooped in closer, hovering so low we glimpsed the maple leaf on its side, the crew hanging about the opened door. Sonny dropped the puppy, gazing up. For an instant I forgot myself and waved. The noise was deafening, blending with the foghorn. As the chopper banked and began to ascend, passing over the ship then heading out to sea, the childishness of what I'd done sank in. Like the itch from a string of bug bites, it spread, then set. Even as the chopper disappeared, its noise stayed with me. In the echo, I imagined its flight path circling over land and touching down at the base.

We watched the ship slide towards port, flags waving in the stinging breeze. I'd just taken a sip of cold coffee when the chopper returned, with that roar like the clouds being put through a blender. It scudded over us, flying faster this time. I watched till the rotors were a daisy twirling out of sight. When I glanced at Sonny, he was staring at me with that wide-open look only a kid can get away with. The puppy had stumbled over some stones and was chewing a plastic bottle cap. We watched him arch his body and leave a deposit. "Oh, gross," I waited for Sonny to howl. Instead he picked a wild aster from a crack in the rocks and pulled off its petals.

"Where d'you think Dad is right now?" he asked the stem. "Aren't we ever gonna go back?"


That second question was quite practical, as it turned out — prickly, too, as the blackberry canes along Hangman's Marsh. It was so called because the British navy had executed people on the rocky shingle hemming it. "Fucking Brits'd hang 'em, right there, see?" Hugh would point. "Then they'd tar the corpses and feather 'em." After two months, we'd only begun learning the names of spots on the island, names Hugh tossed out like shorthand, knowing the stories behind them.

School started in a week and something would have to be worked out.

"You could home school," Hugh suggested one day. He'd been busy all morning, straining dirt from the mercury. Sonny wanted to help; who knows why that stuff attracted him so. He was still nagging for a sample to keep on his windowsill, in a jar like his other specimens — shells, insects, rocks.

"Keep him home? Right," I said to Hugh. Thinking, *What planet are you from?*

He wrapped his arms around me and waltzed me to the sink. Ran us each a drink of water, downing his in a gulp.

"You know best." He held his glass to my cheek, then refilled it. "God, I can't get enough."

*Water, water everywhere, nor any drop to —* an odd little voice crowed inside me.

There was a scuffling and Oreo bounded past our shins. Sonny made a dive for him.

"Arsehole dog. He messed again!"

"Get a rag."

But Sonny wasn't listening. He'd sprawled out, swatting the puppy with the rope used for tying him to the shed so he wouldn't run off.

"We'll work something out," Hugh said, guzzling down another drink. Stepping over Sonny on his way outside.

Sonny rolled onto his back, the puppy gnawing on his ear. "This sucks," he moaned, batting Oreo away. The pup rolled onto all fours, whimpering. Sonny pounded the tiles with his heels. Horrified, I saw tears.

"I'm sick of this, I'm bored," he ranted. "I want to go to a movie. I want to see my friends. I want French fries. I want *real* pizza, not frozen crap. For *shit* sake, I want —" As suddenly as it'd started, like that hailstorm the tantrum passed. He lay there with his arms over his face, sniffling. Perching on his chest, Oreo licked his chin.

"Sonny?" Kneeling, I peeled away an arm.

"Frig off!" was all he muttered.

When Hugh came in a little while later, things had calmed down. Digging out some pop from the fridge, he announced that everything was arranged. The school bus stopped in the Passage; all Sonny had to do was be there on time.

"Let me guess. Wayne to the rescue."

He gave me a funny look. When he reached out to stroke my arm, his hand felt icy.

"I'm not going," Sonny said when we broached it. "School's a friggin' waste of time. Who needs it?"

Hugh vamoosed to the bedroom; I could hear him in there flipping pages — sheet music for a tune the band was supposed to be learning. Notes honked out, random as duck calls. After a few bars, he sauntered into the kitchen, where I was trying to interest Sonny in a book. He played "Shave and a Haircut, Two Bits" to get our attention, then let the sax dangle from its strap.

"You know what they do to deserters, eh Alex?"

"Listen up, Sonny," I rolled my eyes and wanted to laugh. "Here comes a story."

"Take a look out there," Hugh said quietly, gazing from the little diamond-shaped window above the coat hooks. "When they hanged a guy, they'd leave 'im out in the sun to rot, and the birds'd eat out his eyes. Yummy, eh?"

"Bullshit," Sonny blurted out, and I swatted his wrist. But he had this look that he never got reading anything.

"Ask Wayne." Hugh shrugged, grinning. "You complain about your mother's cooking."

Sonny kicked the rungs of his chair. "You're lyin'," he said, but you could see his delight.

A smile worked the corners of Hugh's mouth. Though it was early, he looked bushed.

"A warning, Alex. To guys with the same idea. Deserters — first thing you saw entering or leaving the harbour. Dunno about you, but it'd make me think twice, eh, Mom?"

"She's not your mom," Sonny muttered; I'd swear sometimes he ran on cruise control.

"Thank God," Hugh said, and I swatted him. He caught my arm and tickled my ribs, doubling me over.

"Uncle!" I gasped, laughing like a hyena.

"Movies! Two words; first word," Sonny cut in, chopping the back of his hand with two fingers. Pointing at the ceiling, he gazed up, spinning slowly. Then he fluttered his fingers, opening and closing his fists like Pacman mouths. Twinkle, twinkle, he mouthed at me, turning one hand into a gun and zapping Hugh.


That last week of summer, taking the pup out first thing, I spotted something lying on the ground by the clothesline. It was a large bundle, khaki tarp tied with yellow rope. Camp gear, was my first thought; my second: is this some kind of invasion? Hugh was still asleep. He'd complained of tiredness — a bug, he said, and there must've been something to it, since we hadn't made love for three days. I lifted the bundle; it wasn't heavy so much as awkward. As I tugged at the rope, my breath caught. It was tied with the neat, efficient knots you'd imagine sailors using, or the military. Like the ones Charlie'd fussed over once, tying a borrowed tent to the roof rack the sole time we'd tried camping.

Lugging the parcel into the shade behind the tool shed, I prayed that Sonny wouldn't come outside. The puppy nipped at me as I laid it down. My fingers shook undoing the knots. Inside were clothes — *my* clothes, things left behind in drawers and closets, non-essentials. A pair of burgundy cords rolled as if for a hike; T-shirts, sweatshirts; an ancient, unworn nightie, my old leather jacket, a ratty pair of shoes. As I lifted the pile from the tarp, a note fell out. The writing made my throat tighten.

*You'll need these more than me — Charlie.* He hadn't even bothered to write "from," but what did I expect? Below was a PS, painfully legible: *Take good care of my son, or there will be consequences.*

Consequences. It conjured everything from pitchforks to game show hosts. It stung as I stared at the sky, swallowing back an awful taste.

"Tess?" Hugh's voice spilled out above the waves and the wind and gulls yammering overhead. Shakily I bundled everything into the tarp and stepped out into the yard with it, steadying myself. He was leaning from the porch, his face shaded by the roof. His jeans looked slept in, hanging off him, and he wasn't wearing a shirt. He looked shaken, as if plucked from a nightmare.

It was as if Charlie's care package carried germs. That same week I caught a flu that made everything a dream, a mirage. The wind-beaten clothes on the line lifted and flapped over the sea like terns. Shirts became bodies — headless, legless — doing the deadman's float on the dancing, diamond surface.

Hugh compared them to scarecrows frightening away birds.

"What birds?" I asked at the height of my fever. "What garden?" Scarecrows were useless without a garden.

But you couldn't grow a thing out on the spit — not anything needing shelter or soil. The wind flattened everything, rendered the birds paper cut-outs against the clouds. Sweating into my pillow, I thought of ways to thwart it: like planting hollyhocks against the house. I dreamed of pink crepe-paper blooms bleeding through fog, and fogbanks blooming into stoppers plugging up the harbour mouth. To quench the fiery cattail in my throat I swallowed fog — fog as solid as freighters shouldering past. At the very worst of it, I gulped water: drowning, galloping waves. I drank the harbour dry.

Lord knows how Sonny amused himself those couple of days. Hugh put cold cloths on my forehead and fed me thin yellow soup. I fretted and fussed that Sonny needed scribblers, shoes.

"Sweat it out," Hugh said, shutting out the world beyond the bedroom. "Just try and sleep."

It worked. On the third day I got up in time to see the sun paint the hangman's beach gold, a tarnished gleam to its smooth, grey stones. The sea was amazingly calm, lapping at that steep, slate crescent. Not a peep from Sonny or Hugh, so I took myself outside.

The light pricked my eyes and my mind swam, weightless, with that feeling when you've lost touch and are only half returning to your body. I floated over the yard to the lighthouse, laid my palm against its cold cement for grounding. *Earth to Willa*, a voice murmured: mine.

As a ship slid closer — a monster container ship, its windows pinpricks of gold — I lifted my hand and waved. It took a lot of effort. Had Sonny been there, I'd have made him wave, too. It was like watching the whole world glide past my fingers. The engines' shuddering rocked the balls of my feet, and I grew legs again. Who knows why this ship was special? When ships like it passed, the air always changed. Dishes rattled. Once, in one of his better moments, Sonny said it was like a giant bowling on the harbour floor. As quickly as it entered my range, the ship passed, leaving the smell of bilge, a press of breakers. In the good old days, Hugh had told me, ships left the scent of cargoes: oranges from Jaffa, bananas from Haiti, molasses from the Dominican Republic. There was a story passed down from an earlier keeper, of how his family awoke one day to a sea of bananas, a yellow lagoon; and another time, cabbages. Bald green heads bobbing and washing up.

The mist split then, showing the buildings of the city beyond, dwarfed but *there*. Like King Kong's New York about to be eaten, except on a teensy scale, and no Statue of Liberty holding the fort on the island — our island.

Well before the start of school, the leaves in the hollows began to turn — red-tipped at first, mottled as apples. It felt like a warning.

"Why jump the gun?" Hugh laughed. "Those leaves are green, Willa. You're seeing things."

Other things filled my head, sounds and voices. In my sleep I heard the wind, like a girl singing and men groaning, the squeak of winching rope. I dreamt of bodies swinging in the midday sun, and of tar painted on the rocks and whatever pilings remained of the boardwalk. Sticky and warm, it coated wood that otherwise left slivers in your hands and feet. "Wear your shoes," I'd told Sonny every living day that summer. He never listened.

Two days before school, Sonny started getting ideas; was it something in the air, in those cirrus clouds? He'd spotted a pony, he said, a brown and white one with a mane like a broom, running through the woods above the Strawberry Battery. He hatched a plan to lure it with carrots and lasso it with Oreo's rope.

"What about the dog?" I played along. "Isn't he enough to look after?"

"Moommm! I could ride it!"

CAROL BRUNEAU

"What about your bike?" It hadn't left the shed, where it leaned against a sawhorse. Most of the paths were too over-grown for biking.

"You don't believe me. You think I'm just makin' it up."

Angling for attention, more like it. Though Sonny had always had a thing for horses. "Whoa, boy," he used to yell, riding his bed's footboard, whipping it with his housecoat belt. It had driven Charlie crazy; he'd smack the arm of his chair and holler, "Aren't you supposed to be asleep?"

"It worries me," I told Hugh that evening. We were huddled together drinking tea on the step, watching the stars. "I think he's been alone too much."

"Hardly." He rolled his eyes. "Well, school'll fix that."

"Yeah. But ... a *pony*? D'you think ...?"

Hugh shrugged. *Anything's possible*, his look said. He slid his arm around me, and I leaned into his warmth, the coziness of things being okay.

"Used to be wild ponies out here, right? Well, maybe not wild — somebody owned them. They pastured them in summer."

"You think — ?"

"Who knows? Buddy's got quite the imagination, Tess. But, hey, it might do him good, horse-hunting for a couple days."

I ducked away from him, jostling my tea. My period was due, and I wasn't in much of a joking mood. Though I tried to stifle them, the words sneaked out: "Ever notice, when some-one doesn't *get* something, it feels like a stone in your shoe? Something you have to dump out?"

I was more fretful than exasperated. But Hugh picked up his mug and went inside. When it got cold, I went in too, and could hear him in the bedroom shuffling papers. After a while, he came out for more tea.

"This pony of his, Willa — it's probably a deer." He was trying to reassure me, while apologizing, maybe, or making amends.

Anyway, it didn't matter. Next day, his last day of freedom, there was conviction in Sonny's eyes as he coiled the rope over his shoulder and took off towards the marsh, the puppy leaping for attention.

He came back after lunch, empty handed.

Putting a peanut butter sandwich in front of him, I pulled up a chair. "Sonny?" My voice was quiet, measured. "Do you hear things — at night, I mean?"

"Things?"

"Sounds. Noises."

"Duh." His mouth was full of peanut butter. "Like, um, boats? Buoys? Like, yeah, Mom."

"No, it's more, I dunno —" a pause "— like squeaking."

He rolled his eyes and snorted, wiping his nose on his sleeve. A man trapped in a nine-year-old's body.

"It'll be nice for you, seeing Derek again," I said, changing tack. He gazed blankly. The table stretched between us; God knows what he was thinking.

"You'll need a bath tonight. And — listen — those dishes? You could dry them while I figure out supper."

But first I went up and rooted out his knapsack and cleaned it off. When I came downstairs he was gone, scarce as pavement, as Hugh would say. From the window I could see something moving through the dunes.

"A bear?" I said, as if Hugh were there. Which he wasn't. Once the weather started changing, he spent less time around the house. He had tunes to work on; perhaps they sounded better to him in the tower's echo chamber.

If he was playing, he was playing softly. He could've been anywhere. Sonny and I might've been alone out here — it was bound to happen sometime, Hugh would have to go ashore on some errand or other without us. A matter of time. Time not measured by a clock or flashes of light, but the kind that moves like porpoises underwater. The thought of being left alone out here was a bit like the smell of tar, or the salty damp-ness that settled into my bones that summer.

Flies buzzed at the panes.

"Is it birds you hear, Mom?" Sonny startled me, creeping in. His voice cutting the stillness. "That sound, I mean." He watched me, suspicious. "Planes taking off — that's what you hear. When you're tryin' to sleep? Planes, landing at the base."

"Right." Suddenly I felt tired. "That must be it." I was still sleeping fitfully, getting over that flu. "Now. Those jeans — the ones you hate? Think you can still get into them?"

"Fuck those jeans," he mumbled. "Fudge, I said."

"*Feed the dog.* And if I hear that language once more I'll —"

"What?" There was hate in his eyes. "Ground me?"

Maybe I should have spanked him. There were mothers who would've. Watching him dump kibble into Oreo's bowl, it struck me that he'd grown too big to spank.

"And when you're done that, call Hugh, would you please? Tell him supper'll soon be on."

We went to bed early, all three of us. What luxury to crawl between sheets that smelled like the wind, while the light at the window was still blue. Hugh undressed quickly and crawled in beside me, and when the sounds of Sonny turning over upstairs subsided, we made love quietly, carefully, until I felt myself absorbed by him. That's how it felt, as if every bit of me was blotted up and drawn into him, the way the sun draws vapour from liquid, and lifts moisture from sand.

Afterwards we lay still, listening to Oreo scrabble downstairs.

"Shhh," Hugh whispered, almost asleep. It'd gotten cold, and I rose reluctantly to shut the window. It was that time of year, that shift that feels like jeans you've outworn but hate to switch for new ones, ones not broken in. I thought of sneaking up to check on Sonny, then decided: let sleeping babes lie.

## 16

## DUE EAST

Hugh kissed me awake the first day of school. "Rise and shine," he whispered, getting up.

I lay watching dust motes jig in a ray of sunlight. "Be ready for a fight."

Rolling out of bed, I tugged on my clothes. Stumbling into his, Hugh put both hands on my waist as if to steady himself.

Sonny shocked us, padding downstairs in his jeans and a T-shirt he'd shunned all summer. He looked tanned, his eyebrows sun-bleached, and he was smiling.

"Whatever," Hugh muttered, as Sonny helped himself to some stale Corn Flakes and downed a mugful of juice.

"Good luck," Hugh called out, going up to shave.

Sonny had grown a good two inches since spring, but I tried not to think about that, or about the clouds scudding over the horizon as we set out for the pier. You could still see the moon, a pale eye overlooking the marsh. The sea rolled like dice over the sand, murmuring gently, and we didn't talk, cutting through the wet woods. It was barely seven-thirty, yet he behaved as if this were a trip to the grocery store. I dared not open my mouth; maybe all this was harder on me than on him, the wrinkle school put in our routine.

Wayne was waiting in the boat, drinking take-out coffee. He looked hungover as usual, but he took Sonny's backpack as Sonny climbed in. When we reached the other side, he tapped Sonny's shoulder.

"Have a good one, bud," he said, pointing out the bus stop. It was just across the road, on a flat stretch beside the Kwik Way. Leaving the engine running, he downed his coffee, pitching the cup overboard.

"Comin', Willa?" he hollered. I'd gotten out, and was tailing Sonny to the roadside. "Yo!"

I turned once and waved.

Sonny marched ahead as if I wasn't there, his thumbs hooked in the straps of his loaded-down pack. God knows what he had in there, besides an empty notebook of Hugh's and a couple of sandwiches I'd slapped together.

There were a couple of kids waiting, a teenage girl with a Walkman, and a boy half Sonny's size. Sonny stood with his back to us, kicking the gravel. "What time is it?" the girl asked, and there was a funny sound. I turned to see Sonny throwing up into some goldenrod.

"Gross me out!" the girl sneered, just as the blue-and-white bus rounded a curve, lights flashing. I scrabbled for Kleenex uselessly, corralling Sonny and touching my wrist to his brow. He knocked my hand away, wiping his mouth on his sleeve. The bus stopped, the door swinging wide, and without glancing back, he climbed in.

"Wait!" I yelled. The driver must've seen Sonny's face, because he waved me aboard. Falling into the first empty seat, I could feel the eyes on me, especially Sonny's, full of disgust.

"Where to?" asked the driver, a scrawny man with a comb-over. He looked pissed off *and* amused.

"I'm sorry," I babbled, "but —"

"Don' worry about it." Then he clammed right up, as if I were one of the kids. The kids, meanwhile, twittered like Hitchcock's birds, a clamorous chirping that foretold disaster.

"Slow learner, are ya?" the driver shouted after a while. A joke.

Fifteen minutes and five stops later, we pulled up in front of the school. Damn, if Sandi (what *was* her last name?) wasn't there with a flock of women.

Sonny stomped past me, eyes locked on the kid ahead.

"Far as I go, dear," the driver said once they'd all shoved and stumbled their way off. The bus felt lighter — a whale after giving birth.

"Thanks." Hoping it sounded sincere, I took my time on the steps.

It was like being dropped on the moon; the beaten-down schoolyard with its rusty swings and view of the base, those houses clumped together as if for protection. The air smelled of diesel and trampled weeds.

"Willa?" I imagined a voice like Sandi's calling me back to the fold, in exchange for news. Information. But neither she nor her friends had budged. Maybe I'd turned invisible? Sonny had beelined to the playground, throwing off his pack. He was shaking a pole, causing the kids on the swings to shriek. One of them was Derek.

I turned away, walking quickly down the hill with no clue where I was headed. But at the highway, instead of starting back towards the Passage, I crossed the railway tracks and, passing through the open gates, headed towards Avenger.

*What is wrong with you?* chorused through my head as I marched along the cracked pavement past those faded, look-alike houses. Reaching Number 12, I almost kept going. It was like seeing something dead familiar, watching some aspect of your tiny life on TV. My heart pounded as I glanced up and down the street. Joyce LeBlanc was dragging a tricycle out of her driveway. A radio burbled faintly from somewhere, and the whine of a vacuum cleaner.

The Dodge sat in the driveway, backed in. The lawn needed cutting. The drapes hung crookedly in the picture window. My key lay in a pocket of my pack. What was I thinking? Who knows what I'd have done had Charlie been there.

Something made me walk up and let myself in. It was so simple, it was scary: the key turning, the door opening.

Inside, it seemed brighter than I remembered, despite the drapes. The sun breaking in was like beaten yolks, shockingly cheery. Feeling like a burglar, as if any second an alarm would sound, I scooted to the kitchen. The counter was even cleaner than I expected: spotless. Somewhere, a tap dripped. In the bathroom? The tap in the kitchen was turned off tightly. I checked. The toaster gleamed. My note, penned so exactingly that last morning, was gone, of course.

Moving down the hall to the bedroom was like watching my feet in a movie. Any second the scene would shift, lifting them from the carpet.

The bed was made, an inside-out pair of Charlie's jeans slung over the foot. Apart from this, nothing looked out of place. It was like being in a museum. A film of dust coated the dressers, nothing serious. A few of my clothes hung in the closet, like items in a new-to-you store: worn, but by whom? I flipped through them without much interest, careful not to touch Charlie's things hanging there too.

Steeling myself, I crept to the bathroom. I don't know what I was hoping to find: evidence of someone else? Maybe some hint of habitation — a mess. Hairs in the sink, a razor on the edge of the tub, strange deodorant.

Nothing.

I went and found some plastic bags — in the closet, right where they should've been — then tiptoed to Sonny's room. The door was shut tight. What lay behind it clawed at me. The carpet had lines from the vacuum, and Sonny's Lego airbase was set up. Not as he'd left it, with crashed planes and limbless men, but intact, possibly upgraded. And on the desk, below the window, was a shrine with Sonny's school photo and that picture of us on Family Day, the Sea King in the background, and Sonny's dodge ball and bike helmet.

I imagined Charlie touching these things: his pained smile. His smell, for heaven's sake — of engines and aftershave and a hint of sweat. And his voice: accusing, judging. *Bitch.* Then softer, younger: *Willa? You seen my socks? My shaving soap?*

I pictured him squirting WD-40 on Sonny's bike chain. And I thought of the morning Sonny and I had left, the sky's pale blue before the fog set in.

I wish there'd been something to tidy. But nothing needed attention, except maybe the dressers, and I couldn't bring myself to re-enter that room. It was too full of Charlie; not just his things, but the buzz of him — or my memories of it. The way he'd shivered sometimes in his sleep; the effect of spending too much time around engines, the jittery pull of those dinosaur helos? "Think of your favourite old car," he'd said once, explaining the allure of his job. It had meant nothing, because I didn't have one. Sighing, he'd moved on.

Charlie was so many shades of a person, it struck me, as many blues as the ocean. What colour did that make me, a sponge absorbing each hue? I tried not to think about it, emptying Sonny's drawers and scooping clothes into bags. God knows why, since he'd outgrown most of them.

I didn't take anything for myself. Oh, there were things that might've come in handy, like some old binoculars Charlie never used, on a shelf in the bedroom. But there was nothing I needed, and I'd finished with that room. The time jogged me. The clock on the stove, ever reliable, said ten-thirty, and I wondered how Sonny was making out, hoping his stomach had settled.

Grabbing my collection of bags, I locked up, leaving every-thing exactly as I'd found it. Still, I wondered if Charlie would know I'd been there, if he'd pick up my scent. How could he not?

It was a long time till school dismissed at three, too long to stick around. So I started walking again, turning onto the highway in the direction of the Passage. It had to be a good five-mile hike, with cars and trucks whizzing past. A couple of drivers seemed to slow down and stare; I could've been a tramp carrying a bundle on a stick. But nobody stopped or even waved, and after a while I felt invisible again. A chopper rumbled overhead, coming in for a landing. Hugh would be wondering where I'd got to. Nobody had mentioned me going to school.

Traffic stirred whirls of dust, clouding my head with the stink of exhaust. My heels burned, but by noon I'd left behind the busiest stretch of road and the air seemed cooler, fresher. That grey and white house, where Hugh's friends'd had the party, came into view and I quickened my pace. Paula was getting her baby out of the car. I could've used a drink or a visit to the bathroom, but she either didn't see me or didn't recognize me going by. Maybe it was my baggage.

Outside the Kwik Way, I set everything down and went and bought a Popsicle. It melted faster than I could eat it; most of it fell on the road going over to the wharf. Wayne's boat was tied up, but he was nowhere around. I went back to the Kwik Way to use the pay phone. Hugh would be worried.

He sounded as if he'd just woken up, vague and far away.

My voice was sure to sound different on the phone.

He seemed confused when I explained about waiting for the bus, both of us catching a ride with Wayne.

"Listen — it's okay. Take as long as you need."

"Save him the extra trip, right?"

"Yeah? Oh. Sure. Okay. See ya." No *miss you* or *don't be long*.

Hanging up, I went inside and bought an apple — lunch — and went back to the wharf to eat it.

A good three hours to kill.

The roof of Wayne's house showed through the skinny trees. By now I really needed to pee. Reenie won't mind, I told myself, walking up the road and knocking. I felt a bit weird, especially after passing Paula's. Though it'd been just as well, her missing me. Being around little kids would've reminded me too much of Sonny and his morning's ordeal.

Reenie took forever coming to the door. She looked a little shocked, but kind of glad to see me.

"Willa?" She eyed all my stuff. "Been shoppin', or what?"

She seemed more dressed up than usual — the two or three times we'd met. Her brows looked freshly plucked. She had an interview at a bank — for a job, she said, flitting around in search of her cigarettes.

"I won't stay. It's just ... well, I'm kind of stranded, and ..." oh, hell. "Can I use your bathroom?"

She pointed the way. I thanked her.

"Don't worry about it."

When I came out, she was in the kitchen lighting a cigarette. She nudged her fingers through her permed hair as she puffed.

"Wayne's around somewheres. He could take ya right now if you want. Not trying to rush ya or nothing. I was you, they'd hafta drag me over there. Dunno how you hack it, really, stuck on that goddamn islant." She made a face, though who knows what it meant through the haze of smoke and all her nervous primping. But I got the distinct feeling she pitied me.

I thought of Sandi and Paula, and felt this sudden urge to talk, this longing just to shoot the breeze. Between filing her nails, Reenie sipped what looked like cold coffee from a Garfield mug. She could've been a total stranger, could've been anybody. There was nothing there to invite my urge.

"I went home today," I spoke up, pointing at the bags parked in her hallway.

"Okay?" she said suspiciously.

*Tell her*, I thought; *what's the difference?*

"You know I left my husband."

She shrugged, as if people told her this sort of thing every day. Why was she applying to a bank? She looked like a hairdresser. Despite its hardness, her face had that open yet distant look.

She sighed, inspecting a nail. "Well, I guess if you done that, you had good reason."

My turn to shrug. My neck felt hot. I'd given this away for nothing.

Or maybe not. "Having a kid and all," she murmured, "and Hughie ..."

"Yes?"

"Ah, nothing. I was just gonna say he's ... well, Hugh's like a big kid himself, that's all."

"Oh?" Which is why I love him, I thought, and why things'll never be how they were with Charlie. Something in her eyes kept me from blurting it out.

"Nothing," she said, scrabbling through her purse.

"You guys've known him for a while, I take it."

"Huh? Oh, Hughie and Wayne, they go way back."

She flipped car keys onto the table. I stayed put.

"Yeah?"

She started digging again.

"He's never told you?"

I shook my head, a little confused.

"They grew up together. They did time together, sweetie," she said, deadpan. You could imagine that voice at the circus: *please, clap now for the bearded lady!*

"You didn't know?" She fluffed her hair up off her neck, glancing at the door with its tole-painted Welcome attached to a tiny, twee birdhouse.

My cheeks felt hot. I should've just thanked her then and left. I mean, anyone with eyebrows like that is not to be trusted.

"Nothing serious. Possession," she crowed, a smile cracking her made-up face. "Don't tell him I said. It was just a bit of hash. Frig! Nothing to get pissy over."

"Who's pissy?" I quipped, going along with her, even if it wasn't funny. She had a weird sense of humour.

"They were just kids, him and Wayne. Oh, mother."

"The music," I cut in, and rose to gather up my stuff.

"They been at that forever, too." She pushed her hair back primly, showing a pimple coated with Erase. She said something about a record, her voice sarcastic. Her mouth tightened in a little line. My time was up; she'd run out of patience.

"Listen. Keeps 'em out of trouble, eh?"

"Right," I said, as she followed me to the door.

Wayne was outside peering under the hood of his truck.

"Good luck with the interview," I called as she got into her car. It looked quite new.

"Easy on the clutch in that Tie-oughta," Wayne hollered without looking up. "Now, I s'pose you want a ride."

"It's okay, I can wait for Sonny."

I lugged those ridiculous bags back to the dock and found a patch of grass and flaked out. But I wasn't in much of a mood for sunbathing. Watching the clouds, shivering every now and then at the chill off the water, I wondered about Reenie, why she had it in for Hugh. The chill moved up my arms. Were there things he hadn't told me? Drugs, shoplifting — I mean, who didn't do crazy things as a kid? A teenager, I mean. I pictured myself, a younger, skinnier version, toking off a crumb of hash on a pin, pinching the odd chocolate bar, a pair of flip-flops. With no mom and my father on some other planet, there'd been no one around to notice. I pictured a younger, shorter Hugh rolling a joint, stealing candy, maybe an album. An eight-track tape.

Reenie's nuts, I decided. She's jealous.

The coolness spread through me. Consequences. Punish-ment. I'd never got caught doing those stupid things; who knows how Dad would've reacted? Something would've come to me, though, some excuse, some good reason.

I wanted to call Reenie and tell her she had it wrong, what-ever it was about Hugh.

*An eye for an eye* ran through my head: tit for tat. But as the wind churned up whitecaps, an image of Charlie came to mind. Items from the news he liked quoting, stories from the Middle East, or wherever it is people get their hands chopped off for stealing. Stealing what? A wife and son?

Sick, the stuff that plays through your mind when you're hungry and maybe a bit dehydrated and just want to get home. Especially after seeing someone like Reenie, never mind your kid barfing in a ditch and the house you've left suddenly as spotless as if it were inhabited by Mr. Clean *and* The Man from Glad. Now there's a couple; anything's possible these days.

There wasn't much you could rule out, really.

I shut my eyes, felt the sun pulse through the lids till every-thing swirled orange. When I opened them, my watch said two-fifty. Sonny would be here any minute; we'd have lots to talk about.

But when he got off the bus twenty minutes later, he scowled past me, barely saying hi to Wayne, who hobbled towards us, checking his watch. He was breaking up his day for this, after all. As he mumbled something about his ignition, I asked Sonny,

"So how was it?"

He just fired his pack into the boat, keeping silent the entire crossing.

"Six minutes and thirty-five seconds," Wayne brayed as we nudged the dock. You could see why he and Reenie were a pair. "Good thing Hughie's not paying me by the hour, wha'? Ah, I'm just arsing around. Tell him I'm putting you on his tab."

## MERCATOR SAILING

"Honey? We're home!" I hollered, just kidding. Sonny threw down his pack. Hugh was nowhere in sight, though he'd left a fresh pot of tea on the stove. Pouring myself some, I fixed Sonny a snack — bits of Kraft singles on saltines. Not great, but he had to be starving.

"Eat your lunch?" I fished around. "So, how's your teacher?"

Sonny scarfed down his crackers, not speaking.

"Where's Oreo?" he finally asked, as if the dog had been sent to school too.

"Beats me." I paused, testing the waters. "While you were at school, um, I had this chance to go —"

But he'd jumped up and was leaning outside yelling Oreo's name.

"Hugh has him out for a run, betcha," I called, but he'd disappeared. A little while later, there he was scaling the rocks towards the marsh. It was then I thought of the binoculars, the ones I'd seen this morning. This reminded me, fleetingly, of the house on Avenger, its morgue-like neatness.

If he wasn't out with the dog, Hugh would be up in the light. Crossing the yard, I tried the door to the tower and it swung wide. "Hugh?" I yelled, climbing. Sometimes the sun made him groggy and he'd doze off sitting on the floor, his legs stretched out.

Reaching the lantern was like rising to the top of a huge baby bottle with a bright red nipple. He wasn't there. All around me the world shimmered, a continuous, rolling blue with an edge the sea lacked in summer, a resoluteness. It was obvious why Hugh liked being up here; it made you feel in control. Of what, though, it was hard to say. Just *in control*. The mercury gleamed like a mirror and I paused there, my hand drawn down as if by a magnet. Holding my palm over it, I dangled one fingertip, let it touch the surface, just brushing it. I expected a silky feeling like hot mud. Instead it felt chilly, metallic. Realizing what I'd done, I wiped my finger on some paper towel, balling up the wad and leaving it on the ledge. The sun streaming in made me woozy, and I wondered if the vapour had an odour. I thought of *Alice*: the Mad Hatter and the March Hare having tea.

The only smells were of dust and window cleaner. But I thought of that place in Japan: Minamata. How crows had fallen from the sky and cats jumped into the sea after eating mercury-poisoned fish. So the story in *Life* had said, the article that had run with the photo that was stuck in my memory, of that teenage girl and her mother. Falling birds had been the first sign that something was wrong.

The Danbury shakes, Hugh had called the sickness suffered by those hatters in Connecticut, the ones with red hands from felting beaver pelts. I thought of spills from thermometers, leaky fillings in people's teeth. The symptoms you heard about: thirst, confusion, nutty behaviour, an uneven gait.

Hugh's binoculars sat by the radio. Looping the strap over my head, I scanned the horizon through the salt-stained panes. It felt disorienting; the glasses were probably better for bird-watching. Climbing back down, I started towards the beach with them. Sonny would need coaxing to do his homework. The thought of it reminded me again of the house — Charlie's house — and nights before bedtime. Charlie puttering, oiling the chain on Sonny's bike. He'd been so careful not to miss a link. As if everything had to be perfect, otherwise why bother? Not that he'd been cruel, exactly; he'd probably never "stepped out." But then there was his phone call.

I sat cross-legged on the sand, focusing the lenses. The water spread like a glittery sheet. It was a trick, of course; if there was one thing you learned on Thrumcap, it was variation. One fog bank was not like another, nor one curve of beach like the next, no matter the weather. In a blink the ocean changed, yesterday's blue different from today's, currents like stretch marks. I could appreciate this, having given birth; miles from the sea I could've looked at my belly and seen it.

Watching a sailboat, I tried to make out the skipper, then thought again of Hugh, how it wasn't his nature to watch for lines or wrinkles. His job was to make sure sailors knew they weren't adrift. Simple. He *was* like a big, beautiful kid. Frig Reenie; she was poisoned by living with Wayne.

I wondered if Charlie ever missed me, or had I been like a propeller, invisible when operating smoothly? Marriage suffered the same fatigue.

Endless blue, endless summer, but just as you grasped things they ended. For the millionth time, I wanted Hugh — Hugh moving inside and around and beside and above me, like vapour. Like some sort of holy ghost.

He was boiling water when I sauntered in. Sonny was hunched over a box, the first aid kit open on the table. The bleeding seemed to be from Sonny's arm, till I spied squirming fur.

"Calm yourself, Tess, it's not that bad." Hugh threaded a needle, dipped it in the kettle. "His ear. Must've had a run-in with something bigger. Whaddya think, Alex? A bear on the prowl, or what?"

The pup's eyes rolled. "I found him like this," Sonny cried. "His ear all chewed."

Hugh bent closer. "Hold him tight, now, Alex." His hand kept shaking as he stitched bloody skin together, then swabbed the wound with greyish gauze. "Didn't know I took sewing, did you?"

I stroked his arm. "What other tricks d'you have to show us, Mr. Gavin?"

"Beats me." He patted Oreo's trembling rump. "Now, could we eat?"

"Thanks, Hugh," Sonny actually said.

Nobody asked about anyone's day. Just as well; the bags of clothes showed where I'd been. I would explain without words, later in bed.

"Make sure the dog stays inside," Hugh told Sonny after supper. "You can't leave him wandering all day." Then he said he was going ashore to jam; the guys had a gig coming up in November.

"But that's months away."

"Don't wait up, sweetie. Keep your mother company, bud, and watch the pup. He's too young to be off on his own."


Sonny spent the evening up in his room, the dog scratching to get out. I took a walk on Hangman's Beach, the rocky one, drawn by the slant of light as the sun sank. The shingle was steep, treacherous; one false step and you'd slip and clatter into the surf. Hugh never came this way. But curiosity pulled me, a silly need to see if the sounds in my dreams could be heard out here. In the dead of night, they were cries for help.

Stumbling along, I imagined quizzing Sonny on his multiplication tables. Six times seven, nine times ten? Numbers beat time with the waves. There were no corpses, of course — not even a bone from an animal. The only tar was spillage from tankers, coating the rocks like asphalt.

Not even in my mind did Sonny answer the questions. He was asleep with the light on, the pup curled on his bed, when

I came in at dusk. Turning in, I missed Hugh's smell, his warmth in the bed. Don't be a wimp, I told myself; see what habit does? Think *propeller*. Though things could never be as they'd been with Charlie.

At dawn I woke to Hugh's breathing. Then the morning snapped into place: a lunch to be packed; Sonny roused, fed and marched to the pier. Maybe routine wasn't so bad. Promising to watch Oreo, I kissed Sonny's cheek and started back up the path before he and Wayne puttered out. I didn't look back or wave.

"Come to town with me tonight," said Hugh. He was in his Jockeys, lighting the stove.

For the first time in months, we were alone. "What?" I didn't want to waste it.

"There's a party in town. Food. Music. You'll love it."

I thought of the lighthouse, then of Sonny.

"What's wrong now?" he said, before I could speak.

"I saw Reenie yesterday," I started.

"No rule says you can't. Not like you're stuck out here."

I pinched the flesh above his shorts, making him squirm.

"Nobody has to stay out here without relief," he said, tickling me till I yelped *uncle*. "What was Reenie up to? There's a piece of work, that one. A case." He laughed. "And what a case *you* are." He drew me close. "You're a six-pack."

"No. *You* are. And I'm thirst —"

"Sweetgrass," he murmured and I blushed: it was how he

described my taste. He drew his hand down my back, slowly, making me want more.

Next he was eating cereal with his fingers.

"Put milk on it," I said, to hide my disappointment.

"I'll miss you," he said, "if you don't come tonight."

"And?"

"The dog," he seemed to waver, "still got an ear?"

I wanted to tell him that his sewing reminded me of a toy rabbit Sonny had when he was tiny. But he had a funny look, like he was trying to remember something. He put down his bowl and went to the bedroom. He came back dressed, the sax in its case.

"So, you know where to find me, anybody calls."

It was a joke, since the only people who phoned were his band mates and Wayne, and, once in a blue moon, the Coast Guard checking in.

The day yawned, suddenly blank.

"The dog — shouldn't we have a vet take a look?"

He paused, his eyes puzzled. "Why?"


He was home by suppertime, but didn't bring up the party again till we were doing dishes.

"There'll be lots to drink," he said.

Sonny glowered. He still hadn't mentioned school, clamming up at my questions.

"Derek sit near you?" I tried.

Hugh stretched, wobbling in his shoes as if they were too big.

"Who?" Sonny shot back, bending over his homework. Spelling, thank God.

Hugh made a face; it was time to leave.

"I can't," I said, eyeing Sonny.

"Free booze — not enough to entice you? Your loss, Will o'."

I put on the radio as he left. CBC was all we could get. For an hour or more, they ran a documentary about adobe houses and a colony of poets and the meaning of aging. When it was time for bed, Sonny switched it off and sat there stubbornly.

"And?" I sighed.

"How much longer?" he said, out of the blue.

"What?"

"Derek's dad was there today. He said my dad drove by one day and waved." His pause was filled with harbour sounds. "How come I can't see him? How come — ?"

"Sonny." I avoided his eyes. "You should know —"

"Nothin'! I don't need to know nothin'."

"Anything." I dragged it out, turning its sting on him. "Look. Your father knows where you are. It's not our fault he hasn't tried to see you."

It was mostly true. What I hadn't disclosed was the PS I'd left Charlie: *I'm happy now, and hope you'll respect that and leave us alone.* The two of us. The *fuck* alone, I'd meant, but I could hardly explain that to Sonny.

He stared baldly. When his mouth moved, the look in his eyes like Oreo's, I flicked the radio back on. When he started to cry, I turned it up till the voices swallowed the sound.

*Movies. Two words. First word, one syllable. Second word ...*

Late into the night the radio played news of Haiti, an insurrection. I tried to read, a mildewed copy of a romance, one of those girl-running-from-burning-castle types of books. Another relic from past keepers — or the kept, I thought, getting into bed.

The instant I put out the lamp, it was obvious something was wrong. The darkness at the window was steady, a country darkness. No intrusive flare or cruising softness, only blackness. Shit. I felt almost sick. The goddamn light — a bulb? My first thought was of Hugh wailing away on his sax in some smoky living room. I pictured those wholesome women, Paula and Emily, swaggering around loaded, their eyes on him. Their kids with babysitters. I imagined them shouting over the music, the jungle rhythm of drums. Then I thought of the light, of ships skinning the nose of the spit.

Call me alarmist, but I felt like a kid lost in a mall. My first impulse was to wake Sonny, as if he'd know what to do. Tripping to the kitchen, I dialled Wayne's number, but the line just rang.

"A light bulb," I said aloud. A fuse.

But the flashlight, too, was dead. Tearing upstairs to that rat's nest storeroom, I dug another from under some tangled rope and decrepit gear. I kept digging, for what, I wasn't too sure. An instruction manual? A maintenance guide? Good luck.

From the window at least, the night couldn't have appeared calmer. Never mind the phrase *shit creek* pumping through me.

If there was a manual, surely it'd be here?

Under a pile of oilskins I found a bag — blue canvas, army surplus. I ripped it open, but it contained nothing useful. Only some clothes, a camisole, and an Indian cotton top with faded blue embroidery. As I stuffed them back, something crinkled. It was a photo of a woman, a girl really. She looked young and not all there. Pretty, in a spacy way, with small, even teeth. Airy-fairy; playing with half a deck, Charlie would've said. Her eyes smiled vaguely; her long auburn hair was pulled back from her forehead. It looked like a school photo, posed like Sonny's, with fake books for a backdrop. There was no name on the back, only a date — 21/6/85 — in bubbly writing, and a heart with an arrow through it. Someone's kid sister, or daughter; the daughter of some other keeper. The one Hugh had mentioned, maybe, the daredevil tobogganer.

I tried to picture a girl growing up out here, a girl like the one I'd been. I tried imagining Hugh with a daughter, or a sister. He'd grown up in a house of boys, he'd said; like me. Maybe that girl with the toboggan had, too; that was what had driven her to such crazy things.

There was a noise downstairs. The dog at the garbage, not a raccoon or rats, I hoped. Replacing the picture, I shoved the bag under the sticky heap of old rubber jackets.

Then I remembered the shed.

The pup had got a can and licked it clean. I pried its jaws open, hoping it hadn't sliced its tongue. Already the ear had started to heal, the zigzagged blue thread like a decoration.

"Stay," I hissed, grabbing the shed key from the hook and venturing outside.

The flashlight poked a skinny beam through the dark. There wasn't much of a moon. The only sure things were the granite boulders along the edge of the point, the sloshing behind them. I thought of that foolish girl coasting there. She must've had a name.

The darkness pressed in, with a hint of rain. In the curve of Hangman's Beach, stones clattered, like marbles in a purple velvet bag. The Crown Royal bag my father'd let me have. I thought of gibbets and the noises from my dreams.

The key wiggled in the padlock. Crowded by the dark, I rooted around, fighting a quiet, spreading panic. Be practical. Fuses, spare bulbs. Where *did* Hugh keep them? Idiotic, since I hadn't a clue how to replace either.

Shit. *Fuck.* I'd have to call someone. The Coast Guard.

The shed door bumped behind me. I almost tripped over something — a can. Gas or kerosene. Something flammable anyway; I could see the blazing logo on it.

How had Hugh taken off without leaving so much as a number? My stomach knotted. I hadn't bothered to ask. "Shit shit *shit*," my voice rattled from the shelves. In a jumble of stuff, surprise surprise, I stumbled upon fuses, several kinds. A bulb, too, but when I shook it, it sounded like there was sand inside.

I'd broken into a sweat. Letting the door thud shut, I traipsed to the tower, tripping on my nightie. The flannelette felt clammy. The white concrete loomed like a massive tree. The tower was locked, a fucking Fort Knox.

I was almost to the house when a whistle pierced the dark.

"Sweetie?" The sound of his voice was medicine. A lifeline.

"What's going on?" It lilted on the wind, all in fun, as if he'd caught me playing hide-and-seek, and it was my turn to be it.

I waited by the stoop as his face lit the dark. He was grinning. "What's happening?" he asked again, like someone who'd been lying in the sun all day. That way of his so unlike Charlie's, a warmth that loosened my limbs and soothed: *Tomorrow's another day, why fuss over stuff you can't fix? We have no control, Tessie. What a concept, eh? Get used to it.*

Coming closer, he looked a little different, not quite disheveled, but more relaxed than usual. Not drunk, of course not. All I could smell was the canvas of his coat. He read my look. "Don't panic," he said, squeezing my arm.

Oreo whinged and Hugh swung up onto the step to let him out. The dog skittered around in circles, his white patches glowing in the dark.

"Go on in, now, and I'll git 'er," he said, mimicking Wayne?

"You'll git 'er, will you?" I mimicked back, a shiver in my voice. It was way past midnight; Sonny would have to be up in a few hours.

"Cuppa tea?" Hugh called. "Put on the kettle, Tessie, I won't be long."

Instead I stumbled back to bed and when he crept in to kiss me, closed my eyes and was soon asleep.

But strangers dogged my dreams — people in ships, waving as they sailed by. Their faces were blank at first, murky. Then they took on features. Couples: Wayne and Reenie, my father and his wife. Then Hugh. It must've been me beside him, with all these women — wives — calling out advice. Advice on diapers and weaning, which I had no interest in. All of it ebbing away as I woke to Hugh's rising, falling breath, and that liquid, gliding flash that picked me up and spun me, and placed me back inside myself.

Hugh didn't go ashore again, not for a couple of weeks. The band needed a break. Kenny's wife wanted some "quality" time and another guy was up to his eyeballs in home improvements.

"Did Reenie get that job?" I asked, one afternoon.

"Say what?"

"At the bank," I prompted, and he snorted.

"Lordie. She had to be shitting you. A bank?" He laughed, calling Reenie a hard ticket. A little hilarious, given her hobbies. "She's fucked, that one," he said. "She'd tell you the sky's green, Tessie. Scary thing is, you'd believe her. Piece of work, that lady. Like I said."

Since the day I'd dropped in, I'd started to feel a bit sorry for her, considering who she was saddled with.

"How's Wayne?" I asked, and Hugh looked surprised.

"Ahhhh, I see!" He went for my ribs, merciless. "You've got the hots for him, don't you? Don't you!"

"Right. It's gotta be the way he steers." Twisting away, I rolled my shoulders, thrust out my hip. "My morning fix, don't you know — going over with Sonny." Narrowing my eyes, I flicked my hair. We were by the window, getting dressed.

His face clouded, or maybe I imagined it. "Watch out for him," he said, tugging my ponytail.

CAROL BRUNEAU

"Oh, yeah, as if I'd —"

"What?" His grip tightened, a playful threat. "As if you'd what?"

I leaned my cheek against him, felt the tickle of his chest.

"I don't like it," he whispered, teasing.

"What? What don't you like?" I could hear Sonny on the stairs and the scrabble of claws.

"The way you need people, things." He breathed into my ear, stroking my nape. We heard Sonny check the fridge, the squeak of the can opener. I wanted to ask, *Like who?* but then Sonny bellowed, "Mooooom?"

18

## BY THE STARS

Fall slid up Thrumcap like a sleeve, starting at the end nearest the city and moving over the headland that pushed beyond us into the sea. Frost gathered in the hollows. The fog vanished, giving way to sharper days and nights, and Sonny settled into his weekday routine. He wouldn't talk about school, simply answered *yes*, *no*, and *nothing* to my questions. Just him being a boy; when had he been different? Girls, not boys, gave details; who talked, who had trouble reading. As the weeks passed, Sonny actually became agreeable. It wasn't long before he asked to sleep over at Derek's.

One Friday night all by ourselves, Hugh and I perched on the rocks, watching the stars. Pointing out constellations, he taught me how to find the North Star, which I forgot, gazing at the spritz of light.

When we went inside, he kept his coat on. "That gig is next month," he said.

I'd forgotten all about it. "Coming?" I expected him to say, getting back into my jacket. I'd started dressing in layers, my warmest things marooned like hostages on the base.

Hugh shrugged. "Dunno how long I'll be, Willa. Don't wait up." Then he disappeared into the dark.

Disappointment — anger — stole my breath. There was his sax, the case in the corner. He'd be back, surely, and he'd realize I didn't want to be alone, that I was terrified of something happening with the light.

I made myself turn on the radio. He had things to discuss, that was it. Of course. There was more to playing an instrument than music. The eleven o'clock news came on as I shuffled about the kitchen. The puppy nipped at my ankles, then squatted on his paper. Housebreaking was worse than training a child; how much longer? I wondered. *How much longer?* I watched from the window, listening. Radio voices burbled; something about an accident, something happening at sea. A helicopter ditching, the third such accident in as many months, the announcer said pleasantly. Just outside the harbour; search and rescue, no reports of ... There was a beep and a dash of silence, and the voice gave the time: eleven-o-five, Atlantic Standard.

The chances — what were the chances?

My fingers stumbled dialling Derek's house. I needed to hear Sonny, one grudging but familiar syllable, just in case ...

Derek's mother picked up, clearly ticked off at my calling so late. "Alex and them are watching a movie." There must've been a bunch of kids, then, sleeping over. "Something you'd like me to tell him, or were you just checking up?"

"He's okay, then? Everything's all right?" My mind skipped; what was it her husband did, again? "Everyone there's, um, okay?"

"Yeah?" She sounded incredulous; I felt like an idiot. "Like I said, they're all cosied up to the screen?"

I promised to pick Sonny up by noon, with no clear idea how.

"Take care now," she said, as if she could see me through the phone, miles from nowhere.

I went in and lay on the bed, and almost without knowing it, started to cry. It unplugged a dyke, a reservoir held back for ages, possibly years. They weren't tears of sorrow so much as a breathless gratitude, in spite of everything, for the feeling of having slipped through a mirror. Blowing my nose, I'd forgiven Hugh. I would never lose him the way I'd lost Charlie, though it was a free world and Hugh would come and go as he pleased. A poster came to mind, enough to make me laugh, the type with a sunset, gulls, and the slogan, *If you love something set it free* ... Like most clichés it had a kernel of truth. Don't be so clingy, a voice like Sonny's trilled inside, and a beat later: *If it's brown flush it down. If it's yellow let it mellow.* Trust Sonny to come up with lines like that.

Proverbs aside, I hardly slept, hounded by dreams of disasters. Shipwrecks, plane crashes. Fitfully I combed the island's circumference, salvaging rubble from a downed jet. Pulverized Styrofoam washing ashore, clinging to rockweed like bits of snow. Ribbons of clothing decorated the mess, floating on a red tide. A wallet. Part of a harness, a long greyish strap — a monkey tail from a helicopter, tethered to a vest. In the dream I rescued the wallet, and Charlie's picture was inside. Yes, it was Charlie all right, with a beard. But even as I held it his face dissolved to Hugh's, and when I woke he was spooned against me.

The call came not long after, the Coast Guard telling Hugh the operations at Thrumcap were being reviewed. He wasn't surprised. Keepers were an endangered species, he said, lighthouses everywhere being automated, run by computer. No reason to think ours was special. Ours, he called it, which made me want to pick up the phone and blast someone; had they no idea, the lives they were disrupting? Risking?

Hugh seized my hand and pressed it. His look was the Sargasso Sea, calm and reedy. "Whatever, Tessie. I've been expecting this, you know."

"But ... when?"

He shrugged, as if it hardly mattered. "Might they shut 'er down? Whenever. Won't be overnight, though. No point worrying. Their minds're already made up. Look, things happen. Things come up." He drew me close, pretended to gnaw on my neck.

"Okay." I wasn't convinced, but maybe hoping would make it so. "There must be something you can do, though. I mean, you can't just ... give in."

"Jesus, put you in charge!" He smirked. "You'd give the bastards what for. Rapunzel, up there in the tower." Yawning, he rubbed his jaw. I saw myself in the lantern, vapour fogging the windows, the glare of the sky and mercury bright as tinfoil.

"Maybe we should think about moving," I said, as if light-struck.

"Oh, Tess. Let's worry about it when we have to."


The sky closed in again, grey and drizzly, clouds like smoke above the orange woods, as if everything were smudged with the same dull pencil. Sonny stayed home one Friday because of a sore throat, hiding out upstairs reading comic books — 'vintage' ones, a word he'd picked up. *Read a book*; you had to keep at him. *Don't they have anything in that school library?* He'd glue himself to *The Hulk* and *Batman*, stuff my brother and I read as kids. Show some imagination, I'd say. Climb the hill. Get some fresh air. It was hard not to think of the Lego languishing in his old room, though he'd probably outgrown it anyway.

At least he was occupied and not out horse hunting that afternoon.

It was cold enough for gloves, jackets with sweaters. In a blip of dying sun, the high-rises across the harbour blazed a steely orange as Hugh and I set off on a walk down the beach. I'd have just as soon stayed inside, frying bologna for supper. Cape Breton steaks, Hugh called them, though I didn't quite catch the humour. We hadn't made it to the grocery store.

Moving at a clip, he leapt from rock to rock. The dog kept eating seaweed till I scooped him up; squirming in my arms, he was too big to carry. Hugh's hair blew back in damp snarls, and he was whistling. It was hard to keep up. My sneakers kept slipping, and I pictured one of us snapping an ankle, Wayne coming to ferry the lucky person to Emergency. A bone would set in the time it'd take, never mind the city's proximity. It was like gazing across at another galaxy; those blazing windows had nothing to do with us. Their lights would blink and bleed into dawn, always growing more distant by daylight.

My feet squelched as I trailed Hugh along a mucky stretch. The sand stank like rotten eggs. Clam shells lay like notes ripped from scribblers, some whole enough that I wanted to save them — for what, though, ashtrays and candy dishes? Women like Joyce LeBlanc would know, and Reenie. She could have a house full of painted shells, art made of flotsam.

Hugh stopped and shook out his limbs, almost shivering. He bent and hung his head, his hands pressed to his thighs.

"What's wrong?"

"Nothing. Just a little, I dunno, dizzy, that's all."

An uneasiness burrowed through me. Worry. "*What?*"

"Nothing. Too much fresh air, maybe. Too much of a good thing." He smiled and picked up a knotted piece of driftwood like a staff, poking at litter that had washed up — the daily dose. "Ocean'll take it away," he said in that fake voice — his Passage voice. "What arseholes people are, Willa. Jaysus."

I set the dog down, hauling him away from a rotting bone. Hugh picked his way along like a heron. "Blame it on the boats," he usually said, "foreign vessels. Makes you despair." That's what he'd said once finding a duck wearing a beer can choker, a six-pack of feathers flecked with bunker crude. Right now I was more concerned about him. I thought of that list of symptoms; what were they, again? There must be a test you could take if you showed signs ...

"Hugh — ?"

Oreo lunged, taking me with him. Being on his rope, there wasn't much he could do to warn us.

Hugh spotted it first. Something in the sand at the edge of the water, little waves pulling at it. Straining on his rope, Oreo whimpered then started yipping.

Lying face down, the shape appeared to be a woman. The tide tugged at the strings of her red jacket and locks of hair laced with seaweed. Sand filled the ridges of her jeans. She looked like a swimmer who'd made it through a marathon and fallen asleep. Except for the sea filling her clothes, she seemed flattened, a paper cut-out doll.

Hadn't Charlie said once that drowning victims bloated, gases buoying them to the surface?

That she was dead took a moment to sink in.

Hugh pushed me so hard it knocked the breath out of me. I fled to higher sand. Shaking, I watched him bend over her. Oreo pulled and whined.

"For Christ's sake," Hugh yelled, helplessly. He sounded stricken.

Stumbling towards him, I glimpsed what should've been a forehead, wet hair clinging to something black.

"God damn," Hugh was saying, his teeth raking spit, his voice almost a hiss. "A fucking jumper — you can tell. Every fucking bone broken. It happens when they hit."

"Oh my God," I heard myself whisper. Vomit pooled in my throat.

"Get the dog!" Hugh seemed to weave as he stood over the woman. Yanking her by the jacket he staggered, trying to move her to safer ground. I tried thinking of beached whales that people fought to save.

"I've never seen a body before," I tried to tell him, which wasn't technically true. I'd seen those friends of Charlie's lying in state. Gunshots and bugles had shocked the air at their funeral, bouncing off trees, igniting tears. And I'd seen my mother, though I'd been so little, and she a mannequin inside a big jewellery box on a berth of roses. I'd wanted my father to kiss her awake like Snow White. *How will she breathe?* I'd cried, thinking of insects Jason caught in jars, forgetting to punch holes in the lids. *Honey, she's gone,* my father had said. Gone gone gone: the dark of the closet, later, when I refused to come out.

Somehow Hugh dragged the body towards the dune. I glimpsed the rest of what might've been the face — eyeless sockets, the nose eaten away, and a hole where the mouth should have been. The only thing proving it was human was the clothing. As if she'd been dressed for a hike when something snatched her.

I threw up on the sand.

*Suicide,* Hugh kept murmuring. The pup barked his head off. Suddenly I was plugged with fear. Sonny — was he still inside? Sweet Jesus, let him be in his room.

The smell, when it reached my brain, was like the stench of something an animal, a dog, would roll in. A field of dead clams. The kind of smell you panicked at the thought of getting on your clothes or skin.

Oreo had finally given up, and was licking his paw. Out on the spit, I saw the light come on in Sonny's window.

Hugh seemed calmer now, sort of, though I was still shaking. Thank God he knew what to do. "Come on." He tugged at me. "I'll call the cops and the Coast Guard. Not much else we can do. The cops'll come out, and the examiner. They'll curse her, you watch, for washing up out here and not someplace easy, like under the bridge, or the dockyard."

He didn't need to say he'd dealt with this before.

He went to put his arm around me, but I reeled away and was sick again. When I glanced up, he was kneeling by that filthy, icy water, washing his hands.

The police boat docked at the wharf we never used. Hugh and I met them halfway down the beach. An officer was already taping off the pebbled part where Hugh had managed to roll the body. "Away from the dogfish," he quipped when they reprimanded him for touching it.

I should've run back and stayed with Sonny, who was holed up in the kitchen. There'd been no time to stop and explain anything. But I couldn't pull myself away from the beach. *She needs me*, I thought, ludicrously. She needs a woman here, with all these guys — as if anything more could happen to her. The beefy, uniformed cops in their orange vests barely looked twice at me. It was only Hugh they had time for, and only just.

"But who is she?" I murmured stupidly, as if they should've known. "H-how long —?"

"In the drink?" One of the cops, a younger guy with short dark hair, finally glanced at me. "Could be nine months. Salt preserves 'em, and the cold." His expression was almost sympathetic. "But they're not gonna look like Elvis."

That night in bed I held Hugh's hands, slowly turning them over, studying them. The sight of them carried me out of myself. The most beautiful part of his body, his hands. It almost made me weep, touching his palms.

"There you go," he said, gently. "Read my lifeline. Go on. What does it say?"

He was still jittery, too, but trying to soothe me. He brought my hand to his lips, drawing my fingers into his mouth. Curling my fist in his, he kissed me.

It made me close my eyes, and I gagged as the image of that blackened face swam before me.

"Shit happens, Tessie," he whispered. "Life goes on." Then he paused. "I've got a jam this week," he said, his heartbeat miles away. "Will you guys be okay?"

The body turned out to be an eighteen-year-old. An autopsy showed she died of drowning, and had been in the early stages of pregnancy. Foul play was not suspected, we heard on the radio some time later. Anyone who may have seen the woman was asked to notify police. That's all they said. Her name was withheld pending notification of next of kin. There was no mention of how long she'd been in the water or where she'd come from.

"Street kid? Listen, they're out there. Prostitutes, pushers." Hugh shrugged. "Happens a lot, I'm afraid. More than you'd like to think."

He was cleaning his sax at the table, getting ready to go out.

"She had to come from somewhere," I said, wiping up around him.

"Well, yeah. They usually do."

"Hugh? What if *you* had a daughter?"

"Yeah?" He looked kind of startled. "Ah, Tessie. It's not that I don't feel bad for her, whoever she was."

"A daughter — think of it."

"Um, yeah?"

I thought of the girl in the photo upstairs. "Say, like the one you said went to law school. You know, the one who ... from an earlier family? The one ... you said ... went sliding off the rocks, you know. For fun. Swinging from the lantern and all that."

"Family?" He tugged my hair, kissed my ear. "It's only been couples out here, Willa. Far as I know. Guys and their women. Thrumcap's no place, really, for a kid."

19

## RHUMB LINE TRACK

When he left I went on autopilot, keeping busy — one of those bizarre tidying jags. Anything to take my mind off the dead girl and the light and all the things that could go wrong. As Sonny sulked over his math, I toyed with the idea of tackling the mess upstairs, the piles of junk people had been collecting for, what, a century? What did people have against throwing stuff out? Hugh was just as bad: "Never know when you'll need it," his motto. I was the queen of sorting and trashing. Only natural, after the moving we'd done.

But I thought again of the girl's photo and those clothes, and decided to start downstairs. The bedroom, the closet — the only real one in the house, crammed with Hugh's stuff. There was a cardboard box and a binder full of musty sheet music, with a review of a gig he'd played in Montreal, and a map of Vancouver tucked inside. I opened the box. A tangle of stuff was held down with a paperweight — a beach stone with a painted-on blue jay, not tacky but quite well done, with dozens of brush strokes for feathers. Putting it back, I dug through some papers — old boarding passes, ticket stubs, serviettes from some fast food places, and a piece of loose-leaf folded several times. People say women are packrats, but look at men! Charlie had saved receipts for everything: had he ever thrown anything out? In this regard Hugh wasn't much different, but at least he'd thank me.

The loose-leaf looked to be a letter, with typing on one side. *Haven't met*, it said, *but my family believes you know my sister. The last we heard she was in B.C., but that she was moving east. We haven't been in contact for two years. Friends of hers said if we reached* …The top was missing, and the bottom illegible, as if the paper had got wet, but you could just make out part of a signature: something something *Preston*.

No good comes to snoopers, I know that, but suddenly I was a cat chasing a string, looking for the rest of the letter. Having no luck, I refolded and tucked the paper among some others. There was a bank statement thanking Hugh for opening an account, a receipt for his sax and a pay stub from a hotel on East Hastings in Vancouver, dated a few years back. I picked out a couple of restaurant serviettes. One had scribbling on it. *In this town name marithon missing you like craze. Got ride with some redneck from Alberta. See u soon, OK? Cant wait to u no what. Luv u 4-ever, J.* A chain of *X*s and *O*s looped around the logo, a chicken wearing a cowboy hat. The writing was small and childish, that rounded, bubbly hand like my own as a teenager, *I*s dotted with happy faces.

Just a kid, I thought numbly, a kid who happened to be in lust. How could you blame her? Still, something pulled inside me and the room's starkness sharpened. The poor thing — though every girl went through it, to some degree; who at that age doesn't mistake lust for love? I thought of my high school boyfriend's groping hands. Guys, even guys like Hugh, had no idea how it feels to wear your heart on your sleeve. You had to pity any girl who did. But even as pity swelled, another feeling rushed in; pride; the calm, sweet knowledge that Hugh was mine. It was like winning a lottery and having the world walk by unaware. Blind luck, what some people called grace. The trouble is, realizing what you have makes you muckle on tighter.

There was a *glug*. Sonny stood in the doorway, drinking pop. He stared over the glass. "Mom? What're you doing?"

I closed the box as if it contained kitchen stuff. "Not a thing, darling." But my face was hot, my breath a butterfly high in my chest. "Now, about that long division ..."

"Math sucks hard." His grumble seemed far away.

Sonny stayed at Derek's the night of the party, the big one in November. We nearly froze going over in the boat with Wayne. The plan was to drop Sonny off on our way to town. There wasn't room in the truck — oh, lovely — so he and I rode with Reenie in her Toyota. I hadn't seen her since the first day of school. She hardly spoke, except to ask Sonny about his favourite sports — "Don't have any," he said, "my mom won't sign me up" — and what he wanted to be when he grew up.

"How would I know?" he answered, as if she were a *Star Wars* droid. I'd have answered the same. Reenie *was* a queer duck, like Hugh said.

Derek's mother waved as Sonny disappeared inside. She was a tiny woman, tinier than she'd seemed the day Sonny had come home wearing the fish hook. Reenie peeled off without a word, racing to catch up to Wayne. You could see the two of them in the cab of the truck, Wayne and Hugh. Reenie lit a cigarette, rolling down her window a crack.

"You been to this place before?" she wanted to know as we started over the bridge. I shook my head. "Ah," she said. "Quite the clientele, eh." She smirked, and her mouth had that look, like cement. "I guess the guys'll play wherever people'll have 'em, right? Wayne says that's how youse met — at a dance."

"Um, well ..."

We drove through the city and some subdivisions till there wasn't much but woods. As the road twisted and turned, the harbour came back into view. Reenie slowed down like a little old lady. Finally we pulled off in front of a building that looked like an old school, with a sign that said Silver Sands Social Club. A crowd milled outside.

"Here we go," said Reenie, lighting another smoke as a drunk reeled up to the window and asked if she was going far.

"Just got here, bud," she said, quite patiently. The guy draped himself over her door and she had to give him a push to get out.

"Hey honey, who you shovin' aroun', eh? C'mere, honey, an' I'll push ya roight there agains' the wall."

Drunk laughter followed us up the steps and somebody else stumbled out, diving for the railing. Reenie butted out her cigarette on her boot heel and stuck it back in the package, then pushed ahead like a politician. She popped a piece of gum into her mouth, her jaws working as we pressed inside. There was a crowd and the lights were low, though the band was still setting up. A woman in a backless dress was talking to Hugh as he ducked about, helping Wayne plug things in. "Most of these guys've been drinkin' since noon," she said, sliding a bottle of vodka behind the drums. Darrell, the guy with the bad perm and the Mustang, slid his arm around her, then he went up and spoke to Hugh, passing him something — money, maybe.

Reenie was yakking to some woman with streaked hair; they seemed to know each other. She pointed to someone staggering past and asked, "Who *is* that arsehole?"

"That's my husband!" the woman shrieked with laughter. Reenie doubled over. "Oh my fock!" she howled.

This was going to be interesting. I ordered myself a beer. The band was doing a sound check. You could barely see them for the crowd; the stage was a platform with a disco ball spangling the tops of their heads. I glanced around for Paula, Emily — those wholesome partners. They weren't there, unless they'd worn disguises. Taking my drink to a spot by the picture window, I watched a light blink across the water. Thrumcap, it struck me with a wash of recognition.

Reenie promptly got pissed, copping sips of Smirnoff behind

the stage. Wayne hardly looked at her, which made me think of parties at the Mess, where having a smashed wife put the fear of God into a guy — like having a loaded rifle on the dance floor.

The band started off with a few standards — light jazz. People banged their glasses on the tables. Reenie just kept drinking.

"Elvis!" someone screamed. You could see Wayne eyeing Hugh, Hugh shaking his head. The singer, Danny, scratched his ear and leaned into the mic. The woman I'd noticed earlier talking to Reenie stumbled up and dropped to her knees before him, snaking her hands up his shins. Everyone watched. The disco ball made the place a migraine waiting to happen. Hugh closed his eyes and tilted his head and blew. Opening them, he searched the room. Our eyes met and he smiled for a second before looking away. The woman on her knees crawled to him and I felt myself freeze. She clung to his jeans like a toddler, gazing up adoringly. God, it didn't get more pathetic. Suddenly people were clapping — the entire room — like in some jungle ritual as she pulled herself up, rubbing against him.

The beer in my glass tasted sour.

Slitty-eyed, Reenie was smoking another cigarette, listening to someone discuss her diet. Draining my beer, I slipped over. "Oh, Dorilda ... this is ..." Reenie slurred, and the woman stuck out her hand. "Oh, fock." Reenie laughed, spraying vodka. "Willa — as in them chocolates? Like, you know, Willacrisp?" The woman stared blankly, edging away.

As Reenie dug into the basket of Cheezies on the table, I went and got another beer, then sat down with her. It was too loud to talk. That crazy woman had backed off Hugh, but you could feel all the eyes practically unzipping him.

Between songs I made myself smile at Reenie through the smoky haze.

Suddenly, something about her look egged me on.

"Tell me about this Julie person." The name rolled from my tongue like a hard little candy, and I blushed.

Reenie scratched her neck and played with an earring, a new one, by the looks of the hole which was scaly and red.

"Ah, Hughie got it up for that one." Her eyes darted away, scanning the dance floor. "Tell ya the truth, so did Wayne. Guys, right?" She bit the end off a Cheezie, took another drink, then chewed ice.

"Fucking space cadet, you ask me. An artiste. She had these big ... eyes. Kind of a greeny colour, like, ya know? 'Cept she never looked at you when she talked, she just —"

"So they went out for a while?"

She plunked down her glass, eyeing me. "Fill 'er up!" She laughed raggedly, squinting around. "That what he told you?"

I shrugged, drawing my finger around the rim of my glass till it whirred.

"Oh, they were quite the item a while ago," she said, almost soberly. "She dealt for him, right?"

I looked at her.

"Before you come along — you and *Sonny*," she added slowly, like she was going through a grocery list. I really didn't like this woman.

The band launched into "Love Me Tender." The beer was

warm; saliva pooled in my mouth.

"I thought they were just jazz," I yelled, swivelling around. The floor was packed now with waltzing — staggering — couples. The disco light added a festive sparkle to their groping.

"You gotta give people what they want." Reenie snickered into her empty glass.

A lump as big as a walnut filled my throat. I looked at her. "Did they live together?" The words stung.

"Who? Hughie an' ... Jooolie?" She scratched under the V of her top. She was one of those smokers who look all bone and nicotine. "For a while," she said dismissively.

I wasn't rising to this. Was he crazy for her? The question scalded, but I held it in.

"Ttttt — I wouldn't worry about it," she said, almost gently despite that rasp of hers. Teasing, "It's not like with you. *She* never had a kid."

The music died and someone shrieked, "Okay everybody — the Fifty-Fifty!" The woman who'd been talking to Hugh, the one in the skimpy dress, grabbed a mic.

"What happened?" I couldn't help myself. The image of that childish handwriting, the writing on that serviette, floated up; and suddenly, the photo of the girl, the girl with the ditzy smile. Julie.

"Huh?" Reenie rolled her eyes. "You dunno what's a Fifty-Fifty? Where you been, girl?"

"No, I mean —" A number was hollered and someone ploughed to the front, parting the cheering crowd. Then the band started up again. I had to shout to make her hear: "— to

Julie." The name almost tasted sickly-sweet. "What happened to her?"

Reenie gazed into her glass, upending it and sliding an ice cube into her palm.

"Took off, I guess."

"Took off?" That teeny-bopperish phrase — *luv u 4-ever* — came back.

"Fuck knows." Reenie slowly stood up. She lit another cigarette, then teetered towards the bar. Returning, she slapped down a fresh pack of Players, a drink and a handful of change, then squeezed her hands into her pockets.

"Lose something?"

She grimaced; even in that bad light her ear looked infected.

"Nah ... it's just ... I coulda used that Fifty-Fifty money, y'know?" She paused, and there was silence as she pulled out the earring and stuck it in her purse. Sighing, she fiddled with the fake-looking medallion on its flap.

"I'm leavin' Wayne. Don't say nothing."

I looked at her, confused but not exactly shocked. For the first time it seemed like she was being straight. She even looked like she might cry. Her brows crinkled together, that hardness dissolving.

"It's okay," I said stupidly.

"No it isn't." Chewing her lip, she sounded almost cheerful.

"Things might change."

"Doubt it."

"How come?" I said after a pause jarred by shrieking feed-back.

"You don't wanna know."

She got up, and next she was on the dance floor doing a shaky version of the Twist with one of her girlfriends, the streaky-haired woman whose husband was passed out beside a VLT.

When Reenie slithered over breathlessly knocking back her drink, I reached out and touched her arm.

"Reenie?" I watched her face. "Did you ever meet her brother — Julie's, I mean?"

"What?" She sounded thoroughly gooned now and fed up. Pressing her lips together, she grinned and waved to someone by the door. Turning to me, her gaze was like a snake's. "Look," she slurred. "She came, she took off. No one knows where to, not even Hughie I bet. You asked him?"

My beer tasted almost like vomit.

Reenie fell back, rocking her chair, and whispered; "Tell you the truth? I wish she'd of stayed. Right around the time she took off, Wayne started."

"Started what?" I was pushing now, and I knew it.

"Fucking up, okay? Nothing, right?"

20

## PLANE SAILING

Everyone got too pissed to drive, except Hugh. We went to someone's house — a cabin on a hill overlooking Thrumcap. It had a porch like the Clampetts' and rickety wooden stairs. Out there in the blackness, the light, our light, dotted and dashed; that comforting flare vanishing the instant you glimpsed it, then flashing again just as you looked away.

"Look, Hugh," I nudged him, pointing it out. My voice was woozy and thick, my throat raw from the smoke.

But Hugh wasn't interested in the view. Someone was passing a mirror with lines of white on it, which people snorted through a straw. When it reached Hugh, he hedged, glancing at me, then, looking embarrassed, muttered, "What the fuck?"

When my turn came, I passed it quickly to Reenie.

We slept on blankets spread over the floor, a bunch of us, like at a kid's sleepover: bodies everywhere. Except these ones snored — even Reenie, who whistled through her teeth, I noticed, waking sometime after dawn.

I felt almost normal, though it was like coming to in a battlefield, hard to tell the living from the dead. Wayne lay like a mountain next to Hugh. He had a sheet over him, his wiry chest hair showing and some kind of tattoo, a muddied anchor, above one nipple. Hugh looked smooth and lean lying between us, moving slightly in his sleep, a long, tall boy still sporting a bit of his farmer's tan from the summer. I slid closer and touched the skin below his collarbone.

He was naked. God, maybe everyone was. I had on my T-shirt from the night before; I could smell it without trying. The rest of my clothes lay in a heap near Hugh's head. I reached for them — little mouse movements so as not to wake him — and squirmed into them. Hugh moaned and rolled over, taking most of the blanket, and I lay there staring at the rafters and listening to everyone. It was a jury of bullfrogs conducting a Q&A, the noise of their breathing — Hugh's and Wayne's, and Reenie's whistling in and out. Someone else started in, someone who looked oddly familiar. The guy who'd won the Fifty-Fifty.

Rain drummed the roof. I pictured Sonny in Derek's basement, the two of them curled up asleep in their sleeping bags, the TV screen buzzing blank. Hugh stirred, sliding his arm around me, and I remembered the dog — oh, God, what had we been thinking, leaving him alone all that time? There'd be wall-to-wall poop by the time we got home. My stomach clenched at the thought, and for no good reason, I felt suddenly

CAROL BRUNEAU

hungover. A queasy, leaden feeling, the urge to close my eyes forever and crawl under a rock.

We didn't hear about the accident until a few days later. Sonny had a current events project and brought home a clipping from that Sunday's paper. His topic was harbour cleanup, the argument for building a sewage treatment plant.

"When's it due?" My question sent him into a mope. "Look, you need to buckle down. I'll help, if you let me."

Pouting, he swept the clipping off the table.

Picking it up, I noticed something on the back — a fuzzy shot of some men in headgear, wearing terse expressions. One of the men looked like Charlie. My God, it could've been him. Most of the article was clipped away, except for a couple of paragraphs. Something about a Sea King losing an engine during a routine night flight and ditching in the harbour south of Thrumcap. "Within close range of the light," it said.

A queasiness crawled through me as Sonny scratched away at his loose-leaf, rubbing a hole with his eraser. "Polution sux," he pencilled, glancing up at me. "What's the matter with *you*?" he said, his sneer melting.

"Nothing. Sonny, could that ... I mean, does that look like ...? He's ... Look." I laid down the clipping and he drew his finger over the grainy image as if to rub life into it. "Where's the rest of the story?" I muttered, my eyes feeling jittery.

The next day Sonny brought home the whole section, which Derek's mother had saved. The article mentioned that the crew

had signalled the nearest radio — the VHF on Thrumcap —
and got no response shortly before the emergency landing.
A second chopper had come to the rescue, one stationed on a
destroyer doing sea trials beyond the harbour approaches. A
spokesman for the Coast Guard said no distress call had been
registered, and there was nothing personnel on Thrumcap
could've done besides radio for help. The same person was
quoted as saying the light was "under review."

"Whatever that means." Hugh's breath was a coolness on
my neck as he peered over my shoulder.

After the first snow, I tried reaching Charlie at work; it was
safer calling him there. Sonny needed clothes, boots; there was
no putting it off. I had it all rehearsed — "He's just as much
yours as mine" — steeling myself as someone picked up.

"Jackson around?" the guy's voice echoed up and down the
hangar. I pictured Charlie setting down an engine part and
coming to the phone. After a while, the person came back.
"Not here right now," he said, guardedly, perhaps.

"Okay." I watched through the window for Hugh.

"Any message?"

"Um ..." My mind raced.

"Hello?"

"Can ... can you tell him it's ... nothing urgent; it's ... Willa?"
There was a muffled noise — something nudging the
receiver? — then mumbling.

"Charlie's wife, right?" The voice kept the same, even tone:

operation damage control. "I'm afraid he's at sea. Training, you know. NATO. The bake and shake tour?"

"Oh?"

"Two weeks in the Caribbean, then two in the arctic." It was meant to be funny; I was supposed to laugh. There was a pause — good-natured — as if the guy had all day. "If it's urgent we can message him, no prob."

His son needs boots, I wanted to say. Please tell —

There was the shotgun slam of a door; Hugh outside, locking up.

"By Christmas," I said quickly, "will they be back?"

"Ah," the fellow groaned, clicked his tongue. "'Fraid not. This is definitely an IMC."

IMC? Then I remembered: I'm Missing Christmas.

"Like I say," the guy went on, as footsteps sounded on the stoop, "we can pass on a message. I'm sure if it's important —"

"Thanks," I murmured, cupping the receiver. "It's okay."

"Who was that?" Hugh wanted to know, sticking his coat on a peg as I hung up. He looked dizzy to me, not himself. "A fly in the bath," he quipped, reaching for me. I sank to the table.

"You know, Hugh, I've been thinking, maybe it'd be the best thing ..."

He gazed down glumly. "You've lost me, Tess. Say what?"

"If they did shut it down — the light. Cleaned it up."

He smirked. "Ttttt." That sound Sonny made when he thought you were full of it. "Occupational hazard. Snarfing those fumes, I'm telling you. Who needs drugs, right?"

"It's not funny. You could get checked. I mean, they have tests for this kind of thing, right?"

"Right." He grimaced. "You're always right."

"Hughie." I never called him that. "This isn't something to just blow off."

There was a long, itchy pause. His eyes looked jumpy.

"I'm worried, okay?"

"Ah, Tessie. You're worried," he mimicked, blinking. He downed a mug of water, refilled it. "You don't need to be. I'd know if there was somethin' wrong, wouldn't I? It's a bug. I'll be fine, just fine. So long as you're here, right Tess? Lookin' after me."


That night I dreamt about Charlie; not a shadow or a name, but *him*. He was on a ship in a roiling turquoise sea, surrounded by other ships and aircraft. There were teams, a blue one versus a green one. Charlie was working feverishly to re-attach something to a helo hovering above the pitching deck like a broken hummingbird. The entire tail section sat on a stack of mattresses like the ones in *The Princess and the Pea*. The tailless chopper sagged and hiccupped. The crew was cheering; the females covered their mouths in awe. "Come to me, baby!" Charlie kept yelling, coaxing the pilot lower. "Don't crap out on me now!" Exhaust swirled in his face. The downdraft flattened him as he crawled underneath with his monkey wrench and, deft as a surgeon, re-attached the tail. "Up, up, and away!" another voice bellowed triumphantly, a boy watching somewhere off-camera, from the clouds perhaps.

Or the sea; it must've been from the sea. As the helo ascended — everyone cheering and holding onto their Tilley hats and grinning through their Ray-Bans — a yelp erupted from the stern: "Man overboard!"

The chopper buzzed so low it blew off those hats and gouged a crater in the water. Everyone went silent, freezing as the bear trap descended, swinging; skimming turquoise, and hooking its prize. *Sonny*, I thought, my heart in my throat; I was one of the legion craning over the rails.

But as the boy was swung to safety and deposited on deck, I saw that it wasn't Sonny at all, but Oscar, the dummy used for practice.

Everything had been a prank.

"Sonny?" I screamed, but no one, not even Charlie, could hear. Already the chopper was a dot in the sky, the crew around me busy firing pink torpedoes and smoke guns at the "enemy."

I was putting Hugh's laundry away, that's how I happened to see inside his drawer. Under some sun-dried Jockeys lay a wad of cash and an envelope. They were banded together in a little pile with some pay stubs and receipts for supplies, mostly gasoline.

"What're you doing, Tess?" He startled me, leaning in the doorway. Rain dripped from his face and hair.

"Nothing." It was utterly true. He'd never minded me putting his stuff away. Doing little things was how I kept busy, slipping into routines; the domestic division of labour.

"When d'you expect Sonny?" he asked, oddly. Sonny was at school; he'd be home the usual time.

"Same as always." But my mind had caught on the notion of labour, the other kind. The hours it had taken, in my fuzzy, earlier life, to birth my boy. Clenched teeth, ripping pain; a lie, saying you forgot it. Charlie would have no recollection, having been on a tour, in training. Wherever the choppers went, piggybacked on ships, the technicians went. Pilots, navigators, AESOPS — no wonder I regarded his job as a fable — and always the techies, Mr. Fix-its attached to the aircraft. Like sitters assigned to dotty seniors, or lion tamers keeping the beasts from crashing into the audience.

"What's wrong, Tess?" Hugh came closer, close enough to trace my breast with his finger. Oreo made off with a sock.

Wasting no time, we undressed and Hugh made love to me quickly, relentlessly. For a moment or two it was a bit like being pinned, nailed, to the bed.

"There's a problem," he said afterwards. "Not with you. The lighthouse." The Coast Guard had been in touch again; now the government was nosing in. "Bunch of fucking enviros. Now they say they're worried. It's a crock, Willa. Just a goddamn excuse, nothing else." His eyes slid to my belly, his voice distant.

Covering my stretch marks, I pushed away the thought of moving, instead remembering how I'd felt after Sonny's birth, how it had opened and sectioned me like an orange. Twisting Hugh's hair around my finger, I listened for Sonny now, for Oreo's whine signalling his return.

"Tessie? You with me?" He snapped his fingers, poked my ribs.

"Mercury," he murmured dismissively. "Some dickhead says it's in the paint. What a load, eh? Just to get me out."

"But ... Hugh? You said, about moving, 'Things come up.'"

"Horseshit, I never said any such thing. I'm not leaving, Willa. Why the fuck would I, 'cause of what some dweeb in a suit says? It's all economics. Think they'd replace me? Not a fucking chance. Think of the people out there, all those guys at sea. How would it look, now, if I just fuckin' bailed?"

"Hughie? It's not just about —"

"Look. Far as they know, I'm solo out here, okay? What they don't know won't hurt 'em."

Winter fell quickly and with it a glumness in Sonny that troubled me more than the business with the light. "Look for anger," I'd heard some expert say on CBC; wasn't depression repressed rage, a feeling of helplessness? But Sonny never seemed helpless, even in his foulest moods; blame them on his prepubescence.

There hadn't been a word from his father, and not a cent. I had other worries, too, namely sending Sonny out in the boat; at least it was a short crossing. But we heard reports all the time of lobstermen getting lost and tankers disappearing. December seas were the worst, Hugh said. I wasn't keen on entrusting anybody with my boy, watching Sonny's smallish figure in the bow through binoculars, Wayne's bulk in the stern. As they disappeared around the next island, I'd do my best to visualize Sonny strolling safely to the bus stop.

Hugh kept up his chores in the tower, polishing the lens, straining the mercury. He shrugged off my apprehension, wouldn't listen when I brought it up. He quit keeping the tower locked. "Who'd trespass this time of year?" He had a point, except I worried about Sonny sneaking up there, getting into things. In the distance the city looked dead, a silent, dodgy grey. The harder winter fell, the more I thought of Charlie hovering not over the tropics, but over pack ice.

The wind rattled the branches one day I went to meet Sonny; I liked being there as the boat chopped into sight. He never waved though, wouldn't have if his life had depended on it. Heading home he trudged behind me, his knapsack flapping.

"How was your day?"

"Fine. Terrible." A shrug, a scowl. His second teeth were still too big for his mouth. When I asked what he'd done at school, he said, "Nothin'."

A movement in the bushes caught my eye, a fox with something in its mouth.

"You must've done *something*."

Sonny threw his pack down in the kitchen, the dog all over him. "Where's Hugh?" he wanted to know. His scowl lifted momentarily. "I've been wondering. You know what I'd reeeally like?" I braced myself. "A guitar, Mom. Electric."

The memory of him playing air instruments on the beach flashed back, warming me as Hugh shuffled in. Hanging his coat over Sonny's, he shooed the pack out of his way.

"Hey!" He slapped Sonny's arm, then kissed me. His eyes were bright, his fingers icy on my cheek. "What's with the kid, Tessie? You could scrape his lip off the floor." He poured them each some pop. "So, Alex, who'd you hang out with today?"

"Like, nobody." When he emptied his glass, Sonny's mouth looked like the Joker's on *Batman*. "A kid got caught smoking," he let slip, eyeing us. I noticed a mark on his neck.

Kicking off his boots, Hugh noticed it too. "What happened to you, bud?"

The bruise looked to have teeth marks. Sonny twisted away. "Nothing. It don't matter."

"*Doesn't* matter." He looked about to cry. "Sonny? Who ...?"

"Those girls after you or what? Get used to it, Alex. Good looking guy like you."

Sonny grabbed his pack and ran upstairs.

"Wait a sec," I yelled after him. "What're you —"

"Leave me alone," he screamed back. "I got homework. What's it look like?"

Hugh finished off the pop, straight from the bottle. "I could drink a frigging bucket of that." He smacked his lips. "Look. I'm not telling you what to do, God knows. But don't you think he can figure out his own shit?"

The money wasn't in Hugh's drawer the next time I put away laundry. But I came across the envelope, taking a Thermos of tea to the lantern. Figuring Hugh was there, up I went — quietly — to surprise him. No small feat on those stairs.

But all I found was an ashtray with roaches in it, and a half-empty bottle of Windex on the ledge. The navigation book was there, too, his place marked with the envelope.

There were pictures inside it, photographs. I didn't recognize the people in them at first. The shock of what they were doing stole my breath. One showed Wayne — it *looked* like Wayne, though it was hard to distinguish his features. His head was thrown back, his eyes shut — in laughter or pain, you couldn't tell. In the next shot he was naked, sitting on a bed with a blue spread — I'd recognize that chest and that murky tattoo anywhere — except it looked like he was wearing pantyhose. Well, not quite wearing them; they were pulled up to his thighs. One hand was closed around his penis. There was someone else in the picture, half of someone. You could just make out a blue sweater, a peasant blouse, and jeans; someone laughing, the top of the head cut off, the mouth open, roaring. Reenie, maybe? No. Her hair was a reddish flare against her shoulder, a clasp sliding from it. A curve of belly above the jeans. It looked like the girl from the other picture, the school picture upstairs. Stretched across the bedspread was a shadow — the photographer's?

At dusk Hugh appeared with a bouquet, a mix of treasures gleaned from the beach. Twists of frozen kelp beaded with periwinkles, Irish moss the palest pink, the bunch tied with a ribbon of fishing twine. In the middle of the bouquet was a rose; a white one limp and smelly from riding the waves. Its centre was tight as a bullet, its leaves black. A rose, though, still a rose, like the ones at my mother's visitation.

"It's been ages, hasn't it," he said, "since I brought you that yellow one, remember? Tie a yellow ribbon, Tessie." He laughed, and I pulled the flower from the seaweed and smelled it.

"Where the heck … ?"

"A wedding? People get married on the ferry. Cruise ships. They do it all the time — *Love Boat* and all." He held a corsage of Irish moss to my sweater.

Or a funeral. People did that too, got buried at sea.

"What's the matter, Tess?" His voice was the sound inside a shell. He took my hand, rose and all, and kissed it.

Stalking in to raid the fridge, Sonny eyed the bouquet. "What the frig is *that*?"

In bed Hugh gathered me to him, the way you gather flowers — or weeds — or a sheet off the line. He buried his face against me. His beard felt like thistles. Moving from his arms, I could think only of the photographs — the girl and that pervert Wayne.

"Hughie?"

"What is it?" His voice was thorny, his touch cold. He slid his hand between my legs. "Warm me up, Tess. It's so damn freezing out." He was trembling as his leg pushed mine apart. "I love you, Tessie. You know that, don't you? I love you." Lapping, the word slid ashore, swamping me even as I imagined a finger — his? — lingering on a shutter.

 21

# DEAD RECKONING

The photos burned a hole in my imagination. Now I couldn't let Sonny go alone with Wayne; couldn't bear the thought of him in that boat. Though part of me — a shrinking, nattering part — tried to deny it. In an open whaler? What can happen in five minutes? But nothing eased my disgust. Reenie was still in the picture, which seemed odd. Hugh said she and Wayne were talking about kids of all things. A joke.

Almost worse was wondering why Hugh had the pictures, though fear kept me from asking. Sometimes it's necessary to close your eyes, which is what I did when he touched me. Until the chill of his hand made me think *mercury* and that worry pushed the other, more immediate ones away.

"You're going for groceries *again*?" Hugh was bemused the first few times I accompanied Sonny ashore. But after a while, he seemed almost peeved. Nervous.

Nothing erased those images in my head. Yet I couldn't speak. It was like being small again, a tiny kid being wakened to hear that my mother was gone. Gone where? Back to the hop-si-tal? My little voice, *no no no*, in the depths of the closet, the coolness of a fur coat against my cheek. The crack of light under the door had finally coaxed me out. But then, as now, I could only let myself see as far as it would allow.

One morning close to Christmas I said I was going over to see Reenie, to see how she was. Hugh complained suddenly of a cramp.

"You should call a doctor," I said, alarmed.

"Do you have to see her today? That ricket ... you don't even *like* Reenie."

"D'you want me to phone someone?"

"No," he said, "I'll look into it. I will." Just like that, his pains seemed to vanish, and his mood lifted. "Go on. If you want to see her that bad. Dunno why anyone would, but ..." He stroked my hair and straightened my sweater — his sweater, a floppy Aran that fit me like a dress. He laid his hand on my throat as he kissed me, his thumb pressing my pulse. "Long as you come back. You wouldn't leave me alone out here, would you?" He squeezed my fingers a little too tightly. "Christ, Tessie, you always have this effect on guys?"

As I was getting ready to leave, nagging Sonny to brush his teeth, Hugh dug something out of the freezer. Strawberries, tiny fairy ones left over from the summer. "Say hi to Reenie." He put one on my tongue.

He stood waving while Sonny and I skidded and wind-milled across the yard, sheer ice till we reached the rocky part of the beach. I looked back once, pushing my hair out of my eyes, those floppy cuffs like weights.

Out of the blue Sonny said, "You gonna marry him or what, Mom?" The look in his eyes was like an older man's, my father's, out of patience.

"Huh?"

"Like, duh."

"Should I?" Tucking my hands inside my sleeves, I braced for a question about Charlie.

"Hugh's a goon. An arsehole." His voice was full of dreadful conviction. I swatted at him; without meaning to, clipped his ear. He reeled from me, making a show of it. "You're a goon too!" His yell was worse than a slap.

I wanted to hit him. Instead I tried pulling him to me.

"Le' go — I'll be late!" As he jerked away, I caught the smell of oatmeal and milk.

Wayne was waiting, the fur on his greasy parka spiky with spray. "You comin'?" he said to me, grabbing Sonny's backpack. "Take 'er easy, guys. You go for a swim, I ain't fishing youse out."

Eyeing his mitts on the tiller, I thought of the girl — Julie. What had possessed her?

Waves slapped the bow and Sonny ducked out of the wind. "How's Reenie?" I said, making conversation. Wayne grunted something unintelligible. On the other side I followed Sonny to the road, then started towards the yellow bungalow.

Wayne's truck soon purred beside me. "She ain't home, if that's who you're looking for." He sounded pissed off now, accusing. Their yard was in sight, the Toyota missing. His door slammed and I could feel his bulk behind me. "I dunno what you said to her," he muttered, and without speaking I crossed and doubled back towards the bus stop. I didn't want to embarrass Sonny standing there with the other kids, so I just smiled and kept going.

With the wind pushing me, I walked clean to the base, ending up — crazy as it sounds — once more on Avenger. The car was gone this time. Joyce LeBlanc was digging something out of her mailbox. She looked twice when she saw me, and hollered down, "Willa Jackson? Oh my jeez, is that you?"

I hurried around the curve then cut across someone's yard to get back to the highway. Cars buzzed past. When a bus came along, I flagged it down. Amazingly, the driver — a woman — pulled over. I asked which bus went into the city.

"Hop on," she said.

The bus shunted around for an hour, eventually letting me off on a downtown street crammed with traffic. The air pulsed. Throngs of people shouldered past, disappearing into office towers — women wearing sneakers with pantyhose and suits, men in overcoats. The noise made me edgy, as if I'd been yanked from sleep. I ducked into a store, but the lights and music and blank faces chased me outside again. I walked aimlessly, half expecting the streets to lock into a circle. What a concept, the open-endedness of blocks, lines. I breathed all of it in till my lungs hurt, then headed back to the bus stop.

There was a book shop kitty-corner to it, with used paper-backs, nautical charts, and a cat curled in the window. Going inside to warm up, I took my time perusing the shelves. I was feeling guilty now, ashamed for lying to Hugh. Something caught my eye: a yellowed copy of *A Popular Guide to the Saints*. While my hands thawed, I flipped through it and found Teresa. The patron saint of heart attack victims, her write-up said, and headache sufferers. I'd hoped for a picture, but there wasn't one. Our chit-chat came back to me, the feel of Hugh's tongue tracing my spine. "It's the shadows under your eyes, Tess. The way your neck bends, like a spruce in a gale."

"Okay, then. So who are you?" Watching for bodies, and lightning off the bows of container ships; Hughie, who couldn't dog paddle to save his life.

I started to look for Elmo, then checked the price. Only a couple of bucks, so I paid for it and left, just in time, too, as the bus shuddered up. On board, I found the entry. Poor Saint Elmo, patron of the seasick and sufferers of appendicitis, mar-tyred by men who'd used a windlass to winch out his intestines.

*Willa, call me Willa.*

"What're you so sad about?" His question out of the blue, once, like a squall.

"But I'm dancing inside!" Like a hornet over the marsh, not touching down.

By now it was well past lunchtime. It seemed like the right bus, but we took forever reaching the bridge, even longer cross-ing it. Then I had to transfer. When I finally boarded the bus to the Passage it was almost three o'clock.

Wayne was hiding out in his eco-shed, as Hugh called it. Lately it doubled as our mailbox, the post office dropping stuff there for us to pick up. Wayne had been drinking.

"Sheeesh," he rambled. "I've already been over once. Your little guy wondered where the hell you were. Shark musta ate her, I said."

*Sonny.*

Wayne's look made my skin crawl. It took coaxing to get him to take me across. But he seemed to have forgotten our little run-in that morning. Halfway over, he pulled something from his pocket and handed it to me: a crumpled red envelope. It was addressed to Alex, the writing Charlie's.

The sun was sinking as I slid and skidded through the woods, a rattling tunnel of twigs and animal sounds against the softer push of waves and the port's rumble. That piece of mail weighing my pocket, the noises followed me like the sluggish moon barely lighting the trail.

Sonny was home alone, starving but otherwise okay. Hugh had gone off somewhere to jam; odd that Wayne hadn't mentioned it. Oreo had attacked the garbage. Picking up the mess, I threw supper together, then helped Sonny with some math.

"You smell different," he said, wrinkling his nose. "Weird."

Waiting till his knapsack was packed for the morning, I finally passed him the envelope. It had a strange postmark and inside was a card, which got ripped in his rush to open it. On it was a boat with a Christmas tree for a sail. A hundred-dollar bill slipped out, Sonny barely noticing as he buried his nose in the card.

Closing in on Christmas, Hugh and I talked — not an argument, not a heart to heart, but something in between. It was during a freezing rainstorm; a fire blazed in the woodstove as ice pellets hit the window. The power had gone out; all you could hear was the generator roaring from the base of the tower. We had Scrabble spread out in the candlelight. Too many vowels, not enough consonants. The game was going nowhere.

Hugh said, "You think about him, don't you?"

"Who, Sonny?"

"Charlie. Don't you."

I took a sip of tea. "Sometimes."

"Think you'll go back with him?" It was more an accusation than a question.

My letters clicked together, breaking the awful silence. "Why would you ask that?"

"I can tell," he said.

"Tell what?"

"You've been going somewhere else, haven't you."

Rain slammed the panes. The lamp flickered, the ancient kerosene one we'd begun keeping in the porch.

"Well ..." I hesitated, then it spilled out. "It's not easy, you know ..."

"What isn't?"

"This ... place." I barely knew where to begin. "The way everything leads, well, back to where you frigging started," I tried to joke.

He opened his mouth to say something but stopped, as if he'd forgotten what it was. Closing his eyes, he rubbed his forehead, sighing. "And you're surprised?" I just looked at him. Then he grinned. "What'd you expect? You knew there wasn't a fuckin' bridge." He reached across to pour more tea.

I sat there, swallowing. "Remember ... that girl?" My stomach churned. The rest of me felt tied to the chair.

"Girl? Um, Tess, could we be more specific?" I didn't laugh. "Which one?" He gave me a dull look.

"The jumper," I said quietly, an odd relief rippling through me. It pulled into a knot as the image of the body rushed back. "Jesus, Hugh." It came out a whisper, and there was a pause. All you could hear was sleet and the flames guttering. "What if Sonny'd seen it?"

"I'd jump too, if you left me." His voice was quiet, matter-of-fact, and the force of it took a moment to hit.

Numbness seized me, then let go. "Oh, Hugh." My mouth took over. "Don't be foolish." It was like telling Sonny, *Eat your peas or I'll ...*

What?

"It's not foolish. You think I'm shitting you, but it's true. I'd —"

*Jump*: my brain spun at the idea. Other words, names, clung and spiralled with it. *Julie. Wayne.* Tessie, Elmo.

"Plans," I blurted out, to stop the spinning. "We need to figure something out. If I've got a problem, it's wondering where we'll be. I don't think the island's —"

"I'm sticking by my guns, Willa." His calmness ate at me, then he seemed to relent. "But if we have to leave, there's tons of other lights. Think of all the coastlines — *think* of it."

"— the best place for Son —"

*The world's our oyster*, I waited for him to say.

"We could live anywhere you want," he murmured, rubbing his brow again. He listed places: Cornwall, Brittany, the Ivory Coast, Peru, Australia.

"Somewhere, I suppose."

"It's only a job," he seemed to tell himself, sliding his wooden letters into the box. He gave it a shove, the little tiles clicking like Chiclets. "So we have 'options,'" he said sarcastically, "isn't that the word?"

"I think you should tell them — the Coast Guard types." I stifled a sigh. "I mean, the way you've been feeling? The tiredness, for one." Something kept me from spelling it out.

"Sure, doc. Mom."

The fire settled in the stove. There was a flicker, the lights coming on but dying again, sinking the corners into a deeper darkness.

"Look. I have a son, remember." My voice was brittle. I picked up a letter — one of the blanks — and rubbed it like a pebble, a worry stone.

"No shit. Maybe it's his old man's turn?"

I bristled. *It's not like that.* But the words wouldn't come.

"D'you love me?" he said, point blank. Even in the lamp's wavy light his eyes gleamed, like bits of cellophane in the sun.

"Of course." It had a righteousness that I regretted. "How can you ask?"

He studied the linoleum, then leaned back, sighing. "That girl. That ... 'partner' of mine. Julie. She ..."

*What?* I thought; *she what?*

"... wasn't exactly faithful."

Such a quaint, unlikely word. It made me stiffen, as if the girl had been some kind of pilgrim.

"So ... what happened? Where'd she end up?"

"Gave 'er the boot, like I told you. No big deal, Tess. People come and go, right?" A vague smile lifted the corners of his mouth. "She was ..."

"What?"

"Too clingy."

"Right." I felt stung. "Nice combination."

"Guess I know how to pick 'em, eh?" It was as if he wanted my approval, my collusion.

"How'd you ditch her?" I asked, too bluntly. Despite the chill, my face was burning. My temple throbbed. The photos flashed through my head: Wayne and the shadow across the bed.

"Oh Jesus," he laughed, "there's a story. Got a year?"

The lights flickered again. With a little shock, for the first time in what seemed hours, I remembered Sonny up in his room with candles.

"Better see what that kid of yours is into," Hugh murmured, glancing upwards, eyeing me with that wash of a smile.

Rising, I tried moving on. "We need a date," I said, padding towards the stairs. "They must've given you some idea when."

"Willa." Hooking me, his voice reeled me back in. His face looked sallow against the shiny, black panes. "You're forgetting how things work. Let 'em take for-fucking-ever. It'd suit me.

You know, sweetie, really, it's like fuck-all matters. Crazy as that seems."

Christmas was a baby spruce cut from the tea house garden. Sonny decorated it with stuff that had washed up: shells and bits of rope and wood and salt-bleached tampon applicators. He didn't know what they were; who had the heart to tell him?

I gave Hugh the Saints book and cooked a turkey in the woodstove; it took all day. Hugh played "Blue Christmas" on the sax. His present to me was a round grey stone with an eagle painted on it.

"You don't like it?" he said.

"It's ... amazing." I couldn't bring myself to touch it. "The detail!" The bird's yellow eye seemed to follow me. "Wherever did you find it?"

"A girl down the shore — an artist," he said, pulling on the mitts I'd knit for him.

Sonny spent the day in his room, drawing pictures of battle scenes in the sketchbook he got, from Santa, I insisted, though he'd quit believing by grade three. He taped Charlie's card above his bed, after I'd peeked inside it.

*To my No. 1 Son, LOVE Dad*, Charlie'd printed. *Don't spend it all in one place!!!* Sonny had stuffed the hundred dollars in a sock, to put towards videos — if we ever saw a TV again, he griped.

After dark Hugh and I went outside with the binoculars to view the navy ships in port, lit up like department stores. You could just make them out, like gaudy Northern Lights against the shifty sky. I tried coaxing Sonny to come have a look, but he wouldn't budge.

I suggested he invite Derek for a holiday sleepover.

"Why'd he wanna come here for? Nothing to do in this crappy place."

He ripped a drawing from his book and taped it next to Charlie's card. It was one in a series. Since school had let out, he'd taken to plastering walls with his art — spidery creatures with jagged, bloody wounds.

"God, gory enough for you?" Hugh made us both jump, peering in from the landing. Who knows how long he'd been standing there. Sonny crumpled up the picture he'd started and pitched it; we watched it skitter across the floor. Then he ploughed me out the door, winging it closed behind me. I heard him kick Oreo off the bed.

"Man, that kid's into violence," Hugh remarked, looking up from his book. It was opened to the page on Saint Elmo. "What the fuck goes through his head, you think? You oughta look into it, Tessie. Bad news, any kid acting like that. Where d'you suppose he gets it from?"

22

## BEACONS

We met Derek on the other side when he came over. His mom wouldn't leave till she saw him wearing a life jacket, which Wayne bummed from someone tied up nearby. Hugh had come over, too. Instead of returning with us, he disappeared inside the eco-shed to wait for his friends; they were supposed to jam. This time he had his sax.

Amusing the boys took my mind off things, though I could've left them to their own devices. The dog acted like he'd never seen a child before. That afternoon we took a hike, though neither kid was dressed for it. They pelted rocks at the frozen pond to see who could make the farthest hole. Watching them reminded me of when Sonny was tiny, the hours I'd spent at playgrounds, breathing on my hands to warm them.

After supper we roasted marshmallows over the stove. The boys ran outside waving the flaming ones like torches.

"This is like winter camping," Derek said. "Me and Dad did that once. We froze our butts off." The two of them reeled with laughter. "What do you guys do for entertainment?" he wanted to know. "I can't believe you don't even got a TV. You musta really fugged up at math."

"Fudged." Sonny looked at me. "He said 'fudged.'" They giggled hysterically.

I told myself: *breathe.*

"Man," Derek wouldn't shut up, "I couldn't live with no TV, my mom neither. I'd be dead meat."

Sonny peered into the fridge. "Dead meat's about it." Then they thumped upstairs, complaining.

I made cookies, chocolate macaroons you didn't have to bake, and took them up on a plate.

"Dog turds." Sonny chortled, taking one.

"Shit cakes!" Derek spewed coconut. Sonny's mouth was ringed with brown. "For the love of GOD!" — I lost it — "You two better go to bed."

"Nuttin' else to do," they grumbled.

"Tomorrow we'll show Derek the forts."

"Whoa, baby. Whoop-de-doo."

They were still up there snickering when I went to sleep, the bed a tundra, cold yet peaceful without Hugh.


In the morning they hated the pancakes and pestered me for coffee. ("*My* mom lets me drink it.") The day gaped; eating my pride I'd asked Wayne to aim for three o'clock to take Derek back, figuring Hugh would be with him.

On our trek, Oreo sniffed and lifted his leg at everything as Sonny marched ahead, clearly wishing I'd stayed behind. "What if something happened?" I called, remembering the fish hook incident. "I'd never forgive myself." Nor would Derek's mother.

The path was frozen, the moss like green fake fur with a dusting of snow. Instead of the fort, Sonny insisted on the rifle range. No big deal; the island was strewn with rusty reminders of war, rubble scattered through the woods like bones. Hidden by summer's lushness, in the bleakness of winter they sprouted everywhere, weeds from a forgotten world.

The boys trudged along bleary-eyed. I cursed the inventor of sleepovers. Oreo darted after a squirrel, then squatted on some moss. The trail narrowed to a skid of ice between the alders and tamaracks, their feathery yellow a relief from the greyness. Blue jays yammered, as if warding us off. When the path forked, Sonny veered right, dashing ahead.

"Check 'er out!" he hollered.

"Awe-some." Delight spiked Derek's grin as the machinery appeared, rusted racks and pulleys growing from the trench. "*Fluffing* sweet," he bellowed. The two of them left me crashing through the alders.

"Training," I heard Sonny yell, his voice almost prideful; okay, so there's no TV, but the place isn't a total write-off. "The military used to teach guys to shoot here."

Derek raised an invisible rifle and blasted a tree. "Take that, ya friggin' commie!" They slid into the trench, yanking on a pulley. The whole works looked like undersea wreckage, just left there. There was the crunch of shattering ice. Oreo threw his head back, baying.

"Don't get a soaker," I started to yell. "Hope you've got spare socks." Derek goose-stepped along the frozen length of the trench. Watching them was exhausting, but enlivening, too. It let me forget everything. That's the deal with children: you can disintegrate inside, and they'll glue you back together.

"Not too far!" I shouted. The noise was like an army shooting at gyprock, till the ice gave way to yellowed bulrushes.

"Oh, maa-aan! Check this out!" Their voices rang back. "Awwww — gross! Who farted?" Derek was waving something like a chunk of wood dredged from the swamp. It was a sandal, like something peat people would've worn, those mummies found in bogs in Europe. A Birkenstock, small; a woman's?

The dog crouched there, quiet now, but his tail going like a propeller.

"Call the Smithsonian," I joked. "Okay, Indiana ..."

"Mooom!" Sonny was disgusted. "Don't be such a keener."

Derek was stomping back along the trench, sighting a new enemy. Sonny fired rocks into the trees: grenades. Before I could stop them they scrambled up the opposite bank and into the bushes, flickers of lime green and blue as they wrestled and bayoneted each other. Suddenly there was a whoop: "MOOOOOOOM!" Oreo streaked towards them. I had to follow.

The bunker was dug into a mound overgrown with bushes, its concrete face chalky, its iron fittings dripping rust. What use could it have had — shelter for the fellow setting targets?

"Better not go in," I warned lamely. They were shoving each other, Sonny grunting like a dying man, then yanking on the iron door, yanking with all his might till it gave way. They squeezed inside, their voices a piercing echo.

"Frea-ky."

"It stinks, man."

"Who cares?"

Oreo slid in after them. The hinges crumbled as I swung the door wider, ducking inside. "Get out!" I expected to hear.

A grid of light fell from a grate in the mossy wall. The floor was wet and a dankness rose up: urine? Some initials were chipped into the cement: BG & LM, 1962. In a corner was a pile of singed-looking rags.

"What the —?" Sonny yelped. I could hear the boys' breathing as Oreo whined.

"Come on," I said, "the dog hates it." And, louder, "That roof can't be safe."

The cold, fresh air felt like a second chance, it was such a relief to get outside.

"Hurry up, guys — that's enough," I hollered, and they darted after me. But then they took off through the brush, heading towards blue. You could see a crinkle of ocean through the woods, but the branches were so tangled the boys soon gave up.

"C'mon pup." I whistled. Oreo was rolling on his back as if crazed by fleas.

"Stupid dog," Sonny said, huffing a little. Clicking my

tongue, I dug for a treat.

"He's some cute," Derek said. "If I had a dog, I'd name him Panzer — Panzer Otti."

"O-kay." I whistled again, louder this time. But Oreo kept rolling, his tongue lolling like a slice of ham. His eyes were brown and white alleys. "Heel," I called, grabbing his collar. Then I noticed something sticking out of the ground, half frozen. Unravelled blue wool — the sleeve of a sweater? — and litter. A leaflet, the sort of thing you'd see at the grocery store, advertising yoga classes or tole-painting. It made me think of Reenie. The print was faded, mostly illegible — except one word: Lamaze. Lovely. Instructions on birthing in a swimming pool, swimming while grinning and bearing the interminable.

Oreo snatched the leaflet and started chewing it.

"Silly dog!" My voice quavered. The boys must've heard it.

"*Now*, guys. Let's go. I'm *leaving*."

Oreo snapped as I grabbed the paper and dropped it. I let go of his collar. He started rolling again.

"Not yet," Sonny was moaning. "We'll come home at lunch."

Oreo growled as I caught hold of him.

"You're coming now," I managed. "Derek's mom'll be waiting, and Wayne —"

"Wayne the brain," Sonny tittered. At least he was listening.

But before I could do anything, they ran back to the bunker. Derek scaled the roof while Sonny disappeared inside. Distraught, I yanked the door and it broke from the hinges.

There was something in the corner we'd missed, a smooth grey stone and what looked like a kid's plastic paintbrush, yellow, with hardly any bristles. Sonny picked up the stone, turning it over, rubbing away leaf mould. There was part of a bird on it, what looked like the head of an osprey in a nest, with a tiny, half-formed baby waiting to be fed.

"The stink," Sonny was yelling up through the grate. "Makes you wanna puke."

We could see our breath; I felt Sonny's on my neck. A cold nausea filled my throat.

"Mom? What is it?"

The place was an echo chamber. I shrugged, escaping. The dog was nipping at me, yapping. "The noise," I said, swatting him. My insides twisted like rope. The woods, the barking, the bright blue sky jumped around me.

"So much for a secret hideout." Sonny elbowed me. "Me and Derek claimed it for our clubhouse. Tell the freakin' world about it, Or-e-o."

"Sonny." My voice was feeble. "Like who?"

But he and Derek were already shoving through the branches, Oreo snapping at their jeans. I wanted to hug them, put my arms around both of them and draw them to me, the witch rewriting everything. Comforting Hansel and Gretel, apologizing for luring them into the gingerbread house. I just wanted the warmth of Sonny's hand squirming in mine, if only for a second.

Back at the house, I made grilled cheese sandwiches and,

while the boys were eating, crept upstairs. The blue canvas bag was gone. So were the clothes and the school photo. When I slipped outside, the lighthouse door was locked.

When Wayne came for Derek there was no sign of Hugh. He'd been gone twenty-four hours. Twenty-four hours without the sound of his voice.

*Why are you counting?*

He came home sometime during the night, long after I'd gone to bed. The creak woke me; I held my breath as he slipped in beside me. My body froze as his knees spooned into mine and he moved against me. He smelled of smoke. I lay perfectly still until he stopped and his breathing grew shallow. I barely slept after that, and didn't dream. Instead, over and over, I imagined Charlie rescuing someone, lowering the horse collar to a swollen-bellied mermaid, her seaweed hair fanning out, tangling in the chopper's landing gear. Me in the water, grabbing for the rising cable, the cable swinging over the rising sea. I imagined the burn of spliced metal through my fingers, and slipping under the waves till salt burned my throat. A stinging effervescence like inhaled 7-Up, but hot, not cold. Tears.

In the morning I rose to muffled music, notes that seemed to travel through wool. The bed beside me was empty, the room like a vault. The fire had all but gone out. On the table was a clamshell with a roach in it. I dressed and stoked the stove, plugged in the kettle, made coffee. Then waited. After a while he came in from outdoors, rosy-cheeked, wearing a sleepy smile. I stayed put as he moved towards me.

"Where've you been?" I said, fighting the room's iciness, the slide of his eyes. He shrugged, brushing my shoulder as he went to fill his cup. "Sonny and I were expecting you."

"Ah," he said. "How'd your holiday go?"

As if we'd been to Disney World — anywhere but here. "Excuse me?"

He leaned against the sink, eyeing me.

"In case you forgot, I had the boys?" I thought of the bunker and the rags and painted stones, and my stomach kicked. "Where were you?" My voice was shrunken. I felt weightless as a leaf.

"The city," he said, "here and there. Round an' about." He stared above the rim of his coffee, then his gaze slid.

"One day left of vacation," I said, breathing from the top of my chest. That sting again, like soda. "Sonny's not going to like going back."

"Where?" The dullness of his question stopped me.

"To school?" I couldn't help a little snort.

"Eat shit," he may have said, laughing like I'd missed something, the beginning of a pun. He eyed me strangely, his look almost one of boredom. "Tell Sonny he can eat shit," he repeated, and the fuzziness in my sinuses went cold. "That kid gets away with fucking murder. I can't believe the stuff you take off him.

"If he was mine, I'd —"

"What?" My pulse raced. "You'd what?"

"Look, Tess." He shook his head, smiled wanly. "The guys and me, we've been playing flat out for a day and a half. Recording."

*Eat shit yourself,* I wanted to say, *here's a spoon.* Silence. I could hear Sonny upstairs running the tap.

"My whole life I've wanted to do this," Hugh finally spoke, slouching to the table. He peeled an orange, held out a section.

"Hugh — ?"

"Don't ask — I don't want to talk about it. Never discuss somethin' in the works, sweetie; you'll jinx it. You know I'm superstitious."

Our eyes locked.

"Hugh. I've ... the kids and I, we found the ... the bunker." You could hear the waves scrubbing the breakwater, the grinding ice.

"Yeah? Bet they liked that. Good for an afternoon, eh?"

He sucked at some orange, then held out the last piece. I closed my eyes, shook my head.

"Willa, I don't want to fight with you." He went to touch me and I pulled away. "Be like that," he said. "You'll just hurt yourself."

Covering my mouth, I felt the glide of tears.

"Tessie," he whispered, oh so gently. His breath on my cheek. "Grow up."

We didn't speak the rest of that day or night. At breakfast Sonny started in, filling the kitchen with complaining.

"Mom? Do I have to go back? Why can't I stay home? You could teach me! School's a freakin' waste of time. Make me go, and I'll ... I'll run away."

*Where?* The one advantage to being on an island.

Hugh was washing dishes, doing a lousy job. Porridge stuck to everything.

"I'm not lyin', Mom. Seriously. You make me go, I'll —"

"Alex!" Hugh exploded; the room was a paper bag with the air slapped out of it. "Quit the crap. Quit giving her a hard time. You were my kid, know what I'd do?"

Sonny stopped dead, shooting both of us hateful looks. "Fine. But I ain't going and you can't make me." He and Oreo flew outside so fast there wasn't time to scream about wearing a coat.

"He'll freeze." I was trembling.

"Let him," said Hugh, sneaking his arm around me.

He pulled me close, his hand roving like a spider under my top, cupping my breast. Picturing Julie and her blue sweater, I shrank from him, but his touch was sure. Knowing. Next he was kissing me; shyly at first, timid, almost like Charlie after one of his tours. His tongue was warm and tasted of brown sugar.

"I'm sorry," he whispered into my hair, "I never meant to be a prick." His eyes shone as he pulled my sweater up over my head. "Skin the rabbit!" Then he slid his lips to my nipples, sucking each till it hurt.

I was Alice *and* the March Hare. "But ... Sonny ..." I moaned, my face wet as he slipped to his knees, his hands on my waist, unzipping me.

"Shhh," he kept saying, kissing my belly, working down my jeans. He undid his belt and lifted me, and with all his wiry strength, carried me to the other room. Pulling off his jeans, he stretched close, his hardness throbbing against me as he moved his mouth over my skin, his tongue flicking everywhere, and all of me dissolving, wet, wanting him inside even as a voice screamed *no*, a voice that wept not just for us but for Sonny.

*What about Sonny?*

Yet I pulled his face to mine, my eyes open as he thrust and pushed and we arced against each other; and in one long aching moment it was over and we fell in pieces over the bed.

"Hugh?" My plea broke the rushing stillness. "What if Sonny'd — ?"

"Shhhh," he said, wrapping me in the blankets. "See what you do to me, Tessie? You know I adore you. Don't you."


Sonny came in around lunchtime, blue with cold. Wordlessly, I spread peanut butter on crackers and passed them to him. He dropped one and it stuck to the floor.

"That was stupid," I finally said, "going out without your jacket."

Nothing.

"Where'd you take off to, anyway?"

He licked peanut butter from his thumb.

"Wouldn't you like to know."

I squeezed the plastic jar so hard it dented.

"Sweetheart? Knock it off. That's a good way to catch pneumonia."

"Mom?" He gawked, his mouth full of cracker. "No one ever got sick from bein' cold." Then he pointed at the saltines. "I'll have more of those, while you're at it."

Hugh drew up a chair. "Don't talk to your ma like that." Yet his voice was contrite. "Guess I haven't been here much for you, have I, bud? Things've been rough, hey, Sonny? Well, they're gonna change," he promised, his eyes canted upwards, searching mine.

That afternoon while Hugh was up in the light, I dialled the house on Avenger, God only knows what for. The phone rang four or five times, then the machine picked up. "Can't take your call right now, I'm on the Haitian Vacation — or is it the Persian Excursion? Whatever, good buddies. Leave a message." I was all ready to discuss Sonny, but the brightness of that voice undid me.

"Charlie?" I blurted out after the beep. "I'm so sorry."

23

## MERCURY

Sonny ended up returning to school without a fight. "You can't sit around here all day," I'd finally convinced him, as bleakness washed inside me. Like the tides, the feeling would rise and fall.

"And what about Derek? You need your friends." It wasn't as though he'd never see them, sticking around Thrumcap. But that's how I made it sound, *either/or*, as his father would've said. "So long as the weather holds, no excuses."

Sonny's first week back the days turned balmy, as if someone had messed with the thermostat. The harbour stretched forever, flat and blue. The sun teased the earth and everything melted. Water dripped from the roof, a rhythm against the waves washing the rocks. In the woods birds sang; chickadees dotted the trees. Trails turned unexpectedly to mud.

As things thawed, and with Sonny gone, Hugh started stay-ing around. Spending less time in the tower, he returned to his old self. He wouldn't see a doctor, insisting that he was fine. The easier and more attentive he became, the more things drifted back to the way they'd been that summer, his attentions winding around me like a bandage over slathered ointment, till they worked under my skin again. Aided by the warmth of that quirky winter sun, they drew out any poisons.

Whether I wanted them to or not, I let them. It was easier this way. What were the options? I was defenceless. His presence pushed blue wool and beach stones out of my thoughts, and the shadows from the photos I'd seen. Out of my consciousness, anyway, if not my intuition. But I'd seen enough to know that like most things, love suffers growing pains. It couldn't have been easy for Hugh, either, having a child underfoot. Someone else's child, another guy's responsibility. Not every man would've taken two for one. And where would Sonny and I have gone, otherwise? Knocking on Joyce LeBlanc's door, or Sandi's, bearing cookies: *Remember me?*

With Sonny at school, Hugh would putter for a bit in the lantern, then devote the day to me. He stopped mentioning the band, and I didn't ask. He seemed happy just polishing glass, even though any time now some official might come for the key.

It got so mild we opened windows and lunched on the stoop with the radio playing, CBC voices hovering over the surf. We were kids with a ghetto blaster, except we listened to news, political panels. Talk talk talk: analysis. Once there was a debate over Charlie's helicopters — whether the government should mothball them. I went inside and fiddled with the knob until by some fluke the airwaves co-operated and the golden oldies station came in. Buddy Holly flooded the yard and Hugh put down his soup, taking my hands and swinging my arms in a jive.

It was on the tip of my tongue to ask, *Aren't you worried?* This, and the chestful of other questions I should've asked. At times they pressed like a growth. But I tilted my face towards the January sun, its fickle warmth shouting spring, and thought of love instead.

Thinking *love*, I put all fear and dread in a bottle and cast it into the sea. A grapefruit juice bottle, full of notes jotted on paper. Like a miniature jar in a raffle: pick a problem! I watched the current lift it, carry it before it sank. When it was out of sight I felt surprisingly better. There's something about writing things down; outside of you they lose their grip. They shrink to being no more and no less than scraps of paper in a leaky jar.

And there were other, more immediate things to fret about, like the weather. The prospect of the mild spell ending and winter howling down again, locking us in; weeks stretching by with Sonny moping at home. And the light, of course. I worried about the Coast Guard coming; then where would we be? Worse, though, was the worry of Hugh spending time up inside the lantern. I stopped thinking about Alice and the Mad Hatter, and thought instead of the article I'd seen when I was a kid, sixteen. *Life* magazine, a photo essay. About those Japanese people, their faces and bodies twisted, eyes like E.T.'s, all from eating poisoned fish. And I remembered what it had said about animals getting sick too. Cats going crazy and hurling themselves into the sea, dogs dying and crows falling from the sky.

After so many years, wouldn't the tower be steeped in vapour?

"It must be contaminated," I broached the subject once more, one of our mornings together. "Maybe the Coast Guard knows more than they're saying. Maybe they —"

"Look, I told you — it's just an excuse. Convenient. You watch, Willa. A year from now there won't be a manned light in Canada. It's so fucking predictable. A 'cost-cutting measure.'"

"I know, but —"

"What?" He rubbed my back, a slow, circular movement that made me feel like a gem being buffed. Shutting my eyes, I leaned closer, loosened up. The thought broke through of smooth stones, feathery ridges of paint. It caught me short. The image of Wayne pushed in, and without warning the questions I'd put to sea resurfaced.

"Hughie?"

Perhaps he felt me tighten. I drew an ocean breath, let it out bit by bit. Jetsam floated to my tongue, bobbing up.

"*What?*" His hand on my shoulder pensive, slow.

"Was Julie ... pregnant?" My heart thudded. His hand dropped. His look was a mix of surprise and frustration.

"What've you been snarfing? Jesus Murphy. You're the one after *me* to see a doctor. Willa, Willa, Willa."

Then he cupped my chin in his hands, the way I used to

cup Sonny's when he was small, to make him listen. Hugh's eyes were a bottomless blue.

"Sweetie? It was Wayne's, you know." He sniffed and drew the back of his hand across his nose, arching his brows. "Shit. Maybe you're right, maybe we should be making some plans. No telling what those bastards ..."

I waited, the hollowness inside me drifting, filling slowly as if with salt water, sinking.

"It wouldn't hurt for you to see a doctor. I mean, if there *is* a problem. The last guy," I said quietly. "What became of him?"

His hand climbed, kneading my shoulder. "Oh, Sykes? That was his name. He and his wife more or less shared things. Took the light out at Sambro. Job security. The one place they'll keep manned for a while yet."

"Couldn't we ... ?"

"Sambro?" He gave me the queerest look. "Christ, I don't think so. You'd get washed away. Nowhere for a kid, I can tell you."

"Maybe you could talk to someone." My voice was watery, remote. All I could think of was quicksilver: that gleam like a deadly grey sea.

"Sykes? Yeah, I guess." I knew from his tone that he wouldn't.

"I need to know where we'll be in six months," I said, closing my eyes. His breath warmed my cheek. I waited for him to edge away, but he stayed there, massaging my neck.

"Shhh," he said, the way I would've to Sonny. "It'll all come out in the wash, Tess. Till it does, no point stewing over it."

I nodded foolishly, glancing out at the wash, several days'

worth lifting like ghosts in that faux spring breeze. "You're right — there isn't." And I thought of that saying about gift horses; how you shouldn't look them in the mouth, whatever that meant.

Sonny's teacher used that expression his second week into the term, when I went to see her. He'd been doing so well — no complaints — that I felt suspicious. My visit was like insurance to see that things stayed that way.

"Don't borrow trouble," Hugh said, his tongue touching mine as we kissed before Sonny and I left for the boat. It was a chilly morning, still warm for January but with a rawness, the horizon a muddy pink.

I hitched a ride on the school bus, this time offering to pay. Sonny sat at the back, ignoring me. Every now and then his voice rose above the others discussing Luke Skywalker and *The Empire Strikes Back*.

The schoolyard was the usual wasteland, students milling around. Not a mom to be seen, though, not a single Sandi or Joyce. I squeezed past some kids huddled by the door, and found Sonny's classroom.

"Can I help you?" the teacher said sharply.

She shook my hand. "He's a great kid," she said. "Any worries I had are non-issues. If he was having problems, they've, um, cleared up." A heavy woman older than me, she studied me with her amber eyes, smiling faintly as she pulled out Sonny's math scribbler and handed it over. "Why don't you take it home, go through it with him. I'm sure you'll be pleased." The bell rang and I thanked her.

Passing Sonny in line, I gave him a thumbs up. This called for a treat, something besides tuna or fried bologna, the poor little monkey. Pizza, take-out. Then I imagined asking Wayne to deliver. Outside, the sky had gone white and the wind felt sharper. The air smelled tinny — a hint of snow? The phrase *great kid* rolling through me, I walked all the way back to the dock. The clock inside the Kwik Way only said ten twenty-two; time did funny things when you stopped to notice. Thrumcap was partly hidden by mist: a snow squall, I realized with dismay. Wayne's boat was tied up and his shed deserted. *Pepperoni and mushrooms*, the thought plagued me. The sign in the Kwik Way window advertised hot coffee, sandwiches. All You're Needs, it said.

The island faded in and out behind its greyish curtain, and I imagined Hugh stoking the fire, making coffee. Suddenly it seemed crazy to be marooned ashore. I pictured Hugh grinding the beans. Pressing the grinder's button the way he pressed the keys on his sax, owning it without thinking about it. Such a small thing, yet weren't our lives compilations of tiny details? Tinier than inchworms inching over summer leaves, ending up on someone's shirt and landing miles, or feet, from the tree. You could travel and not get far.

A funnel slid past in the harbour, an ominous, black fin. I imagined the submarine under the surface, the crew like krill inside a whale. A chill settled under my collarbones at the roar, hemmed in by clouds, of the chopper tracking it. Desperate to be somewhere — anywhere — I walked up to Reenie's and rattled the door. Wayne had been up and alert a couple of hours before; with any luck he'd take me across before the snow got bad. With any luck, Sonny could stay at Derek's.

"C'mon in," Wayne hollered from the kitchen. It sounded like he'd been drinking. I stepped inside, steeling myself. He was sitting at the table, slumped there with no shirt on. The sink was heaped with dishes. One of Reenie's decorations hung cockeyed over the window, clutter everywhere. Hugh had mentioned her taking a trip with some girlfriends from the dance.

My eyes darted over the mess. "Heard from Reenie?"

"She's in town now," he slurred. The anchor moved as he scratched his chest. "Could you do me a favour?" He was having trouble standing up. "Pass me that envelope — up there, on the fridge."

I went to give it to him, but he grabbed my hand, placing it on his belly. His eyes rolled. "I'm starvin'," he said. There was spit at the corners of his mouth. He squeezed my fingers till they hurt. "Hughie's one lucky bastard."

Heaving himself up, he wrenched my arm, breathing in my ear. "He's a good buddy, Hugh. Owes me, though. Good buddies share, don't you think, Willa? He don't need to know."

As I jerked back, Reenie's name popped out, as if she were near.

"Shut up about her." His hand closed on my wrist. "The two of 'em, they don't need to know nothing. I've been watching you, don't say you never noticed. I seen you looking, too."

Nausea rose inside, and a feeling that lifted and swung me above his reach. He reeled, flopping down as I peeled his fingers away. My other hand tightened around the envelope. *You fucking pervert.* I was Tweety Bird surveying Sylvester, dizzy from my perch.

"Tell me about her," I said.

"Reenie?" he spat. "She always was a jealous bitch."

"The girl in the picture," I heard myself say. "Julie."

His eyes froze over. "Don't be sticking your fuckin' nose ... What a dick, Hughie. Hookin' up with the likes of you. Any woman that'd take her kid and —"

"I've seen them." My voice quavered. "The pictures."

His hair seemed to shrink off his forehead. "You ain't seen shit."

The cage tilted; suddenly I wasn't so high up. "Who took them? Reenie?"

He licked his lip. "You stunned bitch." Drool slid down his chin. "I know you want it. Hughie on the prowl again? First time I seen you, I —" His chest jiggled as he laughed.

The smartest thing would've been to fly outside — steal his boat if I had to. But numbness pinned me. I was caught, my head in his mouth.

"Tell me," a voice dared, a voice barely mine.

"What, an' crap out on a buddy? I don't think so."

"Maybe when you're sober." My words mixed with a whirr, the furnace coming on.

Outside, it was snowing like crazy, covering the gravel. I felt Wayne's envelope half up my sleeve; stunned, I'd held onto it. The return address was a law firm downtown, the letter a diversion while I pondered what to do, guzzling Kwik Way coffee. An attorney advised Wayne of a legal separation; Reenie's address was there, an apartment number, a street near the bridge.

I could still feel his grip, the scratchy warmth of his skin. Scumbag. *Liar.*

There was a small fleet tied up at the government wharf. I walked over to some men baiting traps. What weather to be going out in; you wondered who set the seasons. I shouted down to a grizzled fellow in a Maple Leafs cap and eventually he scowled up.

"What's your problem, honey?"

"I'd be happy to pay —"

The younger guy in the boat nodded towards the eco-shed. "Buddy there runs a ferry, not us."

"S'pose we could run ya out," said the older one. "This once. Not far, is it."

*Never look a gift horse ...* Taking the man's hand, I climbed down.

"Seen you before, haven't I?" he said, once we'd gotten a ways out. "You're part of that outfit there with buddy, Mr. Ecologize? One of them hippies. Jeez, you folks'd live in hollow trees if you could."

The younger one worked away as if the old guy was talking to the air. The boat stank of engine oil. The chop rocked my stomach. You could barely see Thrumcap for snow. Maybe he was just being friendly, but the man kept staring, flakes sticking to his lashes. It made me squirm.

"I know," he said, as the dock's outline slid into sight, "you're the little one that was expectin'. How's the kid, then? Good thing youse are out here so's the rest of us can't hear the squallin'. Lord Jesus! Like Joel here, eh? Miserable little son of a bitch he was. Hadda leave home to get away from the crying, no friggin' lie."

The snow swirled, making it hard to see. For a minute it was like being in a plane: nowhere. The lump in my throat grew as we finally docked.

"Thanks for the ride." I pushed money at him; he pushed it back.

"Watch yourself," he muttered as I scrambled out, and the son mumbled, "He don't mean the ladder."

As I waved, they were already putting out into that wrinkled, steely grey.

Snow shrouded the woods, covering my tracks. It held in every sound and smell — the sharpness of spruce gum and the odour from the refinery made almost solid. I wasn't dressed for it. Bolts of white capped my head and shoulders, weighing the branches, plummeting without sound. Nothing stirred, except for the foghorn. Its groan was a trail of pebbles luring me, snowblind. It made me think of warmth. The kitchen fire, tea. A box of Bugles I'd been hiding from Sonny. Reaching the pond and the open, slanting snow, suddenly I craved salt, imagined Hugh and me devouring the snack. The silence following the crumbs.

Wayne slid back into my thoughts; how had Reenie kept from picking up a knife?

Twice I stopped to spit into the wiry, white bushes, the Kwik Way coffee like acid inside me. Thirsty, I stuck out my tongue. Snow burned my eyelids. *If I stopped and lay down, who would notice, or mind?* Sonny, perhaps. Imagining myself melting in spring, a wet sheen on the ground, I thought of Hugh and replayed what'd happened. *If I lay in the snow ...* How foolish, though. Not like I'd gone to Wayne's naked, wrapped in cellophane, as Sandi and her friends said they did to please their husbands. "That'd give him paws." "My luck, he'd call the guys in white suits, take a permanent Haitian Vacation." Their voices seemed to screech through the snowy branches, but it was only the container pier, its cranes.

I pictured the cover of a *Cosmo* magazine: *50 ways to please your lover! Keep him coming!* Then thought of that Paul Simon song about fifty ways to leave your lover. *Fifty?* Husbands were different; with Charlie there'd been only one. How many ways were there for Reenie? Wayne's face mooned me. As I reached the tundra of beach the foghorn jeered: *He don't need to know.*

The falling snow shushed the waves. At the water's edge I jammed my finger down my throat and brought up coffee.

Hugh was watching for me. "Where've you been?" He pulled me inside, helped me out of my sweater. Snow left pools on the floor. I waited for him to say he'd been worried. "Wouldn't wanna be out driving anywhere," he said, and my stomach churned as I thought of Sonny.

He poured tea and set what was left of the Bugles on the table. "Surprised Wayne'd go out in this. Should've asked him to stay. With Reenie out of the pitcher he's got nothin' but time."

*Pic-ture*, I wanted to snarl, rubbing my hands together. Almost purple, they ached as they thawed. Tell him, I thought. *Tell.*

He creaked back in his chair, as glad as anyone to be inside.

"Wayne was in no shape —" My teeth chattered. "He was —"

"Poor bugger. Ever since Reenie took off ... fuck. Can't blame the guy. I mean, without Reen ..."

I licked orangey salt off my fingers and laced them around my cup. Hugh kept talking. His voice doodled around me, buzzing off the walls and whitened panes. All about Wayne and Reenie, me and Sonny ... it made little sense.

The tips of my fingers were wizened teardrops.

"Hugh," my voice leapt, still frozen, and he went quiet. "He tried ... he came on to me." The words were a fish out of a lake. Dated, as if from a bad script.

Hugh looked at me, then reddened, his face changing.

"Oh?" he said in the tone he used totting up Scrabble points. *Double word score; sweetie, why not go for triple?* "You must've done something, then." That scorekeeper's voice, so matter-of-fact it took a second to register. "You must've waved some bait."

"*What?* You honestly think —"

"Wayne's not a bad looking guy."

I choked, inhaling tea; he was kidding, right? "If you like fat drunks with disgusting —"

He didn't crack a smile.

"Look. It, it wasn't ... something I expected."

His gaze was like the tower's beam. "What did you expect, then?"

"A ride, as usual. That's all." My brain seemed to float to the ceiling, as if the rest of the room were rocking, shifting.

"I'll bet. Was it good?"

Tea stung my throat; heat buzzed in my ears. *I'm dreaming; that's all it is, a dream. Maybe I'd dreamed Wayne, too.*

But he persisted. "The ride, was it good?" It was like being frozen then dropped into a scalding tub.

"Stop," I bleated.

His eyes were slate. He rose slowly, as if minding his step, and without a word put on his coat. The dog whined at his heels, the storm door thudding behind him.

## DECLINATION

The snow was so thick now you could hardly see out. I folded the Bugles box and pushed it into the fire, then, mustering a sweaty calm, phoned the school and asked for Sonny. The secretary balked at first. "Normally we don't take calls to students."

I squeezed the receiver, breathing. "This is, um, *not* normal."

"Well," she sniffed, "it's chaos here, with the storm. We're looking at noon dismissal."

"Please — he'll have to arrange something."

"Who's speaking? A guardian, or caregiver?"

"His mother."

I could hear her sigh. Outside, the wind howled at the eaves. The snow blew at a crazy slant past the panes and the sound was like insects hitting them.

"Well. Just this once," the woman relented. "In future you should sort things out with your child in advance." There was a clunk as she put down the receiver.

Feeling sick, I imagined Sonny leaving his desk and ambling to the office phone. He took forever, the silence as I waited laced with that pinging noise. It got louder as the snow turned transparent.

"Hullo?" His voice seemed thin and nervous.

"Sonny?" He always sounded younger on the phone. Picturing his face, its spray of freckles, I ached to put my arms around him and hug him till he hugged me back.

"How come you're phoning?"

I hesitated, everything flooding in. Hugh, the snow and ... "The weather outside is ... frightful." I tried my best to sound chipper. His breathing, the sleet beating the glass, a crackle on the line — everything seemed filtered through thick cotton.

"I'm goin' to Derek's after school. He already asked. It's okay."

A buzzer sounded in the background and a high-pitched chirring — that noise of kids, like a zillion birds.

"You don't even have a toothbrush —"

"Mom. It don't matter."

"Doesn't."

"Whatever."

"That line's for emergencies, dear. Someone might be try-ing to call," Ms. Officious chimed behind him.

"Mom, I hafta —"

"Sonny?"

"What?"

"Be good now, won't you."

"Yup."

"Sonny?"

"WHAT?"

"Love you."

"Yup."

"Call me when you get to Derek's?"

Then he hung up.

Sometime in the black between dusk and daylight, Hugh returned. I was lying there listening to the wind driving rain when he crawled into bed. He'd been drinking. I could smell it. He stretched out beside me, pulling at the blankets.

"I'm sorry Willa. You don't fuckin' know how sorry. I'm a shit," he breathed.

I shrank away, but part of me wanted to sing out, *we're all shits*.

He curled closer, his eyes shut, moving under the lids. "You don't deserve it, Willa. You don't deserve this shit. I can't believe Wayne did that to you. I can't fuckin' believe what an asshole ..."

*Wars had started over less*, I thought.

"He's already stepped in once — once too many. The little prick."

"Hardly little," I blurted out, hugging myself.

"What d'ya mean?" But his voice was just a murmur. Pressing his face to my shoulder, he stroked my side. His clothes were damp and smelled like wet dog. "Promise, sweetie," he whispered slowly. "I'll kill him if he tries that again."

I caught his hand, let it fall. "That's what you say."

"Willa. Without you, I'm —"

"Toast? *Merde?*" I thought of Sonny and Derek upstairs hurling insults, boys having fun. Bonding. *Worthless piece of crap*, one had called the other. A giddy despair filled me, a quiet rage. "Piss, poop, crap, dung."

He opened an eye, winced as if nursing a wound, then took my hand and kissed it. His lips were cold as the ocean. "Without you I'm lost. A fuckin' dinghy without a rudder." He grinned a grin not much different from Sonny's. That grin was my undoing.

Something inside me dissolved. "How'd you get home, anyway, this time of night? Good old Wayne. Did he get funny with you in the boat? Get fresh," I mimicked, almost choking. "Put the moves on, the make. Try to toast a weenie, for God's sake!" I thought of that belly, that tattoo. My throat felt parched. My voice rose, sputtering. "Wanna hear a joke? Derek's, to Sonny: How'd the Dairy Queen get pregnant?"

Hugh looked baffled, then scared. His hand lay on my stomach.

"Burger King forgot to wrap his weenie."

Like a car slow to turn over, he laughed, his eyes strangely lit.

"Thought you weren't a drinker," I prodded, and his face went like sand with the moisture drawn out of it.

"Once, maybe." There was a dullness about him. "Not anymore."

"Okay." But my voice was foam riding a wave. "I need you to tell me. I have to know. What did you do to Julie?"

He held my hand so tightly it hurt, his sleeve dampening my wrist.

"You have to believe me, Tess. *I* didn't do anything. It wasn't me."

My need to believe him was an undertow, a suck and pull dragging me out.

"All right." I came up for air. "Then tell me, Hughie. Tell me where you've been."

He kissed me, his mouth sour. He lay back, sighing, a sound that pushed everything from the room. "I can't. What you don't know won't hurt you, Tess. Trust me, all right?" Then he slid under the covers, kissing my navel. "'Pussycat, pussycat, where have you been? I've been to London to visit the Queen.'"

We woke to ice: snow transformed to glass. It creaked from the clothesline. Hugh used a pickaxe to clear the step, the yard a silver glare as if the sea had spilled in and solidified. The Ice Age following the Flood. The hills on the far shore were crystal, too, split from us by a belt of sparkling blue. Even the wind seemed frozen, caught; the world struck with brilliance as if everything had been splashed with mercury. The roads would be treacherous; I imagined Sonny slip-sliding with Derek to school.

Hugh hacked out a path to the lighthouse, then went back to bed. He'd been up just after dawn, wretching. Grudgingly I offered toast, tea. He yanked the covers over his head.

There was an inch of vodka left in the bottle up in the lantern. The sun beamed through the salted panes and the quicksilver glinted, a huge silver bracelet, the giant lens turning in it like a fist. Picking up Hugh's binoculars, I trained them on the sea. A pair of ships sat on the horizon, a helicopter darting between them, like a needle darning them together, gunboat grey melded with chicory sky. Turning the binoculars, I peeked through the wrong end; everything foreshortened, the military manoeuvres squeezed from view, disappointing. Righting the glasses, I looked again. Already the ships had moved, shrinking against the competing sea. I took the bottle outside and emptied it on a rock. The bright trickle melted the ice as if Oreo had passed, lifting his leg.

By noon the sun had turned everything liquid, with the kissing sound of melt and things coming unstuck.

Hugh slept.

I tried calling Derek's. There was nobody there. "Have a good one," the message machine trilled.

At one-thirty I dialled Wayne's, one of the hardest things I've ever done, harder than calling for Charlie. While the phone rang, I remembered something Charlie had told me once, he and his crew picking up a defector, a Romanian stowaway who'd gone overboard into the harbour. The man spat like a rabid cat till they'd wrapped him in a blanket and calmed him enough to drink a coffee. The guy had cried and kissed their hands. Best part of the job, Charlie had said, handling the unexpected. Though things swung both ways.

"Yup?" Wayne sounded the same as ever. "Whassup?" he blurted out, then, "Who is this?"

*Apologize, you piece of crap.* "Willa."

"Oh. Yeah." There was a heavy pause. Then, "How's she goin'?" Not a hint of remorse. Possibly he didn't remember; could he say I made it up? I thought of Julie and the photographs. Pantyhose! A sick amazement held me; maybe the guy was to be pitied. It was all I could do to be civil.

"Alex's bus'll be there by three."

"Like — yeah?"

Another deadly pause.

"Can you ... would you, um, get me first?"

"Put Hughie on."

"Hugh's in bed."

"Wha's his problem?" He cleared his throat. "You poisonin' him or what?"

*Asshole.* "Look. Can you get me first?"

"Huh? Listen," his voice slurred low, "dunno what you're so uptight about. I ain't no fruit, if that's what you're scared of." His laugh was a bark. "Well, that's it, then," he said, as if *he'd* called me. "No problem wit' Sonny. I'll be waitin' for him."

From the next room came the creak of Hugh turning over.


Visualize. Isn't that what we're supposed to do? Picture something as we want it. An orange, for instance. Perfectly round, dimpled, whole. The colour of the sun meeting the horizon.

If we believe it, so it is — or might be.

I set myself on a course of tidying then. *Re-prioritizing*, as Charlie would've said. The importance of tiny things: shelves clear of greasy stains. Baking soda in the fridge. Dust-free treasures in Sonny's window. I scanned his room for other details: clues as to his happiness — or misery — but it was a map with no key.

The god of small things ruled the clock, folding everything inside a tissue of safety, and almost before I knew it Oreo yipped and Sonny was bursting through the door.

"You okay?" Dropping everything, I grabbed for his waist. He batted my arms away.

"Like, yeah? Why wouldn't I be?"

He smelled like someone else's house. Fried food and carpet. Oreo licked him all over, then reared back, barking.

"Freakin' dog. Derek has a hamster. Lucky bugger."

I stroked Oreo's snout. "There's a boy. Watchdog." Never mind that Oreo would've licked anyone breaking in, and wagged his tail. But suddenly I thought of intruders: men at night, rowing ashore from ships; climbing the shingle, surrounding us ... It was an idle fear, yet comprehending this meant believing it even as my weight shifted over loose stones — the whole world shifting in ways I wished it wouldn't.

"Mom? What's for supper?"

"Gimme a second, I'll figure it out." In my heart perhaps I was plotting. Visualizing. A lifeboat landing, rescuers with oars. *Heave ho. All aboard. ROW!*

But the detail god stepped in again. Easier to plot this way, like sliding a knife through cheese. Seeing the bubbles in a piece of bread. The things you glimpse through the bottom of a glass, which you're paralyzed to turn right side up.

Sonny's birthday crept up like a thief. "When is it, again?" Hugh asked five times if he asked once. "Should we plan something?"

To steady myself, I'd visualized cosmic bowling, pizza; kids roaming a black-lit bowling alley, lobbing balls into the wrong lanes, neon squiggles across faces.

*A shark derby? Kayaking through ice floes? A picnic!* I thought. Landing en masse on Devils, Sonny and a horde of boys scaling the icy shingle, tailing Hugh and his sax. I imagined wailing notes as the kids fell into the sea like mice. Hugh's singsong as he hauled them out, tramping over the cloven prints in the sand to safety. The sand itself glittery-black as ground coal. Hence the island's name.

Keeping a light meant harbouring things: superstition. Criminals, ghosts. Like the ones on Hangman's Beach, deserters hung out to dry. But the only moans and groans lately came from the saxophone. Wailing riffs Hugh played after dark; stitches of tunes picked up and dropped. He'd gotten out of practice. It happened in winter. The isolation, he said.

I quit coaxing him to see a doctor. He couldn't have anyway, once the weather closed in again. In the torpor of mid-January, the prospect of the birthday drifted and beached, washing up in my dreams. Night after night Sonny marched across the flat, grey tabletop of Devils to the side where waves overtook land, and all was ice.

One day Wayne had mail for him. It was from Calgary, our forwarding address scratched in Charlie's hand. A card "for Alexander" with a cowboy on it and a twenty-dollar bill inside. It was signed, Sharla & Howard (Grampa), with a note from my father: *Get your mum to bring you out sometime. Like to see you before you're all grown up!*

Like a tree or a hedge?

Sonny added the money to his stash, and out of the blue confided how he'd got that mark on his neck months before. A girl had done it, he said after his bath. A grade six.

He left the water for me to drain. Wiping up wet footprints, I imagined the glow from the window being picked up by a passing ship, and myself on a flutter board out there, knocking against the rocks. Kicking.

Following more footprints to his room, I ambushed him. "So. This girl —"

"This girl *who?*"

"What was she trying to do?"

He snapped a piece of yellow rope at Oreo. A whip. "She tried to kiss me."

"And? Did she have any luck?"

His face went pink.

"Then what did she do?"

He shrugged his shoulders to his ears, glaring. That look, like Charlie's, as if a target had popped up, a snare; gears were about to engage.

His face and ears glowed red. "Nothing, okay?"

I slunk downstairs and he followed. Hugh had made tea and there were enough cookies for us each to have one. We were almost out of groceries but for some tins, things nobody would eat, like cocktail wieners. *Baby birds*, Sonny called them.

"Who's the card from?" Hugh wanted to know.

But Sonny piped up, "A scavenger hunt! That's what I want. You could bury things."

"Good luck," Hugh said. After a round of freeze, thaw, and freeze again, the ground was rock-hard, bare.

"Why can't it be in spring?" Sonny complained. It was what Charlie had said when I was pregnant, as if Sonny's arrival were up to me.

During these short dark days it was hard not to feel stuck, harder still to summon the memory of green without feeling disconnected, a deep and distant longing. That inchworm hue of fiddleheads and the spruce buds Hugh had picked, tossed, and caught like peanuts. "Save you from scurvy!" He'd put one in my mouth; I'd spit it out. The least of my worries, scurvy. But I'd thought of Sonny who reviled things green.

At bedtime Hugh conceded, "You could do a scavenger hunt if we had snow."

Weariness overtook me; all I wanted was sleep. "But you'd need prizes. Ones worth digging for. And a pack of kids, for competition."

He traced my nipple with his finger, and I covered myself. He looked away — disgusted? "It's the hunt that counts. Alex could use the lesson."

I rolled over, studying an icicle at the window. In the light's flash it gleamed like a blade. The mattress jiggled as he coughed, a thickness in his throat.

The night before Sonny's birthday Hugh took off, and while he was gone someone called. "We're s'posed to meet," the guy said, impatient. "I've been waiting at the dock."

"About a gig, is it?" I could hear him squeezing the receiver.

"You tell him Darrell called. Got his stuff. And tell him, he stands me up again, he'll be swimming."

Before I could get a number, he hung up.

"What's your problem?" Sonny asked when I stepped outside to watch for Hugh. Sprayed with stars, the night was freezing, the city a distant twinkle — so distant we could've been the only ones alive. Giving up, I went and got into my nightie, pulling on a sweater over top.

Hugh returned just after Sonny went to bed. He came in smelling of the cold, his eyes shiny. In this world of ice, the sight of him snatched my breath. There was always the hope of a melt even as I relished solidity; my love dangled in the possibility of everything being liquid.

"All clear?" he said, puffing a little. "Alex isn't still up?" He went back outside, then trundled in some gear — a black bag shaped like an elephant gun, and a dusty amplifier. It smelled like an ashtray.

"Shh!" He put his fingers to my mouth. "It's supposed to be a surprise. He said that's what he wanted, remember? That shit about turning ten, or whatever."

He unzipped the bag and slid out a guitar. It was thin and horned, the colours of a Doberman pinscher. Speechless, I forgot about the phone call, the voice on the other end. A draft travelled up my legs as I moved my feet trying to keep warm.

"Oh, Hugh. It's ... he'll ..."

"What? He won't like it?"

The draft climbed through my innards. "He can't play a note!"

"Yet."

"The cost, though," I fretted. Birthdays for us had been Lego and Duncan Hines. When I was small, Barbies — bought by Dad — and grocery store cake.

"Look, it's no big deal. Got it off a buddy of Wayne's. He just wanted to unload it."

He knelt and plugged everything in. The light on the amp blinked, a tiny red eye. Then he hit the strings with a crash like a roof collapsing. I stifled a shriek of laughter.

"For shit sake, Tess." He glared. "Let me get it outta here before he sees."

I helped lug the gear to the lighthouse. "He'll be over the moon," I murmured, tugging on Hugh's arm. But he gave me a look as if I'd spoken in another tongue.

From somewhere overhead we caught the boom of a passing jet. I thought of Charlie, how, if he'd sent anything, it was late and I'd need to go all out, making up for it with the cake. Chocolate, though it'd be a challenge baking one in the

woodstove. A giant hockey puck is what I imagined: a theme.
Except Sonny hated sports.

25

## PILOTS

After breakfast, Hugh tied a bandana over Sonny's eyes and the three of us trooped to the lighthouse. A little extreme, though I didn't say anything. Climbing those steep, slippery stairs, Sonny didn't complain. He was a good sport.

"You won't believe it, sweetie," I whispered into his ear, steering him by the shoulder. At the top, he yanked off the blindfold, blinking in the sun rippling off the water. His face looked pale, almost bluish like skimmed milk. Spying the gig bag, he whipped down the zipper and pulled out the guitar, almost dinging the light's huge lens. Hugh winced.

"Holy crap!" Sonny kept saying. "Wait'll I tell Derek."

"Come here and I'll show you a G chord," Hugh said, but Sonny ignored him. He was kneeling by the juiceless amp, twisting knobs then frantically strumming. His fingers thudded the strings like a clawless cat picking a screen, not remotely musical.

"After school, Sonny," I cut in. "Maybe Hugh'll give you a lesson then."

The idea of a party had fizzled; the feeling of being stranded out here, caught in an icy limbo, had that effect. Plans became pilot whales, dark shapes that surfaced and dove, and, if they did come ashore, died out of the water.

"I wanted a go-kart party," was Sonny's first comment when I met him coming home that afternoon. Wayne didn't bat an eye, but that wasn't unusual. He no longer spoke on our crossings, but he seemed to be keeping score. I could see him calculating Hughie's tab.

The cake was cooling on top of the fridge.

"*Derek's* mother took him and all the grade fives go-karting."

"The whole class?" I rolled my eyes. "Where were you, then? Ah, Sonny." I sighed, wiping down his lunch bag.

Hugh had the gear plugged into the outlet for the toaster and was noodling around on the guitar, bending and stretching notes in a tune I recognized. Johnny Cash, "Ring of Fire." He glanced up at Sonny, a guarded look in his eyes as his fingers curled over the strings.

"What birthday is this, again? You won't learn to play by bitching."

I looked at him.

"Complaining. When we were kids," he said, "you got a swat on the arse for each year."

He took a swing at Sonny. Dodging it, Sonny grabbed the guitar, aiming it like a rifle. He blushed, with the same look as when Charlie had got him the bike. The look I'd had taking Sonny home from the hospital all those years before. Joyful but scared, grateful but not at all sure what to do with the gift. It was then, maybe more than at any other time, that I missed having a mother.

An expression of shame — guilt? — crossed Sonny's face. Hugh yanked the cord from the outlet.

"Fine, then. My mistake, kiddo. Thought you'd at least *act* interested."

I put my hand on Hugh's wrist. His eyes had a shadowy look.

"I'm just saying. Jesus. I went to some effort here, Alex. Next time I'll think twice."

I dug Sonny hard in the ribs, and he blushed a deeper pink. Hugh's mouth was a flat line.

"C-can you teach me 'Jeremiah Was a Bullfrog'?"

"Sonny," I laughed nervously, "where'd you ever hear that?"

"Derek's," he said, gazing from me to Hugh. "His mom sings it."

"O-kay." I waited for Hugh to laugh. Instead, he slouched away, and next we heard him in the bedroom opening drawers. For one dizzy moment my heart bottomed.

Sonny rammed candles into the cake.

"You could've said thank you," I muttered.

He stared back, his bottom lip pushed out. The candles were burned down, all I'd found stashed at the back of the cupboard. At least there were enough, with four spares: fourteen in all, mostly pink. Saved from some other birthday, someone else's cake. Someone we'd never know and likely wouldn't meet. A girl, a teenager, I imagined, with Patty Duke hair and a miniskirt. I pictured somebody sticking those candles, new, into a pink cake. Licking icing off her chapped fingers: a mother. Lighting the candles then carrying the cake across the darkened kitchen; people singing, *How o-old are youuuuu?* A swat for every year. A big, fat swat across the butt. I thought again of my mother and a time so faint maybe it hadn't even happened. A time with no swats but coins baked in a cake — dimes wrapped in wax paper — and candles. Three or four. The present was a baby doll with a tiny hole in her lips for a bottle, another tiny one to pee out of. Sonny was hunched over the guitar, glowering at the strings. I squeezed his shoulder.

"I'm sorry, darling." Not for a second did I think it was enough.

He was on his third slice of cake when the phone rang. After a crackly pause, a voice asked for him, just as faint, and disembodied.

"Charlie?"

Another, brittle pause.

"Put my boy on, would you." There was a breaking sound like foil being crumpled.

"Come back on after. I want to ... there's something I've got to say."

*Saaaaayyyyyy*, the word echoed with squirrelly feedback. Another pause.

"How are you, anyway?"

"All right," I murmured, thrusting the phone at Sonny.

Hugh was licking chocolate from his thumb, about to cut himself more cake. He gazed up at me, haunted.

"Yup ... Yeah, sure ... Uh-huh. Okay ... Not bad. Sucks ... You too. Yeah, okay ... *Okay!*" Sonny mumbled, his lips pressed to the receiver. He kept turning his back, then every few seconds glancing over at me with this funny look, as if checking to see if his answers added up.

"His dad," I whispered to Hugh, my throat tightening. The blood rose to my cheeks. Then Sonny handed me the phone.

"Your turn." His voice was bright with hope.

"Charlie," I said, avoiding Hugh's gaze. Forcing myself to sound calm, measured, though my heart was pounding. My eyes roved, then flicked away. There was a clatter as Hugh dropped the knife.

"Willa." A windy sound came over the line, like dry leaves shifting.

"Good of you to call." I couldn't keep sarcasm from creeping in. "Where are you?"

"Kuwait; some sort of —" the line crackled. "— the blessed land of sand." He let out a parched little laugh and sniffed. "I can't stand this," he said, and I supposed he meant the desert. I thought of the heat, and Sonny's need for a parka. This seemed as good a time as any to raise it.

"Now, about Sonny — there's things he could use," I began, remembering boots, jeans. "You should see, he'll soon be taller than —"

"I miss you," he interrupted, and there was a crackling silence.

Hugh stared from the table. In the yellow light his face was pale and there was chocolate on his mouth.

*Me too*, part of me wanted to say, cupping the receiver.

"Well," Charlie's voice faded in and out. "So long then. Oh, and the cheque's in the mail."

If he said goodbye, it got lost. A piercing zing split the air. Dangling the guitar by its neck, Hugh raked out another crashing chord before shoving it at Sonny. Sonny chewed his lip, his hand freezing over the fret board.


The guitar ended up hardly leaving its case. It could've been a Lego man forgotten under the bed. God knows, with winter locking down there was loads of time to practise. Once or twice, nights when you couldn't see the breakwater for blowing snow, Hugh got out the sax and tried getting Sonny to play along. There was no predicting. Curled over Sonny's shoulder, Hugh showed him chords, his fingers guiding Sonny's on the frets.

"Try this," he said, running through some old Zeppelin, "Stairway to Heaven" or "The Immigrant Song," things my brother and I listened to as teens in the basement. Either the songs were too hard, or Sonny didn't like them.

"Show me some Wham! 'Wake Me Up Before You Go-Go'."

Hugh rolled his eyes. Then, to please us maybe, Sonny picked out a jingle from the radio.

"Not bad." But then Hugh disappeared to the bedroom. We sat there in the kitchen, Sonny and I, listening to notes through the wall as he blew something on the sax, no competition against the wind and the foghorn. Snow worked like a megaphone, or a blanket pinning the noise close to the rocks and the pitching swells. We felt it rattle the floorboards, watched it shake the dishes. Hugh's music was no match at all.

Maybe it was the cold, the boredom, but he played less and less, and when he did he barely moved his body; forget that wrestling dance. It was as if he'd fallen out with the sax; as if he'd won, and it had given up. Like someone he'd grown tired of.

With a sickening tug I thought of Julie; imagined myself picking up the phone and spilling my suspicions. But love — that icy inertia — prevented me. Who'd have believed? He's not right, I'd have explained. But who would've listened? He's suffering, and doesn't know it. But what then? It was like walking the island's edge backwards with no choice but to fall or leap off. An avalanche of ocean flooding over as I sank, filling every cavity with its freezing effervescence. Burying me alive.

The first week of February it snowed every day, not just dustings, but a couple of feet. School got cancelled five days straight. Drifts piled so high against the doors that one morning we coaxed Sonny to climb out a window and shovel off the stoop. Then Hugh went out and tunnelled paths to the shed and the lighthouse.

I tried to cut a pathway to the front door.

"What for?" Hugh hollered from the angled shade of the house, as the clouds cleared temporarily and the sun sparkled down. The snow-covered boulders made me think of the Rockies set against dazzling sky; the delineation of land and sea as crisp as a blue and white flag, not a shade in between.

I stood my shovel in the snow and flopped onto my back, moving my arms and legs, grinning at the sun. Its brilliance made my head ache. "Sonny?" I yelled. *Come make an angel,* a child voice urged inside me. Hugh's shouts, Sonny's laughter sifted from around back. The dog's yapping. *Ka-POW! Geronimoooo. Suckerrr.*

Wading through waist-high drifts, I tried rolling a ball for a snowman, without any luck. The snow was so powdery it squeaked.

The barking rose as I pushed to the back of the house. Hugh was crouching by the porch, a mitt over his eye. Oreo yapped even harder when he saw me. Sonny skulked by the shed.

"Nearly took my fucking eye out," Hugh muttered as I peeled his hand away. The skin was pink with the start of a bruise.

"Sonny!" I screamed. But he disappeared behind the shed then clambered towards the boulders.

Oreo flicked snow with his snout, nipping at the sparkles. His tail was a plume.

"Sonny!" I yelled again, setting off more barking.

Paying no attention, Sonny started climbing the boulders, sliding into crevices.

"Get back here!" But it was no use.

Hugh's eye began to swell. I pressed a handful of snow to it.

"I'm okay." He beat snow from his mitts. "Why don't you go on in and put some coffee on? That'd be nice, wouldn't it? I'll be in in a bit."

"God, Hugh, I'm sorry ... I'm —"

"Not your fault," he cut me off. His eye looked like a boxer's and his toque had ridden up, perched now on top of his head. Awful, but his appearance made me want to laugh.

"Really, Hugh, I know he didn't mean to. Sonny wouldn't —"

"That kid of yours is a piece of work." He smiled saying it, but his tone stung me. Pushing down my scarf, I looked at him.

"Sonny?" I bellowed. "Mind those rocks! One slip and —"

"Doesn't know his own strength," Hugh said through his teeth, still smiling. His eyes the same spitting blue as the water. "Tea'd be just as good — whatever." He stumbled, reaching around to goose me.

He came inside a little while later, stomping snow into the porch. I spooned the last of the coffee into the filter; he shook in salt. His cheeks were rosy, the eye flaming now. His breath smelled metallic.

"Where's Sonny?" I said over my shoulder. "Not on the rocks, I hope."

"Nah."

"Did you get him back?" Trying to make light of it.

"Huh?" He winced. "Oh yeah."

Oreo was still yapping out there.

"Quit teasing the dog," I muttered under my breath, pouring the water.

Hugh poked a split of wood into the fire and went to change. I hadn't had a chance to do likewise, and the knees of my jeans were stinging wet. Squatting by the oven door, I warmed myself while the coffee dripped, then put on a couple of eggs and tuned in the radio, waiting for them to boil.

Oreo's barking got louder. Maybe there was a ship coming in, or he'd spotted a whale. As I went to the window, there was a tinkling, a chime of icicles breaking. Glass. Moving to the porch, I glimpsed a hand poking from the shed window, the top of Sonny's Canucks toque.

Wobbling into my boots, I ran outside. The wind bit through my sweater, the yard stretching like a field. Closer, I saw blood — Sonny's hand reaching through the shattered pane, groping for the padlock. His pale wrist, the spikes of glass glinting blue. Everything dazzled — the sun blazing off whiteness and the sparkling crush of sea and a little spill of red on the snow. For a split second I lost myself, falling backwards, breathing salt. Then, as if it were somebody else stumbling up, I called his name. His face was pale and frightened; his hat kept slipping over his eyes. The key — it took a second to realize — was there in the lock. It turned without a hitch and as the door swung to, Sonny fell outside. His nose was running, his breath coming in jerky sobs as he sucked at his hand, at the gash below his thumb. His mouth looked red. Dripping to the snow the blood was as bright as the lantern.

Sonny's sobs turned to whimpers. "It stank in there, Mom! Like, like — fish. Like an outhouse. It was so — dark. Dark as a hole. I hate him. The *fucker.*"

My *watch your mouth* leapt idiotically, fizzled. Tears jiggled from his lashes. Something inside me stiffened, as if enfolding a lump of shale.

"He tried to bust my arm. He did! Mom! He grabbed me, like *this.* Shoved me against the wall. He tried to kill me, he did!" It tumbled out, his voice rising. "He's — such — a — fucking — asshole!"

"Sonny!"

"He could've, he *could've* busted my arm."

I got him into the kitchen, ran his hand under the tap. The water ran pink. I glimpsed, or thought I did, the paleness of bone. Grabbing the dishtowel, I wrapped it and held it tight. Red oozed through.

The first aid box was on the fridge, unopened since Oreo's run-in with the fox. Gripping Sonny's hand, I rooted out a dingy roll of gauze, the last, battered-looking alcohol swab. He cried and flinched as I cleaned the cut, then staunched it with gauze, wrapping it and winding on adhesive tape.

He put his head down, cradling his thumb, sniffling at the bloom of pink through the bandage. The tears left salty streaks and he rubbed them away.

Footsteps sounded overhead. The toilet flushed. The eggs knocked together in the pot, steam spitting on the burner. The radio cackled, and Sonny blew his nose on his sleeve. Suddenly

Hugh filled the doorway. Without speaking he strode over and lifted the lid off the eggs. He'd put on jeans that needed washing. His T-shirt sagged as he spooned an egg into a shot glass.

"He needs stitches!" I cried out.

He set the egg in front of Sonny. "Try Wayne, then."

The shot glass had a devil's face with googly red eyes that seemed to follow you.

"It'll be healed by the time we get there!"

Hugh's eye was red as Mars. "He shouldn't've cut himself. Shoulda been more careful." Hugh whacked the egg open with a knife.

"It could've been his wrist."

"So? He shouldn't've —"

"What? Thrown a snowball?"

"Butter, Alex? A speck?" His voice was *cheerful*. I thought of our very first night, Hugh offering "A speck of tea?" and Sonny saying, "I guess so. What the heck's a speck?"

"Alex?" he said. "You were s'posed to pull a Houdini."

Sonny gouged out the yolk. Hugh mixed powdered milk in the yellow juice pitcher, and set down a glassful next to the egg. Sonny pushed it away.

"You need your protein, Alex. Bones and teeth. Right, Ma?"

His tone made my blood go cold.

He smiled, his teeth stained. He needed a shave, and as if reading me, he rubbed his jaw. His skin looked transparent, a tiny blue vein pulsing at his temple. The whites of his eyes the very liquid blue as the light at the window.

I clenched my mug as if we were riding a round-bottomed lightship tossing to tunderation, as he'd joked once. "Sonny didn't lock himself in there. He didn't do this to himself."

Hugh fixed me with a gaze, puzzled, haughty, then glanced at Sonny. "Drink up, kiddo. You been dreaming, or what? Got to be careful on those rocks, Alex. I told you, didn't I?"

Sonny started to cry again, his mouth full of egg.

Hugh went over and hiked up Sonny's sleeve, roughly, I couldn't help thinking, compared to how he'd cradled a gull that'd washed ashore once, its wing broken.

"Hmmm," he said. "We could try stitching it dog-style. Eh, Tess?" His expression the same as when he searched for the right note on his sax.

"If you go near him again, Hugh — I swear — I'll tell."

"What, Tessie?"

I could smell his hair, the wood smoke scent of his skin. "I'll tell. What happened to Julie —"

"What *about* Julie?" His eyes were the bottom of that rocky shingle. "Go ahead, say it. *What* happened to her?" His hand moved to my shoulder. His fingers felt like gears. "I can't believe it. Can't believe you'd think —" Then he lifted Sonny's hand, inspecting the bandage. Brushing Sonny's arm as if brushing off sand.

Sonny shoved his milk away and ran upstairs.

"I'm serious." My voice as tiny as the shudder of a pilot boat.

Hugh cracked an egg on the counter, started peeling it. "You tell, Tessie, and you know who'll be sorry."

My stomach clenched as he reached for me.

"A speck of egg, Willa?" His voice had a lilt — regret caught there? — a smugness, as he flicked a bit of yolk onto a saucer, no bigger than a bead. "Here, sweetie."

I gave the dish a little push.

"Lay a finger on him, and I'll leave." The words hissed like the spray that rides whitecaps. Covering my mouth, I fled to the bedroom.

If birth is an act of self-immolation, then so must be love. You don't choose to throw yourself into the sea — or into the ring of fire. But sometimes, maybe you have to sink — or burn — before anything can save you. Before you can save yourself.

That night was clear and cold; the kind of night when stars beam an icy perfection and all the world seems out of reach. The wind died, leaving the drifts and our snowy paths carved against blackness. Just before dusk, the crows came. Frightening at first, then mesmerizing. The noise started a long way off, a ruckus from the woods: a fevered cawing, croaks and chirps. Then it closed around the house, a veil of sound echoing over the marsh till the radio's warble was a breaking thread and in disgust Hugh switched it off. He wasn't speaking; he moved about sullenly as if the place had been taken over by squatters.

At supper, Sonny's eyes were crows about to peck out mine.

The noise — the real crows — drew me outside, from the deadly silence of the house into the frozen air. I tried coaxing

Sonny to come too, but he holed up in his room. Even before reaching the pond I could hear it, a rustling muted by that racket; the birds' descent like nightfall, from that distance a gleaming shroud settling over the trees. They seemed to be waiting — for the island's snowcap to slide away? For a party somewhere in bird heaven? For a famine? I wondered. More than a murder of crows: harbingers of something. Plague?

As I punched through the cardboard snow the sound of cawing and of ice grinding against the breakwater moved through me, instilling a cold worse than any weather. But the rustling drew me like a silky thread through a needle and before long I spied their hooded shapes in the branches. There were hundreds of them, perhaps a thousand: a shifting, swaying blanket of feathers. I thought of those bodiless sick people, cholera victims, and black-veiled nuns; as if all had risen and were calling from every branch and twig. The noise swallowed me, and the sky became feathered; the tarnished indigo of wings, alive with hooded eyes. I'd have given anything to have run back and found Hugh — *my* Hugh, not the false one in the kitchen — and to stand with him witnessing this visitation, as if every crow living and dead had come to roost. I thought of Minamata and crows falling from the sky. The snow burned through my jeans as I watched, bedevilled, till the moon rose and one by one the birds shut up and melded with the woods. Then, pressed by the weight of snow and a gnawing, hungry fear, I trudged back to the point.

A fire spat in the stove as I crept in. Hugh and Sonny were

sitting at the table, the Scrabble box between them, unopened. Hugh turned the pages of a book, barely glancing up. Holding up his bandaged thumb, Sonny doodled on a paper bag, a cartoonish figure in a cape and mask, dragging a spiked ball and chain. Neither looked at the other. Neither spoke, as if a shatter-proof wall had grown between them.

"You won't believe it, what I saw." My voice scratched the poisoned silence. Without looking up, Hugh said, "Okay."

A feeling of suffocation swelled inside me, as if I had to struggle for air, still clinging to the wonder of those wings fanning the sky.

"One crow sorrow," Hugh said uninterestedly, turning a page. "Isn't that how it goes?"

The tightness inside me opened. Something seemed to slip.

"So many. I've never seen anything like it."

"Every winter. Good nesting spot, nothing odd about that." His voice was like wet felt. "No big deal."

Sonny creaked his chair out to lean down and stroke Oreo, who'd nudged his empty bowl across the floor.

I said nothing. It was all I could do to keep myself together. Hugh closed his book and went to the bedroom, slamming the door. Shutting my eyes, I stood there, rocking slightly as the dog leapt up. He could smell them, maybe: lost souls.

"How cold is it, upstairs?" I whispered.

Sonny looked baffled.

"Two in the room might help, would you say?"

He made a face, wary.

"Our breath, darling," I said as brightly as I could. "We'll warm it up with our breath, okay? Two is always better than one."

We found ourselves lying upstairs, a frigid gulf of floor between us, Sonny in his bed and I in the spare one that smelled and felt as though an age had passed since it'd been slept in. We whispered to each other in the dark, our voices crossing that chilly divide, mine so false and cheerful. As long as he responded, I felt pinned between those musty sheets. As moonlight scaled the wall his breathing turned whispery, but I persisted. "School tomorrow, betcha any money. Back to it. No more sleeping in, mister."

"No." His drowsy protest breached the chill. "They can't make us go back ... yet." He seemed to sleep-talk, then his breathing slowed to that shallow snore that made me want to huddle close and keep watch, like some sort of fairy, or angel.

I woke sometime later in the dark. There was a strange smell in my nostrils and sweat traced my skin, though the room had got colder, so cold my hands trembled pushing back the covers. But the mattress beside me felt warm, as did the stretch of pillow beside my head, even as I shivered. There *was* a warmth, lingering somehow even as it evaporated, as if someone had just risen, yet hung back, watching me.

"Hugh?" I called out, my tongue thick with sleep; the presence was so strong I almost felt something stroke my shoulder. My breath clouded the air, and it was so cold. Of course there was no one there at all, only Sonny sound asleep in his bed. But — I'd felt it. The silent hum of somebody in the room, somebody besides Sonny. From somewhere downstairs I heard the clink of glass, creaking footsteps; where that sudden, chilling warmth had been now there was only emptiness.

Sometime before dawn the temperature must've risen and the rain started. But it fell only long enough to melt the top layer of snow, until the cold bit down again to glaze it silver.

26

## SAINT ELMO'S FIRE

First thing in the morning I phoned Wayne, to make sure he'd be coming. His drawl conjured awful things. I couldn't help picturing him crawling out of bed, naked.

Sitting on the edge of the tub, I peeled the gauze from Sonny's hand, afraid to look. The gash had closed and blackened. There was an ancient bottle of Mercurochrome in the broken cabinet above the sink. I opened it and tried to wipe the wound. Sonny jerked and batted my hand away.

"It's fine," he kept saying, but after a bit of a struggle he let me give it a quick dab. Then I wrapped his thumb in the last of the gauze. I made coffee while he got dressed. He dawdled like a geriatric. The view outside was a solid glare, sea smoke swirling over the water. Sonny came downstairs dragging his pack. I tried to make him eat something.

"Someone should look at that hand," I murmured, stealing

around getting ready. He shuffled into his coat, which made his arms look like sausages, and he hauled on his pack. No hat, no mitts.

"Do you have a test? A make-up for the one you guys missed the other day?" I said quietly, bringing my leather jacket and boots in to warm them.

Sonny was waiting in the porch.

"You seen my belt?" Hugh's voice boomed behind me, and Sonny shot outside. Hugh's face was pale, his brow lifted above his swollen eye. Limping in, he poured coffee. There was a noise below the window as Sonny rushed past, like eggshells being crushed.

"Have you seen my belt?" Hugh caught my arm. "Alex should keep his goddamn hands to himself. You know I don't like people touching my stuff." I imagined Sonny running ahead now, smashing through that icy crust.

I thought of Charlie rooting around once for some work gloves. *Wha'd you do with 'em, Alex? Kid, I'm gonna throttle you!*

Charlie hadn't meant it, though; of course he hadn't.

"You know who you remind me of?" I asked, all the same.

"Willa?" Hugh sounded more leery than angry. "*He's* out of the picture. Forget him." It was like a cold cloth pressed to my chest. "Come here," he said, tugging me to him. "Maybe you know what he did with my belt."

"D-don't you have things to do? I've got to catch up with Son —"

He let go, and I shrank from him, shivering. The kitchen creaked. As if miles away, the sea sounded like icy milk being drunk through a straw. Peering out, I could just see Sonny disappearing past the drifts by the marsh.

"You must be hungry," I said in a whisper, and he slouched towards the fridge. He rooted through it, sniffing at leftovers. "Where'd the bacon go? That little fuck eat it all?"

But I'd thrown on my things and made it to the porch. Outside, my feet slid easily through the tracks punched in the snow. I could hear the boat's engine from the crown of the hill. Sure enough, as I rounded it they were already putting out. The two of them in the open boat, sea smoke swallowing everything, till I couldn't see them any more. There was nothing to do but go back.

Hugh's face brightened; his smile made me cringe.

"Don't worry, Tessie. We'll take a run over this weekend, okay? Wayne'll be up for it. With no one around, he's got nothing but time."

No one. I thought of my dad out west, and my brother, wherever he was. Then I thought of Reenie. When you're sinking — drowning — the nearest floating object will do; the least likely port becomes a haven. My eyes burned. My throat felt dry. There was a rattling inside me, a humming, as if I were above water now, high above water but losing altitude. Falling through clouds.

"Hugh? What made you do that to Sonny?" my voice rasped. "Put him in the shed?"

He looked startled. "He was doing me a favour, I asked him to get me a ... hammer. The rocks, Willa. He went too close ..." His voice changed. "Christ, what that kid gets up to. You don't know the half of it. Better watch him. Don't mean to interfere, but. Fucking kid never listens. Never *quits*. There's something wrong with him, Willa. Wears you out just being around him, that pissy energy, that attitude, rubbin' everything the wrong way. Willa," he seemed to plead, running his hand up my sleeve. His palm as cold as granite. "Dunno what the big deal is. Thing wasn't even locked."

I opened my mouth. "His arm —"

"I'm *so* tired." He closed his eyes, his fingers lingering. Like a blind man's, reading my arm, the tiny mole — a birthmark — inside my wrist. It made me think of a barnacle, a tiny creature attached to a rock, and then, oddly, of Charlie: moles on his back, a scar from an injury he'd got at work.

"I know you are," I said, my voice far away. "The weather — maybe when it warms up, things'll improve."

"You have no idea." He pulled away, bitterly. "Do you."

I was a crumb swept off the table suddenly, a crumb not even worthy of Oreo.

"What, exactly, d'you think will improve? What d'you mean?" He stared, slurping coffee. Then he moved to the window, hunching there; one bare foot on top of the other, arms folded tight. His chipped blue mug dangling from his finger. "What you don't get, Willa, is the *greyness*. Hunh? The fact that there's no beginning, no end? Not like you'd have it. See, things're like one big grey sheet, is what I'm trying to say." He kept nodding as he spoke. "There's no one thing that's right — or wrong either."

I stared; this was asking me to make sense of everything, and of nothing. Backing away, I felt raw, and everything was bleak. Dumping out Sonny's milk, I noticed that the counter — such as it was — needed scouring. So did the tiles, the whole house.

"The thanks I get," he was murmuring now, a bitter version of his old, teasing self. "For rescuing you, and that freaking kid of yours."

Clenching my teeth, I switched on the radio, which was tarred with grease, feathered with dust. Sonny'd been playing with the dial again. Music spurted out. "The Way It Is." Fading in and out, the fast, tinkly piano made me want to turn the cupboards inside out, purge the place. Not just of flotsam — all the worn-out, cast-off tackiness that filled its rooms — but of my presence and Sonny's.

"It's early," he said softly. "Let's go back to bed."

I didn't budge.

"Well. Fine, then. If you don't feel like it." He tucked in his shirt haphazardly. His jeans stood out from his hip bones; and I realized with a little shock how thin he'd gotten.

"I'm gonna grab a ride with Wayne," I said, my voice like somebody else's, an echo.

"Hmm?" He smirked. "Island girl scores trip to mainland. What'll you do there? Hitchhike to the mall and shop? Right."

I didn't answer, picturing myself by the Kwik Way, my thumb stuck out. Veiled from him by sea smoke. Except, in my imagination the air was fallish, damp but not biting; and everything around me was muted, earthy, not silver-plated and slick.

"Can't hear myself think," he muttered, turning down the radio. Before I could escape, he came and stood behind me, sliding his arms around my waist, crossing his hands over my belly.

"Come on, Tessie — please." He breathed into my ear. "Don't be pissed. It was nothing, you know, yesterday." As I tried to pull away, he caught a handful of my sweater, clutching it. He swallowed; I could hear the spit in his throat. "You keep me alive." His words slurred together, as if sub-zero mist had blown into the house.

"That's what you say," I whispered, just loud enough for him to hear.

In the bedroom I lay like a mannequin as he shed his things, moved, naked, against me. His breath roared in my ears as he tugged at my clothes. His hands roved. He knocked and he knocked, but I would not let him in. After a while he went limp, then curled against me. A stowaway clinging to a good luck medal, a relic from his homeland, a foggy memory now. I lay like cargo awaiting landfall until he turned, and I could tell by the way the mattress moved that he was crying.

I went up and ran a bath, and when I stole back downstairs, he was gone. A trail of holes in the snow led to the tower.

Oreo licked at me, following me to the dresser. He whined for a treat as I slid the drawer open. The wad of bills was gone, all but two fifties. Pocketing them, I went and called Wayne.

By the slur of his voice, I figured he'd gone back to bed after ferrying Sonny, or was already on a toot.

It's urgent, I told him; a problem at school. I'd be more than happy to pay him for his trouble.

"Fuck. All right," he grumbled.

CAROL BRUNEAU

I hung up just as Hugh shuffled inside, kicking snow from his boots. His eyes were red and miserable.

"Haven't heard a tune in a while," I said, as brightly as I could. A tiny part of me still trying to be nice.

"What's up?" He sounded contrite.

Oreo's tail swished like a windshield wiper. I could've concocted something, anything. Sonny falling, banging his head, punching a kid or saucing the teacher. All I did was shrug, waiting for Hugh to speak. When he didn't, I pulled on my jacket and a hat from upstairs, a brown and white toque thick as quilt batting. Forgetting the dishes, I left before he could ask where I was going.

Once I got past the pond, I reached for the envelope in my pocket, the one from the lawyer with Reenie's address. If I had to walk there, I'd find her.

Wayne's face looked like a torn overshoe. He was in rough shape, but coherent. I handed him a fifty, which he pocketed with a smirk. He even cracked a joke or two as we set out through the freezing mist. For a minute I couldn't see land — neither the island nor the shore — and I had the sense once more of being nowhere, of moving through clouds or sleep. "What're you and Hughie up to these days?" he leered, wiping his nose on his sleeve. When I didn't answer he clammed up again, as usual.

When we reached the other side, he pulled a letter out of his back pocket. Its postmark was in Arabic. He watched as I opened it and slid out the cheque that was inside, made out to me, for five hundred dollars. *I don't want Alex going without,* said the note. Though there was no salutation, Charlie had signed it with love.

Wayne actually offered to drive me to the school, which, steeling myself, I took advantage of. He offered to wait while I went inside; his saintliness made me want to vomit. I said it might take a while and wouldn't be fair, holding him up. He picked at his chin, and for an instant, a blink maybe, looked regretful.

"Gimme a shout, then," he bellowed as I jumped out. "Any time before dark."

It was a half-hour bus ride to where Reenie was staying. I almost missed the stop, mulling over Charlie's writing, his blocky signature on the cheque. As if there might be more, penned in indelible Bic.

Once I started walking, it wasn't hard to find the place. Just under the bridge, a dumpy, brick apartment building, one of a cluster like shoeboxes. I buzzed #4, which had the name A. Smeltzer taped underneath it. The lobby door was open. There was no answer at first, but after a few more buzzes a voice echoed down — Reenie's.

"Who is it? I don't want any."

I followed it up a scuffed set of stairs. "Reenie? Reenie Tobias?" I called quietly, a little out of breath.

"Yup?" She peered anxiously from a doorway. The hallway was carpeted in dingy red and smelled of cat pee. "Jesus Christ — Willa?" Her voice had a huskiness; she wasn't exactly overjoyed to see me. Not that I'd expected her to be. But for a minute I felt like an invader, and wanted to flee.

She seemed plumper, and as usual was wearing too many earrings. She had on sweatpants and a tube top with a shirt tied over it, and around her neck a gold chain with a little crucifix. Her face looked awful, as if she'd been on some sort of binge — non-stop bingo? — and she'd had her hair done, chopped and permed till it looked fried.

After a bit she stepped back to let me in. The place was cramped and stuffy, a TV blaring somewhere. Reenie went straight to the narrow kitchen and lit a cigarette off the stove.

I followed her into the tiny living room. The blinds were drawn, the walls a dismal green. The TV sat on a plastic milk crate and a cheap flowered couch lined one wall. A black velvet painting of the Last Supper hung above it. There was little else in the way of furniture, but lots of ornaments. A clock made from a varnished slab of wood with a decoupage Christ on its face, and plush figures from *Sesame Street* — fuzzy red Elmo, and Kermit the Frog — in various sizes, one adorning the TV. A few items looked vaguely familiar: a tole-painted cat and birdhouse and a miniature sled with dried flowers glued to it.

"It's a friend's place," Reenie said warily. "A sublet." She kept eyeing my backpack, as if hoping for something — a housewarming present? Food? Shit, it hadn't even occurred to me. What did you give someone like Reenie anyway? Unpainted wood, maybe: cut-outs of squirrels with acorns, hearts. Things for people whose fingers never stopped, for people who felt guilty not being party to their own gifts.

She sat at the wobbly dinette suite, gestured for me to sit too.

"I got nothing much to offer you," she said, as if I expected a fuss. "What's wrong?" She eyed me suspiciously. "How'd you know where to come, anyways? You've been talking to Wayne, haven't you."

"Um, well ..." The envelope had been in my pocket nearly a month.

"How is he?" She spoke as if the room was bugged.

"All right, I guess." I saw him in their kitchen gooned up and half-naked. I pushed the image away. "Reenie. I need to talk to you."

She twiddled an earring, tapped her cigarette, glancing towards the door with its dangling chain lock. Voices echoed from the hall — a family, perhaps, a mother herding small children, arguing.

"Reenie — I need to know ... what, well, exactly *happened* to that girl."

"Girl?"

"Julie."

"Who's Julie?" She rose to turn up the TV, cranking it so high the window rattled. Through the mini-blinds the glass looked streaked and there were the shadows of birds — pigeons.

"You told me, that time —"

"Oh. *Her.*" Reenie's eyes narrowed. The blue eyeliner made them crooked.

"Wayne sent you, didn't he." She sounded frightened — no, pissed off. I waited for her to tell me to leave, but she didn't.

"Look — I'm asking ... I don't mean to bug you, but ... I need to know. I mean, listen, we can't just let this *go*." My face was hot, the stuffiness of the place getting to me.

Reenie sighed, raking her cigarette over the ashtray. She turned the shiniest hoop in the curve of her ear, studying a spot on the wall — the traitor, perhaps, in the black velvet painting.

"He screwed around on me, okay?"

Remembering Wayne in the photos, I faked surprise. "No!"

She faced me then, the skin above her eyes bald as rock. "The two of them, missy, where you been? You want to know the truth. They both screwed her, both of 'em gave it to her, right. I thought you knew. No big frigging deal." She laughed sarcastically. "But don't go running to anybody, sayin' I said so." *A shadow across a dingy bedspread.* The image flared like an ad. More voices burst from the hall, men's this time, discussing mufflers.

"When ... when was this?"

She lit a cigarette off her old one, exhaled. "I dunno, coupla years ago. Me and Wayne, we were having problems." She spoke as if it were my fault — or I was blaming *her*.

"Okay ...?"

"She got pregg-nant, then got rid of it. A write-off, this chick. Trust me." She flicked back a frazzled lock. "I mean, *I* wanted Wayne to get a blood test. You know, with all them diseases going around these days." She laughed, as if having described a thwarted shopping spree.

"Well." I felt sick. "You must've —"

"Must've what?"

My head felt dangerously light. "Well ... been worried."

"Look. It happened a while ago, okay? Case fuckin' closed."

"Yeah, but ... that girl, I mean, after ... ? Her family! The cops ..."

It was almost as if Julie were there in the apartment, hiding in a closet.

"Oh?" Reenie squinted, holding her cigarette aloft. Her mouth had a greyish look. She started to speak, then slouched back, blowing a chain of rings. "It's none of your fuckin' business. I mean, wouldn't worry about it," she said bitterly. "If I was you?"

"You were me what?"

"I'd move on too, Willa. Go back to my hubby, or whoever. Hear he's a real nice guy." I gawked at her. "Wouldn't know him from a hole in the ground, of course. All's I know, maybe he's a first-class arsehole. Like, forget him too, right?"

Speechless, I reached for her Players. I wanted to break them.

She caught my wrist, then dropped it. "Like I told you before, look out for Hugh." Putting down her cigarette, she picked at a nail. I still hated her, pitied her too. That hardness, those flaky earlobes, that brittle hair. She must've known, though she didn't let on. "Can't trust that one as far as you can throw 'im." Her lips tightened like a bingo player's, or a *Jeopardy* contestant's. "Like Hugh? Like shit?"

There was a clanging; air in the pipes or the radiator coming on, as if the place needed heat. I noticed a smell, like rancid chicken. It seemed to come from the vicinity of the couch.

I should've just risen then and left. But Reenie smiled, of all things; her look reminded me of a rabbit. And it hit me that, despite the apartment, despite her hair — heck, despite the apparent lack of a jar of Maxwell House in the cupboard — she had climbed. In the oddest, most unsettling way, she dangled high above me now, free to look down.

There was nowhere for me to look but up.

"What do you mean, can't trust him? Reenie. Tell me." As if I needed it repeated.

The smell grew stronger. Sure enough, there was a Kentucky Fried Chicken snack pack mouldering under a cushion.

"Nothing you haven't already figgered out."

She shocked me by laying her hand on mine. I jerked it away.

"Hughie's whacked, Willa. Plain and simple."

"It's not really his fault," I blurted out, in spite of everything. One last bleat of denial. An excuse? "It's, well, it's the mercur —"

"What? Is that what you think?" She snorted. "Fuck, girl, you're more full of it than ... It's all the acid him and Wayne did when they were kids, right? Growing up? I told you. Wonder they're not both dead, like, you know." Her voice soured, as if she'd bitten into something nasty. "Or in prison. My fuck, the stuff they're into ..."

I could almost taste it too. My stomach knotted like a fist. I stood and tried to zip up my jacket.

"Ever notice?" Her eyes had a funny look, as if she were talking to herself. "Some people? Guys especially? Get away wit' blue fuckin' murder."

She chewed her thumbnail, gazing at the TV, an ad for some kind of mop. Her eyes had a naked glitter. I wondered then how she was getting along, paying for things.

"Did you ever get on at the bank?" I said, idiotically. Embarrassed. Ashamed, for both of us. Her gaze didn't move from the screen. I felt for the fifty in my pocket, that and a few coins. The coins would've been insulting.

"Wonder the cops aren't onto them," she started rambling. "Shows you how stunned the cops are, right? I mean, drug city. Not exactly your smooth operators, them two ... You know, I thought — when that chick, when she disappeared ..."

I sat down again, my zipper dinging chrome. A draft scooted up my arms. "Julie?"

Reenie shrugged, smiling as if she pitied me.

"What did they do with her, Reenie? Where *is* she?"

The TV was a distant burble.

"You should ask Wayne," she grunted, and I thought once more of the photos and what he'd tried on me. I looked away.

"How long were you guys married?"

She opened her mouth, then sighed. "She's dead." She sounded exasperated. "And you know it."

My stomach kicked. That clanging started up again, like monkeys wielding wrenches.

"Where?" I made myself ask.

"Hughie could tell you better than me." She waited, eyes level with mine. "Berthed, far as I know." An ugly little laugh broke from her. "Far as I ever could drag outta Wayne. Some-place in the harbour."

Red nylon swelled before me, filling, emptying, moving in the water like a jellyfish.

"Huh?" She looked at me as if I'd spoken, then got up and shoved the chicken box into the garbage.

"The body ..." It took all my strength to say it.

Reenie picked up a dusty fry. "Wild, the shit you can drag out of Wayne — stuff you'd rather not know. Stuff you could live without, right."

"He told you she was ...?"

She looked about to tell me to fuck off. But her voice cracked. "That was *it*, you know, when Wayne —"

"So it *was* his."

She rolled her eyes, and my bowels twisted. "Doubt *she* knew whose it was."

Bitterness filled my throat.

"Maybe you should go back to your base."

"That's hardly your business." It sounded shrewish and small.

"And this is yours? Wayne's *my* husband, for *fuck* sake!" She shoved over to the window and played with the blind, watch-ing something below. "You'd best go home," she said, her voice raw — with sarcasm or regret, I couldn't tell. "And don't you breathe a word, missy. They find out I told you, and I'm screwed. Your life won't be worth shit either, if you squeal."

Nausea hummed, rising inside me, as if I'd been viewing everything through the wrong lens. The couch, the décor, and all the rest. "But, how can they —?"

"Stand each other?" Light striped her face, and she seemed far away. "Go home to your little guy," she said then, almost sappily.

As I fled, her voice tailed me through the thin door: "Watch yourself, Willa." The bolt shot behind me with a clink.

Making it outside, thinking of Sonny, I vomited into the dirty snow beside the step.

27

# LANDFALL

The wind hurled litter along the curb. The sky had a muzzy look. It had warmed up a little and almost felt like rain as I waited by the bridge. The bus took forever to come and when it finally did, it only went as far as the Superstore. I got off and started walking, watching for another bus, but none came. It was almost three o'clock; I needed to race to meet up with Sonny. Already the sun seemed low, a bilious glow over the harbour. My chest tightened. Near the base I stuck out my thumb, desperate, and a rusty station wagon stopped. The driver was an old guy in a green mesh ball cap.

"Where you headed, honey?" he shouted as I slid in. He drove about twenty kilometres an hour, cars backed up behind us. "I'm just going as far as that house up ahead," he said. Suddenly I felt so exhausted, I almost wished the sticky bench seat was a couch. "Don't get too comfy," the man joked. He was missing teeth. "Gonna have to kick you out soon." He laughed, not entirely in fun, it seemed. He had a plastic coffee cup stuck to the dash and kept reaching for it, though it looked empty.

"Ya wanna ride?" he muttered, out of the blue, as the house loomed close. When he pulled over, his fly was open. Jumping out, I started walking fast. He leaned on the horn as he passed.

In a couple more hours it would start to get dark. The string of passing tail lights made me queasy again, but somewhere inside I felt glad for them. People going home. Normal people; husbands, wives — and kids, I imagined. Whining from back seats, *What's for supper?* My feet couldn't move fast enough.

Walking backwards, the wind like a brace, I stuck out my thumb again. Drivers streaked past, their faces blank, but finally a woman in a pickup stopped. She had fluffy yellow hair and seemed nervous. You almost wanted to pat her stubby hand on the wheel.

"I'm just going up's far as the bingo," was all she said. "Kinda chilly to be hoofin' it."

"Can't thank you enough," I uttered when the Kwik Way appeared.

She gave me a frightened look, forcing a smile. "Get inside and get yourself a hot cuppa." It made me want to cry. As she pulled away, it was bright enough to read the neon-pink sticker on her tailgate: EVE WAS FRAMED.

When I finally rounded the hill, Wayne's place was in darkness. Kicking the shoulder, I sent a loose piece of asphalt skittering across the centre line. Already the skies above the island were a muddy orange, the woods dusted black. As I traipsed back along the dip in the road, the wind shrieked and chopped the water. It ate through my jacket. Plans hatched and fizzled as a thought warmed me; Sonny had gone to Derek's. It was possible, even likely. I'd phone, then meet him there. Maybe Derek's mother would help? When we were ready, we'd go back for the dog. Oh God, the dog.

Another, feebler plan took hold. I'd jot a note on the back of Charlie's envelope; leave it like an IOU. And I'd borrow a skiff and row across. Because maybe Sonny was there, and hadn't gone to Derek's at all. Something riffled inside me, not relief, but something almost soothing. I'd pin the note under a rock. Charlie's postmark would be a clue to my desperation. People did worse, way worse, than borrow things in dire situations.

As I scanned the government wharf — sweet God, let there be something with oars — a popping sound broke from the water, a sputter. Bright as a toy, that hopeful green, a boat was coming in, a lobster boat with traps piled high in the stern, so high the wind rocked them. As it got closer, I recognized the guy at the wheel and his son, the surly one; the men who'd given me a ride before.

A van swerved to avoid me. Scooting to the shoulder, I watched as the boat swung towards the dock, then I started running. "Hey! HEY!" I yelled, waving. The wind threw back my shouts till I was standing on the dock, right over them. Both men peered up, looking frozen. The younger fellow grimaced.

"Great," he muttered out of the side of his mouth, "if it isn't Ms. Hollow Tree."

A gnawing had started in my gut, and my face felt stiff.

"It's my boy," I shouted. "He's over there alone, and ... and ..." As if it were a rainy lunchtime on Avenger Place and I'd overshopped.

Waves slapped below. The men seemed not to hear me. The son was securing things with ropes, the father hollering about the traps.

"Please!" I shouted down and the father squinted up, rubbing the sides of his jaw. His fingers were like cigars.

"Already she's blowing pretty bad," he growled. "Weather people are calling 'er a bomb. Rain, I guess." He coughed a couple of times, a smoker's hack, then licked his teeth.

"Well, if we can make it quick. Whaddya think, bud?"

"Get in," the son said, hawking over the side.

The flame from the refinery jumped in the distance, the reflection jittering over the falling darkness as we pitched through swells. This was a sheltered part of the harbour, but it felt like we were ploughing through drifts. The spray cut like a razor. As we closed in on the island, you could see ice breaking up, the black currents snaking through it.

"You're cracked living out here this time of year, miss," the father observed above the hiss and slosh. He sounded scornful now. His voice and the wind numbed my ears. I tried to answer but my lips felt frozen, the way they might after a long, painful, dentist appointment. Thank God he kept quiet after that. Before too much longer we sheared in along the dark ribbon of water; and soon enough bounced alongside the dock.

"Take cover, dear," the old guy hollered. "What're you gonna do? You want us to radio for youse?"

Waving him off I nearly fell, scrambling out. The wind pushed my hand as I raised it in thanks. It screamed from the north, swinging the power line like a skipping rope where it emerged from the woods. I swear the pole was almost moving.

The snow had melted, turning the path into an icy sluice-way. I grabbed at branches, sliding and pulling myself along. It took forever to cross the island. By the time the pond appeared, the sky had gone from purple to black. As darkness closed in, panic rose inside me.

From the marsh the house looked to be in darkness. From somewhere, as if muffled by wood, came the sound of barking. A solitary, chilling repetition, the only dog in the neighbour-hood. But as I twigged to it the wind blew it away. I tried going faster, till a timid relief flicked through me. There'd be a light, wouldn't there, if Sonny had come home; the light in his room. Whether or not —

I tried not to think about Hugh at all as I skidded over the rocks.

The tower pulsed its slow, searching light. It seemed like someone about to stop breathing, about to expire, as it flashed and flashed again. And yet a calm settled inside me. The house was wrapped in silence, the back door unlocked. The wind tore at the windows, the eaves, a grinding noise that amplified the stillness of the kitchen. Emptiness seemed to well from the floor, the room ringing like a vault. Oreo's spot beside the stove was empty, a dust bunny moving in the draft. I switched on the light and it blinked and wavered; the shabby fixtures leapt out in odd relief. The dog's blanket was grey with hair. The clock, hanging lopsided as ever above the hotplate, said 5:45.

I dialled Derek's. The phone rang and rang before his mother picked up. She sounded edgy, short. Suppertime. You could hear the clank of dishes, a man's voice, kids.

"Hate to bother you, but is Alex —?"

"Huh?" The woman's voice was scratchy, impatient: "He's s'posed to be here?" Before I could answer, she yelled out, "Derek? You know where Sonny is? It's his ma?" The man grumbled something, then she came back on. "Sorry. Um, Derek doesn't know where he is — oh, wait — what, honey? He went right home? Okay." Her hint of concern seemed to harden, turn almost accusing. "He should be there. They got out the usual — didn't youse, Derek? Look," she said, "my husbant just got back?" There was a jostling, a pause, and a child, maybe Derek, yelling, "Dumb-ass!"

"Well," said the mother, sighing. "Hope you find him. Sure, he'll turn up."

*Turn up* — as if Thrumcap were a street with fences and sidewalks. But she sensed my fear. "Don't worry," she murmured. "He's prob'ly gone to Mikey's house. You know what kids're like. Here," she said, and read out a number.

I was looking at Oreo's empty bowl. Her voice jumped like a cricket's as I dropped the receiver.

The yard was like a flooded rink, a slick, greenish grey under each revolving flash. I held my breath, listening for barks. I couldn't hear a thing above the surf and grinding ice. I closed my eyes, listened harder, then started back towards the pond. The feeling in my gut was as if a stone had dropped there. At the head of the beach I hesitated, almost choosing the path to the tea house hill. Sonny's name caught in my throat as I stumbled over the icy sand, fighting the urge to scream. *Where are you where are you where are you* pounded through me. Sonny's face swam in my head. It pulled me along, beyond the pond and up into the woods onto higher ground where clumps of thawed moss made for easier going. There was no moon, not even a sliver rimmed with frost, only swirling blackness, the branches snapping. My feet moved as if they weren't mine, led by instinct striking its own trail.

Then I heard it; a sober, hopeful yip, its sharpness piercing the wind. Another, and another, deepening into a nervous braying. My feet moved faster, even before the sound caught hold. The path levelled and I followed it through the bending spruce, my stomach in my throat. The barking got louder, more insistent, and I watched for a flash of white through the trees.

"Oreo!" I called, hoarse with fear, burying the urge to scream, *Sonny!*

As I pushed through the branches, faster faster faster, a pounding started in my ears. There was a whimper, frantic sniffing, the dog lunging, leaping to lick my face. With a shock, as if I'd been sleepwalking, I realized where we were. The dark shapes of gears and pulleys loomed through the bushes, set against a break of sky. As Oreo jumped and nipped, his tongue was so warm I thought it'd meld to me. In the same instant, my heart buckled as he sat back on his haunches and bayed at the trees. "*Sonny*," I cried, then louder: "*SONNY!*" The woods closed around me, and I remembered the bunker, where he and Derek had played, and God-knows-who-else had conducted what? Target practice, war games, love?

Tearing at branches, sidestepping, squatting, as if squeezing from one airtight chamber to another, I inched through the woods, stumbling on the moss. The shelter looked the same as when we'd discovered it. Pulling in breath, I pushed the sagging door aside.

"Mom?" His voice was like a sparrow's, tiny, frozen, and his face was pale and frightened. Huddled in a corner, he squatted, gripping what looked like a pencil. There was a smell, a sourness, as if fear had rubbed itself into his clothes. Falling to my knees, I crawled towards him.

"Where were you?" he kept crying as I folded him to me. His body as big as mine. His hair tickled my cheek, a cold little shock. "I was scared, Mom. I was scared shitless that you'd ..."

Prying his fingers open, I took the pencil from him.

It wasn't a pencil at all, but a sharpened stick, the kind used to fasten a hair clasp. It made a hollow little sound, hitting the packed earth.

Slowly I found my voice. "Did Hugh — ?" Sonny shrank from me and I tightened my embrace. "Did you see him?" My heart pumped. You could almost hear the wind pulling, loosening roots, splitting the ground.

His eyes widened, not with fear, but something beyond it: trust? Their expression was like the expression in the eyes of the girl in the black and white picture etched in my brain. The photo from Minamata of the girl and her mother, the girl's flat body, twisted hands and feet floating on a dark, fathomless surface. The mother's arms a berth. The deep black pool; the serenity of that yielding.

At sixteen, I'd almost wanted to be that girl. Until now, I'd wanted to put myself, if not inside her damaged body, then in her place, in someone's arms, arms that would not let me sink, but would keep my buoyed, afloat.

"I'm freezing," Sonny whimpered, "I want to go home."

I thought suddenly of him in the chopper on Family Day, how he'd stood there on the brink, a thousand feet up; how, if he'd fallen or jumped, there was only the monkey tail and not a thing I could've done to save him, except for jumping too. Wasn't the fall through clouds motherhood? The ring of burning atmosphere, an airy abyss of caring, of loving someone more than you could ever love yourself. A leap, one I'd set myself up for the day of Sonny's birth. Passing the torch, too. Loving without the float of stronger, wiser arms meant leaping from the cargo door without boom or harness.

A wave passed through me: the feeling of walking over a grave. I was the mother in the photo, or at least now I knew a little, just a little, of how she, and my own mother, must've felt. The instinct to shield one's young as bloody as a bear's.

"Hugh didn't ... he *didn't* — ?"

"What?" Sonny eyed me miserably. "He wasn't even there."

I tugged at him; clumsily we squirmed to our feet and ducked out into the wind.

"What were you thinking of, coming here?"

He dodged my arms.

"I didn't want to see him. I was scared, when you didn't come. I thought —"

"What? What did you think?"

"That he, he done something to you."

"Shhh," I whispered, touching his cheek. The dog nipped behind, crashing through brush as we struggled against the wind. It would've helped if he'd been on a lead, pulling us. Though taking the path to the spit felt like waking someone or something best left asleep. I couldn't think about what might be waiting, but with the trees bowing and whipping we couldn't stay in the woods.

I'm not sure what I expected to find when we got there.

The tide had come up, pushing cakes of ice against the rocks and slicking everything with spray. Twice Sonny almost lost his boots and by the time we made it to the house our clothes were damp. The sea foamed through cracks in the breakwater, fingers of it pulling at the edges of the yard. But, thank God — yes, there *was* a God — the house was as I'd left it, the kitchen light blazing, but otherwise cold as a tomb.

Sonny balked in the porch, whispering, "He's here, isn't he."

"Sonny. Alex. *Alex* Jackson." I put my hands on his shoulders, drawing him close. But he strained away, blinking; studying the initials, dates, scratched in the doorframe. *A.P. '19-'48, G.S. '49-'85, H.G. '86-'88.*

"When I got home I seen him in the lantern. That's how come I took off. Didn't wanta talk to him, I just —"

"But you said he wasn't here. Sonny? Shhh," I whispered, trying to keep calm. It was as if something had grabbed hold of both of us and wouldn't let go.

"Mom?" His voice was faint, almost a whine against the sloshing surf. "I just want to go home."

The wind was like a subway train, a howling shriek through a tunnel. The house groaned around us, as if being pushed. You could hear the waves crashing. I locked the door and pulled him upstairs. It seemed cozier up there, somehow. His knapsack sat on the floor, his lunch half eaten. I'd had nothing since breakfast. We split the remains of his peanut butter sandwich, then got into his narrow bed, the two of us in our coats. For an instant the air seemed to change, charged by the distant shudder of engines, but the sound was swallowed by the wind.

"This is silly. I could go down and make a fire."

But Sonny caught my arm. "Tell me a story," he said. "From when I was a kid."

"You still are," I whispered back.

His weight against me, he closed his eyes and waited.

"When you were a baby," I started, "your dad ... Well, you hated going to sleep; you'd yell at bedtime. Don't you remember?"

The window pulsed, the glass pushing in, then something creaked and the light blinked. He went still.

"You'd scream bloody murder when your father and I ..."

"What?"

"Hm?"

"When you what?"

Above the roaring surf and that screaming wind, I imagined plundering engines: rotors.

"What is it?" He pinched me.

"Nothing." I put my finger to his lips as if he was tiny. "Go to sleep."

"Mom?"

"Yeah?"

"Can people read other people's minds? Derek seen this guy on TV."

"Mmm." I stared at the ceiling as the wind made a ripping sound. "Can you read mine?"

"I dunno." He shifted, hooking his arm through mine, nudging me to the edge. His face was a soft moon. "Wish I could read Dad's right now."

The thundering outside got louder. A container ship, it had to be.

"Can you read Hugh-the-arsehole's mind?" he said.

"Stop it." I shook him gently. "Go to sleep."

"Can you?"

"Oh, Sonny. If I could've ..."

"Well," he burrowed close, "that's *real* useful." He sighed, and it crashed down around me, the weight of my blindness. My stupidity. The pair of us squeezed into this mouldering little bed in a place that should've been condemned. I could barely open my eyes to the rest, the truth like needles.

The light overhead blinked again, went out completely for a few seconds, then came back on. Sonny shut his eyes. Before long his breathing grew softer.

What sleep I got was fitful, that feverish, half-awake state where every fear is amplified, every creak a footstep. Perhaps I dreamt, or merely imagined, Hugh coming in and stoking the stove, and climbing the stairs to find us. Then I pictured him in the lantern, as if I were a hovering gull; he was slowly, methodically draining the mercury from the trough, straining it, then pouring it back, grinning as the lens resumed its revolution. In my mind's eye the whites of his eyes were quicksilver, a mirror of the sky.

I came to, with the feeling that his lips had brushed mine, a chill so real I trembled. The light in the room had gone out, there was nothing but lashing darkness, not a flicker from the tower. Only Sonny's breath and the pillow's musty smell and the dog curled at our feet brought me back. The wind was raving, raving like all the world's crazies out of control. As I lay there it rocked the house, and with every shriek the waves seemed to slap louder. God knows what the tides were doing. I thought of the woods, spruce bending, snapping; the copper beech in the tea house garden. The house itself like a hollow tree being battered, silenced. Nothing so much as a hum from the fridge below.

The dog stretched, warm as a hot water bottle. Letting Sonny sleep, I crept to the bathroom. From the window everything looked black, glossy, the tips of boulders like heads floating in darkness. Trying the light — nothing — I peed loudly. There was a clanging as I turned on the tap. The toilet wouldn't flush.

Downstairs, there was no sign at all that Hugh had been back. There was kindling in the porch and some split wood, though the stack had gotten low. I scrounged up enough for a fire as the dog whimpered by his dish. I tried the phone: nothing. Stupidly I tried the radio. Useless.

The glow from the open burner lit the gloom as I fed in bits and pieces, watching them burn. A stick for every kiss; one for every secret, every story. *A penny for your thoughts*, Hugh had said once. The fire became a pool, a fountain. Smothering, it dwindled, and I looked for paper. Sheet music, a little stack of it under some cheat books. Balling some up, I stuffed it in and the flames leapt, wavering in the draft.

The storm had got worse, throwing rain at the windows. The house moaned like someone sick in bed, the wind a death rattle. Water beaded the sill like shiny caulking. From upstairs came tearing, like something being peeled away, shucked. Shingles from the roof? There was a pounding, like boulders knocking together. The noise was almost deafening. The only place scarier would've been out at sea. I imagined the bell buoys breaking from their moorings and rocking to the bottom. The darkness all around a billowing, ripping blanket.

When the sheet music was gone, I went into the bedroom. The closet door wouldn't open at first, as if the frame had shifted. The box was still there, but empty. Not a scrap or scribbled note. But as I flipped it over, starting to rip the cardboard into pieces, something slipped from a bottom flap. It was the photograph of Wayne and the lost girl, the shadow like a stain on the spread between them.

Piece by piece I fed the cardboard into the fire. Turning the photograph over, I laid it on top of the fridge. If there'd been one of Hugh — his face, I mean — I would have burned it. In my heart of hearts, yes, I would've. Probably.

The shadow was evidence enough. If not for Sonny, I'd have taped the photo to the fridge. *A lifesaver, Wayne.* Hugh's voice flooded back, and a movie-like image of sinking ships flared. It was easier than picturing him, as the cardboard burned to black and darkness swelled again.

There was the generator, of course, sitting out there in the base of the tower. But the gasoline was in the tool shed. I stuck my feet into the nearest boots and bundled up. Seawater licked the steps, covering the bottom one as I ventured out, slipping on the ice underneath it. The rain was like a washer's spin cycle, gusting in wild, spitting rounds. Both boots filled, and I thought crazily of something Hugh had said about lining his boots with bread bags as a kid; Sonny had just stared. The yard was a lake, the sea boiling over the rocks. Foam swirled like the head on dark beer, a brew dotted with floating bits of trees and wharf. The wind shoved me like a skate bug, a mayfly. The shed tilted as if afloat. It seemed to move as I grasped the latch. The wind ripped the door away. Objects bobbed out, scraps of firewood, a tennis ball, a piece of Styrofoam buoy. Sonny's bike was submerged past the chain.

There was a squeaking, timbers rubbing rock. I lugged the jerry can from the shelf; it was reassuringly heavy. I waded towards the tower, then, remembering the lamp in the porch, looped back to get it. The water had risen almost to the top of the steps. Against all odds there was kerosene, and I ducked into the kitchen. Matches.

Sonny was kneeling in the hallway, his hands buried in Oreo's ruff. A keening rose from the dog's throat. Sonny pulled his hands away and clamped them over his ears to shut out the roar. He was still in his coat, and he was shivering.

"The water's come up," I said as calmly as I could. Sonny pressed his hands tighter, shaking his head. "Sweetie. The tide's awfully high, but it'll turn, right?" My voice was a straight black line. "Go on upstairs, darling. I'll be right back."

The wind was like a squall of sirens now, a fleet of emergency vehicles.

"Mom?" His lips moved. I could barely hear him.

There was a grinding noise, and something seemed to buck.

"Sonny, listen." It was like forcing my voice through a sieve. "Go on up now, okay?"

As he stomped upstairs the embers settled in the stove; foolishly, I considered dousing them. A finger of water slid from the baseboard and a little trail seeped in from the porch. I struck outside again, gripping the lamp in one hand and the gas in the other, for ballast.

The tower loomed out there like a pillar of ice. The torrent shoved at my knees and I clenched my belly, bearing down, planting each foot, step by step, the ten or twelve yards to the light. The door wasn't locked; maybe Hugh's haphazardness was a mercy. Water slicked the cement, spreading towards the generator on its dolly, less than a foot off the floor. Lighting the lamp, I swung it up onto the windowsill. My fingers were frozen sticks uncapping the gas tank, lifting the can. A funnel would've helped; half the gas sluiced over the engine. But I replaced the cap and groped for the cord, gave it a yank, then another, harder, and another, getting nothing but a splutter.

Just outside, waves slapped the concrete. Straightening up, bracing my foot, I gave one final yank, as Charlie had done with the lawn mower. Like a miracle, the thing burped and roared to life. The noise bent my eardrums, driving back the shrieking and pounding. Creeping around, palms pressed to the sweating walls, I opened the panel, hesitating over two thick switches. Closing my eyes, my pulse drumming my ears, I flipped the right-hand one.

Who knows what I expected. An explosion? A landslide, the sea cascading?

There was a whirr, a sputtering buzz, and the hatch overhead filled with brilliance. Seizing the lamp, I started back to the house. The flashing beam lit the yard and what was left of the breakwater. Before my eyes the tool shed rocked, swaying like a buoy. Then it toppled, pieces swirling away as it drifted beyond the house.

Somehow I made it back to the porch. Inside, water lapped at my ankles, moving over the floorboards. I emptied my boots, shoved an old coat against the threshold. A trickle followed me into the kitchen, a snail crossing the linoleum. My brain spun, trying to pinpoint high tide. Unlike Hugh, I'd never paid that much attention. Dropping the jerry can, I re-lit the lamp and set it on the table. A ghost of warmth still came from the stove.

"Sonny?"

I could hear him bumping around upstairs, surely the best place to be? The light from the tower bloomed and waned, painting the windowpanes that oily, sea serpent green. The smell of gas clung to my fingers; how long till the generator would need refilling? The can was almost empty.

"Sonny!" I shouted again. "The tide, when's it turn?"

The trickle from the porch pooled in a dip in the floor. Another snaked from the cupboard below the hotplate and met it, then branched towards the puddle by the window.

*Fire, heat*, I thought crazily, tearing the cover off Hugh's book — the one on navigation — and pushing it into the stove. An acrid stink filled the room.

Suddenly the walls seemed to waffle and breathe. The pool widened, then a tiny spring seemed to well between the floorboards. I was thinking of the fishermen, the older fellow's last words, what he'd said about radioing.

The thought flashed of the house drifting like Noah's ark, only with the three of us: Sonny, Oreo, and me.

"*Sonny!*" I yelled up. "Get your knapsack. Grab your stuff."

The puddle slanted and gently spread towards me.

"Sonny! Quick! Sweetie? *Leave your gear* —"

His footsteps on the stairs. Down he came like a robot, the dog at his heels, his pack over his shoulder and a ratty-looking gym bag in one hand. It bulged like a python that had just eaten. As he set it down, the hallway seemed to tilt.

"My pitchures," he said, glancing upwards. Wrinkling his nose. "What's that hum?"

"Nothing, it just Hugh's book —"

"My *Punishers!*" he yelled, starting back up.

But then the floor moved, I swear, and the water slid back.

Another smell rushed in: the heavy, fishy smell of salt and rotting wood. Suddenly the house seemed to sweat, beads of wetness springing from corners and edges. They shone in the greenish light. We watched, mesmerized, like the crew in a leaky submarine, a U-Boat popping its rivets, bursting at the seams. Then a *rip* shoved us to the stairs. A grinding racket, like the lid being torn off a box, and a train rushing in.

## 28

# ANCHORAGE

There was a *crack*! A gush as the storm raged in, the wind rearranging everything. Furniture scraped overhead. Rain raced down the stairs, a little waterfall. Slicking the ceiling, it showered down, streaking the wallpaper.

I threw Sonny's boots at him, grabbed his hand.

As a small tide leapt towards us, the kitchen window buckled, rain and glass slanting in. A rising, glittering spectacle, the floor was a pool of diamonds for a suspended moment. Then water burst through the plaster above the sink; the hiss sounded like a bus braking. There wasn't time to grab anything as we fled to the front door. The case with Hugh's sax rocked near the foot of the stairs, already warping. The water was past our shins, the jamb swollen. As we yanked at the door things swung in a drunken *do-si-do*, the house coming unglued like a cereal box.

Oreo yipped and splashed as the door caved inwards. The smell was like seaweed and the spines of starfish left to rot in tidal pools. Somehow we got out, with the dog thrashing behind us in the dark. I don't remember flying off the step or treading water, only the pulse-stopping cold and Sonny screaming, "Here boy here boy come come come."

Sonny's hand clenched mine as we pushed, half swimming, choking, towards the tower. The dog paddled in mad circles around us, his eyes rolling. It took everything to fight the current nudging us towards the cove, Sonny's limbs like ropes entangled with mine. An image flashed through me of the boats anchored off the spit that summer day, the divers sliding under the waves. As Sonny pushed free of me, I imagined, fleetingly, debris at the bottom. Secret, scary things, dumped mines and mustard gas? Creatures, wreckage. An orange buoy floated by, and a stick that looked like a table leg.

As the white of the tower loomed closer, closer, my limbs were weightless, dead, as if all sense had leaked away.

Sonny made it first, the dog clawing to get in. Somehow Sonny braced the door against the flood and lashing gusts, Oreo scrabbling ahead as my feet touched concrete and I pulled myself inside.

The generator chugged and roared, and the dog balked, whinging. Then he shook himself, shook and shook. He was a shivering mess of dripping fur.

There was a scratch on Sonny's hand, another on his cheek. As I wiped the blood away, the dog gave another shake. The sea had slid past the threshold, swirling around the footings.

Oreo bent to lick at it. Water lapped over his paws and the toes of our boots. The sound was like a pack of animals drinking. Oreo thrashed as Sonny lifted him and tried wrestling him up the first set of steps. Our feet were ice blocks on the metal rungs. Somehow I managed to grab the dog in my arms, bracing his forelegs, and boost him to the first landing. I felt Sonny at my heels as we scrambled the rest of the way up, borne by invisible hands into the lantern. Light swamped us, its brilliance pushing back the ruckus below, and derailing the wind.

Sonny licked blood from his hand. His lips looked purple, and a puddle spread under his feet as he grabbed for the radio, the VHF. I barely remember wrenching the mic from him and fumbling with knobs. At first all we got was a hiss, then, like life from another cosmos, a voice leapt out.

"No no no," Sonny kept yelling — it was a struggle to hear anything over the racket — "we need channel sixteen." As he pushed my hand from the controls, the same voice blared in and out. Something about the Mounties, the Coast Guard.

"Major interdiction, 0200 zulu. Four, four, thirty-seven north. Six, three, twenty-five west —"

"Channel 10. *Shit!*" Sonny's teeth were knocking. "Must be the navy." He tweaked the knob. Had Hugh shown him how to work the thing?

Broken by static, the voice filtered back. "Operation Search and De-stroy." It sounded like laughter. Then nothing. As I gazed out, a crack of lightning whipped the rocky shingle of Hangman's Beach, jagged and white as the surf. It lit the top of a big tree by the marsh and in its flash the pine was a masthead. I thought of Saint Elmo in Hugh's book, how such a flash on a ship signalled the saint's protection.

Fighting tears, Sonny twiddled the dial, his fingers blue.

Without warning, a woman's garbled voice burbled, "Coast Guard, go ahead, over."

"Mayday! Mayday!" Sonny shrieked.

"Help!" I yelled behind him, the lightning branded into my eyes.

The voice, maddeningly calm, didn't waver. "Go ahead with your coordinates, over."

Oreo's bark had shrunk to a whimper; perhaps he'd seen the lightning too and was listening for thunder, each hair an antenna. Sonny eyed me desperately, shaking his head. My limbs, coming to, throbbed under the soaking weight of my clothes. Despite all that wet, my hands still reeked of gas. The smell brought back Family Day: the reek of fuel inside the chopper.

Elmo, I wanted to cry. Seizing the mic, I formed the words, "Thrumcap Light." Forcing calm. "We're flooded." It sounded surreal, deadpan, even as I watched for another flash. Gaping down at the house, I saw the roof hanging like a blanket, like a sheet of melting ice about to slide off. In the same instant the wind lifted one corner, then hurled it towards the cove, and I let out a shriek.

"Stand by one," the voice ordered flatly, then, "Steady. Give us five; we're sending a chopper, over."

"Over," Sonny stammered behind me, watching the roof. It was riding the waves now, a rippling, sequined float, its shingles like scales. I couldn't tell if he was laughing or crying, his face almost angelic, lit by the beam. He was shivering, grinding his teeth. Pressed together, kindling our shared warmth, we stared down at the house. The walls staggered and swayed. A hollow stump without limbs, it danced, uncertain, shy, as the tide tore at it. Water poured from the bottom windows like flames, and Oreo's whinging picked up. Just above the treetops, beyond where the lightning had flashed, the first traces of dawn smudged the sky. The shapes of things swung in the current. A chair, a bed frame, part of the stove. I thought once more of Elmo — his real name Erasmus, the name his mother would've used? — and whatever faith he'd died for. I thought of the fuzzy red doll in Reenie's apartment.

"What time is it?" Sonny shook me, and I remembered things like days and hours. As he leaned into me, his jacket was a soggy hide. His voice far away, wispy. "High tide's at six."

"The dog," I said in a blur, peering down through the hatch. Oreo gazed up, his ragged ears cocked, ridiculous. As if in a dream, I slid down and managed to scoop him up. He growled and writhed, his teeth grazing me as I heaved him up that last flight. Passing through the opening he snapped at Sonny. The smell of wet dog was everywhere, the only thing that seemed real as I squatted beside the door to the ledge and pulled it open. The smell blew away as I crawled outside. Wind ripped at the railing, dissolving my senses. The memory of another smell, the bunker's fetid dankness, rushed in instead. That, and the thought of Sonny squatting there in the dark. Yet the streaks in the sky brightened. I could see the top of the breakwater now, a path of stepping stones. Numb, I crawled back into the lantern, and we counted them, one for each hour we seemed to wait.

"How come they're taking so long?" Sonny kept moaning. At one point he knelt and peered into the mercury. Like Narcissus, I thought before snapping to, almost but not quite thawed.

"Don't!" I heard myself yell.

For once he listened. The wind had stopped screeching; suddenly it was a moaning whistle. Beyond the tips of the boulders the harbour rolled and seemed to flatten slightly. Oreo lay down and licked himself, strummed his banjo, as Hugh would've said. Sonny flopped down and buried his face in his fur. For a single, rushing instant, I allowed myself one thought of Hugh — beautiful Hugh: his hands and eyes. Even as it fled, replaced, pushed, by another — the lilt and slur of his voice — there was a slow, watery squeal as the walls of the house buckled and folded.

Watching boards and shingles swim away, we might have missed the chopper's approach. Sonny spotted it first, a teensy dragonfly against the pink sky. Crawling out onto the plat-form, I pulled myself up to the railing and, stretching my arms out like a tree, started waving. I thought of us queued up on Family Day, Charlie, Sonny and I; the mirage of solid, level ground, tarmac. The dark shape whirred closer, then, dipping its nose, bore in. It wasn't anything like a dragonfly. Cheery as a candy cane, its fuselage red and white, it descended, hover-ing. Freezing me in its hurricane, its roar stopped everything.

I barely saw the helmeted rescuer and his basket, didn't hear Sonny's shouts as he crawled out behind me and was plucked and winched to safety.

The downdraft was like the weight of the ocean. It drummed out everything as I was hoisted into the net. I couldn't open my eyes. All I felt were thick arms around me, legs too, perhaps, and the swaying, slow release of being lifted. Like a fly being pulled into a web, though Sonny bragged afterwards that *he'd* felt like Spider-Man.

Suddenly my knees hit metal and I was shoved inside, into the rattling, roaring belly of the bird, and I opened my eyes to see Sonny wrapped in blankets. I glimpsed the top of the rescuer's helmet before he disappeared again.

"My dog my dog my dog," I think Sonny was shouting, his voice wobbly and almost inaudible.

One of the pilots yelled, "We don't have all day, bud."

The chopper lurched. There was a shout, and a tangle of fur appeared through yellow mesh and was tossed in, and before Sonny or I could move, Oreo spilled towards us, the whites of his eyes showing, his jaws snapping. Next, the rescuer was unhooking himself.

"We're gonna land at the base," the flight mechanic might've hollered, stuffing blankets around me. "Havin' a nice day?" I think he shouted, as if they did this all the time. Old hat, saving women and kids from calamities. "That old place was bound to go anytime," he yelled some more, handing us earplugs. I read his lips: "Frigging death trap, middle of a neap tide. You guys out there picnicking, or what?"

As we lurched and climbed, I caught one last glimpse of the view below, through the glass between the pilots' heads. A wave pushed a raft of shingles. One of the men turned, and I saw a patch of the island. It looked stepped on, as if the trees had been flattened by giant feet.

The man mouthed something to Sonny. "Been in one of these birds before?" it looked like.

"Yup," Sonny mouthed back, his arms around Oreo's neck.

The dog was scrambling to sit, his claws scrabbling. The rescuer shook his head, as if all this was mildly entertaining, then he fiddled with equipment, ignoring us. It seemed odd, even amid the chaos, that no one asked why we were alone out there, or if there was anyone else. They'd have known of the lightkeeper; should've wondered where he was. My stomach rolled and once more I remembered Family Day, the taste of hot dogs, and that sensation of being carried like a kitten, the scruff of its neck between the mother's teeth. But my fear had been left on the spit, washing behind. There was no time to dwell on it as we skimmed over the water, already closing in on the refinery. Seconds later we hovered in a whirlwind, then, almost too soon, began descending.

Part of me could've stayed up there forever and simply vanished into the ozone, anything to avoid re-entry. But before I knew it we were landing, with the blare of rotors and that typhoon force gale like a field of windmills going full tilt. Sonny strained against his monkey tail, hanging onto the dog.

"We'll file a report," the pilot yelled once we'd touched down. Pulling the plugs from my ears, I felt the weight of gravity, yet I was giddy, too, as if the storm had robbed me of oxygen. My eyes felt singed, my ears blocked as if with snow. As if separated from my body, I jumped down after Sonny onto the tarmac. He half-crouched, gripping Oreo by the tail. The runway glistened like plastic wrap as the sky opened. There were things strewn around, pylons scattered as if somebody'd thrown them, and strips of siding. In my giddiness I was Mary Poppins, except empty-handed, sodden. An umbrella, a carpet bag would've grounded me, armed me; anything better than the nothingness I carried now.

A memory of Hugh's smile scraped my heart. The air felt damp, the wind carrying the faintest hint of warmth, and thoughts played of how I might've worked things differently. How I might've packed our belongings, mine and Sonny's, and simply left one morning — the last day of summer, perhaps, or the first day of school.

"Some freakin' weather, what? Don't think anyone expected that," somebody shouted out. "Hadda be a Type Three, what I saw. 'Magine, a bust in the middle of that. Better them than us."

"Out Cow Bay, you mean?" one of the crew was saying, as they strode alongside us. "A tonne of coke. In gym bags, if you believe it. Jesus Christ!"

Someone let out a laugh. They'd already distanced themselves; you could hear it. Mission accomplished; now on to the next.

"Self-cleaning oven, cats like that. Guess they nailed a woman, too, eh?"

"No shit. No accounting, eh?"

Removing his headgear, the pilot remembered us. "You two okay? Someone'll be along to check you out, make sure nothing's busted. Oh, and they'll need some kind of statement."

Sonny had split away; already he was marching towards the hangar, a greenish blur in the distance. He'd let go of Oreo and the dog bounced beside him, sniffing out the wind. How great, how much easier, really, to be canine: at home anywhere and even when chained, free.

"Off limits, bud!" somebody yelled, but Sonny ignored him. I wanted to ignore the guy, too, trailing behind, flopping along in my boots. My feet hurt; the smell of gas still clung to my fingers as if it'd permeated the skin, a smell that conjured other scents, salt and the perfume of bodies, even blossoms.

"If someone c-could call us a cab," I muttered, the most dignified thing that would come to me. I imagined getting in, telling the driver, "Just drive."

There was a Sea King parked on the tarmac, idle but positioned for take off. Pushing ahead, Sonny stopped to gaze at it. Oreo nipped at his hands — his poor hands, almost frozen. Catching up, I caught them in mine and started rubbing them. A crew was coming towards us, men in coveralls and Kevlar vests, carrying helmets and headsets. Four of them. They were talking and laughing; the shortest one kept shaking his head and muttering. The man next to him gave him a cuff and as he looked up, he stopped.

At that instant, perhaps a plane passed over; his features clouded. His hair looked longer. It couldn't be, I thought. But it was him. It was Charlie, and even at that distance I felt myself shrivel. I expected him to turn and disappear back into the hangar, or pretend not to see me, simply act like I was someone else, a complete stranger, and keep going towards the chopper. But he didn't. As he came closer, his helmet was tucked against him. He was staring at the ground, saying something to his buddies. His buddies had stopped talking. When he glanced up he raised his hand, a stiff, somber salute. His face was pale, his expression confounded. I wanted to turn and run.

Oreo crouched, wagging his tail and baring his teeth. Before I could stop him, Sonny raced towards his father. Charlie bent down and so did Sonny, that crazy animal leaping and pawing at them. The dog must've sensed something; maybe he wanted to protect Sonny. Pushing Oreo off, the two of them straightened up. Father and son. Sonny came up past Charlie's chin. As they moved towards me, Charlie's face was a poster of grief and astonishment, stodgy disbelief.

I shut my eyes and stood there on the tarmac, that endless, firm stretch of concrete. Letting the wind fill my ears, I waited, certain that Charlie would keep going. I waited for him to fire an insult, throw a flare. Instead, the air around us seemed to soften. I could hear Oreo's panting, Sonny's breathing. I blinked and there was Charlie's face not far from mine. It looked rough where he'd missed a spot shaving, creased in all the same old places.

"Jesus Jesus Jesus," he kept saying under his breath. The smell of fuel and soot and faulty wiring seeping around me.

Charlie's buddies stayed silent. Then one of them started clapping, another groaning.

"That's one wicked bug you've got, Jackson. I'd say you're grounded."

"Get the hell outta here, before you pass it on."

"Too sick to fly, corporal. Don't you have a maintenance sched at home to follow?"

"Here we go. Operation Underwear."

"Operation G.I.O."

"G.I. *Joe?*" Sonny piped up. He was hanging off my arm now, trying to pull me closer, the three of us doing a two-step with the dog.

"Get off it, bud." Charlie's voice was low, wary. Despite its pallor, his face had an odd sheen.

"Operation Get It On, Jackson. Or off — whatever."

As Sonny pushed and pulled at me — this child, grown so much taller — for a second I felt dull and three-footed as the twenty-year-old I'd been once, drinking coffee from a Styrofoam cup. But the feeling passed as I gripped Sonny's arm, holding back. Suddenly I thought of my mother, of all people — what I remembered of her anyway — and how she'd started to cry when I'd held out those pieces of my hair.

"It's okay." Charlie kept nudging Sonny. But then he did a strange thing, a very strange thing for him, and unwelcome. Stepping closer, he put his finger to my cheek, drawing it along my jaw to the pulse below my ear. Letting it linger, he shook his head. His sigh was like blowing sand. Then his hand dropped to Sonny's shoulder. He kept shaking his head, the shadows under his eyes battle grey.

I made myself look into those eyes; my own were stinging.

"I don't believe ... *you'll* never believe ..."

He shrugged, the same shrug as when something had gone missing in the basement. He held up his hand. "Save it, okay? There'll be time for talk, I guess." His voice changed, but it was still sardonic: "I mean, what're the chances, eh? God damn." There was a deadly pause, and the weight of his arm brushed my shoulder as I backed away.

"Shit happens, Willa. Doesn't it. Shit happens all the time. Maybe now we're both used to it?"

Flushing, he pushed his helmet down on Sonny's head, snorting at how it almost fit.

It wasn't that we considered giving things another try. There are no second chances when you fall the way I had; there could never be a second with someone like Charlie. But what he offered was a little reprieve, when he didn't have to, somewhere to stay till I figured things out. Only because of Sonny. It lasted a few weeks, not quite a month: a silent truce. A ceasefire?

Amnesty.

We'd been back on Avenger a couple of weeks when the call came one afternoon. I was there sorting stuff, things Sonny had outgrown, things we'd need. I almost missed the phone, rummaging downstairs for boxes. Not that I didn't hear it; the house was dead quiet. It always was now, as if waiting for us to leave. I tiptoed around, hardly playing the radio, even when Charlie was at work. Nothing was really mine anymore. I was a guest, a phantom boarder.

I felt a little out of breath, picking up the phone.

There was silence at the other end, and I knew right then I should've let it ring. The silence was full of echoes and the sound of breathing, as if the person was calling from a bus station, or an aquarium. When Hugh finally spoke, his words were a slap.

"I knew you'd go back."

He must've felt my urge to hang up. "Wait," he said, and for a second his voice was a hook, my heart an open loop.

"Where are you?" I heard myself ask.

A long, windy pause. I swear you could hear his thoughts ticking. Missing, then slowly, slowly engaging.

"Remand," he said. "You don't want to know, Tess." Then: "Couldn't we talk?"

I held out the receiver — held it as if it were toxic — and waited. *Hang up*, the voice inside me pleaded. Instead, I put the phone back to my ear, listened to him breathe.

"Are you okay?" It came out a squeak. Pathetic, really.

Oh, to have shut my ears, and found myself somewhere, anywhere, else.

At the edge of my brain, the word *posting* lapped, and I visualized Charlie coming home, boxes everywhere, cardboard wardrobes plugging the hall.

Hugh coughed and didn't answer.

"Have you seen a ... I mean, there're tests they can do, right? Remember?" An echo of Reenie's voice crept in: *You believe that crap?* My own was tiny, quavering. "Blood tests," it murmured. "You really should get it checked out. Even if —"

Hugh laughed, and it was full of bitterness. "Right." His voice deepened, as if he were speaking through a funnel. "Matter of fact, Tessie, they've done 'em. All that shit about vapour and whatnot? You were right. Thought I'd come out clean as a fuckin' whistle." Another laugh echoed over the line. "Now I'm thinking, okay, there's my defence."

It was just like Sonny plea-bargaining to stay up late.

I pictured my Hugh guzzling tea, complaining of being tired and thirsty, staggering on the stairs. Suddenly I felt exhausted — that tiredness when all you want to do is lie down and sleep like Rip Van Winkle.

"I should've listened, Tess." He sniffed. "It's just like, I dunno ... imagine, coming out with, 'The girlfriend says I'm bein' poisoned.'" The way he spoke reminded me of Wayne. There was a beep and I felt like a party-liner listening in. All I wanted was to put down the receiver. He must've known, because he started talking faster, as if running out of minutes.

He was rambling, and even as I listened for Sonny coming in from school, something he said caught my ear.

"You have to believe me, Tess. I wouldn't lie to you. You know that, don't you? It was Reenie, Reenie who did it. She shoved her. Swear to Christ, that's what happened. Wayne saw her, too. I know what you're thinking ..."

My fingers melded to the phone. I just stood there as his words bumped and skidded together. There was nothing I could do to stem them.

"The two of 'em," he kept insisting, his voice a murmur. "Her and Julie. Got into it one night, all right? Reenie tore a strip off her, you know," he paused, as if losing steam. "Because of Wayne, right? They were outside. By the breakwater. The bunch of us, we were — it was icy, you know, and —" His voice eddied, clinging to dead air, before slipping beneath the surface.

As I set down the phone and moved from it, it was as if he could see me. Drifting to the kitchen, I turned on the radio, the sound a jumpy rattle, the easy listening station that Charlie favoured. I tuned it to one that played loud, shredding rock.

Something good, something blotto, to sort and pack to.

They were playing that U2 song, "Where the Streets Have No Name."

When the last of Sonny's Legos were boxed and ready to give away to any kid who wanted them, I went back to the phone. It only took a second to get the number. The hardest part was dialling. Like looping the rope of a noose over a branch.

Just one kiss, one last kiss ...

"Tell me what you know," the detective's voice was earnest, gruff but pleasant.

It primed me for another call I had to make, one I'd put off even longer.

"Willa?" Sharla — Dad's wife — sounded incredulous, thrown for a loop actually, but sweet. She ran from the phone yelling, "Howard, *Howard!*"

"No, no, no, you'll stay here," my father insisted. "How much is the flight?"

"It'll be a short visit, just until I —"

"No way. We've waited this long to see you guys, you're not getting off that easy."

"Dad? Listen — it's only going to be Sonny and me. Charlie and I, well ..."

Oddly enough, music got me through those last couple of weeks, once I lost my phobia about playing the radio. It passed the time, right to the end; that and cleaning. You can't stay idle once you've got a plan. Something good to clean to: that's the thing.

The roll of paper towel was just opened, the cleanser blue as the sea in its spray bottle. I was all dressed up, already in my coat — overdressed, like Heidi, the Swiss girl who wore everything she owned climbing the mountain to her grandpa's place. My father had read me the story not long after the funeral. "It's a girl's story," my brother had complained, uninterested.

I wanted to be ready, not wasting a second once Sonny got home.

Charlie was working; I'd planned it this way. Our suitcases, mine and Sonny's, were parked by the door, along with some boxes.

Grabbing the Windex, I went out to the living room to watch for Sonny. With any luck, the cab wouldn't be far behind. The tickets were in my pocket; I'd checked three times to make sure.

If I were Reenie, I'd have smoked two packs by now.

I started on the picture window, spraying cleanser and watching it run. Charlie would need things clear, whether or not he'd appreciate it. As I rubbed and wiped, my arm moved in an arc like one big windshield wiper, and I couldn't help thinking of that song, "The Wheels on the Bus," that Sonny had liked as a toddler.

When was the last time my dad had seen him? Sonny had been six, maybe, or just turned seven.

A herd of kids waddled up the street. Little kids in rain suits, sausage legs whisking together as they waded through the slush by the curb. A mother came up behind them pushing a stroller, and I almost waved, thinking it was Sandi, or whatever her name had been. But it was somebody else, someone new.

As she inched past, moving like a snail in that little tide of bodies, I started cleaning again, polishing, really, looking out in time to see Sonny throwing a snowball, just as the cab came creeping up.

Somewhere in the house, Oreo barked, then leapt at the door to greet him.

"You too, bud," I said, my hand trembling as I put him on his lead.

"Got everything, Sonny?" And he nodded, even as I dug one last time for our tickets, and the slip of paper with that Calgary address.

# ACKNOWLEDGEMENTS

As always, thanks are owed to Bruce Erskine for lovingly keeping us afloat; our boys for the rock ('n' roll); the rest of my family, and friends Sheree Fitch, Pam Donoghue, Cindy Lynds-Handren, and Dawn Rae Downton for tossing lifelines and buoys, and Jane Roberts, whose willingness to hike any-time anywhere helped birth *Berth*. This one's for all of you.

I'm also grateful to those who shared time and expertise: Chris Mills of the Nova Scotia Lighthouse Preservation Society, and Master Corporal Pat McCafferty and other mili-tary personnel at 12-Wing Shearwater, Canadian Forces Base Halifax; John Chambers of Emergency Measures Organization Ground Search and Rescue (Nova Scotia); Shawn Brown and Gwen Davies; Robert McGrath and Bjorn Haagensen.

Huge thanks go to the Canada Council for the Arts, for providing assistance, and to others for their support: my agents

Don Sedgwick and Shaun Bradley; Jane Buss and Mary Jo Anderson, and, in particular, Marc Côté, for his patient encouragement and dedication. Thanks, as well, to Margot Metcalfe and my editor, Steven Beattie.

Two books in particular helped as references in the writing of *Berth*: the Reverend W. Hall's *Navigation in The People's Books* science series (New York: Dodge Publishing Co., ca. 1912), and Annette Sandoval's *The Directory of Saints: A Concise Guide to Patron Saints* (New York: Penguin, 1996). The photograph of Tokomo Uemura and her mother, referred to throughout the novel, was made in Minamata, Japan, in 1972, by W. Eugene Smith. But the inspiration for the book mightn't have come without Richard Forsyth's class trips to McNabs and John Ure's tales about living there. Thanks to both for planting the seed.